GOLD RUSH

A 1970s NASCAR ROMANCE

REBEKAH BUCKLEY

INDEPENDENT PUBLISHING NETWORK

First Edition August 2024

Cover design by Rebekah Buckley
Cover Photo by BublikHaus/Shutterstock
Edited & Proofread by Becky Clapham

ISBN: 978-1-80517-823-1 (Paperback)
ASIN: B0CTDJY3FK (eBook)

I didn't miss out on a family life because of racing. I had one because of it.

RICHARD PETTY

For those whose dreams have changed direction.
Keep chasing them, you might end up somewhere beyond even the
wildest of them all.

content warnings

Car crash
Serious injuries & blood
Medical procedures
Sexual harassment & assault
PTSD, anxiety & panic attacks
Mild violence
Manipulative relationships
Recreational drug & alcohol use
Intercourse & sexual acts

one

ADELINE
December, 1974
Malibu, California

ADELINE GOLD LOVES SPEED. THERE'S NOTHING MORE liberating than the wind in her blonde hair as she races along the Pacific Coast Highway. Foot heavy on the gas pedal of her cherry-red Chevrolet Corvette, she accelerates smoothly to 80mph; top down, radio loud, screaming the lyrics to *Tiny Dancer* at the top of her lungs. A tingle of adrenaline trickles through her limbs and as the winter sun bounces off the ocean blurring past her, she's tempted to throw her hands in the air like she's on a rollercoaster.

She feels free.

Until she gets pulled over by a cop.

She sighs as the cop in question, Officer Tommy Valance, approaches her car with a certain swagger that oozes a seniority complex. Adeline sees right through it, and has done since the first time he pulled her over, yet he continues to make sure it's turned on before he leaves his car.

"Addie, Addie, Addie," he mutters her name with an exasperated sigh and his thin, pink lips part to reveal a row of uneven yet unnaturally white teeth under his porn-stache.

"*Officer*." Adeline smiles sweetly, resting her sunglasses on top of her head. She's already leaning across the car and digging in her glove compartment for her licence and registration.

She knows the drill.

"I can't keep letting you off the hook, Adeline. This is it. Next time, I'm gonna have to write you up," Officer Valance warns, looking over her documents briefly. If he's seen them once, he's seen them a hundred times.

Adeline bats her eyelashes. He's soft on her because of who her father is and she plays into it because, who wouldn't?

"It won't happen again, Tommy, it's just that I'm running late to meet my dad."

"It's like fuckin' deja vu, Goldilocks." He peers down at her incredulously, but then a sad smile sweeps across his face. "Too many accidents happen on this road, Addie. I don't wanna be pulling up to your car in a wreck."

"I promise, it *will not* happen again," Adeline reiterates, looking him in the eye as she speaks.

Tommy gives a satisfied nod and taps the shiny red door between them. Adeline frowns. She wishes people would stop pressing their grimy mitts all over her car as and when they please.

"On your way then, princess," Tommy says, before pointing a chubby finger at her. "No more speeding. And tell your old man I said hello."

Adeline waits for him to climb back into his cruiser before she revs her engine, wheels spinning as she tears off down the road muttering to herself.

"In your dreams, Tommy boy."

The less her dad knows about her driving offences, the better. Being an adrenaline junkie is a condition of Adeline's upbringing, after all. Her mother left when she was three years old and so her father, a champion NASCAR driver, took her everywhere with him. Travelling across the country – speedway to speedway –

she would sit in the stands with her father's best friend, Tobias Shaw, a pair of ear defenders engulfing her tiny head as she cheered her hero on. Her young brain never comprehended the danger of the sport and she always hoped she would follow in her father's footsteps; except Michael Gold had seen too many tragedies over the years and the last thing he wanted was his little girl behind the wheel of a souped-up race car.

So now Adeline gets her kicks out of speeding down the PCH and keeping her frequent run-ins with Officer Valance a secret.

She pulls up to the beach house to find her usual spot is taken. There are three other cars in the driveway, one she recognises as Tobias', and the other belongs to Stan Reynolds, driver and bane of Adeline's life. He's had it spray painted red, white and blue – his lucky colours, apparently. They're both in-your-face muscle cars that Adeline finds ridiculously ugly; there's no need to modify a car *that* much. The third is a sleek, steel grey 1969 Lamborghini Miura. It's a beauty, and Adeline lets out a low whistle as she climbs out of her own car and peers through the window. There's no hint as to who it belongs to but she's not surprised to find a random car parked outside her house. Her dad and Tobias prefer to conduct any business from his home office so Adeline is used to it.

"Dad, I'm home!" She calls as she pries her key from the lock and steps over the threshold of their Malibu home, one of three properties the Golds used to split their time between. Not so much anymore.

"Hey, Goldilocks!"

Adeline enters the spacious living room to a crisp sea breeze filtering through from the open back door and Stan lounging on the couch flipping through a copy of Hot Rod magazine between spoonfuls of chocolate pudding.

"Don't you have a condo you pay rent for?"

She gave up acting surprised to see Stan in her house a long time ago. With how often his car is stationed out front, he may as well live there.

"I like it here." Stan wiggles his eyebrows at her as she appears in front of him. "Your refrigerator is always stocked."

"Funny, I always thought you drivers had to be in peak physical condition?" Adeline asks with a perfectly shaped eyebrow raised and her voice laced with teasing judgement.

"I went for a run this morning, this is my reward," Stan mumbles through another mouthful of pudding. There's a gloop of it dripping from the corner of his mouth, and Adeline taps her own face to let him know but he doesn't catch on. It's only then that she spots the two empty cups he's already gone through on the coffee table and she groans in annoyance.

"You're buying me more, Stanley."

"Maybe you should just hide it and I won't be tempted," he retaliates, poking his tongue out at her, smeared with chocolate. Adeline grimaces. How her teenage self once had crush on the man she'll never know. "Your dad's in his office. Big meeting with Toby about signing Billy to the team."

"Billy Brooks?" Adeline asks, her interest piqued.

"No, Billy the Kid. Yes, Brooks," Stan scoffs, rolling his eyes. "He's in there too, by the way," he adds with a sly smile.

William Brooks, Billy to his inner circle, is fairly new to the NASCAR circuit. Although he's been driving for years, karting and drag races mostly, his professional career really took off in 1973 when he signed with Christopher Lennox at Hard Strike Motorsports. It was clear from the first race that the team wasn't a great fit for the young driver. Adeline remembers watching him race and by the looks of it, bad communication from the crew led to car malfunctions and poor lap times despite Billy's strong driving. It didn't help that all their money and attention went on their top driver, Rex Harlow, but Billy had signed a year long contract for the 1974 Cup Series so he was stuck.

It's no surprise to Adeline that as soon as his contract was up, Billy would be scouted by her father and Tobias. After his retirement from driving, Michael still lived for speed, and with his racing days long behind him, he teamed up with Tobias and they formed Shaw & Gold Racing. Adeline still follows him across the country to get her NASCAR fix. It's just now, at twenty-five, she prefers to keep her eye on the drivers as opposed to their cars speeding around the track.

"He's here?" She tries to keep a calm demeanour, but the thought of him being in her house has sent a buzz of nerves rushing through her veins. The Lamborghini outside is his, she realises, and suddenly he's become ten times more attractive to her. Stan's chuckling at her; he can see right through her cool as a cucumber act. He finishes his last spoonful of pudding with a flourish before he answers.

"Yup. I wasn't gonna give you a heads up at first and just watch it all unfold. Maybe make some popcorn. But I'm feeling nice today so you're welcome."

"I haven't seen him since he crashed our end of season party," Adeline says absently.

"Oh, you mean since you spent the whole evening making eyes at each other?" Stan recalls, not for the first time, with a grin and teasing raise of his eyebrows.

Adeline has only been in the same room as Billy a handful of times and they've never actually spoken to each other, but she's *always* been aware of his presence and he's been aware of her too if the soft smiles they've shared have been anything to go by. Harmless, subtle flirting.

Not subtle enough though, considering Stan has been teasing her endlessly about her little crush.

Adeline tries not to get her hopes up. Most of the young, single drivers will flirt with anything with a pulse so she takes everything with a grain of salt; low expectations, no disappointments. Adeline prides herself on not falling at their feet. Did she sleep with a few of them in her rebellious late teens? Sure, but not one of them has ever stirred up the warmth she feels in her belly every time she sees Billy.

Because Billy Brooks is something else.

Adeline glares at Stan and prepares a snarky comment in her head but before the words can leave her lips she hears the door to her father's office open. Her eyes widen in panic as she stares at Stan who is, once again, no help whatsoever. He shrugs his shoulders and kicks his feet up onto the coffee table, ignoring Adeline, and casually runs his hand through his beard. Pouting as he goes back to reading his magazine, Stan acts like he's deep in thought. It's not convincing.

There's faint conversation down the hall, and for a few seconds it sounds like the voices don't seem to be growing any louder. Adeline breathes out a small sigh of relief as she deliberates what to do. Her eyes dart between an oblivious Stan and the hall where Billy is, still out of view. In the end, she decides she's not prepared to meet the potential love of her life *just* yet and makes for the stairs.

"You never saw me," she hisses to Stan, whose only response is to flap his hand around in midair without even the slightest glance in her direction.

Upstairs, Adeline locks herself away in the bathroom. She grips either side of the sink and stares herself down in the mirror.

"Are you done being a fuckin' pansy?" She questions her reflection. Her electric blue eyeliner has smudged under her bottom lashes so she gently wipes it with her finger and then tousles her hair, trying to tame the windswept locks.

She's got this. Maybe.

Maybe Billy's an idiot like Stan and she can get over her little crush by tomorrow and everything will be cool.

As Adeline exits the bathroom and peers downstairs, she sees the four men gathered around the couch in the living room. Her father's familiar laugh cuts through his conversation with Tobias while Stan seems to be chatting enthusiastically to Billy, reminiscing by the sound of it. It's probably been a while since they've seen each other properly. A lot of the drivers attend the same karting meets early on in their racing careers and then maintain those circles into NASCAR, except Adeline is under the impression Hard Strike were never a fan of Billy, or any driver on their team for that matter, fraternising with the enemy. That's never stopped some of them before, though.

The hum of voices carries on whilst Adeline weighs up her options. If she's quiet enough, she can sneak across the top of the stairs to her room without being spotted.

"Hey, where's Addie? I'm sure I heard her car pull in earlier?" Michael says. Billy turns at the mention of her name and the corner of his mouth rises into a small smirk. Adeline's pretty sure they can't see her from where they're standing so she lets herself admire him from afar. He's in slacks and a cream wide-collared shirt and Adeline has already decided that he dresses better than any NASCAR driver she's ever met. It's a fair judgement considering she walked in to Stan sitting on her couch in stained, grey sweats. Billy has pulled his outfit together with a plaid sports jacket and sunglasses perched in his beautifully fluffy, chestnut hair. He's illuminated by the soft, golden glow of afternoon sunlight that pours through the windows – a dream in Adeline's eyes. It's a shame she's pulled from her moment of drooling by Stan betraying her.

"She's upstairs."

"Fuck you, you fucking snitch," she grumbles to no one in particular before sheepishly padding down the stairs. Billy is already looking at her by the time she reaches the last step and Adeline loses her footing ever so slightly, much to Stan's amusement.

"Ah, there she is!" Michael beams and extends his arm, waiting for her to join them. "Billy– sorry, can I call you Billy, William?" Billy nods, his eyes never leaving Adeline. "This is my daughter, Adeline."

Adeline gives her father an unimpressed glance for introducing her by her full name and then switches on what she hopes is her most charming smile for Billy.

"Just Addie is fine... Adeline usually means I'm in trouble."

Billy laughs and holds out his hand. Adeline hesitates but forces herself to reciprocate and that buzz of adrenaline from earlier returns with full force as their palms mould together. She glances up from their hands to meet Billy's gaze, unwavering on her face and so, so blue, and she wonders for a moment if he feels it too.

"Well, Just Addie, you can call me Billy." His voice is like honey. Adeline almost whimpers; just eight words and she's putty in his hands.

"Alright then," Michael starts and Adeline pulls her hand away from Billy's with a coy smile. "Now everyone has been properly acquainted, we should probably get back to work. Stay as long as you like, Billy. God knows Stan always does."

Adeline stifles a laugh as Billy tilts his head in question.

"This is Stan's home away from home," she says with a roll of her eyes. "At this rate, I wouldn't be surprised if he's spending Christmas with us."

"I am, actually," Stan replies, grinning. "Your dad invited me earlier. You're in Cali for Christmas too, right B?"

"Uh, yeah. Michael offered, but I promised Delilah I'd go to her parents' house in the Hills."

Delilah? Well, that's brand new information.

Adeline tries to keep up with who's single and who's not when it comes to NASCAR drivers; she's not about to get caught as the *other woman*, thank you very much.

And apparently, Billy Brooks is taken.

And also notoriously private.

A notoriously private flirt, her brain adds unhelpfully, and this is exactly why she never gets her hopes up. Stan catches her eyes as Adeline tries to hide the flicker of disappointment on her face and he shrugs apologetically.

"Okay, well, I have things to do," she lies, dragging out the 'o' as she makes a move towards the stairs. "It was *lovely* to meet you, Billy. I'll, um, I guess I'll be seeing you around a lot more now."

She's already halfway to the second floor when he calls out his goodbye.

In her room, Adeline rifles through her vinyl records until she finds the one she's looking for. She carefully places it on her turntable, drops the needle and turns the volume right up before she settles into the cushioned seat of her bay window.

When they moved into the beach house, back when she was fifteen, her only request was that she had a bedroom with a sea view. It's something she's grateful for now as she lights a cigarette and sits listening to Carole King. And with every wave that crashes to the shore, she comes up with a reason why falling for Billy Brooks would be a very bad idea.

two

ADELINE
Christmas Eve, 1974

"WHAT DO YOU KNOW ABOUT BILLY BROOKS?" ADELINE ASKS as she winds a string of multi-coloured lights across the branches of the six-foot Norwegian fir they managed to fit in the bay window. She stretches the wire around as far as she can reach and then passes it over to her best friend, Norah. The redhead stops what she's doing and glances at Adeline with one sharply raised brow.

"What do you *want* to know about Billy Brooks?" Her light, husky voice is teasing as she questions Adeline, who does her best not to spit out every question sitting on the tip of her tongue. Not an easy thing to do around her best friend of eight years.

As Shaw & Gold's only female driver, Norah Ridley has a way of getting things out of people. She's a few years older than Adeline, but none the wiser, and she dishes out advice like an agony aunt. She's pretty good at it, most of the time.

Norah drags a chair across the living room and stands on it to wrap the last of the lights around the top of the tree. She nods at Adeline to plug them in and then the girls are blinded by the glow of the bulbs encased in coloured plastic.

"Perfect," Norah says, hopping down from the chair and grabbing the tub of metallic baubles and velvet bows. She looks at Adeline expectantly, waiting, and suddenly Adeline has no time to think before she speaks.

"How long has he been with Delilah?" She blurts.

All hope of subtlety is gone. She may as well have a flashing neon sign above her head that gives away her intentions.

"Ah," Norah sighs and falls back into the chair. "The Delilah situation is... complicated."

The familiar heaviness of dread enters Adeline's body. She winces, shoulders slumping as she sits down cross-legged on the floor and begins to sort the Christmas tree decorations into piles, grateful for the distraction.

"Is it too late for me to retract the question?"

"Nope, no take-backs," Norah quips, "I met Billy when we were twenty-two, and they've been on and off, and then on again, for as long as I've known him."

"Oh." Adeline tries so hard to play it cool but her efforts are futile when she knows Norah can read her like an open book.

"They've known each other since they were kids, Addie."

"I get it."

"Billy always feels like he struggles to meet new people, form strong connections, y'know? We all know what that's like, being on the road so sporadically like that eleven months of the year. So he just kinda gravitates towards her time and time again because it's what he knows. It's safe."

Adeline huffs, and then groans. Crushing on Billy Brooks has literally turned her brain to mush.

"Wait. How do you know all this?"

"I've known him for a while, he tells me things."

Adeline doesn't buy Norah's answer. She stares at her friend with the big, puppy dog eyes that usually make her crack. Just as predicted, Norah heaves a sigh.

"*Fine*. I slept with him, like, five years ago. His pillow talk got... emotional," she confesses.

Adeline's mouth forms into a small frown, gut twisting as she processes the information. She blinks rapidly and glances up at Norah.

"Don't look at me like that, Adeline. You asked."

Adeline scoffs at her for using the full name card.

"Like what?"

"Like you're thinking what I did with Billy was anything more than a one night stand."

"Well," Adeline says, "was it?"

She has no right to feel jealous, but her heart still pounds with it. Plus, she is a little hurt that Norah never told her until now.

"No, Addie. He and Delilah were off at the time. We got drunk at a race meet and he kissed me, and I went with it. One thing led to another and well... we broke the desk in his motel room." Adeline gapes at her as she adds, "I'm pretty sure he was back with Delilah not even a week later."

"Okay, well, you could have spared me the details. You broke a desk, Norah? Seriously?!"

Adeline wishes she could rewind the last two minutes, maybe ask a safe question like *'what's his favourite flavour of ice cream?'*

From that story alone, she's on the cusp of deciding that maybe she would be better to get over whatever feelings she has for Billy. The alternative would be getting into something that is inevitably going to be very complicated, and Adeline doesn't *do* 'complicated'. Not anymore.

"I know what you're thinking, Addie, but Billy's a good guy. He just needs to get his shit together and end it with Delilah for good," Norah says.

Adeline believes that Billy is a good guy. She's heard nothing *but* good things about him. She's seen him shake the hand of everyone in the room and heard he always buys a round of drinks for the pit crew at the bar after a race. Friendly with everyone, even his rivals, people say.

Well, fucking clearly, Adeline thinks, glancing at Norah with narrowed eyes. She wonders if he's slept with anyone else she knows.

"If you need incentive to go for it, he's *really* good in bed, Addie. I hope you get to experience that if anything." She's wearing her signature Norah Ridley smirk and Adeline rolls her eyes.

"Gee thanks, Nor," she laughs as she climbs to her feet and begins arranging decorations on the tree now they're organised to her liking.

"And if you want my honest opinion of Delilah, I don't think she deserves someone as great as him in the slightest. But, you do. After–"

"Right, well thanks," she says quickly. They lapse into silence and Adeline takes a deep breath before she speaks again. "Why did you keep this from me?"

She doesn't want to fight, but she's trying this new thing where she's honest about her feelings. It's worked out great so far if you count the one time she told Officer Valance his moustache made her feel uncomfortable. He had shaved it the next time she saw him and then she told him it looked worse and he grew it back out again. Honestly, she has that man wrapped around her little finger.

Adeline passes Norah the bows and they work together to fill the branches.

"You don't tell *me* everything," Norah counters after a moment.

Well, that Adeline can't argue with. Not even Norah knows how many times Adeline has been pulled over for speeding. She does, however, know about each and every NASCAR driver Adeline has slept with, the good and the bad, so understandably she feels a little put out.

She's about to reply when they're interrupted by Stan. He's carrying two amber glass mugs of mulled wine, each garnished with cinnamon sticks, orange slices, and star anise.

"Alcohol to soothe your boy troubles, Goldilocks." He grins as he hands her drink over.

"I don't have boy troubles," she grumbles, bringing the cup to her lips. Red wine and spices immediately fill her senses, and then the strongest hit of alcohol envelops her tongue as she takes a sip. "Jesus, Stan! What did you put in this?"

"Like, half a bottle of brandy. It's how Toby made it last year," he replies with a shrug. "Why are you all frowny, anyway?"

"She found out I slept with Billy," Norah answers, blowing on her drink before draining the cup like it's juice and not ninety-five percent red wine and brandy.

Stan's eyebrows nearly hit his hairline.

"You only just told her? Did you tell her that he fucked you so hard you broke a desk?"

"*You* knew?!" Adeline gasps.

"I know everything," Stan says and throws an obnoxious wink in her direction.

"God, you're both insufferable." She knows she sounds like a moody teenager but she doesn't care. Adeline hands her drink off to Stan, freeing her hands to put one last bauble on the tree. "I'm goin' outside," she mumbles.

With that, she grabs her mulled wine back and swipes a packet of cigarettes up from the coffee table.

Outside, the fresh air seeps into Adeline's lungs like the first breath after swimming underwater. She kicks off her house shoes and wanders down to the beach, the grainy sand between her toes cool and grounding. The coastal wind whips through her hair as she struggles to light a cigarette, and in the end, she gives up and makes herself comfortable on the sand.

Adeline loves Norah like a sister but sometimes she hates how easily the redhead breezes through everything. Norah radiates confidence like she's the fucking sun. If she wants something, she'll just go for it; she has to in a world so dominated by men. Nine times out of ten she gets it. Adeline overthinks almost every move she makes despite her whole low expectations outlook on life. By the time she's ready, the opportunity is gone.

If she wants Billy, maybe she needs to be more Norah.

That's easier said than done.

The crisp December breeze picks up around her and suddenly

Adeline wishes she hadn't been so hasty in leaving the house. She's only in a thin striped jumper and denim overalls, and they're flared so the cool air works its way under the denim to her legs. She shivers and attempts to light her cigarette again. Anything to stay outside until she can feel the warm buzz of the brandy from her mulled wine filtering through her veins. Only then does she think she'll be able to face Norah and Stan without feeling stupid for getting so worked up over Billy.

She wants to enjoy their Christmas Eve traditions without the image of Billy Brooks fucking her best friend on a shitty motel desk invading her brain like a zombie virus. She grimaces and shakes her head until the thought dissolves.

"It's getting cold out, sunshine."

Michael mumbles his words around the half smoked cigarette hanging from his lips, hardly loud enough to be heard over the crashing waves. Adeline realises then that she probably should have lit hers before she left the house, and she curses herself for not thinking in her rush to get out. The small smile she musters as she turns to look at her father properly soon blooms into an amused grin. It gives way to a laugh, real and loud, when she notices the hideous Christmas sweater he's wearing.

"You look ridiculous," she says through her giggles. Maybe the brandy is getting to her quicker than she thought. "I'll be in soon. Just enjoying the sunset."

Michael replies with a short nod.

"We're starting charades in a minute," he calls as he crosses the beach back towards the house. "If you don't wanna be paired with Stan, I'd hurry."

Adeline's mood picks up once they're two hours deep into the games and drunken fun of the evening. There's no more mention of Billy, much to her relief, and she and Norah win charades. Of course.

Now they're huddled around the kitchen table, dregs of Michael's good whiskey and melted ice in their tumblers, and a Monopoly board overflowing with little plastic buildings. The game has been going on for the better part of two hours but it's finally reaching its end, where it's very clear Adeline has won but they keep going until everyone else is bankrupt. It's tedious and stupid and Adeline is loving each and every moment someone lands on one of her properties.

"Okay, Reynolds. Pay up," she slurs with a smug smile. She reaches her hand out and beckons for his remaining cash.

"Are you sure you didn't cheat?"

"How would I cheat? Dad's the banker and he takes his job very seriously," Adeline argues, "you're just a sore loser."

"On that note," Michael says, pausing to chug back the last of his whiskey. "I'm off to bed."

He scrapes his chair back across the kitchen floor as he stands and moves around the table to kiss Adeline on the forehead and then does the same to Norah. Before he goes, he ruffles Stan's hair like he's a child and not a thirty-year-old man. He'll say it's the liquor but Michael loves them both like they're his own.

"Merry Christmas, you gremlins."

"I think I'll hit the hay too," Stan says, stretching his arms high above his head and forcing out the most over the top yawn Adeline has ever heard. "Big day tomorrow."

Adeline arches an eyebrow.

"You and I both know you're going to spend the whole day camped out on the couch eating, Stan. Don't even try to deny it."

"Like I said, big day. Happy Christmas, Goldilocks. Hope Santa brings you something nice."

He says goodnight to Norah and disappears upstairs to the guest room he's claimed as his own.

"What about you? Up for one more drink?" Adeline asks Norah, shaking the whiskey bottle enticingly. She's probably one too many drinks over her limit and her best friend clearly knows it too as she grabs the bottle out of Adeline's hands before she loses her grip on it.

"I'm going to turn in for the night, Adeline. *You* – need to get into some pyjamas and drink a gallon of water."

"Yes, *mom,*" Adeline giggles and rolls her eyes but she's lucky to have a woman like Norah in her life.

Norah ends up supervising as Adeline changes and gets settled into bed with two glasses of water and painkillers for the inevitable hangover she's going to have.

"I love you, Addie. You know that right? You're my best friend."

"Yup, you too, Red." Adeline smiles sleepily, the old nickname falling from her lips easy as anything. "Happy Christmas, Nor."

It's 2am and Adeline can't sleep. The house is too quiet and she has a hundred and one thoughts swimming around her heavy head.

Christmas is always a funny time of year. Adeline loves it on the surface. The fun of decorating the house and the games and the food. God, she *loves* the food. Although it's a joyous day she spends with her weird, little makeshift family, there's always the lingering ghost of her mother – and she's not even dead.

Adeline heaves a sigh and ends up tiptoeing downstairs for more water, shivering as her skin erupts into goosebumps as soon as she leaves the warmth of her bed. She bought a red, silk camisole and matching shorts as a Christmas Eve present to herself. The set is gorgeous but it's doing very little to keep the chill off her arms and legs.

She pads around the kitchen as quietly as she can, but it's not until she's refilled her glass with chilled water that she notices the saucepan of leftover mulled wine on the stove. Maybe a little glass of that will warm her through and send her off to sleep. Flicking on the burner, Adeline stirs the wine and throws in another cinnamon stick and a few cloves for good measure. She loses herself in the motion of stirring as the warming wine sends tendrils of steam from the pan and fills the kitchen with its sweet, spiced scent.

With the house so quiet, she can hear every sound. The waves lapping at the sand, the creak of the pipes, and the tyres of a car crunching across the stoned driveway.

Wait.

Adeline turns down the flame and creeps to the front door, her heart hammering against her ribcage. There's nothing nearby that she can grab as a weapon so she curls her small hand up into a fist – she's known to pack a punch, it'll suffice – and she waits. The car engine cuts off and someone steps out, their footsteps hurried on the stones and growing louder as they approach the door. Adeline holds her breath and then there's the softest knock on the front door.

She deliberates for a few moments. Does she answer the door and possibly get murdered? On Christmas Day of all days too. Whoever it is outside huffs out a breath, their footsteps retreat back to their car, and before she even realises what she's doing, Adeline swings the door open.

"Oh, shit." The person jumps a little and turns back to the house. "I wasn't expecting anyone to be awake."

Adeline blinks, her eyes adjusting to the darkness outside. She can just make out the warm tan coloured coat he's wearing and the overnight bag in his hand. Her breath hitches as her gaze meets blue eyes; they glisten in the moonlight, a hint of sadness in his stare. Adeline swallows thickly, her mouth suddenly dry despite all the water Norah made her drink, and when she finally finds her voice it comes out as a quiet whisper.

"Billy?"

three

BILLY
Christmas Eve, 1974
Beverly Hills, California

BILLY HATES CHRISTMAS IN CALIFORNIA. THE HEAT OF THE mid-afternoon sun is only just made comfortable by the soft breeze rustling through the palm trees above him. He misses the snow and the cosiness of being wrapped up by the fireplace in his parents' Brooklyn brownstone; home comforts that he hasn't indulged in for a long time.

His parents are in the Bahamas for two weeks with his younger sister and even though it's too late to join them, the better option may have been to just go back home and spend Christmas alone. At least he saw his family before they left; a small gift exchange and lunch at their favourite restaurant before he flew out to Los Angeles for his meeting with the owners of Shaw & Gold.

Billy is trying to do the right thing. The good thing. Because he's not in love with Delilah anymore but the least he owes her is a half decent Christmas before he inevitably breaks her heart. Although, as he stands on the front step of the Jones' Beverly Hills home, he's about two seconds away from turning on his heel and bolting.

Never mind that he and Delilah grew up together in Brooklyn Heights, just two houses apart and a childhood spent in each other's pockets. Never mind that they were in all the same classes at school or that their wedding was planned and their kids' names were picked out by the time they were eighteen, or that there was a brownstone waiting to be inherited.

For the longest time Billy felt like the cat who got the cream – his future with the fiery redhead, the true girl next door, was pretty much set in stone. It's Delilah's parents who continue to push the marriage agenda. Billy's are a tad more laid back, supportive of his life choices and the fact that his career is his priority. They show up for him and Rosie more than either of them could ever hope for. It's something Billy is, and always will be, extremely grateful for.

Billy rocks back and forth on the balls of his feet, puffing out his cheeks and clicking his tongue against the roof of his mouth before exhaling heavily.

"Stop fidgeting," Delilah hisses beside him.

Billy glances at her briefly, his eyes trail over her as he takes in the hairdo she took forever to perfect. It's an over-styled beehive that makes her look older than her twenty-nine years and exactly like her mother. Unfortunately, her efforts in beauty don't hide the fact that even her voice grates on him now. Was it always *so* high pitched?

He hops from foot to foot, growing impatient as they wait for someone to answer the door.

"For fuck's sake, William. Just stay still."

Billy sneakily flips her off and sighs. Looking to the sky, he says a silent prayer and hopes for a fucking Christmas miracle. It appears his pleas go unanswered as Loretta Jones answers the door.

"Lilah! William! Come in, come in."

Billy plasters on a smile and Delilah gives him a light shove to make him move.

The Jones house has never changed, Billy realises as he walks through the door. They moved to L.A. in the late-sixties, claiming New York was too busy for them now they were older. Everything about the place says the owners have a lot of money and very little taste. So much so, it hurts Billy's eyes if he stares at the carpet for too long.

He takes Delilah's fur coat from her on autopilot and hangs it in the hall closest alongside his own suede jacket. When he steps back out and closes the door Delilah's already gone, following her mother further into the house.

The day drags. Billy's sanity is hanging on by a thread by the time they gather in the glorified second sitting room for afternoon drinks. Loretta calls it the parlour. Billy tries his best not to roll his eyes at that and then realises that actually, he might do better just gouging his eyes out. It would save him the pain of looking at the carpet for the next two days.

Still, he makes polite yet tedious chit-chat with his in-laws for the next few hours. Delilah's father, Jack, asks him how his little racing hobby is going and Billy tells them he's just signed with Shaw & Gold.

"And they're good, are they?" Loretta asks, topping up Billy's glass a little too generously with sangria.

"They're one of the best NASCAR teams right now, yes," Billy replies tersely.

At least Jack has given up on his quest to seduce Billy into the world of finance. Working on Wall Street is Billy's idea of hell, even if Jack's years as a New York Stock Exchange broker are the reason the Joneses can now afford their Spanish-style villa.

"*It's good money, son,*" he would say, "*it'll make you into a real man.*"

Billy was laughing when he received his first NASCAR earnings; Jack wouldn't know good money if it smacked him in the face.

Dinner, the only thing about the holiday Billy has been looking forward to, goes slightly better than the rest of the afternoon. Loretta's cooking is quite possibly the one tolerable thing about her. She always uses old Italian recipes, each one passed down through her family and the best thing Billy has ever tasted. They gorge on bread and antipasti, an indulgent pasta dish, and then tiramisu for dessert. Billy thanks her earnestly when she brings out a moka pot and her best little espresso cups and saucers at the end of the meal. Is it bad that her mother's food is what he's going to miss most when it's all over with Delilah?

They play card games well past midnight and after the eighth game of rummy, Billy zones out. Conversation flows around him, talks of plans for the New Year. It's all white noise until Delilah gushes about how excited she is to watch him race this season and Billy can't help himself as he laughs. It's so loud and abrupt that suddenly all eyes are on him.

"Sorry," he chokes, "it's just– when was the last time you *actually* showed up for a race, Lilah?" His harsh, accusatory tone doesn't go unnoticed by Loretta who looks all about ready to lurch forward and slap him into next week for speaking to her daughter that way.

"I came to that one in New York, remember? The, um– the karting one?" Delilah fumbles over her words as Billy stares at her, unimpressed.

"That was seven years ago," he deadpans, draining the rest of his coffee. He doesn't know how much longer he can sit through this farce of a family Christmas. "I'm going for a smoke. Dinner was lovely. Thank you again, Loretta."

Fishing his pack of Marlboro from his back pocket, Billy leaves the room and escapes the uncomfortable silence lingering in his wake.

He gets a moment to breathe out on the porch. It's a clear night and the stars are out in a ridiculous show of splendour. Billy steps out further into the darkness of the yard to search out the constellations. Eyes up and spinning slowly, cigarette smoke travels around him in soft wisps from his parted lips as he focuses on Orion, then Gemini and Taurus. Hundreds of thousands of tiny twinkling lights that never fail to make him feel so small and remind him why he's always been so fascinated with astronomy.

When the moon landing happened Billy was like a kid on Christmas. It was an event and he watched in awe with his sister, parents, and half the neighbourhood crowded around the crappy TV at the diner down the street. He'd had dreams of working for

NASA when he was in middle school, but then he fell in love with cars and the electrifying high of motorsports and the rest was history.

He still reads books on the subject in his spare time, the childlike need to learn anything and everything about it will never leave him.

Billy's stargazing is disturbed by Jack calling to him from the porch and he internally groans when he hears what he's been dreading since he walked through the door.

"So, when are you kids gonna tie the knot?"

Billy squints as he heads back toward the house and he sees the cigar hanging between Jack's fingers, the same one he's been smoking for years. It's clear the older man has been waiting for this all evening. He springs the question on Billy every time they get together and by some miracle, Billy always manages to avoid answering. It seems that despite the tense moment at the dinner table, as far as Jack is concerned, Delilah is still destined to be a Brooks.

"Uh... I don't think–"

"Nonsense. Here." Jack holds the cigar between his lips, his aged cheeks hollowing as he inhales deeply. His hand dips into the pocket of his slacks and Billy instantly feels the acidic burn of bile rising to his throat. It's like his whole life flashes before his eyes when Jack holds up the ring and the diamonds glitter under the dim porch light. "This was my Ma's, and her Ma's before that."

No, no, no, no.

"Sir, I... uh. I can't," Billy stammers as he stubs out his cigarette, hand shaking. He's *always* managed to avoid it going this far and now he feels trapped and unsure of what will be worse, saying no or going through with it.

He thinks back to the advice Norah gave him in Tulsa as they lay naked in a crappy motel room. Vulnerable and exposed in more ways than one, Billy had poured his heart out to her as they smoked through a whole pack of cigarettes and raided the awful selection of liquor in the minibar; "*Don't leave it too late, Billy, whatever you do. You'll end up sucked into a life with her like a star into a black hole and then what are you gonna do? You'll be tied to her for the rest of your miserable fucking existence."*

Well, he fucked that up, didn't he?

Five years it's taken him to see sense. To see that Delilah, to put it lightly, is a bitch. She's like a robot, devoid of emotion except for when it's to guilt-trip him into getting back with her. Each time she seems to morph into a different, no, a *worse* variation of the girl he once fell in love with.

"William, son? Take the damn ring," Jack sighs.

There's an agonising pause while Billy weighs up his options. In the end, he thinks *fuck it* and bites the bullet.

"I can't. I... I don't love Lilah anymore."

It's barely a whisper but Billy knows Jack heard. He looks up from his feet to see Jack's worn features twisted in anger, or hurt, Billy can't tell.

"Does she know?"

"I was going to do it after Christmas," Billy admits. He looks down at the ground again, kicking about a stone that's come loose.

"I'd like you to leave my house now, William." Jack's tone is low and steady as he speaks. "You can let my baby down easy after the holidays. I'll tell her you're not well, that you've gone to a hotel for the night. I assume you're planning on going back to New York?"

"Sir–" Billy starts but Jack doesn't want to hear it.

"Just leave."

Billy nods, shame warming his cheeks. He hurries through to the hall, unnoticed by Delilah and her mother, and grabs his jacket from the closet. It's not until he's outside that he lets the relief wash over him.

Climbing into his car, he revs the engine and reverses out onto the road without hesitation. His eyes cloud over, lashes damp, as he's suddenly overcome with the emotions he's been forced to hold back. The streetlights around him blur through salty tears of alleviation and he has to swipe across his eyes with the back of his hand.

Billy feels free for the first time in years, and he's never looking back.

BILLY

HE'S SPEEDING ALONG THE PACIFIC COAST HIGHWAY BEFORE he even realises where he's heading. It's late and he'll be surprised if anyone is awake to let him in. He figures he'll just sleep in his car if he has to; he'd rather that than spend Christmas morning alone in a shitty, last minute hotel room.

The sea glistens under the bright, partially lit moon as he zooms past. With each mile he covers, the tiny shrapnels of lingering regret get swept away with the wind, replaced with easy-flowing adrenaline that pumps through his veins. Billy laughs, loud and joyous out the open window. It's full of reckless abandon as he curves around the bend at full speed and onto the last stretch of road that leads to– well, it leads to Adeline Gold and the smile he's seen every time he's closed his eyes for the last two weeks.

He's tried to stop himself from thinking about her; from reaching into his memories for the first time he ever saw her. The darkened room, the way her hair fell in delicate tendrils around her face and the gold glitter shimmering on her eyelids. Some of it had made its way down to her cheeks and every time it caught the light, she caught his eye.

Adeline caught the eye of so many others too. Billy wasn't surprised considering the tight little mini skirt and low-cut, iridescent blue halter-neck top she was wearing that night. It did *everything* for her and added to the ethereal beauty that reminded him of a pixie.

The stone driveway crunching under the weight of his tyres draws him out of the memory as he pulls up outside the beach house and cuts the engine. The house is in darkness and for a split second, Billy second-guesses himself.

Before he can change his mind, he climbs out of the car and grabs his bag from the trunk. His feet carry him to the front step and he raps his knuckles gently against the white wooden door.

He waits.

And he waits.

With no sign of anybody coming to answer the door, Billy sighs and heads back towards his car. He pulls his jacket tighter around his body, the December chill sinking bone-deep now the adrenaline is wearing off. He's probably tired enough to sleep anywhere but he *was* kinda hoping for a bed. Or a couch, he's not fussy.

He's dreaming of curling up on *something* soft at least when the door swings open, causing his shoulders to flinch.

"Oh shit." He spins on his heel and kilters slightly off balance on the uneven stones. "I wasn't expecting anyone to be awake."

Adeline's tired, hazel eyes search his as he takes a step forward into the dim light filtering out from the house.

"Billy?"

"Uh...hi?" Billy winces, "sorry, I shouldn't have just shown up here, but–"

"No, no. It's fine." Adeline smiles, bright and welcoming as she ushers him into the house. He's grateful she doesn't ask why he's turned up at such a ridiculous hour and his shoulders loosen as he steps inside with Adeline close behind.

"Thanks," he says, feeling awkward as he hovers in the entryway. He runs a hand through his hair, a nervous habit.

"It's no problem. I was up anyway," Adeline replies quietly as to not wake the rest of the house. "I'm just warming some mulled wine if you want some?"

"At 2am?" He questions as she closes the door behind them.

"Couldn't sleep," she murmurs, appearing in front of him again. Billy's gaze flicks down to her silky little pyjamas and the way they're doing absolutely nothing to protect her from the cool night air. He shifts his weight, trying to will his cock to chill out as it twitches at the sight of Adeline's pert nipples protruding under the red fabric. Tongue darting to the corner of his mouth, Billy licks across his bottom lip like a predator eyeing up its prey.

He doesn't even really know her, not *well*, but the things she does to him; he'd almost forgotten what it's like to feel this way. Heart racing, palms sweaty, it's like he's a schoolboy with a crush except he's twenty-nine and wants nothing more than to feel Adeline against him, run his hands over her soft curves and *taste* how sweet he just knows she is.

"I know that feeling," he says instead but she's already turned her back to him, leading the way through to the kitchen.

He follows, watching her hips swing left to right as her bare feet pad across the hardwood flooring. Her blonde hair cascades down her back in messy waves and Billy assumes it's the aftermath of a more styled do from earlier in the day but it still looks good, slept in and loose. He almost can't help himself as he imagines how it would feel clutched between his fingers and he has to stop walking for a moment to collect himself.

Adeline must notice he's stopped following her as she peers over her shoulder, large doe-like eyes watching him carefully. She bites her lip, a teasing smile blooming across her features, and Billy has to bite the inside of his cheek to stop the efflorescent groan in the core of his chest from slipping past his parted lips.

"You coming?" She asks and then turns to walk away, her hips swaying just a little more than before as she disappears into the next room. Billy nods even though she's gone, the thudding of his pulse in his ears is loud, distracting. He takes a breath, focusing on the way his lungs expand, calming his overtired, overactive brain in the process.

"Chill out, Brooks," he mutters as he places his overnight bag by the stairs and wipes his clammy hands on his trousers. When he joins Adeline in the kitchen, the scent of cinnamon and clove hits his nostrils immediately, warm and festive. He takes a seat at the large table, his fingers tapping out a random tune across the oak and his leg bouncing up and down restlessly. It's a reminder that he desperately needs sleep but he's revelling in the fact that he's spending time alone with the girl who's occupied his mind for the past year.

"Do you wanna go for a drive?" He blurts as the side of his brain fighting to spend more time with Adeline wins out over the side begging for rest.

"In your *Lamborghini*?" Adeline drawls with a sly, little smile. Billy nods, pulling the keys from his pocket and dangling them from his pointer finger. "Fuck yeah!" It clearly comes out a little louder than she intended and she covers her mouth, giggling through her fingers. The sound is like music to Billy's ears, a wide smile on his lips that eventually gives way to laughter of his own.

"Yeah?"

"Fuck. Yeah," Adeline whisper-shouts this time. "Who needs sleep?"

Me, Billy thinks, *I need sleep.*

"You might wanna change out of your pyjamas first," he says with a smirk, "as cute as they are."

"You think my pyjamas are cute, Brooks?" Adeline asks, eyes flicking up from the pan of mulled wine to meet his. There's a daring sparkle in them and Billy knows now that she caught him looking. "I could always keep 'em on for you, but I might be a little... chilly, don't ya think?" Her tone is sweet and Billy almost groans; she's playing him like a goddamn symphony.

"A little," he murmurs dumbly as Adeline pulls two hip flasks from the cabinet behind her and places them beside the stovetop.

"You put the mulled wine into those and I'll be right back," she says, dragging her fingertips across his shoulders as she passes him. Billy suppresses a shiver, turning his head to watch her leave.

"I'll wait for you in the car," he whispers and Adeline sticks her arm back around the door to give him a thumbs up. Filling the hip flasks with shaking hands, Billy is giddy with anticipation, spilling drops onto the countertop and then wasting precious time searching out a rag to clean his mess. He breathes deeply as he wipes down the surfaces, an attempt to chill the fuck out, before he makes his way out to his car and starts her up quietly.

Heat on, he fiddles with the radio to find the perfect late-night station as he waits with fidgety hands. A knock on the window pulls his attention away from dials and buttons and he looks up to see Adeline pulling a stupid face, her tongue hanging out and her eyes crossed. Billy laughs as she climbs into the passenger seat; the difference between Adeline and Delilah is startling now he's spent a little time with the blonde. Seeing how she acts, carrying herself like she doesn't give a fuck what anyone else thinks. She's like that first sip of ice-cold lemonade on a hot summer's day, sharp and refreshing and everything Billy needs.

"Where to, Just Addie?"

"Surprise me," she says, flashing him a toothy grin; more awake now with her bright eyes and flushed cheeks. The pyjamas have been swapped for flared jeans and a thin, roll neck sweater, a faded denim jacket thrown over the top to keep off the December chill. With her hair pulled into a ponytail and a fresh face, the whole thing is gorgeously effortless, and Billy is starting to think that Adeline could probably wear a trash bag and look good.

They chat for a little while as they drive away from the coast. Billy steers clear of anything to do with Delilah or the Christmas Eve from hell he's just experienced. Instead, he listens intently to Adeline, relishing in the way she babbles excitedly about her own day, from the food to the games and everything in between, and Billy finds himself wishing he'd just said yes when Michael offered to spend the holidays with them.

"What do you usually do on Christmas Day?"

"Mimosas and stocking gifts first – obviously," Adeline replies, grinning over at him. The streetlights illuminate her face with each one they pass, a soft orange glow catching the browns and greens of her eyes and making it hard for Billy to look away.

"Obviously."

"Then it's pretty much a repeat of Christmas Eve. You're gonna love it." And doesn't that warm something in Billy, loosening the knot in his chest further as he thinks about spending the holidays with people he can actually tolerate. The conversation falls into a natural lull and Billy turns the radio up just a little, enough to hear the song *and* Adeline humming along to it quietly. It's hard not to stew, not to let his thoughts fester in the quiet, and he must be frowning as they pull into a parking spot at Topanga Overlook because Adeline peers over at him in the low light with a gentle frown of her own.

"Do you wanna talk about it?" She asks softly as Billy takes a swig of his mulled wine. The spices, and the brandy, flow through him; a welcome, soothing remedy. Adeline has been sipping from hers throughout the journey, her hip flask almost empty and her cheeks glowing with a rosy hue from the alcohol. Billy sips from his once more before tipping it towards her in offering and her fingers wrap around Billy's hand as she pulls his drink towards her mouth.

"I'd rather not," he murmurs, gaze tracking over her face until it lands on her mouth. He can't take his eyes away from her lips as she drinks from the flask, his hand still tucked under hers as she lifts it. Suddenly, all Billy can hear is his heart thumping as his blood rushes south and he has to shift in his seat as his trousers begin to grow tight across his cock.

Stifling a soft groan, he can't help but think he shouldn't be doing this. He hasn't officially broken up with Delilah yet, and even if he is already over it (if he's being honest, has *been* over it for a long time), he knows that doesn't make *any* of this right. It's a potential disaster waiting to happen, dragging Adeline into the middle of what is likely to be a messy break up. But the thing is, and he's realised this just now as he watches a drop of mulled wine sit daringly on Adeline's bottom lip, Billy is on a speeding train and there are no brakes, not when it comes to Adeline Gold.

He studies her for a moment longer, picking out the green flecks of her irises in the glow of the single, dim streetlight on the overlook, and decides he would be stupid to not act on his feelings. At this moment, at least. He may come to regret it later, but he figures it'll be worth it in the end and he's gone too long living by someone else's rulebook.

Leaning across the centre console, Billy's fingers brush against Adeline's cheek as he pushes away loose hairs, soft wisps of blonde fallen from her ponytail. A slow simmer of desire works its way through his limbs as his eyes flick across her dainty features and settle back on her peachy lips, stained with wine. Adeline's breath hitches in the silence and she lets out a whisper of a whine as she leans in and Billy closes the gap.

When he presses his mouth to hers it's slow and tentative; just a soft press as he learns the shape of her lips, of her smile, against his own. Adeline sighs, her mouth parting just enough for Billy to sweep his tongue along the seam of her lips and the simple move flips a switch in them both. She moves across the car with ease, landing in Billy's lap as he reaches down to release the seat and create more room. He groans into the kiss, of relief and arousal as she settles her weight on his aching cock.

"Sorry," she whispers as she shuffles back a little but Billy keeps his hands on her waist, holding her still as he rolls his hips beneath her, chasing the feeling. His fingers tease at the hem of her sweater as Adeline weaves her own into Billy's hair, raking her nails over his scalp and down to the nape of his neck in a way that's so utterly distracting, Billy moans softly, almost meekly into her mouth. Pushing Billy's jacket from his shoulders, Adeline begins unbuttoning his shirt, fingers fumbling, neither of them wanting to stop. She smiles against his mouth once more – *victory* – as she pulls open his shirt just enough to trace her fingertips over the firm muscles of his chest and she pushes further, licking into his mouth with renewed fervour.

The kiss is everything. It's quick and electric, blowing all his expectations of what it would be like to kiss Adeline out of the water. His tongue pushes against hers, their breaths hot and heavy and Billy's senses are going into overdrive. He can taste the cinnamon and brandy of the mulled wine lingering on her lips and tongue, smell the floral notes of her shampoo and feel the softness of her skin under his fingertips as they dance across her waist. Adeline keens into him, a gasp slipping from her mouth as Billy's cold hands brush up the sides of her body under her sweater and settle on her breasts. The pads of his thumbs circle teasingly over her nipples and Adeline whimpers.

"Coulda warmed your hands up first," she mumbles and a chuckle-cum-moan fights its way up from Billy's chest as Adeline begins to move above him.

Billy's more than aware they're making out like horny teenagers in the front seat of his car but he's on a high he never wants to come down from, euphoric and light and so fucking enraptured by Adeline.

When they eventually break apart, they're both flushed. Adeline's lips are pink and kiss-swollen as she heaves out a warm breath and Billy brushes his thumb across the dewy skin of Adeline's bottom lip. He can't bring himself to look away from her; she's gorgeous, bright-eyed and thoroughly taken apart, and everything he hoped she would be. If this is all he gets, then he's a lucky man, he knows that much. Adeline pecks a kiss against the pad of Billy's thumb as her fingers trail across the light stubble of his cheeks, watching him just as intently.

Billy sighs. He was desperately unhappy this morning, dreading the day ahead and wishing he could be anywhere but California. But now? Now he feels like he can start to breathe again. He buries his face into the crook of Adeline's neck, peppering her tanned skin with light, tender kisses.

"Happy Christmas, Adeline," he whispers.

"Happy Christmas, Billy."

five

ADELINE
January 5th, 1975
Malibu, California

"*WHAT'RE YOU DOIN' T'MORROW?*" BILLY'S VOICE COMES through the line rough and low, lazy with his words. Adeline kicks her legs against the kitchen counter where she's perched with the phone cord stretched from the wall. She balances the receiver between her ear and shoulder as she scoops out a helping of chocolate pudding from the cup in her hand.

They've spoken on the phone every night since Christmas Day. Tonight, they've been talking for three hours about everything and nothing and so much in between. Their conversation has flowed so easily that Adeline thinks maybe she's been waiting for someone like him her whole life.

"Why? You wanna take me out, Billy Brooks?" she replies, licking a drop of pudding from the spoon. Her belly swoops when Billy huffs out a laugh, quiet and soft and directly into her ear.

"*I do, actually. I'm only in Cali for another day or two. I got some things to take care of back home before the race at Riverside.*"

"Where's home?"

"*New York,*" Billy says, "*Brooklyn.*"

"Billy Brooks from Brooklyn, huh?"

Billy laughs again, a little louder this time, and Adeline can picture the way his face lights up and his eyes crinkle at the edges.

"*That's me. So what d'ya say, Adeline Gold, you gonna let me take you out?*"

"I suppose I could do that," Adeline teases, "pick me up at seven?"

"*I'll be there.*" Billy replies, his words stretched around a yawn. Adeline glances at the clock. It's past midnight and she knows Billy has a sponsorship meeting early tomorrow.

"I should let you get some sleep."

"*Hmm? Yeah. I'm not hangin' up first though.*"

Adeline groans as she hops down from the counter and tosses her finished pudding cup into the trash. She twists the phone cord around her fingers as she paces back and forth across the chequered linoleum, listening to Billy's amused chuckle that comes in response.

"I hung up first yesterday, it's your turn."

"*You keepin' score?*" Billy asks. The question is threaded with a thick, sleepy Brooklynite twang so prominent Adeline feels a little silly for not noticing it before.

"Maybe."

"*You're gonna be trouble, aren't you?*"

"Why don't you stick around and find out?"

"*I intend to. See you tomorrow, Adeline.*"

"Goodnight, Billy."

Headlights illuminate the front of the house as Billy swings into the driveway, the tyres of his Lamborghini crunching over the stones before he kills the engine and the night is once again filled with the soft crashing of waves and distant traffic. Adeline is waiting by the window, twisting the rings on her fingers out of nerves. It's been a while since she's dated like this and she *really, really* likes Billy. For once, she's letting herself be hopeful that whatever happens between them is real and more than the short term flings she's so used to.

"Have a good date, sunshine," Michael calls through the house as Adeline shrugs on her jacket. He's no doubt on his way from the kitchen to his office with a TV dinner on a tray to eat while he works, a habit Adeline has fought against time and time again to no avail.

"Thanks, Dad. Don't wait up!"

Adeline flicks her hair over her shoulder as she passes the mirror by the front door. She gives her outfit a once over, rolling her miniskirt up just a little higher and pushing her boobs up in her bra until they sit perfectly, and then she pauses and takes a deep breath. With her eyes closed, she psyches herself up as she listens to the sound of Billy's footsteps growing closer. Then they stop and retreat again and Adeline giggles as Billy mutters to himself before he approaches the house once more. Even though she's waiting for it, the loud chime of the doorbell makes her jump.

"Hi!"

She's breathless as she answers the door, almost losing her balance and crashing into Billy as she swings it open. He steadies her easily, his large hands warm as they settle on her waist and he leans back to get a good look at her.

"Hi," he whispers when his eyes finally meet hers, shining icy blue in the dim light of the entryway behind her. Adeline's gaze sweeps over him too. She takes in his pants, tight over his thighs and flaring out over his boots, and the intricately patterned knitted polo half hidden under his leather jacket.

"You look–" Adeline starts.

"You look–" Billy says at the same time, chuckling as they cut each other off. "You look beautiful."

"Thank you. You look good too, I like what you've done with your hair." Adeline fights the urge to run her fingers through the soft-looking waves, reaching her hand for Billy's instead. "Shall, uh... shall we go?"

Billy nods in response, smiling softly as his fingers curl around hers, and he leads her to his car. He opens the passenger side door and waits for her to settle in the seat before he jogs around the front, flashing Adeline a dopey smile as he joins her. He's nervous too, and just as bad at hiding it.

"So where are we going?" Adeline asks once they're on the road, passing through Malibu in a blur of midnight blue sea and orange streetlights.

"Dinner first, obviously," Billy says, "and then I wanna take you to my favourite place in L.A." He glances over from the driver's seat, all lopsided grin and earnest eyes. "You trust me, Addie?"

And the thing is, she does. He could take her anywhere, to the fucking moon if he wanted, and Adeline would follow. Already, Billy oozes something soft and lovely. Something Adeline's needed for a while now.

Her nerves settle further as they drive into West Hollywood. Billy's talking away beside her, telling her all about his meeting and how excited he is to be partnered with Gatorade this season. When they eventually pull into a space outside the restaurant, Adeline turns to him in shock.

"This place is booked out for *months*, Billy. I've been trying to get a table since August!"

"Didn't you hear? I'm Shaw & Gold's new golden boy." Billy winks, a cheeky grin blooming gorgeously across his face when Adeline rolls her eyes. She's seen the papers, of course. Ever since she could read Adeline's been scouring the sports pages for any mention of Shaw & Gold and their drivers. The big articles get framed in her father's office, everything else is tucked neatly in a photo album.

"I wouldn't let Stan hear you say that," she laughs, "it'll be a terrible knock to his ego."

"I've known Stan Reynolds for fifteen years, Addie. Nothing will ever shrink that big head of his, trust me."

"I'll take your word for it," Adeline replies as Billy climbs out of the car. He opens the door for her again and helps her to her feet like a perfect gentleman.

The restaurant is dimly lit and cosy, a little Italian place tucked between bigger establishments on Sunset Boulevard. It immediately reminds Adeline of her favourite place in Little Italy – she's pretty sure the back rooms hide mob headquarters but the spaghetti is to die for – and for a second she feels a longing for New York; for the bustling streets and the hidden gems they have to offer.

The hostess greets them with a soft accent and leads them to a table at the back. In the candlelight, the place feels dream-like, with its red and white tablecloths and quiet piano soundtrack. Adeline slips into her seat, stomach rumbling and ready for food, and Billy reaches across the table to entwine their fingers as they skim the menu.

"I'm really glad we did this," Billy murmurs, cheeks flushed a delicate pink as he meets her gaze. The blush stays but his nerves seem to ease as the date goes on. Adeline loses time, sitting opposite him, basking in his laugh and the way his eyes light up when she laughs too. The tables around them clear out and new faces fill the seats, one by one, until their waiter subtly slides their bill onto the table and they take it as their cue to leave too.

"Do I get any clues about where we're going next?" Adeline asks as Billy holds the door open for her and his hand slips casually across her lower back as they step out into the parking lot. The restaurant was toasty inside and Adeline takes a moment to let the cool L.A. breeze wash over her.

She feels pleasantly full. Full with good food and whispered conversation, soft touches of hands across the table and Billy teasing and gentle as he skimmed the toe of his shoe over the curve of Adeline's foot and further up her calf until he reached the top of her knee high boots.

"Look up," Billy says as they reach the car. Adeline does, blinking into the darkness. Above her, hundreds of stars twinkled into her vision, a cluster at a time as her eyes adjusted. There's always been something so magical about the night sky, vast and filled with more than the human eye could ever comprehend.

"To space?" She asks, incredulous.

"Kinda, you'll see."

The winding roads of the Hollywood Hills give it away, through the dust and the green to Griffith Park and the observatory.

"To space," Adeline says with a smile. "This is your favourite place?"

"Ever since I saw *Rebel Without a Cause*."

"Understandable. James Dean had that effect on people," Adeline chuckles as Billy kills the engine.

Higher up in the hills the breeze holds more of a chill, whipping through Adeline's hair as she wraps her jacket tighter around her body. Billy pulls her into his side, shielding her from the cold as they walk towards the observatory, the white architecture stark in contrast to the dark sky. As they get closer, Adeline notices groups of people milling around, some on blankets and sipping warm drinks.

"What's all this for?" She asks, just as Billy pulls two tickets out of his jacket pocket. Adeline peers over at them, squinting to read the text in the dim light. "*Laserium*?"

"It's a laser show," Billy explains, his words coming out a little timid, bashful. As if he's embarrassed by the date idea he's clearly taken the time to think out. "I've been meaning to come see it and I thought... you're gonna love it, I promise."

"I'm sure I will. Come on, let's find a good spot."

They collect a blanket from one of the stewards and settle onto the grass somewhere in the middle of the crowd. Billy leans back on his hands and Adeline slots between his legs, her head dropping back to his shoulder.

"Warm enough?" Billy murmurs.

"Mhmm" Adeline hums, snuggling into him. She tilts her head further, peering up at Billy through her eyelashes. She knew it before but being this close, it kind of blows her away how beautiful he is; all full pink lips and high cheekbones.

"Is it crazy that I already know I'm gonna miss you when I'm in

New York?" Billy says, glancing down. His mouth is a whisper away from Adeline's, all she has to do is pucker her lips and she'd be kissing him. The thought makes her nervous even though they spent hours kissing Christmas Day and longer still on the front porch when he left with Stan the next day. "Adeline?"

"Yeah?"

"I said I'm gonna miss you, when I'm back in New York."

"I'm gonna miss you too," she whispers, craning her neck a little more.

Billy gets the message, closing the gap. Adeline feels his smile against hers, the slight graze of teeth on her bottom lip as he kisses her soft and slow. It's so gorgeously delicate. Billy works magic with his tongue, drawing little breaths from her as he deepens the kiss. He brushes his fingers along her jaw, tucks a lock of hair behind her ear and Adeline's a goner.

The show begins and Adeline is briefly aware of the bright lights among the stars and psychedelic music echoing around them, but she's mostly wrapped up in Billy and trying not to think too much about how the night is nearly over and the two weeks she has to go without him once it is.

ADELINE

January 19th, 1975

Riverside International Raceway, California

THE FIRST RACE DAY OF THE SEASON IS ADELINE'S favourite. Energy is already high from qualifiers, morale is up, and the drivers are itching to race after the winter break. She heads to the team garage with two cases of Gatorade in her arms and buzzing with adrenaline as she watches the stands fill up. The hum of anticipation and the smell of motor oil and beer fills the air and Adeline wants to bottle it up.

Norah finds her as she's passing their neighbouring garage, cornering her for the third time today. Only this time, her best friend is wearing a petulant pout and a frown as she takes the top case of drinks from Adeline and falls into step beside her.

"Please, Addie. It's killing me. Just one tiny, little detail and I'll shut up forever."

Adeline raises an eyebrow.

"I find that hard to believe," she replies, "and we've been talking since Christmas, I told you this."

"But then he took you on a date and I've heard absolutely

nothing about it. Which is a total crime against friendship, by the way."

"I thought we decided we were okay with not telling each other everything?"

"I changed my mind," Norah replies flippantly.

Adeline laughs and Norah grins like she's just won the lottery.

"We went for dinner and then he took me to the observatory, it was very lovely," Adeline says, feeling a little coy about the whole thing.

"And then…"

"And then he drove me home and I haven't seen him since," Adeline answers honestly. Billy had left her with a promise to call from New York and the kind of kiss that sent sparks from her toes to the very tips of her fingers, every bit of it slow and explorative. Adeline's been thinking about that kiss for two weeks.

"Ugh, you're no fun," Norah whines.

"And *you* have a race to think about. Quit pestering me about my love life."

"What's this about a love life, sweet Adeline?"

The curious voice of Billy's crew chief, Gabe, comes from somewhere behind them as they approach the refreshment tent. Norah promptly dumps the case of Gatorade she was carrying on the table and heads over to her car, spinning to blow Adeline a kiss. The redhead's eyes slide over to Gabe and Adeline has a front row seat as the mechanic winks with a flirty little smirk on his lips and Norah blushes so hard she almost stumbles into Stan.

"Warren," Adeline says once her best friend disappears further into the crowded garage.

"I haven't seen you in two months and all I get is '*Warren*'? Damn, girl."

"Sorry, Gabe. I feel a little all over the place today," Adeline sighs, and throws her arms around him in a quick hug. She scans the room over his shoulder, looking for Billy. She expects to find him swarmed by press and NASCAR bigwigs; his first race with Shaw & Gold has people excited. Gabe diverts her attention back to him as he pulls back from the hug and holds her at arm's length, a knowing smirk on his face.

"Brooks, right?"

"What about him?" Adeline asks innocently.

"Well, the guy's been following you around the room with his eyes for like, an hour now – looks like a lost puppy dog. Figured there must be a lil somethin' somethin' going on there." Gabe shoots Adeline the smug, toothy grin she's come to both love and hate, wiggling his eyebrows. Adeline's cheeks burn as she avoids his gaze and Gabe laughs triumphantly. "I love it when I'm right."

"Yeah, yeah. Lap it up," Adeline replies.

"Look at you! He really got you in a spin, don't he?"

"It's new and exciting, leave me alone!" Adeline pouts, squealing as Gabe hooks her under his arm and ruffles her hair.

"I'll leave you alone the day Norah finally agrees to go out with me," Gabe says.

"She still playing hard to get?"

"Like you wouldn't *believe*, Addie."

"I'm sure she'll come around."

The mechanic looks unsure but Adeline knows her best friend. Gabe has had Norah from day one, she just likes making him sweat.

"I hope so 'cause she is killin' me," Gabe groans, whipping a rag out from his back pocket as he begins backing up towards the pit. "Billy was being held hostage by Tobias last I saw. Go get him, tiger!"

Adeline rolls her eyes but finds herself grinning as she searches the garage again. The frequent phone calls have been great, enough to tide her over the last couple of weeks, but she's missed Billy like crazy. To the extent where she found herself closing her eyes and listening to the soft, gravelly texture of Billy's voice over the phone just to imagine he was there with her. They say absence makes the heart grow fonder and Adeline has never felt so head over heels about anyone like she does Billy Brooks.

God, she can't wait to see him again.

It only takes a moment of meandering through the garage before she finally spots him, hidden by his car with Tobias, who appears to be giving one of his ridiculously egotistical, dry-humoured pep talks. Adeline watches on, chuckling when Billy stares at his boss like he has two heads. Understandable. Tobias' words of wisdom are never *that* encouraging. The pep-talks are usually her father's forte.

She catches Billy's eyes just at the right moment and he mouths '*help*' to her across the roof of his Dodge Charger. Adeline considers playing with him, pulling a face and pretending to really think about it, but she can't watch him suffer the curse of a Tobias Shaw pre-race chat any longer.

Billy's face lights up the moment Adeline approaches. He pushes off the hood of his car to meet her halfway and Tobias pauses mid-sentence.

"–Brooks? Are you listening?"

"Yeah," Billy says absently, "something something, go fast, something something, win. I gotcha."

He engulfs Adeline into a hug, solid and warm as he squeezes her breathless. She sinks into it. Too many weeks apart has her committing the feel of his body to memory, every firm muscle and soft curve under his racing suit, as Billy noses into her hair.

"You, Adeline Gold, are a menace," Tobias grumbles beside them. There's no venom behind his words so Adeline shifts in Billy's arms to grin at him. "I've always said you're a distraction but your father never listens– oh, Reynolds! There you are!" He cuts off his own complaining to dash after Stan, shouting in his wake, "go fast and win, Brooks!"

"Thank you," Billy breathes once Tobias is gone. They step back from each other but their hands stay touching, lingering in place on shoulders and hips. "Pretty sure he was one pep away from getting in my car and driving the race for me."

"You get used to him," Adeline says, chuckling as she watches Tobias trap Stan in the refreshment tent. Billy snorts and flashes her a smile that makes her heart swell, that familiar flutter in her belly returning.

For the first time in two weeks, she takes in the sight of him up close. His hair is damp, presumably from his pre-race shower, the longer strands at the front settled into gentle curls that lick his forehead each time he moves.

Everything about him is *so* soft. That's how Adeline would describe Billy. From the dimple of his chin to the scrunch of his nose when he smiles to the gentle way his fingers brush tentatively across the small of her back. She can't remember the last time she met someone like him. Every other man she's had the pleasure of dating, or sleeping with, has always had this bravado about them; a macho man persona that they think will really get her going. When really, it's men like Billy.

Adeline's gaze falls as she takes a moment to admire him in his racing suit. It's a garish combination of fire engine red and golden yellow, the team colours, but Billy wears it so, so well. Much to Adeline's delight, it hugs him in *all* the right places. Skimming her fingers down from his shoulders to his chest, she traces the outline of the Shaw & Gold patch neatly stitched to the pressed fabric before she moves to the various other patches sewn down the left hand side – NASCAR, Goodyear, Gatorade and then right above the yellow band that wraps around Billy's torso is his name embroidered in white cursive lettering.

"Not that I'm against you admirin' me, Addie. By all means, admire away, but do you wanna maybe go somewhere quieter?" Billy slowly flicks his tongue over his bottom lip and Adeline becomes momentarily distracted. Again.

"Hmm?"

"We're being watched," Billy stage whispers, gesturing across the room with a cock of his head. Adeline glances in the same direction to where her best friend is very obviously pretending to be busy. Norah is a lot of things but subtle is not one of them.

"Yeah, let's go," Adeline says.

Billy looks around to make sure no one else is paying too much attention, sliding his hand into Adeline's as he leads her out of the crowded garage. Privacy in a busy sports venue is hard to come by but they slip into the darkened walkway between garages. Billy backs her against the wall as soon as they're deep enough into the tunnel that they're sure to go unnoticed.

"Hi, my sweet girl," he says in a hushed tone. He rests one hand against the wall by her head while his other hugs her waist, ruching up the fabric just where the seam of her t-shirt gives way to skin.

The air between them is charged, the tension so desperate to be broken, and Adeline swallows thickly as Billy stares down at her. His pupils are like moons, taking over his irises, and his tongue darts over his bottom lip, leaving it dewy and so *damn* kissable that Adeline almost whimpers.

Billy's fingers skim across her exposed midriff and Adeline shivers. The lightness of his touch sends a sharp, static tingle through her limbs. He notices, of course, a small smirk tugging at the corner of his mouth as he dips his head to meet her gaze.

"You good?"

Rendered speechless, all Adeline can do is nod. There's a knot in the depths of her belly being pulled tighter every time his hands drift across her skin, a lethal combination of lust and anticipation. Billy presses in closer until they're cheek to cheek and his rough stubble rubs over her jaw deliciously as he speaks, low and rumbly in her ear.

"I need you to say it, Adeline." She has a strong urge to roll her eyes at the use of her full name but the way it drips from Billy's lips like molasses is enough to hold her back.

"I'm good," she squeaks. Her legs are like jelly and there's the warm, slick feeling of arousal pooling between her thighs.

"That wasn't so hard, was it?" Billy chuckles, his lips ghosting over her ear. Adeline can feel his smile brush across her skin and she knows he has her right where he wants her when he draws back, cupping her face in his hands. As his cloudy eyes flit over her features, Billy sighs like he can't quite believe how lucky he is, and then he leans in. Adeline's eyes are already fluttering closed, lips parting in anticipation as Billy's nose gently nudges hers.

She's been so patient; it's been a long two weeks and Adeline can't wait any longer. She kisses him, pressing hot and firm against his mouth. Billy's hold on her waist tightens and he pushes his tongue past the seam of her lips, deepening the kiss. Adeline sucks in breath, taking everything Billy gives until they're left panting, mouths no longer moving against each other.

"I missed you, Addie. Fuck, did I miss you."

He slides his hands under her shirt, palms scorching on the soft skin of her belly. Adeline's t-shirt rises with the movement, exposing her bralette. It's all cream silk and lace and Billy groans as his fingers dance over the delicate material, his thumbs brushing over her pebbling nipples. A lightning bolt of desire zips straight to Adeline's core and she gasps, fumbling for Billy's hands and guiding them to the fastening of her jeans.

Billy pauses, pulling back with a heaving breath and a steady gaze.

"You sure?" He asks tentatively and Adeline nods, catching her bottom lip between her teeth. "I wanna make you feel good, Addie, but you gotta tell me you want this. With words, sweetheart."

Yes, she wants this. Good God, does she want this.

It's not the time, nor the place, but all rational thinking went out the window the moment Billy kissed her.

"Please, Billy," she whispers, and that's all it takes for Billy to sink to his knees, kissing his way down her bare stomach as he goes.

Adeline's breath catches in her throat as he painstakingly undoes every button of her high-waisted jeans, his fingertips tickling her thighs as he shimmies the denim down her legs. Billy peers up at her through his lashes, his eyes dark and wanting.

"You look so pretty from down here, Addie," Billy says, hushed and intimate as he pushes her panties to the side and slides his middle and pointer finger through the heat of her. As he slicks up the digits, his thumb drags along the crease of her thigh, closer and closer until he finds her clit. He strokes over the sensitive bud, so *ridiculously* delicate with it that Adeline whines, bucking her hips against his hand to chase the small jolt of pleasure the soft touch triggers.

Billy chuckles lightly as he stands back up. His large hand hugs her thigh as he lifts her leg, hooking it around his hip.

"Ready?"

"*Please*," Adeline gasps. She knots her fingers in Billy's hair as she hauls him closer, mouth slotting over his to muffle the inevitable moan about to slip from her lips. Slowly, Billy pushes one finger into her, working her gently until she relaxes around him; wet and writhing. He keeps up a steady rhythm; once then twice, three times as his tongue drags against hers. Then he stills, buried inside her, and Adeline lets out a soft whimper.

"*Guh–*" She tears her mouth away from Billy's, frustrated, and huffs out his name.

"You want another one?" Billy asks, wiggling the fingers of his free hand as he cocks his head to the side, tongue tucked into the corner of his smirking lips.

Adeline nods, half expecting Billy to chastise her for not using her words. Instead, the smirk turns into a grin and suddenly she feels so *full*. Billy mutters something about how tight and warm she is but it's all background noise as Adeline tries so hard not to cry out at the spine-tingling sensation of him pushing and dragging his fingers in and out of her so *agonisingly slowly*.

"Brooks, you down here? You got a visitor," a disembodied voice calls and Adeline is grateful to be shrouded in the darkness of the tunnelled walkway. It doesn't stop the small thrill buzzing through her at the risk of getting caught though, and the adrenaline only further fuels the euphoric feeling fizzing in her brain.

"*Shit*," Billy hisses, but instead of stopping, he picks up his pace. Adeline gasps at the abrupt change, the attack on her senses amping up just that bit more.

"Brooks?" The call comes again.

"*Oh–* please don't stop, Billy. *Fuck*. So good," Adeline whispers through laboured breaths, though the tail end of her sentence comes out louder than she intended and Billy is quick to cover her mouth.

Whoever came to fetch Billy gives up, their footsteps retreating, and the two of them simultaneously breathe out heavily in relief.

"I wasn't gonna stop, you know. Not when you're trying to suppress such pretty sounds," Billy mumbles, kissing her thoroughly. "Can't wait to hear just how loud you can be for me, sweet girl."

He curls his fingers, adjusting the position of his hand in a way that hits just the right spot. Adeline feels the coil in her belly start to unfurl, the low hum of pleasure rippling through her limbs and she chases the feeling. The soft flutter of her pussy around Billy's fingers tells her she's close and she keens, grappling for him and digging her nails into his biceps.

"Uh– yes, *yes*," she moans softly, "Billy, m'gonna come."

Billy's lips find hers once more and it's *so* lazy and slow it's like a stroll, the way he kisses her, clashing tantalisingly with the way he's fucking her with his fingers. He's so *fucking* good. It's like he's worked out what makes her tick in a matter of minutes; taking note of every reaction, each small jerk of her body and how her breath hitches in her throat when he hits a particular spot.

Adeline rolls her head back, hitting the wall as her eyes flutter closed and she starts to come undone. Her orgasm washes over her like she's been caught in a downpour, the pleasure soaking through to her bones. She's completely lost in it, nothing in her ears but rushing blood and the pounding of her heart. Billy takes a hold of her jaw with his free hand, fingers pressing lightly into her cheek.

"Look at me, Adeline."

She quickly complies, her eyes shooting open. Swimming in bliss, she holds Billy's gaze as he keeps up the relentless drag of his digits, his thumb stroking over her over-sensitive clit. She doesn't see the second wave coming, her senses overridden with *Billy, Billy, Billy.* He's everywhere, mouth and hands and body pressed in close as he pushes her into the abyss. All Adeline can do is whine helplessly in place of the moan that's caught in her throat.

"Holy shit," she rasps as her vision refocuses on Billy's shit-eating grin. He watches her, beguiled, and slides his fingers free. As he brings them to his mouth and sucks them clean, he groans like she's the sweetest thing he's ever tasted.

She quirks an eyebrow. "You good?"

"So good," Billy replies, surging forward to kiss her, his lips dewy and mouth hot.

Once her chest has stopped heaving and the hazy feeling in her head clears, Adeline pulls up her jeans and adjusts her shirt. Billy swipes his wet fingers on his racing suit, eyes glazed as they travel the length of her body and he gnaws on his bottom lip.

"What?"

"It's nothing," he murmurs, seeming so shy now. Billy is a lot of things but Adeline didn't think shy could ever be one of them.

"You better go see who your visitor is," Adeline says softly, cupping Billy's cheek.

"Probably my mom. She always used to stop by to wish me luck and then Hard Strike banned visitors from the garage. I wouldn't be surprised if she's talking Stan's ear off as we speak."

Adeline chuckles. He always speaks so fondly of his parents, it makes her a little nervous to meet them.

"Go, Billy. Don't leave her waiting," she urges. "I'm gonna find the bathroom but I'll see you out there."

"Okay," Billy nods, but hesitates still, bouncing on the balls of his feet.

"Go!" Adeline laughs, giving him a gentle push in the right direction. He dips his head to press a quick kiss to the corner of her mouth before he jogs back along the walkway. Adeline watches him go but she waits until he's disappeared around the corner to squeal and spin herself dizzy like a lovesick teenager.

seven

ADELINE

SHE HEARS THE COMMOTION HALFWAY DOWN THE HALL. THE room she and Billy left not forty minutes ago, thrumming with pre-race activity but otherwise calm, has descended into chaos.

"What *the fuck* is going on?" She asks no one in particular as she re-enters the garage.

Nobody answers her so she weaves her way into the middle of the space to see who the hell is arguing thirty minutes before a race. When she finally fights her way through and spots Billy at the centre of it all, her heart drops. There's a woman, an older looking redhead, screeching at him. She's jabbing him in the chest with her pointy, manicured nail, babbling on and on while Billy stands there taking it.

"I'm here, aren't I? Isn't this what you wanted, William? I've made the effort to support you and you can't even pretend you're happy to see me."

"Maybe that's because he's not," Norah murmurs and Adeline suddenly realises it's Delilah.

She knows more about Delilah now. Billy told her what happened over the last of the mulled wine on Christmas Eve, once

Adeline had clumsily clambered back into the passenger seat of his car, clothes askew and thoroughly kissed. Their kissing turned into conversation, turned into hysterical laughter, turned into tears when Billy – overtired and on the verge of tipsy – finally let his guard down. Adeline listened, hand in his, fingers wiping tears from his face, and then helped him devise a plan; the best way to end things with Delilah for good. She wasn't getting him back this time and if a little bit of that was Adeline being possessive over a man she barely knew, well, who could blame her?

Now, as Adeline steps into the commotion, she's not sure that plan worked. She reaches out as she moves closer to Billy, staying hidden behind him, and traces a single finger down the length of his spine. He tenses.

"It's me," she whispers, catching the minute slump of his shoulders at the sound of her voice. Billy grapples for her hand and holds on tight. The man who just made her come twice with wicked fingers and a mouth to match is gone in the blink of an eye. He's small, sunken into his shell as he stands there, letting Delilah prod and poke him. Adeline hates it. Seeing the way she treats him first hand makes her want to slap the presumptuous redhead silly and tell her she never did and never will deserve a man like Billy.

So, she does.

Stepping around him, she makes herself fully visible to Delilah. And though she may be small, Adeline has no qualms about getting up in her face. Billy tugs her back, telling her it's not worth it, and more people start to gather around. She glances around to Billy who looks like he wants nothing more than for the ground to swallow him up.

"Oh, look, here she is. I take it this is the little bitch you left me for," Delilah sneers. If she's hoping to get a rise out of Billy, it works.

"Woah, hey! Don't you *dare*."

"I'm not wrong though, am I, Billy? You think I don't know you ran straight to her on Christmas Eve?" Delilahs's voice grows louder, she clearly doesn't give a shit who sees or hears her outburst. Norah steps forward, ready to defend Adeline too but Delilah turns on her just as quickly. "Don't you start. I know he slept with you as well. Fucking NASCAR whores."

There's a collective gasp. Adeline raises her arm but before she can follow through with her actions, someone lifts her into the air. Their arms are wrapped tight around her middle and she flails, kicking out as they drag her away.

"Not a good idea, Adeline."

"Put me down, Gabe."

"Not until you've cooled down," Gabe says. He holds her flush against his chest and no matter how much she thrashes about, she's not able to free herself from his grip.

"I'm not gonna cool down until *she* leaves," Adeline huffs. She's all hot and bothered and now she has no one to take it out on. "How dare she show up here all fucking high and mighty because she's shown up for him for the first time in seven *fucking* years, and when they're not even together anymore, as if he was suddenly going to go running back to her. The fucking audacity."

"Are you done?"

Adeline breathes out heavily. In her rage and Gabe's attempt to stop her from doing something stupid, her hair has fallen across her face and as she sighs, the long blonde tendrils float up into the air before gently falling back over her eyes. She watches through them as Delilah is escorted from the garage and her anger gives way to embarrassment. Billy's going to regret everything. She's just proven he's gone from one crazy to another.

"Yeah, I'm done."

Gabe places her back on the ground and Adeline straightens herself up just as Billy approaches them. He looks upset, his lips pulled into a sullen pout.

Here we go, she thinks as she prepares herself for Billy to tell her everything has been a mistake, that *she* was a mistake. Instead, she's taken by surprise when Billy crashes his lips to hers in a kiss that's so intense, it nearly knocks her off her feet. Her arms automatically wind around him and her hands roam his back. He's tense again, muscles rigid under her fingertips. They ripple against her palms as

Billy suddenly picks her up and she squeals into the kiss as her feet leave the ground once again. Adeline weaves her fingers into his hair, the curls at the front dry now as she twists them softly. Billy melts into the touch and the hurried, frantic kiss transitions into something more delicate. Shallow breaths and slowed hands as Billy nips at her bottom lip and presses small kisses across her mouth in quick succession. When he pulls back, slightly breathless and cheeks pink, he stares at her in awe.

"You okay?"

"I am now," Billy breathes between sweet pecks as he places her back down. Around them, everything moves in the pre-race whirlwind she knows so well. Adeline looks up at the man in front of her, tenderly traces the sharp lines of his jaw and the slope of his nose, and wishes they could stay in their bubble. She sighs softly, breaking the spell.

"Come on, golden boy, you've got a race to win."

eight

ADELINE
February 16th, 1975
Daytona International Speedway, Florida

ADELINE'S VISION IS FUZZY AS SHE WATCHES THE FLURRY OF cars zoom along the stretch of track she's stood beside. She refuses to tear her eyes away though, fixing her gaze on the green and orange Dodge that's about to make its 100th lap. They're halfway through the Daytona 500 and Billy is so far ahead you'd think he was behind with the way he chases the other cars around the speedway as they try to catch up with him.

She forgets all about the cigarette between her fingers as she concentrates on the action unfolding before her. It burns slowly, ash falling at her feet until she feels the heat of it against her skin.

"*Fuck,*" she hisses, dropping the butt to the ground.

She always does this; lights one up, inhales a couple of drags, and then gets so swept up in the thrill of the race that she ends up with cigarette burns. Without something to do her hands get fidgety so she makes the same mistake again and again.

Adeline glances at the ground and stomps out the stub with the sole of her Converse as the cars whizz past her once more. She looks up just in time to see Billy's car fly over the asphalt, sending her heart thudding in her chest. These races often feel like a concert when she's this close to the action and every time Billy drives past it's like she's front and centre of the crowd and the lead singer is balancing on the edge of the stage singing just to her.

It's exhilarating; watching the man she's falling for drive like his life depends on it.

For Billy, it probably does feel that way after he came second in the Winston Western 500 last month. He would have been happy with the result if he hadn't been beaten by Rex Harlow by an eighth of a second, his ex-Hard Strike teammate riling him up to no end on the podium. Adeline wasn't happy with the result either; seeing Rex succeed was like a kick in the teeth.

The determination to win is evident in Billy's driving. It's enough to make Adeline swoon, knees weak, the embers of desire flicker in her belly. It's the speed, the control Billy has behind the wheel. Adeline can picture his face, hard and focused as he makes lap after lap. There's a reason she's always found herself falling into bed with these men. It's just this time, there are big feelings that come with it.

It terrifies her and thrills her all at once to find herself this deep. She feels *so* naive for even thinking about love this early on and with her parents as a prime example as to why falling hard and fast isn't as exciting as it always seems, well, it's all the reason she needs to question just how much Billy means to her. Adeline has no solid memories of her mother and father's relationship but she knows it was turbulent and the stories she's heard over the years told her it wasn't ever the epitome of stability – or love for that matter. At least not in those last years.

Still, the words are always on the tip of her tongue and she thinks about it a lot as she finds herself tumbling into the beautiful, terrifying unknown with Billy.

The other thing – the thing that worries her most – is that Adeline doesn't exactly have a track record for lasting relationships.

Each one has been fleeting, a moment in time that either stops abruptly or fades out slowly like the last beats of a song.

She doesn't want that with Billy.

Adeline wants her relationship with Billy to be a whole damn movie score; orchestral and thunderous, transitioning from one piece of music to another so seamlessly that she doesn't even know it's happened.

Maybe she's getting ahead of herself.

Maybe, it'll all come crashing down.

The crunch of metal pulls her out of her spiralling thoughts as though the universe could hear her and she quickly grounds herself. Taking stock, she focuses on the spongy turf beneath her feet as her eyes adjust under the bright Floridian sun and she finds the yellow flag being waved across the track.

It's the smell of burning rubber that sends the little tightly-wound ball of anxiety unfurling in her gut. She cracks her knuckles and balls her hands into fists, nails digging into her palms as she searches the track for the collision. When she spots his orange and green Dodge drive past on the back stretch, following the pace car leading everyone around the track, her whole body softens.

Billy is okay, she thinks, relieved.

Except she still can't see Stan or Norah's cars anywhere and her pulse thunders in her ears all over again.

Heavy footsteps tread across the gravel walkway behind her and Adeline turns to see her father jogging over to the small grassy area she's hidden on, away from the tense energy of the garage and pit. It's quiet enough for her to concentrate on the race but close enough to the stands that she can still vibe off the energy of the crowd.

"Who was it?"

"None of ours, sunshine," Michael replies, watching her carefully as her eyelid twitches with lingering, mild panic.

"Okay. Good. That's good. Not *good* good obviously but as long as no one is hurt then–"

Her father steps forward and pulls her into a bear hug to stop her rambling. Pressing a kiss to the top of her head, Adeline squeezes him tightly. It never gets any easier, the unknown after a collision.

"It doesn't look too serious but there's debris covering most of the track on the east side," Michael explains as he runs a gentle hand over Adeline's hair. "Stan was heading into the pit when it happened so he's gonna wait it out there. I think Billy and Norah are on their way in too if you wanna come say hi?"

Adeline nods against his chest and falls into step with Michael as he tucks her under his arm. She couldn't have positioned herself further from the Shaw & Gold garage if she'd tried and she breaks away from her father halfway around the track, her strides longer and steps quicker, until the team's cars finally come into view.

Everyone sits in their vehicles, ready to go again at a moment's notice unless the race gets called off, and Adeline hurries along the row of cars to the front where Billy is. Gabe is checking over his tyres and Adeline whistles to grab his attention. His head shoots up instantly – the roar of the engines are white noise to most of them now – and he's wearing a smug, toothy smile.

"How long have they got?" Adeline shouts.

She's giddy, eager to see Billy even if just for a moment. Gabe peers out over the track, assessing the situation, and turns back to her with a shrug.

"Ten minutes maybe," he replies.

"I'll take it."

Billy jumps when Adeline knocks on the roof of his car and he grins as he lowers the net in the open space where a window would be.

"Tinkerbell!" He's giddy, high on the adrenaline of the race.

Adeline rolls her eyes, giggling. The nickname Billy's been testing out is sticking it seems.

"Hi, hot stuff."

"What're you doin' here?"

"Wanted to see you," Adeline replies as Billy reaches his hand out and links his glove-clad fingers with hers. "How is it out there?"

"Perfect. The track feels great and I'm winnin' ain't I?" Billy chuckles. It's faint, muffled by his helmet but along with the smug, lopsided smile he's wearing it's still enough to release a kaleidoscope of butterflies in Adeline's tummy.

"Careful, you'll jinx it."

"Nah. Not when I've got you as my good luck charm, Addie."

"You're a sweet talker, Billy Brooks."

Adeline wants to kiss him more than anything but with his helmet in the way she has to settle for flipping the reinforced plastic of his visor down and pressing a kiss to it with an exaggerated smack. There's a smear of lip balm in the shape of her lips as she draws back and she curses under her breath, trying to wipe it clean with her sleeve only to make it worse with each swipe of her arm. It doesn't help that Billy is watching her, his eyes filled with amusement.

"Oh, God. Please don't crash because of that."

The helmet shifts in her hands as Billy laughs loudly.

"If I do, it'll be worth it."

"Billy!" Adeline gasps, swatting him across the arm. "Don't say shit like that. Gabe, have you got a–"

A clean rag hits Adeline square in the face as she turns to find the mechanic and she grumbles out a quick thanks as she gets to work, wiping down Billy's visor until it's sparkling.

"Thanks, sweet girl," Billy says softly once she's done. "Wish I could kiss you properly."

"Only a hundred laps to go. I'll be right here waiting."

She reaches for his hand again and gives it a small squeeze of reassurance just as someone announces that the race is about to continue.

Adeline flashes him a bubbly grin and he winks in place of a kiss as she steps back. Billy reattaches the net in the window, giving it a tug to make sure it's secure before he revs his engine and leads Stan and Norah back out onto the track.

Only a hundred laps to go.

She watches the rest of the race with Michael. They grip onto each other tightly, Adeline's fingers dig into her father's arm in a way that's sure to hurt but he's too polite to say anything. Holding her breath in the final moments, Adeline only lets it go when Billy zips over the finish line in first place. She's an instant mess. Euphoria exudes from her in laughter and tears, and the excitement doesn't dissipate as Stan and Norah finish close behind him.

Adeline celebrates with the rest of the crew during Billy's victory lap and watches from the sidelines as he's whisked to the podium. She's dizzy with emotion and growing impatience. It itches up her body as she waits, greeting her heavy head and the tear tracks dried on her aching cheeks. The brief glimpses of Billy she gets through the crowd aren't enough as she fights back the urge to push her way through, to barge her way to the front just to kiss him stupid.

Gabe appears beside her and gives her a gentle squeeze on her shoulder, taming her jumpiness as he watches on.

"Your boy drives like he needs it to survive."

"Maybe he does," Adeline replies, eyes never straying from the podium.

Champagne spills from the bottle as Billy pops the cork and attempts to guzzle the foaming liquid. It drips down his stubbled chin in waves, soaking his racing suit. Even more so when he laughs around the bottle, his eyes shining in the flash of the cameras.

Adeline has lost count of how many times she's cried since the chequered flag waved, but seeing Billy take his trophy and hold it high above his head makes her eyes water all over again. She beams through the tears, clapping and cheering and hoping Billy can hear her above the cacophony of noise.

It feels like forever before she sees him duck out of the spotlight, shoving his trophy into the hands of whoever will take it. Billy makes a beeline for Adeline wearing a look of determination on his face as if getting to her is a race in itself. He weaves through people until he's almost close enough to touch and then, without warning, he swoops in and lifts Adeline clean off her feet. She yelps, giggling wetly as he spins her around and buries his grin against her shoulder. His smile stretches from ear to ear, lighting up his whole face as he places her back on the ground. Then it falters and his brows furrow in concern as he cups her tear-stained cheeks in his hands.

"You're crying."

Billy gently brushes her stray tears away with the pads of his thumbs and Adeline sighs at the warmth of his skin against hers. Her face fits so well in his palms, like his hands were made to hold her.

"You won," she croaks and swallows thickly. "They're happy tears, I promise."

"Oh, sweet girl," Billy says, lips pressed to her forehead. "Come with me."

He takes her hand and leads her out of the crowd and into the empty garage, away from prying eyes. Adeline's nose twitches at the lingering scent of motor oil. It's in the air, clinging to every surface and woven into the fibres of Billy's racing suit as he pulls her close the moment they're alone; a reminder that she's right where she belongs.

Chest to chest, fumbling blindly through the garage Adeline slides her hands into Billy's hair as they kiss. Her fingers tug and grasp at the sweat-drenched strands curling at the nape of his neck and Billy moans as his mouth moves over hers with a delicate eagerness. His tongue drags along her bottom lip, the sensitive skin fizzing and tingling in its wake, and Adeline pushes in closer. She slides a hand down Billy's shoulder to his chest, her fingers working to open his suit as he cages her in against a work bench at the back of the room.

She deepens the kiss, hungry for it, and tastes the remnants of expensive champagne on Billy's tongue. Adeline suddenly wishes she had a coping mechanism that wasn't smoking half a packet of cigarettes to get her through a race, but if Billy tastes the fading tobacco in the kiss, he doesn't say anything; just hauls her up onto the work bench where she lands with a soft *unf* and wraps her legs around his middle.

Adeline's teeth graze over Billy's bottom lip and she sucks it into her mouth, letting it go with a quiet pop. She studies his face as she draws back, her gaze flitting from his red, kiss-bitten lips to the tiny creases of happiness in the corners of his eyes. He looks dishevelled, as one does post-NASCAR race, but add in the way Adeline's fingers have roughed up his hair and his irises are nothing but a thin ring of smokey-blue around his pupils and it makes Adeline want to do things she really wouldn't like an audience for.

The noise outside is getting closer though, so she settles for another quick kiss. It's softer this time, just a tender press of their lips and quiet breath shared between them. Billy trails tiny kisses down Adeline's jaw and drops his head to her shoulder.

"M'so proud of you," she mumbles into his hair, conscious that their quiet moment is coming to an end.

"There he is! Brooks!" Stan hollers across the garage, followed by more voices as the rest of the team filters in. Billy glances over his shoulder and groans as Adeline lets her legs fall from around his waist.

"You were my good luck charm, y'know? Couldn't have done it without you," he says even though it was *all* him; Billy's competence behind the wheel is a product of his own skill and tenacity.

She's all out of tears but the pressure behind Adeline's eyes is still there and she surges forward for one last kiss as Billy lets her go. Stan whistles, the sound echoing in the vast space, and Billy flips him off without looking.

"Save a dance for me at the party later?"

"I'll save a hundred dances for you, Tinkerbell."

Adeline watches him retreat from her perch on the workbench until he meets Stan halfway and he playfully rough houses Billy across the garage to the others. Gabe spots her and waves; big, stupid swipes of his arm through the air as he flashes her a toothy grin. Norah meets her eye across the room, cocks her head to the side and arches an all-knowing eyebrow. In return, Adeline brings her fingers to her lips, smiling at the faint sting Billy's stubble has left on her skin.

nine

ADELINE

THE HOTEL ROOM IS QUIET APART FROM THE OCCASIONAL flip of a page as Adeline lays on the bed reading. She's been ready to go for almost an hour but Norah is taking her sweet-ass time getting ready for the party in the bar downstairs.

"It's fine," she'd said, *"we'll just be fashionably late!"*

Adeline hums as she reads over the same line again and again, never fully taking it in. Her mind is elsewhere and she's quite enjoying the Billy of her daydreams. If only her best friend would hurry the fuck up and she could go be with the real thing.

"You really like him, don't you?" Norah interrupts the quiet from the bathroom, looking at Adeline through the mirror as she applies her make-up.

"Huh?"

"Billy," the redhead clarifies. "You're humming and you've got that far away look in your eye, it doesn't take much for me to put two and two together. At least, I *assume* you're thinking about him."

Adeline closes her book, her brows knitted together as she watches Norah brush a peachy pink blush over the apples of her cheeks.

"Am I that obvious?"

Norah huffs out a small laugh as she swirls even more blush onto her brush and taps the excess off on the side of the sink.

"Ridiculously so, Addie. You wear your heart on your sleeve and you can't control your damn face for the life of you."

Well ain't that the truth?

Adeline flops back against the pillows with a weary sigh.

"I think I might be falling in love with him. Is that crazy?"

She twists a strand of hair around her finger as she waits for Norah to tell her that it's absolutely mad; the most stupid idea she's ever had, of *course* it's crazy–

"It's not crazy," Norah says nonchalantly and Adeline sits up again.

"It's not? But we've spent such a small amount of time together," she counters, falling straight into a lifelong habit of trying to convince herself the very thing she's questioned is true.

Norah appears in the doorway, the hems of her red bell-bottom jeans a stark contrast against the putrid-brown hotel carpet. They balloon over her feet as she bends down to pick up two heel options, holding them up for Adeline to see. Adeline points to the ones on the left and Norah nods in agreement.

"It's not crazy, Addie," Norah says in a tone that brooks no argument. "Why don't you spend some time in New York with him? He's seen your world, why don't you let him show you a bit of his? You can easily drive down to Richmond from there."

"I don't know, Nor."

Adeline's relationship with New York is… strained at best. Norah finishes buckling her heels and fixes Adeline with a look that means she's about to dish out some tough love.

"You can't follow your dad around forever, Adeline. I know you feel like you have to protect him but he's a grown-ass man."

Adeline curls her fingers, pressing her nails into her palm before she attempts to answer calmly.

"But since my mom left–"

"Since your mom left *when you were three-years-old,* you've been his number one priority and you've always put *him* first in return. Above everything. But it's been twenty-two years, Adeline. He won't hate you for taking time to be a twenty-five year old and live a little. And it'll probably do him some good too. When was the last time your dad went on a date?"

"I see you're wearing Gabe's favourite lip colour," Adeline muses.

"Don't change the subject. If you go to New York, you can spend some proper time with Billy. Away from us and not in a garage; really get to know each other."

The thought of spending quality time with Billy sounds like a dream and Adeline can already picture it; wandering around the city or staying cooped up in his apartment and really getting to *know* each other. It makes her go all gooey just thinking about it. That's all she'll do though and she tells Norah so.

Norah rolls her eyes but says no more as she picks up her purse and looks herself over in the full length mirror.

"Okay, let's go."

Adeline's mood has shifted after her conversation with Norah. She's craving a drink and a dance and a certain looseness in her body only a combination of both can supply.

Which is why she bristles when in the elevator down to the ground floor Norah turns to her sharply, as if she's had a sudden thought.

"Maybe it's time you did something for yourself too," she says, "when was the last time you even sat at a piano."

"I said I'd think about it," Adeline replies through gritted teeth and a forced smile.

"That's all I ask." Norah reaches for her hand as the elevator arrives with a soft chime and the doors slide open.

The Shaw & Gold celebratory post-race drinks are obligatory, no matter the outcome. When one of their own *does* win though, it gets a little wild. Adeline tries to warn the hotel staff in advance when she makes the booking but it's never enough to prepare them for the carnage. *Respectful* carnage; they're not ones to trash the place.

So it's no surprise that the party is already in full swing when they arrive at the bar. Adeline assesses the crowded room and spots Stan and Gabe setting up a beer pong tournament. They've pushed two tables together and are arranging an array of different shaped and sized glasses at either end. Fuck knows where they found a ping pong ball but she leaves them to it, weaving in and out of people as she heads further towards the bar.

The best thing about these events is that it's not just *her* racing team that attends. The place is filled with various pit crew, drivers and execs who happen to be staying in the same hotel so it's always a great chance to network. The worst thing is that they all have scantily clad women hanging off their arms and Adeline has to fight the recoil of self-consciousness as she takes in their busty chests and flat stomachs. Instead, she tries to focus her attention on finding Billy, and luckily, she doesn't have to look far.

"Holy shit, Tinkerbell. You look incredible!"

The first thing Adeline notices is that Billy is already half gone, words slurred and pupils dilated in a drunken haze as he suddenly appears in front of her. The second thing she notices is that his happiness is radiating from him like a solar flare, blinding in the lopsided smile now a permanent feature on his face. Billy runs his fingers through his hair, the soft-looking strands – half damp, half fluffy – fall into waves atop his head.

"Hi," Adeline giggles sweetly and Billy groans in response. He reaches for her, fingers skimming along her cheek as she meets him halfway. The kiss is more a collision of mouths than anything else; a tipsy fumble of wet tongue and dull teeth that Billy grazes along her bottom lip as he sways back with a deep sigh. He holds her gently as his glassy eyes flit from her lips to the glitter on her eyelids, and Adeline swallows down the lingering taste of beer and a liquor she can't quite put her finger on.

"You're *so* pretty," Billy murmurs in awe.

"You're pretty out of it, huh?"

"*Noooo,* I am perfe–" He hiccups, grimacing before he tries again. "I am perfectly– good. Adeline."

Glancing around, Adeline is hoping to find Norah nearby but she's already settled in with Stan and Gabe, draping herself around the latter and trying her best to distract him while he aims the ping pong ball.

Adeline wraps an arm around Billy's waist and he cuddles in close, nuzzling into her hair.

"Come on, Billy. I'm gonna get you some water to drink while I catch up."

Billy responds by pressing a warm kiss to her temple and, thankfully, being cooperative as Adeline drags him to the bar. They squeeze into a spot towards the end, where the walnut bar top bends around to meet the wall and they're likely to be waiting a while. Adeline doesn't mind, happy to watch the bartender make drinks and her friends have fun.

Billy, it turns out, is not.

He leans across the bar and reaches for a clean looking glass and a bottle of whatever he can get his hands on. Adeline is momentarily distracted by the way the near-sheer fabric of his shirt stretches over his back muscles as he moves and the desire itching at her fingers to reach out and touch; to run her palm over the strong, smooth plains of his back.

Her pining is halted abruptly when Billy almost drops the abandoned bottle of vodka he found behind the bar mid pour and it clinks against the glass before he catches it again.

"Billy," Adeline sighs, "I'm not really in the mood for straight vodka tonight."

"I was gonna add orange juice for you," Billy counters, whines really, as Adeline pries the bottle from his hand.

"Where were you gonna get orange juice from, pal?"

"The nice lady behind the bar, *obviously*."

"That still means we gotta wait," Adeline giggles and Billy groans impatiently.

"They're taking too long," he mumbles, leaning over the bar again. This time, he cups a hand around his mouth and bellows.

"*Excuuuuse* me! Can we get a drink for my pretty friend, please! She'll have a– *shit,* Addie, what are you drinkin'?"

"Jack and Coke, please! Oh, and water for him!" Adeline shouts down to the bartender. She's an older lady with a knowing smile who rolls her eyes but chuckles, clearly won over by Billy's playful charm, and lets them know she'll be right down.

The weight of Billy's arm falls across Adeline's shoulders as he pulls her close and he grins his bright, cheeky grin down at her before pressing a kiss to the top of her head. It's ridiculously affectionate, a softly intimate gesture that makes her insides swoop like she's gone ten rounds on the biggest ride at Coney Island.

Billy's subtlety doesn't go amiss, though. Adeline knows now that putting on a show was what he did with Delilah, or what *she* wanted of him. Nothing was just for them; no secret touches or smiles hidden in modest kisses. So with Adeline, when they're not alone, it's all linked pinky fingers, giggled whispers, and a firm hand on the small of her back. Even tipsy, Billy seems to be keeping to his self-appointed rules of public affection; the messy kiss he greeted her with aside. Adeline has a feeling that'll change again as the night goes on.

A few moments later, their drinks are placed down in front of them and Billy adds them to his room tab with a boyish smile and an overly polite, "*Thank you , ma'am.*"

They fall back into the sea of people, meandering their way to a table where Billy deposits their drinks. He flops back into a chair and spreads his legs, stretching his arms up so his shirt rises and reveals the little sliver of tanned skin above his belted jeans. Adeline's gaze follows the sharp line of his hip lower before Billy clears his throat. When she looks back up, he's smirking.

"Drink that," Adeline says firmly, cheeks flushed as she slides the glass of water across the table. "And then you're gonna dance with me, golden boy."

And boy, do they dance.

The night goes by in a blur of dancing and drinks and then more dancing. She dances with Billy; with Stan and Norah and Gabe, and anyone else who concedes to her fluttering eyelashes and flirtatious pleas. Song after song Adeline twirls and spins until she collapses onto Billy's lap hours later, exhausted. Her feet throb in her platform boots and the moment she kicks them up from the floor, it feels like she's floating.

Billy is mid conversation when she lands on him but one of his arms snakes around her waist, holding her securely, while the other rests on her bare thigh with no second thought. Adeline settles against him, her whole body thrumming with adrenaline and her clothes cling to her sweaty skin. It's no surprise that she finds gold glitter on her fingers when she dabs at her cheeks, her mascara is probably smudged to hell too but she's too happy to care.

She only realises she's drifting, head lolling and curled cosily against Billy the human space heater, when said space heater presses a warm kiss to the side of her neck exposed to him. Adeline hums sleepily, stretching awake. Billy's lips are soft as they work their way along her jaw to the spot just below her ear, sucking gently until his tongue swirls – warm and wet – over the inevitable mark he's just left. He coaxes out a whimper from Adeline's parted lips, the music loud enough to hide the sound but Billy smiles against her skin and she knows he still heard it.

"Come back to New York with me?" Billy murmurs, his breath hot over her ear. His voice is low and husky, shot to pieces from singing and screaming along with her to every song played over the shitty speakers.

Adeline silently curses Norah for being so goddamn right about everything and she chews on her lip as she thinks it over; as if there's anything to think about. Her relationship with New York is rocky, yes, but it's *home*. And she hasn't been back in a *really* long time.

"Okay," she whispers, turning in Billy's arms to kiss him in their dark corner of the bar. Once, then twice as she says, "I'll come to New York with you."

ten

ADELINE
February 18th, 1975
Brooklyn, New York

NEW YORK IN FEBRUARY MEANS SNOW. NOT FRESHLY fallen, crisp, white snow either, but sludge. Piles of grey, gritty snow that's been driven over and shovelled and trodden on by thousands, and Adeline loves it. But then she thrives in the cold weather; the frost biting at her fingertips and the chill in the air that gives her cheeks and nose a natural rosy glow.

The snow has made coming back to New York easier and being with Billy helps mask the apprehension she usually feels each time she returns to the city. The niggle is still there though, the nervous ball of energy in her stomach that makes her study each face she passes. It fuels the overbearing anticipation that one day she'll be met with an older face that mirrors her own.

Wrapped up in her favourite suede and sherpa coat, toggles fastened all the way up to her knitted scarf, she follows Billy single file through the dirty slush. Trying to keep up with the speed of his long strides grows tiring after a while though, and she finds herself slowing down, trailing behind him by a good few yards.

"Are you still with me, Tinkerbell?"

"Just," Adeline calls back to him, her voice lost to a sudden blare of sirens and the honk of a car horn.

Hello, New York.

Billy stops to wait for her and as she gets closer, Adeline notices that his nose is pink too. His dove-grey eyes are glossy under cold-induced tears that stay dormant until he blinks and one trickles down his cheek. Adeline reaches out as she meets him and swipes her gloved hand over the droplet before it drips from his chin, pressing her lips to his cheek in its wake. Their cold noses brush against one another as she pulls back and Billy chases after her, grinning against her mouth as he kisses her.

They're not far, Billy tells her as they keep walking, his apartment only a couple of streets away. Adeline is careful with her steps now, speeding up a little to keep up with him. Her eyes are cast down as she concentrates on her feet hitting the pavement one after the other, her strides reaching over snow and skirting around icy patches. She has a talent for sensing other people approaching and dodges around them all while making sure she doesn't lose sight of Billy in her peripherals.

As much as being back in the city is jarring to some extent, Adeline is excited to be there. She spent the whole plane ride from Florida imagining how their short stay is going to go, imagining Billy's home and the hidden parts of him she's going to be privy to. She knows how important Brooklyn is to him. His apartment is just two blocks down from his parents' house – his childhood home – and his sister lives in a student apartment two blocks in the other direction. Everything that means something to him is right here. A million miles away from the NASCAR bubble they live in for eleven months of the year.

Even if they only have a few days before they have to drive down to Virginia for the next race, Adeline has embers of joy flickering through her veins as they round the corner and Billy's building comes into view.

"It was a brewery back in the day," Billy says as they finally come to a stop. "The company didn't survive prohibition so they sold it. M'pretty sure it became a dress factory after that and then they turned it into housing in the early 60s. Careful on the steps, sweet girl."

Billy climbs up to the doors. They're old fashioned and grand looking with intricate iron bars raised across the glass and oversized, shiny brass doorknobs on either side. He sets their bags on the damp ground before delving deep into his pocket and pulling out his key. The place differs so much from the modern Manhattan skyscraper the Gold's call home when they're in the city and as Adeline begins her ascent she stares up at the old, red-brick building in awe.

In her eagerness to see inside, she doesn't notice the slick patch of black ice on the second step. Her foot skids backwards and it all happens in slow motion but she's still not quick enough to grab the railing and she goes down with a whine and a hefty thud. Her ankle twists and her chin clips the top step when she hits the ground.

There's a second thud as Billy drops their bags again and hurries down the steps to where she sits in a heap, gloved hand pressed to her mouth.

"Fuck, Addie! Baby, are you okay?"

Concern floods his features, his lips parted and eyes wide as they flit erratically over Adeline's face. His gaze lands on her chin where she can feel warm blood seeping down over her jaw. Adeline tentatively pulls her hand away, her cream glove now red and clinging to her skin.

Great, she thinks and her eyes well up in shock even though she's too stunned to actually cry. Instead, she looks up at Billy with her bottom lip wobbling and groans.

"Come on, I got you," he murmurs softly, bending down to cautiously tuck an arm around her back. With a tight hold on her hand, he hauls her up to her feet and takes her weight, leading her inside. Adeline collapses into a threadbare armchair in the lobby, grimacing when her damp jeans stick to her thighs as she sits back.

"I'm gonna take the bags up first, you gonna be okay?" Billy asks as he brushes Adeline's hair from her face, fingers barely skimming her skin. He looks down at her like she'll break if he makes the wrong move.

"I'll be fine, Billy," she mumbles.

The building has no elevator, so once Billy makes the journey up and down the stairs to deposit their bags, he does the same again with Adeline in his arms. She only feels a little bit ridiculous as he hauls her up each flight of stairs with relative ease, her body tense in his arms. Billy squeezes her tighter and places gentle kisses in her hair every time they reach a new landing until she relaxes, at least a little bit.

"This is bullshit," she grumbles as he carries her over the threshold of his apartment. She's annoyed with herself more than anything. Adeline Gold, the woman who can wear platform boots for hours without so much as a stumble, injures herself not even an hour into being in the city. She knew there was a reason she doesn't come back often, that New York has it in for her, and this is doing everything to prove her point.

The adrenaline from the fall is dissipating, the numbness wearing off and giving way to a harsh throbbing across her jaw, and her ankle isn't faring much better. Billy settles her on the couch and, despite protest from Adeline, strips her down to her panties and baby-tee to give him better access to her ankle, previously hidden by long jeans and thick, wool socks. He leaves her for a moment and Adeline melts back into the deep brown leather, listening to the sound of Billy's footsteps elsewhere in the apartment, back and forth until he kneels in front of her, a first aid box and ice pack laid out on the coffee table.

"M'gonna take a look, okay? Let me know if it hurts when I move it."

"I will," she mumbles as he takes her foot in his hands. He manipulates her ankle, slow and gentle, tilting her foot up towards the ceiling. Adeline tries her hardest to hide the obvious grimace of pain on her face, looking anywhere but at Billy and clenching her teeth.

"*Adeline*," Billy warns sternly in response to her foolishness. She lets her gaze fall to him as he peers up at her from the floor. The small twist in her stomach is automatic and warmth creeps up her neck and across her cheeks at the thought of what else he could do from down there.

"If I tell you it hurts, you're going to tell me not to walk on it and then we can't do anything fun," she says, petulant and pouting.

"We can still have plenty of fun, Tinkerbell," Billy muses as his hand trails from her ankle up to her calf, fingers dancing over her skin teasingly. Adeline holds her breath, the twist of arousal in her belly tightening as he works his hands higher. She's left with goose-bumps when his warm palm massages her thigh just once before he retreats, smirking up at her. "As long as you keep this elevated and iced," he quips.

He places one delicate kiss on her swelling ankle, his scruff tickling her skin. He'll probably shave again before the next race but Adeline loves the slightly unkempt look on him. It makes him look older, a little more rough around the edges compared to the clean-cut NASCAR driver the world is so used to seeing.

"I don't like you very much right now."

"Yeah, you do," he hums and Adeline wants to slap, or kiss, the shit-eating smirk from his lips. Anything for a distraction as she grits her teeth again, jaw tight while Billy wraps her ankle securely in gauze. She shivers a little, her bare legs prickly with the cold.

"I'm also starting to think this has gotten a little unfair."

Billy quirks an eyebrow. "How so?"

Seemingly satisfied with her ankle, he pulls the coffee table a little closer and stuffs a cushion under Adeline's foot to keep it elevated, the ice pack draped over the joint – not helping with the chill. Billy settles himself onto the couch beside her and busies himself with prepping a cotton pad with alcohol solution.

"Well, you've seen me in my panties multiple times now, and every time you've been fully dressed. I'd call that unfair, wouldn't you?"

"I think you need to stop being a brat and let me clean this cut on your chin," Billy responds, voice low as he delicately grips her jaw and tilts her face towards him. His fingers barely graze her skin but his intentions are still clear and Adeline shuts her mouth. Billy chuckles as he presses a soft kiss to her closed lips. "Thank you, sweet girl."

She breathes deeply as Billy swipes the cotton pad over her cut, hissing as he presses gently and wipes the dried blood away.

"*Shit.*"

"Sorry, sweetheart," he whispers. "Almost done."

When he is, he blows cool air lightly across her chin. Adeline's eyes fall to his lips, pursed and pink, and she dips her head to kiss him. Fast and sweet.

"What was that for?"

"Just because," she replies, her nose scrunching as she smiles.

"You're fucking adorable, Adeline." He says it quietly, as if the words were only meant for himself, as he peels the backing from a Band Aid and lays it over the cut.

"Not with this monstrosity," she huffs with a frown as her fingers graze over her chin.

"You're beautiful."

"You have to say that, we make out and stuff."

"I say it because I mean it," Billy answers simply.

"Well, you need to get your eyes checked."

Billy laughs, loud and rich. "Pretty sure my eyesight is perfect, Tinkerbell. Wouldn't be able to drive cars for a living if it wasn't."

"Okay, smartypants." She pulls a face, but nothing can stop the smile that graces her lips. Billy narrows his eyes, pensive as his cloudy-blue irises give way to pools of black and he takes her face in his hands. He swipes his tongue slowly over his bottom lip and Adeline follows it with her gaze, unable to look away until he kisses her and her eyes flutter closed.

There's no messing about. Billy's tongue darts across her lip and into her mouth while her brain is still catching up. His nose is cold, its icy tip brushing her cheeks when she kisses back, leaning into him, but his hands are *oh so warm* as he pushes them up along her bare legs. Billy pauses their kissing, only for a moment, to carefully slide his hands under her thighs and shift Adeline's body around so she ends up lengthways on the couch, her ankle propped up on the arm. Then he lowers himself over her, solid and safe, as his hands bunch up her t-shirt and he slides his way up her body. He mouths at the soft skin of her belly, thumbs stroking the underside of her breasts.

"Look at you," Billy hums appreciatively, cupping her in his palms before he slinks further up to her mouth and along her jaw.

Adeline digs her fingers into the soft leather beneath her and whines as Billy lips latch onto her neck, his breath hot on her skin. She feels like she's burning up, Billy's mouth and hands only adding more fuel to the fire blazing in the pit of her stomach. She'll never get tired of this; of his kisses and the way he so tentatively and adoringly explores her body. There's so much she wants him to do to her; so much she wants to do to him. She wants to feel his tongue between her legs, lips wrapped around her clit. She wants to make him feel good too, to hear the same soft, small sounds of pleasure fall from his lips at her doing.

They make out for as long as it takes the winter sun, high in the sky now, to cross from the coffee table to the couch, warm on the top of her head and exposing the specks of dust in the air above them. The pain in her chin and ankle is still there, a steady ache and a dull throb but it's nothing she can't handle.

Billy draws back, leaving her with one then two soft kisses on her lips. He stares down at her with eyes that match his kisses and Adeline reaches up to run a hand through his hair.

"Thanks for taking care of me," she murmurs.

"Always, Addie. Are you hungry? We didn't have breakfast before leaving Florida."

"I could eat."

Adeline watches over the back of the couch as Billy rummages through his kitchen cupboards for a good five minutes before the best edible thing he finds is a half-eaten packet of cookies. He does find some painkillers though, and pops two pills, handing them over with a glass of water and a kiss. Adeline takes them while Billy disappears into another room and emerges again with an old pair of running shorts. He helps her into them before pulling a blanket out from a basket by the window and draping it over her legs to keep the chill off.

"I'm gonna run to the store, stock up for the next few days," he says. "Any requests?"

"Strawberries? Oh, and cherry soda, please."

"You got it. Don't you dare move from the couch, Adeline," Billy tells her with a raise of his eyebrows and a firm point in her direction. Adeline throws him a lazy salute as he rounds the couch and drops a kiss to the top of her head.

Once the front door closes and she's sure Billy is long gone down the stairs, Adeline pulls the blanket around her shoulders and hobbles over to the large industrial windows. She waits for him to appear outside, deliberately avoiding the patch of black ice as he skips down the steps. He lights a cigarette and pulls his coat tighter around his body as he starts down the snow-lined street and Adeline sighs, watching until he's out of sight. She feels so goddamn lucky to be here, in Billy's space, with *him* in such a way she never thought she would be.

Their connection is undeniable, palpitating and so vibrant that she feels it constantly thrumming through her when he's around. Now, alone in his apartment, the dread she feels whenever she's back in New York is slowly seeping through the cracks. The love-hate relationship she has with the city is out in full force, the constant fear of running into her mother, although unlikely in Brooklyn, has her on edge.

It's only ever happened once before, outside Macy's at Christmas the one year Adeline had decided to spend it in New York with friends instead of on the west coast with her dad. Stéphanie Dubois – petite and blonde, dressed immaculately – was standing on the street chatting to a friend and Adeline remembers picking up on her mother's French-American accent like she'd heard it just yesterday.

In reality, it had been seventeen years, give or take if she included the time she showed up to Adeline's makeshift home school graduation a couple of years prior. She knows her dad keeps in contact despite the heartache her mother caused them both. He keeps her up to date on Adeline's well-being as if she cares, and maybe she does, but Adeline doesn't want the woman knowing how her life has turned out. If Stéphanie wanted to know, she would have stayed. Or at least called once in a while.

Adeline sighs and looks around, truly taking in Billy's apartment for the first time. It's huge; exposed brick walls and tall ceilings with so much light filtering in through the windows. There's a mezzanine level that looks down over the living room, the bedroom she assumes, and the place is so cluttered with knick-knacks that she can't wait to explore.

For now, she starts at his record collection, a fingertip running over the spines until she lands on *Tapestry*, the Carole King album she listened to the day she met Billy and tried to convince herself not to fall in love with him.

How's that going for you, Addie, she thinks as she slides the record from its sleeve. She drops the needle and it crackles to life as she limps around a little more of the living room, studying posters on the walls and a cabinet full of trinkets until her ankle begins to throb again. Reluctantly, she retreats back to the couch, retrieving her planner from her bag on the way. She sits with her leg up on the cushion again, the warming ice pack back on her foot, and reaches for Billy's landline on the side table. She rifles through the pages until she finds the right page and dials the hotel and extension for Norah's room in Virginia. It rings and rings and then clicks as it connects.

"Norah's room, Stan speaking. How may I help you today?" Says the man she was least expecting to answer the phone.

"Hey, moron. Why are you in Norah's room at..." she glances at the clock in Billy's kitchen, "10am?"

"Oh, hey Addie! We're having a–" Stan is suddenly cut off, there's clattering and grumbling and then Norah's voice on the other end of the line.

"Addie! Have you been thoroughly fucked yet?"

"If you mean thoroughly fucked over by a patch of black ice, yes," she mutters.

"Shit, what happened?"

"I didn't even make it two steps up to his building door before I ended up on my ass, Nor. Cut my chin, sprained my ankle, New York is great. Billy wrapped it and he has me resting on the couch with an ice pack while he gets groceries."

"How domesticated." The smirk in Norah's voice is shouting, loud and clear over the phone. "That sucks though, Addie. Billy was really excited to show you around his favourite parts of Brooklyn."

"Don't tell me that," Adeline whines, "I'm gonna feel even more guilty for being a clumsy mess."

"There's plenty you can do indoors too," Norah reminds her and then because she knows Adeline so well she jokingly adds, "less chance of running into the she-devil too."

That's the catalyst and suddenly all the worries and apprehension Adeline's been feeling spills out of her mouth. Of course, Norah knows all the right things to say; reminding her that chances of bumping into her mother are slim, she needs to share her worries with Billy, and most importantly, she needs to make sure she still enjoys these few days with him despite all of this. The company and familiarity of her best friend, even just over the phone, does wonders to ease Adeline's anxieties.

She needs to start seeing New York in a different light, she knows that. At least Brooklyn feels safe. It's going back to Manhattan and the apartment there, closer to her mother's Midtown and Upper East Side territory, that's going to be a whole new ball game.

eleven

BILLY
February 19th, 1975

IT'S STILL DARK OUT WHEN BILLY WAKES TO SOFT, RED SATIN caressing his skin. Adeline has migrated across the bed in the night, her body half on him, half on the mattress and her messy, blonde hair is splayed out across Billy's chest, tickling the base of his neck gently each time she moves. Her leg is hitched up over his and Billy breathes out a quiet chuckle as he realises she's using him to elevate her ankle; the pillow he'd set up for her at the end of the bed now nowhere to be seen. A familiar warmth stirs in his stomach as he stares down at her. Adeline is pouting in her sleep, a tiny smile pulling at the corner of her lips, and he wonders what she's dreaming about.

Him, he hopes.

Billy lies there for an hour, his fingers tracing over the soft skin of Adeline's arm in patterns not dissimilar to the speedway tracks he has memorised. The alarm clock to his left confirms it's only 3am when he eventually stops staring at the ceiling. His insomnia is back – not that it had ever really gone – but he'd gone fewer nights awake with the moon and inky-blue sky recently. It's usually worse during race season; different cities, different beds, never really settling into one place before he's on to another. That's why he often finds himself running though tracks, mentally driving the course, counting each lap. It's like counting sheep but for race car drivers.

Billy's lost count of how many times he drove around Daytona in his head the night he'd shown up at the Gold's beach house. By the time that race had come around he knew the track like the back of his hand but he didn't sleep a wink. The unfamiliar bed and knowing Adeline was only two rooms away played havoc with him. But now, even in his own bed with the girl of his dreams literally moulded to his body, his brain just won't shut off.

He huffs out a breath now, loud in the stifling quiet of the night and peers down at Adeline, wondering how she's so deep in sleep when she spent yesterday afternoon napping between periods of eating, reading and making out.

"Addie," he whispers, brushing her hair from her face and tracing a line down her small, very cute nose. She stirs a little, her lip twitching at the sound of his voice but then she snuffles and her breathing evens so Billy tries again, singing softly this time. *"Tinkerbell..."*

"Wha– shhh," Adeline mumbles, her mouth warm as her lips smush against his chest in an attempted kiss to placate him.

"Are you awake?" He asks, kissing the top of her head. Beneath the bed sheets, his fingers linger at the bottom of Adeline's sleep shorts, tickling the skin in the crevice between her thigh and butt cheek. The sensation makes her shiver and Billy smirks into her hair.

"You're really annoying, did you know that?" Adeline drawls through a yawn as she peers up at him. Her eyes are sleepy but they sparkle teasingly in the dim glow of the streetlight outside.

Billy's own eyes sting. They've been open for too long; too long staring into the darkness. In normal circumstances, he'd get up, maybe put a record on, make himself a tea and smoke through half a packet of cigarettes. But he's been aware of Adeline clinging to him for the last hour, if not longer, and that was enough for him. Enough of a comfort to at least try to rest.

"Billy?" Adeline whispers when he doesn't answer.

"Sorry, I uh–" he falters, clearing his throat as he sits up. Adeline moves as he does, shifting gingerly to straddle his lap without hurting her ankle. She holds his rough cheeks with her soft hands and kisses him.

"Can't sleep?"

"Insomnia," he admits. "It's been getting better, I don't know why..." Billy trails off and leans into Adeline's touch. He turns his head until his mouth comes into contact with her palm and peppers kisses right across her hand. Adeline combs her fingers through his hair at the same time and he sighs, selfishly wishing he had woken her sooner.

"I'm sorry," Adeline murmurs, pressing her lips to his forehead. They're warm against his skin and Billy feels the tension he's been harbouring gradually wash away. He's beginning to crave the comfort Adeline's presence brings, the ease with which he can be vulnerable in a way he never could with Delilah. Somewhere along the line he learnt to put up a front, until day by day she slowly started chipping away at it and in the end his feelings were written all over his face much to her abhorrence.

"Not your fault, sweet girl," he breathes.

"Can I do anything to help?"

A distraction would be good, he thinks as he slides his hands to her hips. The silky satin of her pyjama top slips against her skin, revealing her midriff, gorgeously soft and supple under his finger-tips. Billy's lips curl into a suggestive little smile as he tilts his head to the side in thought. As much as he would *love* to sleep, he'd love to make Adeline squirm a whole lot more.

"Wanna play a game, Tinkerbell?"

"What kind of game?" Adeline replies, words breathy as Billy's mouth sweeps along Adeline's jaw. He nuzzles into the soft spot, where her neck meets her ear before sucking her earlobe between his lips. Adeline's head falls to the side and she makes the silkiest little sound in the back of her throat.

"I want to know everything about you, Adeline Gold," Billy murmurs, twisting so he can lower Adeline carefully to the mattress and hover over her. "You get one kiss for every fact you can give me."

"I like the sound of this," Adeline grins, surging up to kiss him. "That was a fact."

Billy laughs, shaking his head. "I'll ask you questions. No more cheat answers and I refuse to kiss you for something I already know."

"That's not fair. A fact is a fact whether you know it or not."

"My game, my rules," Billy says with a groan as Adeline's hand disappears beneath the sheets and she pinches his ass in retaliation.

Trouble.

He captures her fingers as they retreat, linking them with his on the pillow above her head before he starts the game off simple. He asks her what her favourite movie is, her favourite song, and kisses down her arm for each answer she gives him, sucking and licking at her goosebump-ridden skin. When Adeline begins struggling for answers, he changes tactics.

"Tell me your favourite childhood memory," he prompts, hushed and low in her ear.

Adeline's pulse quickens against his lips as he kisses down her neck and Billy plays to her reactions, tongue dragging hotly along her shoulder. He pushes the thin strap of her top to the side and her back across the pillow so he can work his lips across her collar bone with no obstacles while she answers.

"It... it was a little while after my mom left. I think I was four years old." She stops. Billy lifts his head from the crook of her neck when she swallows thickly and he squeezes her hand, encouraging her to continue. "We have a ranch down in Georgia. My dad needed to get out of New York and he stepped away from the racing scene for a few months."

Billy remembers that. He was ten years old at the time but he remembers his own father saying how much of a shame it was that Michael Gold decided to drop out of the championship that year when he was on track to win the whole thing.

"We went down there for the summer, I helped with the animals, learned how to ride a horse. Pretty much lived outdoors the whole time. If he was trying to take my mind off of everything, it worked. I like to think it did the same for him too," she says with a small shrug.

A small wave of guilt washes over him. He's lucky enough to have grown up with two loving parents. He knows Michael gave Adeline the best upbringing possible but he can't imagine what it must be like for a little girl to go without a mother figure. Billy assumes that's why she's so attached to Norah, the redhead is a few years older and able to provide a little guidance. He doesn't know what to say, nothing sounds right in his head. So instead, he strokes the back of his hand across Adeline's cheek and kisses her softly.

"Billy, can I ask *you* something?"

He rolls off of her and props himself up on his side.

"Of course, Tinkerbell."

"Where do you think you'd be right now if you hadn't started racing?"

Billy doesn't miss a beat when he answers. It's hard not to, considering his life had been laid out for him when he and Delilah started going steady at fifteen.

"Working on Wall Street, married to Delilah, one kid with another on the way." He shivers at the thought of such a monotonous existence. "Dinner every Friday at her parents' house, assuming they never moved to L.A."

"And you didn't want that?"

"Not with her. Not in the end," he murmurs and Adeline's adorable, confused frown appears on her face.

"Why did you stay with her for so long if that was the case?" She pauses, panic stricken. "*Shit.* I don't mean to pry, tell me to shut up if you don't wanna tell me."

Adeline moves to cover her mouth but Billy intercepts, grasping her hand in his. He kisses each of her fingertips softly before he replies.

"Not at all, sweetheart." He wants nothing more than to be honest with Adeline. She has one of those faces that makes him want to spill his deepest darkest secrets. "We were set up from the start and I settled, simple as that. I barely saw her towards the end, which I guess opened my eyes a little." Adeline raises an eyebrow and Billy laughs. "Okay, a lot. It took Norah, and my sister, to make me realise that my relationship with Delilah was pretty toxic. I bought her an apartment, did you know that? And then she trashed it while I was out of town and I got stuck paying for the damages."

Adeline's eyes grow wide at the revelation.

"Jesus, Billy. And that wasn't enough to tell you to get the fuck out?"

Billy shrugs, smiling sadly.

"I loved her a lot back then. Enough to–" he starts but stops himself from saying anything more.

He wants to tell Adeline everything, needs to, seeing as some of it still affects him, and in turn their relationship. But how does he tell her that Delilah ruined sex for him too? How she made him feel like he didn't deserve the pleasure of sleeping with her, taking her orgasm or three before disappearing for hours, leaving Billy lying awake waiting for her to get home. He's sure it's why he's holding back with Adeline. It's ingrained in him; make her come, sort himself out later. Not that he thinks focusing on his girl's pleasure is a bad thing. He'll always put Adeline first in any scenario, it's just who he is and watching her come undone is the best thing in the world. But it's taken its toll, the lack of intimacy and the years of Delilah dismissing his needs.

"Y'know, Delilah sounds an awful lot like my mom," Adeline says after a while, saving him from elaborating further for now. He's glad, unsure of how much heavy conversation he can handle at three-thirty in the morning.

"How so?"

"The ranch I mentioned, my mom wanted it so my dad bought it for her. I think she only went there once or twice before she got bored of it."

"Oh."

"Yeah. Dad continued paying the upkeep– the employees and the vets fees, everything. Even after she left," Adeline sighs and peers over her shoulder to the window. "It's the same with our Manhattan apartment. It was *her* dream to live in the city, not his. When he realised that I saw it as home too, he could never bring himself to sell it. Though, I can hardly bring *myself* to go there anymore. It's been years but it feels like it's only a matter of time before I run into her."

Adeline's hesitation in agreeing to come to New York with him suddenly makes a world of sense. Cue his overthinking, his brain telling him that she only said yes just to please him. The worry takes form in tapping fingers, gnawing teeth on his bottom lip. Adeline must sense it as she first reaches for his hand to still his jumpy fingers before she cradles his cheek. Her thumb brushes lightly across his lip and kisses him, eyes closed as she rests her forehead against his.

"I want to be here, Billy," she whispers, "I want to be with you and get to know you. The good and the bad, all of it."

A soft little smile blooms across his lips. "Thanks, sweet girl. I, uh. I kinda feel like I need a reset. I'm gonna shower real quick and then I guess we should get a couple more hours sleep." He rolls out of the bed and makes it halfway to the adjoining bathroom before Adeline stops him.

"Hey, hot stuff?"

Billy turns just as her gaze sweeps over his body, her eyes sparkling as they land on his. She looks at him like she knows something, or like she can tell there's something he's not telling her. It wouldn't surprise him, she's proven herself to be ridiculously observant.

"Yeah?"

"I'll face my fears if you face yours."

He ponders over her offer and saunters back to the bed, holding his hand out. Instead of shaking it, she reels him into a kiss. A tender press of her mouth until she swipes her tongue across his bottom lip and deepens the kiss. Billy mumbles the word '*deal*' as soon as he gets a breath.

When he comes back from the bathroom ten minutes later, Adeline is starfished across the bed snoring.

It takes Adeline a few minutes to find the key. Billy leans against the wall, arms crossed over his chest as he waits, watching her intently. He nods at yet another resident as they give the blonde a sideways stare, moments away from telling them that they're not trying to break in. Though, with the way Adeline is muttering to herself, he's not sure they'd believe him.

"How's it going, Tinkerbell? We're starting to look suspicious."

Adeline glances at him – it's more of a glare, actually – as she loses her place on the keychain and starts over.

"Blame Michael Gold for insisting I carry every fucking key I own on one fucking keychain," she grumbles before she cheers triumphantly. "Got it!"

She unlocks the door and hobbles inside. As he follows close behind, Billy blows out a low whistle as they emerge from the small entry hall into the large open plan living room. The place looks immaculate and he assumes despite neither Adeline nor Michael having been there in a while, a maid or cleaning service has still been on the payroll. Though vast, it's a cosy space. A little stuck in the 60s but it works with its dark wood accents and warm toned furnishings, a stark contrast to the light, airy feel of the beach house. The conversation pit in the middle of the room is clearly the centre-piece; a four-sided sunken couch surrounding a coffee table with three steps leading down into it. Billy wanders around the perimeter taking every part of the room in through inquisitive eyes. There are picture frames on nearly every surface, baby Adeline with blonde ringlets, Michael Gold with his racing teammates, Christmases and birthdays and championship wins.

"When were you last here?" He asks, picking up a photo of Adeline holding a large vegetable, looking no older than eight and with the biggest gappy smile.

"A year ago, maybe. We only tend to stop here if we're nearby but Dad prefers Malibu, and I go wherever he is," Adeline replies as she disappears around a hidden corner. Billy is about to follow when he hears the soft tinkling of piano keys. Adeline curses and travels through the octaves in quick succession as she complains about how out of tune the piano is. He sneaks up behind her, hands landing on her waist.

"You play?"

"I used to. We don't have a piano in Cali, or Georgia actually, so I don't get to play as often as I'd like. It's like riding a bike for me though."

Billy reaches around her and taps a few keys. He doesn't know how to put notes together for the life of him, even on an out of tune piano. He brings his mouth to Adeline's ear.

"Play me something?"

"It'll sound terrible," Adeline laughs softly but she sits down on the piano stool anyway and cracks her knuckles. "Any requests, lover boy?"

"Just that you never call me that again," he quips.

"Oh, you didn't like that?"

Billy shakes his head and Adeline stares up at him expectantly.

"What?"

"I'm waiting for a request, come on."

He stares back, bewildered as he tries to summon a song, any song.

"Something by The Beatles? Elton John? I don't know, Addie, what can you play?"

"Anything."

"Anything?"

"I've got a good ear," she shrugs and starts playing.

Billy recognises the opening – slightly off – notes of *Your Song* and he watches in awe as Adeline's fingers dance across the keys. It's magic. *She's* magic. He can't tear his eyes away from her.

Stepping up behind her, he places his hands on her shoulders. His fingertips drum softly against her collar bone before they sweep her hair to the side and he dips his head, lips pressing a hot, open-mouthed kiss on her neck. On the one spot he knows will make her falter. She does, hitting the wrong key, and even out of tune the dud note is obvious.

"Keep playing," he hums, teeth nipping at Adeline's earlobe. His body feels hot, and the gentle thud of his heartbeat quickening fills his ears; a metronome to Adeline's song.

"Bit difficult when you're doing that." She breathes out a ragged giggle as she glances over her shoulder at him, her complexion a soft pink.

"What about if I do this?" He asks, feeling bold now as he shrugs off his jacket and sinks to his knees. He pulls the piano stool out a little and Adeline's mouth falls open as she watches him crawl across the hardwood floor until he's in front of her. Her playing slows as she peers down at him.

"Billy…"

"Just… do as you're told, Adeline," he murmurs, as he unties the lace of her boot.

She's wearing a cute miniskirt and thick wool tights, and once her shoes are off, he motions for her to lift her hips. It doesn't take Billy long to slide the tights and panties from her body. He kisses up her calf and then tucks his hands behind her knees, gently pushing her legs apart.

"Billy," she says again.

"Keep playing, Tinkerbell."

"This is torture." She grumbles petulantly as she bites her lip and picks the song back up. Billy's plan was to drag it out, but as soon as he trails his lips further up her leg, he's growing just as impatient. She's already so wet for him and he makes a little noise at the back of his throat, so quiet it gets drowned out by the music. His lips leave her thigh and he turns his head until his nose brushes her clit, heady and warm. Adeline's fingers still on the piano and the room falls silent apart from her laboured breaths and the whine of his name that slips from her lips as Billy wraps his own around her throbbing bud and sucks, tongue swirling slowly and indulgently.

Adeline makes a sound that sends blood rushing to Billy's cock, already swelling and aching under the denim of his jeans. He removes the hand he'd settled on her hip to palm at himself; a poor attempt to relieve some of the pressure, to hold off until he's made her come first.

It's when her legs tense around his head and her fingers – given up on the piano – weave through his hair, that he can't take it anymore. He withdraws from her pussy, lips dewy and stubble no doubt glistening with Adeline's slick.

"What're you–" she slurs, pleasure-drunk as Billy stands and lifts her into his arms. Her legs wrap tightly around his middle as he kisses her, letting her taste herself on his tongue.

Carrying her through to the living room, he skips down the steps into the conversation pit and carefully drops her onto the couch. Her hazel eyes, now dark with lust, study his face intently. She's waiting and all Billy can do is stare at her.

"Billy?" She blinks, lip under her teeth as her gaze flits down to his crotch, so obviously hard now.

"Fuck it," he mutters, mostly to himself as he tugs his sweater over his head and shucks off his jeans and underwear.

He stalks forward and lowers himself over her, dipping his head to kiss her all slow and searing, taking his time because if he's going to do this, going to face his fears like she said, he's going to do it right. He pushes up her blouse and kisses down her body, warms her up some more with his mouth and fingers. Then when he slides into her inch by inch– and Jesus, she's all hot and tight – she gasps and writhes against the couch cushions, smiling up at him softly as she cradles the back of his head and pulls him down into a kiss. He takes it, takes all the pleasure and the hedonistic chase of his own orgasm and he thinks *yeah, I'm gonna let myself have this one.*

twelve

ADELINE
February 22nd, 1975

"COME BACK TO BED." BILLY'S VOICE IS HUSKY, THICK WITH sleep as it echoes through his apartment.

Adeline knew he would do this, seek her out the moment he realised she wasn't beside him anymore. But he had looked so comfortable sleeping, sprawled out in the bed with the duvet wrapped around his legs like he'd had a fight with it and lost. She figured it best not to wake him after he'd slept so poorly the other night.

"You're the one who mumbled something about pancakes before falling asleep last night," Adeline replies as she continues to chop strawberries. On the counter sits a bowl of batter ready to go and there's a skillet heating on the burner.

"Baby, come back to bed," he repeats and Adeline almost drops the knife in her hand when she peers over her shoulder.

Billy walks across the kitchen completely naked, his cock hard and curving up towards his abs, and his pink lips are wrapped around a half-smoked cigarette. His eyes trail over her and suddenly she feels naked too, standing there in a soft plaid shirt of Billy's and nothing else. She turns back to the strawberries, a poor attempt to hide the rosy glow of her cheeks but she can still feel Billy's eyes on her; sense his darkened irises devouring her through hooded lids, the sultry bedroom gaze she swears has become a permanent feature since their little tryst in the Manhattan apartment.

Adeline thinks back to that afternoon, the hesitation from Billy to go all the way. She didn't know why until after, when they laid on the couch with their legs tangled, sharing kisses while Billy told her everything Delilah did to him, no detail spared. He was so unabashedly vulnerable with her, and Adeline promised him there and then that she would never deny him of pleasure like Delilah had. Never make him go without the intimacy he so clearly craves.

The warm press of Billy against her back brings Adeline out of her head; lips on her neck as he leans around her and stubs out his cigarette on the corner of the sink.

"You're insatiable, Billy." It comes out as a breathless laugh, a quiet reaction to his teeth grazing over her skin. Billy bites down gently and then swipes his tongue over the same spot, warm and wet.

"Only for you, my sweet girl. I'd have you every hour of the day if I could," he rumbles.

Adeline rolls her eyes but she's dying inside, heart pounding so fast she's sure Billy can probably feel it against his own chest. No man has ever spoken to her with such open desire like he does and it's just as intoxicating as his kiss. Unfortunately, they have to be in Virginia by early afternoon if Billy's going to make it for the qualifying laps; they don't have time for this.

"Go put some clothes on," she sighs reluctantly, "we gotta be on the road in like, two hours."

In response, he presses his hips firmly against her ass, trapping his cock between their bodies. Billy's arms snake around her waist, fingers deftly unbuttoning Adeline's shirt – *his* shirt – until it falls open. He grasps her chin, tilting her head until his mouth meets hers in a playful kiss. He pulls at her bottom lip with a smile, tongue teasing before he withdraws it and kisses her softly, just a small chaste press of his lips. Billy's left hand lands flat over her bare belly, thumb caressing her skin as he mouths lazily at her neck.

"Y'know," he murmurs, plucking a berry from the chopping board and popping it into his mouth. "I like cream with my strawberries."

"Do you even have any?" Adeline asks as Billy peels himself from her back and wanders over to the refrigerator. She steals a peek at his peachy ass as he walks away, lip catching under her teeth as she momentarily drifts, thinking about the way she likes to grab it when he's buried inside her.

He walks back to her with a can of Reddi Whip in his hand, shaking it slowly. Adeline expects him to return to his spot behind her, but instead, he moves to the stove and turns off the burner. She raises an eyebrow at him; can almost see the cogs turning in his head as he slides his jaw from side to side.

"Whatever you're about to do, *don't*," she warns and Billy grins, his finger poised on the nozzle of the cream can. He stops in front of her, hand moving to cradle the back of her head as he sways forward and pulls her into a scorching kiss, the kind that always leaves her a little frazzled, and then skims the tip of his nose across her cheek.

"Get on the floor, pretty girl." His voice is rough and rumbly in her ear. Billy has her wrapped around his little finger so naturally, she complies, lowering to her knees. She's eye level with his cock, the tip of it red and dripping a pearly bead of pre-cum. Adeline is so close to wrapping her lips around it when Billy speaks again. "Lie down for me, Adeline. Take the shirt off first."

The dark, hardwood floor is cold, her back only partially cushioned by the skinny floor runner Billy has covering the length of his kitchen. She feels exposed as she lies back, but then, Billy is completely naked too. He towers over her, cock in his hand as he fists his length a couple of times and his head lolls back with a stuttered groan. Then he's on the floor too, knelt at her feet with a boyish grin and the can of cream poised to attack.

Adeline scrunches her face up in anticipation and Billy laughs, loud and delighted, as he squirts a line of cream up the centre of her belly. She flinches, a giggle-filled squeal escaping her lips.

"*Holy shit,* that's cold!"

Billy stifles an evil little chuckle as he finishes up the last little blob of cream on her sternum and then dips his head, replacing the freezing cold sensation with the warmth of his mouth. He licks along her skin, tongue flat and leaving a sticky residue until he comes to a stop below her breasts. He looks up at her, eye glinting and a Cheshire Cat smile as he rests his body over hers and plants a sticky saccharine kiss to her lips. Adeline hums at the sweetness that clings to Billy's tongue.

"This might be the most ridiculous idea you've ever had," she giggles. She goes to snatch the can up but Billy gets to it first. "Gimme the can, I want a go!"

"Hang on, Tinkerbell. I'm not done."

Adeline huffs but lets Billy continue with his fun while she thinks about where she's going to decorate him with cream. She tilts her head to the side to get a better look at him; every part of Billy Brooks lights a fire in the pit of her stomach. Her eyes wander over his toned arms, muscles rippling as he repositions himself, and up to the contemplative expression he's wearing on his face as if he's pondering over the same thing as he slowly eyes her up.

She's shocked out of her thoughts when Billy pipes a perfect swirl of cream over her left nipple, his tongue perched between his lips in concentration as he pulls the can from the peak of the cream mound with a flourish. The laugh that escapes Adeline then is loud and unrestrained. She snorts as Billy giggles against her chest, unable to control himself while he licks and sucks her clean.

"Delicious," he beams, smacking a loud kiss to her lips before he draws back and sits on his heels.

"Okay, my turn," Adeline says, like a presumptuous kid who's had enough of sharing her toys. She wiggles her fingers for the cream can and gets Billy to lie back too as she straddles his legs, making herself comfortable. Carefully, she dispenses cream along his v-lines and stops just before she gets to the base of cock. Billy hisses, propping himself up onto his elbows to playfully glare at her. Adeline quirks an eyebrow as if to say '*I told you so*'.

"You gonna keep looking at me like that or are you gonna lick the damn cream off me, Adeline?" Billy tries to regain the low, authoritative tone he used when he told her to get on the floor but his smile betrays him.

Adeline scoops her hair to the side and lowers her mouth to Billy's hip. She takes her time licking the cream from his skin, peppering kisses along his prominent muscles. Billy shivers beneath her, his abs tensing. He's so hard, whimpering every time she accidentally grazes his cock as she leans over him. She pauses when he slides his hand between them and wraps his fingers around himself again. Part of her wonders how long it will be until Billy feels comfortable enough to tell her what he wants from her, what he needs to make himself feel good. He's getting there, and now they've had sex she hopes he knows that Adeline is present and willing. For now though, she carefully holds his jaw in her fingers, kissing him how he deserves to be kissed.

"You want me to help you with that?" She asks softly, sitting back just as he bucks his hips, thrusting into his hand. Billy nods, still looking a little unsure. He swipes his tongue over his bottom lip and takes a deep breath.

Adeline takes it easy. She cradles Billy's hand in hers, guiding his palm down his length, before she shuffles back and sits herself between his legs. Lowering her head, she peers up at him briefly before licking up the underside of his cock, keeping her hand on his as she stretches her lips around the tip and collects the leaking pre-cum on her tongue. Billy lets out a deep moan when Adeline sucks him down, moving their hands to stroke what she can't fit in her mouth. With his free hand, Billy tangles his fingers in her hair and guides her head down to take him deeper. He's heavy against her tongue, throbbing. Adeline hums around him and he curses under his breath, his chest heaving.

"Fuckin'– *Jesus*, Adeline," he rasps, finding his voice again as he lifts his head to look down at her. "Fuck you look pretty with your mouth around my cock. Doin' so well, sweet girl."

Adeline pulls away from his dick with a pop, her cheeks blazing. That goddamn Brooklyn twang never fails to make her blush. Keeping their hands moving lazily over his length, she catches her breath for the briefest moment under Billy's lustful gaze. His usually clear blue irises are just a sliver around the black of his pupils and framed by dark, long eyelashes. He's utterly gorgeous, laid out for her like this.

She works her way from the base of his cock again, gentle kitten licks along the underside until she takes him in her mouth again, hollowing her cheeks as she goes. Adeline knows what he likes now, what makes him so responsive. She hums, spit dripping over her chin, and Billy's grip on her hair tightens. He pulls hard as his cock pulses against her tongue, hot and slick.

"A-Addie, fuck. So perfect, so fuckin' good, baby," Billy babbles, head thrown back against the floor again. "Please... please don't stop. M'so close. M'gonna–"

He spills into her mouth, moaning and cursing through laboured breaths. Adeline swallows him down, licks him clean with a grimace. She's usually a spitter, not a swallower, and not even the lingering taste of whipped cream can help this time.

"Okay?" She murmurs as she kisses her way up Billy's body.

"*Christ*. The mouth on you, sweetheart," Billy utters, voice quiet and hoarse. Adeline giggles, mouthing at his chest as she curls herself into his side. "Thank you for..." he trails off, clearing his throat.

Adeline tilts her head back to kiss his stubbled jaw, then his mouth, soft and slow. She rolls above him and they make out on the kitchen floor, Billy hands skimming her back, lips on her clammy skin. They lose time, and it's not until Adeline glances up at the clock on the wall that she realises just how much time they're lost.

"Shit, Billy! We gotta move!"

It's a mad dash after that. Billy goes to collect the car he keeps in the city from a private parking lot downtown while Adeline finishes packing their things. She makes a few pancakes for the road, cutting them into snack sized pieces, and puts them into a Tupperware container with the chopped strawberries and stuffs it all into a bag with a flask of coffee.

She leaves the cream.

✢

It's a six hour drive to Richmond, Virginia. They're cutting it fine, probably should have hit the road yesterday but neither of them wanted to leave their little bubble. She would usually be frustrated at the setback but then she replays Billy sauntering towards her naked and the sounds she coaxed out of him and the hour wasted fucking around on the kitchen floor suddenly seems so, so worth it. The whipped cream she can still smell in her hair despite shampooing it twice, however…

Adeline is just wrapping her scarf around her neck, careful of her chin, when a car horn sounds from outside. She hurries to the window to see Billy climbing out of a yellow Volkswagen Beetle that looks at least a decade old, if not older. She was hoping he maybe had another sports car hidden away, they'll be lucky if they get to Virginia by tomorrow in a bug. Billy spots her, waving with big sweeps of his arms and a wide grin.

Two trips with their bags and a still-limping Adeline later, Billy just about manages to close the trunk and he beams at Adeline proudly.

"This is Gertie."

"And does Gertie go more than thirty miles per hour?' Adeline asks as she opens the passenger side door and peaks inside. When she reemerges, Billy is behind her.

"You bad mouth Gertie again and I'll make you walk to Richmond," he threatens jokingly, eyes bright and mouth twisted into a playful smile.

"You wouldn't dare."

Billy kisses her gently, smirk pressed to her lips as he mumbles, "wouldn't I?"

"Are you sure you don't want me to drive some of the way?"

"Nope. You're still limping, sweet girl. I don't want you to put more strain on your ankle," he replies, moving round to the driver's side. "Get in, map's in the glove compartment."

Adeline rolls her eyes and lets out an exasperated sigh. She loves driving, hates navigation. If they get lost, that's on Billy.

He drives very sensibly all the way down the I-95 through to Washington. Adeline falls asleep a couple of hours in and when she wakes up again, they're surrounded by open roads and nothing but fields, and Billy is speeding. The faster he goes, the more Gertie rattles but Billy doesn't seem particularly fazed as he shouts along to the onslaught of rock songs the radio is churning out. Fingers tapping along on the steering wheel, he's oblivious as Adeline watches him fondly. His Ray-ban's are perched on his nose, skin glowing in the low winter sun as it filters through the windows. She's falling so hard for him, there are moments she has to pinch herself as a reminder that this is all real.

"It's rude to stare," Billy says, glancing at her with the ghost of a smile that she can't quite read.

"Well, you got handsome all over your face. It's quite distracting," she retorts as Billy pushes his sunglasses into his hair and fixes her with an unimpressed stare. Even so, he links his fingers with hers and brings the back of her hand to his lips.

"You're ridiculous," he murmurs, before peering up at the nearing road signs. "Looks like we're almost there."

They drive straight to Richmond Fairgrounds Raceway and Billy makes it for his qualifying lap by the skin of his teeth. The place feels eerily quiet the day before a race, just drivers and track staff, but there's anticipation in the air, bouncing off the empty stands. Michael and Tobias are waiting by Billy's Dodge when they walk into the Shaw & Gold garage. Tobias performs an overdramatic check of his watch when he sees them, foot tapping on the asphalt.

"Okay, Toby. Cool it with the theatrics," Adeline says with a grin. She embraces her dad in a quick hug, squeezing him tightly as Billy heads straight to the locker room to change.

When she catches up with him he's pulling on his driving suit, hair mussed and undershirt twisted in his hurry to strip. Adeline helps zip him up, securing the velcro and placing her hands on his chest. He kisses her while they're alone, dizzying as he picks her up and gives her no choice but to wrap her legs around him.

"See you on the other side, Tinkerbell," he whispers, smiling against her mouth before he places her back on the ground.

"Be careful."

Billy nods, dropping one last kiss to her forehead, then pushes his helmet onto his head and jogs back out to his car. Adeline moves as quickly as she can to the lower side of the track where she can watch him. She's just about tall enough to rest her arms on the barrier there and she props her chin on her hands as she waits for his lap to begin.

She's not alone for long.

"Didn't take you long to fall into bed with Brooks."

Adeline doesn't have to look to know it's Rex Harlow sidling up beside her. She steps to the side as the sickening scent of his cologne infiltrates her senses. It's like he's doused himself in the stuff.

"Shut up, Rex."

"After all the effort I put into getting you to go on a date with me just for you to turn me down time after time. Go on, princess, tell me what it took for him to win you over."

Adeline glances up at him. He towers over her, his features hard and tense despite the disgustingly suggestive smile he's wearing. Rex is everything Billy is not; a bulk of a man with dirty, short, slicked back hair, a patchwork of tattoos and an ability to make her skin crawl.

"Ever think that maybe the issue was that you're you?" Adeline smiles sweetly, edging back further when Rex crowds into her space. She likes to keep her interactions with Rex brief, if not non-existent. On instinct, she turns quickly to make an escape.

"Pretty sure that's not what you were saying when I had you under me, sweetheart."

Adeline stops in her tracks and has to stop the physical repulsion fighting its way to her throat as she's reminded of the worst night of her life. She pulls her coat tighter around her body, hiding herself from Rex's leering gaze as much as she can.

"That was three years ago, Rex, and I've never regretted anything more," she says indignantly. Her words are drowned out by the sound of Billy's car finally whizzing around the track and she's furious that her attention is on the man who ruined her and not the man she's half way to falling in love with.

Adeline's history with Rex, if you could even call it that, is something she wishes she could forget. Norah had warned Adeline to stay away from him. She knew of his reputation; how sleazy he was, preying on women like her but a lot of alcohol and a lack of judgement – and rippling muscles that looked one arm movement away from tearing his shirt – got the better of her. It turned out, Rex had her right where he wanted her, even when she decided that's not where she wanted to be.

"And yet, I can't stop thinking about it," Rex muses. He takes a step forward and Adeline takes one back.

"Please, Rex, just leave me alone. You already got what you wanted." She catches Billy crossing the finish line and beginning his drive back into the pit lane, lap now over, and hopes he sees where she is. Instead, Tobias rounds the corner. Adeline's whole posture must change because Rex follows her line of sight over his shoulder before reeling back around.

"I'm not done with you, Adeline." His words come out in a growl, low and menacing, and then he's gone, stalking towards the Hard Strike garage. Adeline turns her back on him as soon as he's gone.

"Is he giving you trouble again?" Tobias asks, tentative as he approaches.

"Nothing but the usual," she gets out before Billy appears out of nowhere, none the wiser to her encounter with Rex. She's swooped under his arm and as he places a warm kiss on her temple, she peers up at him with a soft smile.

"Not that this isn't lovely," Tobias interrupts as Adeline takes the moment, steady and safe against Billy, to calm down. "But I booked out the hotel restaurant for a team dinner so–"

"Yeah, we're comin', we're comin'," Billy laughs, nosing into Adeline's hair.

Tobias rolls his eyes.

"Oh no, your attitude is rubbing off on him," he complains, pointing an accusing finger at Adeline before he trudges away, exasperated.

Later, Adeline wedges herself between Billy and an exhausted looking Stan at the dinner table.

"You could at least look like you're happy to be here," Adeline says as Stan picks at the bread roll on his plate.

"I had a date with room service and a pay-per-view in my underwear," he replies glumly.

"Aw. Well, lighten up, buttercup. You got me instead."

"Norah, swap places with me?" Stan calls down the other end of the table where she and Gabe are sitting so close she may as well be on his lap. She's tearing up pieces of bread, shoving them into her mouth and deliberately ignoring Stan.

"So, Stanley," Adeline starts with an amused grin. "What were you doing in Norah's room the other morning?"

"Looking for Gabe," he answers, pained.

"And did you find him?"

"I did."

"Were they, uh... were they in a compromising position?"

"Gabe answered the door with nothing but the bedside table bible covering his junk. I think I've been scarred for life." Stan picks up his bottle of Coca-Cola and gulps back half of it.

"If you couldn't handle Gabe naked, I guess I won't give you a play by play of what me and Billy did on the kitchen floor this morning," Adeline says casually. At the sound of his name, Billy joins the conversation, arm slung over the back of her chair.

"There was whipped cream involved," he adds with a roguish smile.

Stan promptly chokes on his drink.

thirteen

ADELINE
March 6th, 1975
Rockingham, North Carolina

ADELINE PULLS AT THE ZIPPER OF THE METALLIC RED jumpsuit currently clinging to her body and huffs out a sigh of frustration. She's lost track of how many items of clothing she's tried on and to be honest, she could have spent longer pacing the racks of the thrift store but Norah got impatient.

In her best friend's defence, they *were* headed for the mall down the street until Adeline spotted a dress in the thrift store window and then just kinda... got sucked in. Who can blame her with some of the shit people donate to these places, though? Ten minutes into browsing and Adeline feels like she's hit the jackpot when she finds a pair of Levi jeans in her size *and then* she finds a hand-knitted sweater with a motif of a smiling penis embroidered on the front and picks it up for Billy. She's going to wrap it and give it to him for his birthday.

She climbs out of the Lycra and chucks it on top of her ever-growing 'no' pile in the corner. With just three things left to try on, she looks at her reflection in the fitting room mirror and gives herself a stern talking to; God knows she needs it.

"You're allowed one more opportunity to pick out a flaw, Adeline. *Any* flaw, but that's it so... use it wisely." She points to herself, stepping closer to the mirror. Her eyes fall to the scar on her chin for a moment. It's not as prominent as it was but she traces her finger over the white line gently as if it would still hurt to touch, and even though she complained when it happened, Adeline doesn't mind the little memento she has from Brooklyn so much. She's a firm believer that every scar is a story and now she laughs whenever she recalls face planting the steps.

"Are you talking to yourself?" Norah's voice floats over the dividing wall of the stalls and Adeline can hear the amusement in her tone.

"...maybe."

"Dork."

"Oh, like you've never been caught talking to yourself before?" Adeline replies, rolling her eyes. She knows for a fact that Norah has some kind of pre-race mantra she likes to mutter to herself before she gets in her car. Adeline likes to call it a NASCAR exorcism which usually earns her a scowl and a middle finger in the face.

"I know you just rolled your eyes," Norah says, "are you nearly done?"

Adeline makes a small humming sound in response and picks up the pair of dark bell bottoms from the bench beside her. If they don't fit, she's going to cry. The ads literally ask if she's ever had a bad time in Levi's; her answer is no and she intends to keep it that way. She squeezes them up over her hips and pulls the zipper closed before fastening the two buttons at the top.

"Oh, thank fuck," she whispers as she twists to see how they fit in the back. Does she need another pair of jeans? Probably not, but she'll never not get joy out of a new pair.

"The Levi's fit?" Norah is outside the stall now, tapping her foot impatiently under the curtain.

"Yup... well, kinda. They're a little tight but they make my ass look great, so..."

"That's a win in my book," Norah replies, "and I'm sure Billy will appreciate it. Maybe it'll get him out of his funk."

Adeline sighs and pokes her head around the curtain.

"We fucked in the shower this morning and he still looked miserable when he went to see Gabe. My ass in these jeans won't do a thing," she says, ducking back inside the stall. "I don't think it's just the race that's bummed him out, he said he feels old."

It's been a week and a half since Billy won in Richmond, four days since he came fourth in Carolina, and it's exactly three days, 13 hours, and 23 minutes until his 30th birthday. Not that Adeline is counting or anything. Although that *is* the purpose of their shopping trip, she needs to find the perfect gift and the perfect outfit for his party.

"Thirty's the new twenty," Norah says assertively, as if it's more to convince herself than anyone else. It's her thirtieth next.

"Try telling him that. He won't stop going on about how his age is going to affect his driving." Adeline puts on a deep voice as she mimics him. "'*It's all down hill from here, Tinkerbell,*' he says as if there aren't drivers in their forties still placing in the top ten," she scoffs.

"The thing with Billy is that he doesn't realise how good he is," Norah replies, "he just drives because he loves it. Nearly every driver I know wishes they could drive like Billy Brooks. Even guys who have been in the game a long time, like Rex, they see him as a threat. He's *that* good."

"Yeah, well, try telling him that. Maybe I'll get more than a grunt out of him next time I seduce him in the shower."

The next race, in Tennessee, isn't until March 16th so they're all staying in North Carolina until then. It makes sense considering the hotel they're in right now has a big ballroom that's available Saturday night and Adeline really, *really* wants to throw Billy a party. She had to painfully flirt her way through adjusting the dates of their stay, and Adeline is a horrible flirt. She cringes when she thinks back on some of the things she said to Billy when they first started seeing each other. But at least now she gets to distract herself with party planning, especially after her run in with Rex has put her so on edge.

He hasn't bothered her since, but his departing words make Adeline want to throw up every time she thinks about it. There was a real threat there, low and menacing, but the thing that confuses her the most is that he had left her alone until now. Their interactions pre-Richmond consisted of him greeting her and Michael at NASCAR events; obviously very professional and courteous as if he hadn't done an ounce of wrong in his life. She hasn't told anyone what he actually said, but she knows Tobias mentioned the interaction to Norah, and she only knows this because it became really fucking obvious when the redhead started hovering around her at the speedway and doing a very bad job of acting inconspicuous. No matter how good she would be behind the wheel of a getaway car, Norah Ridley would make a shit spy.

"Did you manage to find Rosie's number?" Adeline asks. She's given up trying on clothes and shimmies back into her turtleneck sweater and denim overalls.

"I did. When are you going to call? I think I saw a payphone down the street."

"Woah, no! Not yet! I need to, like, psych myself up for it!" Panic laces her words as her voice goes up in pitch.

Norah arches an eyebrow.

"Didn't you say you were going to call his sister because you could handle that? I can always get you George and Eleanor's number instead?"

"No!"

"*Addie.*"

"Norah."

"His party is in two days, you need to call her."

"And I will," Adeline huffs. "Once I've written a script and prac-tised it." Adeline may seem tough (she had absolutely no problem squaring up to Delilah, after all) but ask her to make a phone call to a stranger unprepared and she *will* burst into tears.

"Do you do that every time you book our hotels and travel arrangements?" Norah questions as they dump the clothes they don't want into the returns bin and head to the checkout.

"That's different, I already have those scripts memorised."

Norah doesn't warrant that with a response. She goes first as they reach the small checkout desk at the front of the store. The only thing she ended up with is an old biker jacket with a random gang emblem on it and she voluntarily – and very enthusiastically – tells Adeline that she's going to wear it with nothing else for Gabe later. Adeline makes a mental note to ask Norah how that's going. Good, by the sounds of it, but she and Gabe have what Adeline is dubbing a flirtationship with a lot of benefits. One of these days they're either going to realise they're in love or it's all going to end in tears. Gabe's, probably.

When it's Adeline's turn to pay, the girl at the counter eyes the knitted penis sweater for a moment and then looks up as she huffs out a laugh.

"Nice," she nods and Adeline just smiles at her with her lips together, cheeks round and pink.

"It's for my boyfriend," she says, she doesn't know why. "It's his birthday on Monday."

The girl doesn't say anything else as she rings up the items and the awkward silence that follows is excruciating. Norah fails at hiding the short, gruff chuckle in the back of her throat. Once they're outside, Adeline looks at her friend pointedly, waiting for the inevitable tease.

"What?"

"Go on, I just know you're *dying* to make a comment."

"Actually, what I was *going* to say is that you should borrow my sewing kit to make the dick look like Billy's. Or I could do it, I have an excellent memory."

Adeline snorts in response but tucks the idea away for later as they head to the mall. It takes another four stores before she finds a dress and another three before she's all but given up the hope of finding the perfect gift for Billy. Then they get to a camera store and she pauses. Glancing inside, she hovers until Norah has enough of her overthinking and all but shoves her inside.

"*Do* it," she urges when after a browse of the shelves Adeline stops in front of the Super 8 video cameras.

"I don't know, Nor."

"He's sentimental as shit, Addie. Give him this and you'll have home movies for years." Adeline shoots her a sideways glance. "Don't look at me like that. You're both so obviously head over heels with each other, it's sickening."

Norah fakes a gag but her face immediately breaks out into a soft smile before she turns to the sales clerk who's been hovering like a fly at a barbecue.

"I'd recommend the Kodak," he says, eager to make a sale. "It's a great camera and I'm sure whoever it's for will love it."

"See, even…" Norah squints at his name tag, "Henry here thinks it's the perfect gift. Thank you for your input, Henry. Very helpful. I'll be sure to mention your fabulous customer service skills to the manager."

She flashes him a flirty smile and Henry stutters. "I, uh… I am the manager."

Adeline struggles to hold in her giggles as she glances at Norah and follows Henry to the counter to pay. At least she's bought Billy *something* good, although she has a feeling that as soon as he opens it he'll tell her she shouldn't have.

Back at the hotel, Adeline hides the camera and film cartridges she bought with it under the bed, along with the sweater. She nabbed Norah's sewing kit too, putting it with everything to remind herself to do that later. Billy is still at the garage with Gabe so while she's alone, Adeline heads down to the hotel ballroom.

The space is huge. High ceilings and intricate panelling on the walls that lead to a stage. There's a large marble-top bar to the side with moulded gold accent in the metalwork that runs along the base. It's the kind of luxury she looks for in every hotel she books; Tobias' tastes have rubbed off on her over the years. With that go big or go home attitude, Adeline has bought far too many balloons and decorations to fill the room with. Plus, the hotel has a lighting rig and disco ball, and the man on reception reluctantly agreed to have it working by Saturday after she convinced him that a party is not a party without colourful lights and a disco ball.

Adeline is wandering the floor, working out where to put everything, when the door opens on the other side of the room. She jumps initially, her heart only settling when she turns to see her dad walking towards her. He's still in his usual autumn-winter wardrobe of double denim, not yet transitioned to the spring-summer light wash jeans and Hawaiian shirt she's so used to seeing him in. Although, Adeline swears there could be a blizzard outside and Michael would still adorn the palm trees and hula dancers if he could.

"Thought I'd find you in here, sunshine."

"Hey, where have you been?" She squeezes him tightly. Life is always hectic during race season, things have to fit around races and travel and she can go a couple of weeks without seeing him between if his schedule is particularly busy. She'd be lying if she said she didn't miss spending the one on one time she would have as a kid but she gets it.

"Queens – scouting a new driver," he replies and Adeline tilts her head, brow furrowed quizzically.

"Another one?"

"This kid's amazing, Addie. He's only karting right now but I think with a bit of guidance, he's gonna be giving Billy a run for his money."

"Oh, wow."

"Yeah, exactly." Michael follows her as she continues working her way around the room. "How's that going? You and Billy?" He asks it tentatively, as he does most things when it comes to Adeline's personal life. As close as they are, it's always something he's stayed out of; if Adeline needs to talk, she knows where to find him for awkward responses and outdated fatherly advice.

"Good," she says.

"Just good? You're throwing a birthday party for the boy, that says better than good to me," he quips and Adeline blushes. She doesn't quite know how to tell her dad that she's the happiest she's ever been. That kind of talk is reserved for Norah, usually, and occasionally Stan.

"He's great. I think I..." she trails off with a soft shrug.

"You seem, uh," Michael pauses as if he's trying to find the right word, "settled."

Adeline laughs. Settled is definitely her father's way of saying 'in love'. She thinks about Billy and all it takes is picturing his face for her stomach to flip and heat to creep its way up her neck. Then the Billy in her head smiles, big and wide, his nose scrunching and light blue eyes glistening. She pulls herself out of her heart-eyed daze and sighs, catching Michael watching her with a certain fondness.

"Yeah," she says, "I think I am."

BILLY

"DUDE, WILL YOU STOP PACING?"

Billy glares at Gabe in response. He won't stop pacing, no, because he keeps replaying Sunday's race in his head trying to work out where it all went wrong. But Gabe doesn't get that. He took one look under the hood of Billy's Dodge and told him the engine had overheated, simple as that. They're in the speedway garage, empty now apart from the jacked up car, Billy and Gabe, who's lying on his creeper with his eyes closed, slowly rolling back and forth.

"Can you look again?"

"B, I am telling you, it was just the engine. It overheated; slowed you down. I've drained and flushed the radiator and replaced the coolant *and* I'll take her for a drive before Tennessee to make sure she's runnin' okay if that'll stop you pestering me about it," he offers as he wipes his greased up hands down the front of his navy boiler suit and stands up.

"Yeah, okay," Billy sighs, resigned. "Thanks, Gabe."

Gabe pats him on the shoulder and goes to clean up. He's taking Norah on a hike this afternoon, which are two things Billy never thought he'd hear in the same sentence. He waits until Gabe is gone and then pops the hood himself. He has absolutely no reason to suspect someone tampered with his car but he checks anyway. Nothing looks out of place but an uneasy feeling clings to his chest like a leech. Grabbing a flashlight and the abandoned creeper, Billy lies back and wheels himself under the car. He has no idea what he's looking for but he feels like he'll know once he finds it.

"Please don't tell me you're changing career paths, I like my men driving the car rather than under it."

Billy smiles; probably the first to grace his lips since he showered with Adeline this morning, and even then it was only out of the pure bliss he felt as he came.

"Hi, Tinkerbell."

Adeline approaches the car but Billy's too far under to see anything except for her Converse clad feet when he tilts his head to the left. He tinkers at nothing for a few seconds longer until Adeline clears her throat and taps her toes. He can picture the way her arms are probably crossed, head cocked to the side with that impatient little pout on her face.

"Come out and kiss me. I've missed you."

Billy slides himself out from under the car in a flash, a wolfish grin on his face. He jumps to his feet, kicking the creeper away, and then his hands are on Adeline's cheeks, capturing her lips in a feverish kiss. She's soft, mouth tasting like cherry soda and spearmint gum as his tongue moves across her lip and meets hers. Adeline lifts herself onto her tiptoes, her hands wandering over his back and into his hair, and Billy breathes out a small moan.

"Missed you too," he mumbles, quick and breathless. He will never, ever get tired of kissing Adeline; the plushness of her lips – often smooth and glossy, the small sounds he always pulls out of her and the deftness of her fingertips on his body.

Tugging on her bottom lip gently, Billy smiles into the kiss before he slows it down and dances his fingers down her arm. He links his right hand with hers, his thumb softly, slowly, caressing her skin as he walks her backwards and presses her against the hood of his car. Adeline lets out a surprised squeak when Billy lifts her to sit on the very edge and wedges himself between her legs. His lips leave hers, becoming soft brushes of his nose along her jaw, and Adeline tilts her head back in anticipation. He kisses her, wet and open-mouthed, just below her ear then trails his tongue down to the base of her neck, relishing the breathy moan that leaves her lips. His growing erection is straining against his jeans as his grinds against her languidly and she locks her legs around him.

Billy's had fantasies about fucking Adeline against his car, each one of them swimming through his mind now as he makes a move to unclasp the fastening of her overalls. While he's busy with that, Adeline's hands slide south as she presses a messy kiss to his lips. Her fingers work to undo his jeans, ripped and dirty from working on the car, until she can tug them over his thighs, taking his boxer shorts with them. Billy groans into her mouth, steeling himself against the hood of the car as she wraps her fingers around his cock and strokes him dry.

"Norah's invited us on a hike with her and Gabe," she says breathlessly before she spits into her palm and Billy goes slack-jawed, cursing when she slicks up his length at an agonisingly slow pace.

"Sw-sweetheart," he stammers.

"Hmm?"

"*Fuck*– you're killin' me here, baby."

"Am I?" She asks, smiling salaciously as she buries her free hand into Billy's hair. Her fingers are magic against his scalp, and the combination of her massaging his head as she fists over his cock makes it extremely hard for Billy to concentrate.

"Does Gabe know tha– that we're going with them?" Words strained, he raises his eyebrow. Billy was under the impression that Gabe had intended their hike to be romantic, not crashed by him and Adeline.

"Well, I just told him on my way in so... he does now," Adeline quips, shrugging. An infectious, cheeky smile blooms across her lips as she starts to slide her hand faster, right down to the root and up to the tip, thumb swiping the dribble of pre-cum before she repeats. Billy kisses her, hot and heavy, and mumbles against her lips.

"Where're we goin'?"

"Morrow Mountain State Park. Norah said it's about an hour's drive north so we'll be heading off soon."

"Is that why you suddenly decided to accost me in the garage, couldn't wait 'til later?" Billy jokes just as she pulses her hand around him gently, sliding her palm along the underside of his cock to his balls and making him grunt loudly. His brain must short circuit because the next thing he knows he's coming, eyes squeezed shut as his whole body shudders. He bites his cheek to suppress the volume of the moan he lets out and with laboured breaths, he rests his head on Adeline's shoulder, utterly wrecked by a quick handjob. He pulls himself together just as Adeline finds a random rag to clean up with, tossing it in the trash once she's done, and he tugs his pants back up.

"You, Adeline Gold, are somethin' else," he breathes, surging forward to plant a quick kiss to her forehead.

Adeline's hazel eyes sparkle mischievously. It's accompanied by a sweet smile as she hops down off the car and saunters towards the exit, sparing him a glance over her shoulder.

"Come on, golden boy. We don't want to keep them waiting."

He insists on a change of clothes once they get back to the hotel. It's warm for March so he ends up in a pair of shorts – too short, really, but Adeline won't shut up about how good his thighs look in them and he quite likes the attention – and an old band tee with the sleeves rolled up. He has to keep pulling the shorts down as he walks through to the lobby but it's too late to change now, Norah and Gabe are already waiting in the car.

Billy squeezes into the back seat after Adeline, cramped and uncomfortable but they spend most of the journey talking quietly between themselves and making out, much to Gabe's disgust. He plays it up but then Billy will catch his eye in the rearview mirror and he grins.

"Are we there yet?" Adeline pipes up. Her head lolls against Billy's shoulder as she drags her fingertip up and down his arm, drawing patterns and shapes out of boredom.

"The last sign I saw said we were, like, half a mile away," Norah tells them and before long, they're pulling into a space in the parking lot and piling out of the car.

The fresh air filters into Billy's lungs and he's such a city boy that he forgets what it's like being in the trees, with dirt under his feet and blue sky above.

"We've only got a few hours before the sun sets," Gabe says, "you guys wanna do the short route around the lake so we don't get lost?"

"It's like you think we've never hiked before," Adeline scoffs but she slides her eyes to Billy and shakes her head, pulling a face that very much says 'I've never hiked before.' He chokes out a laugh, tucking her under his arm as they set off.

The trail Gabe leads them down offers hills and pretty views, and once they've made it halfway around the lake, he and Gabe fall back as the girls walk up ahead. Billy's gaze trails down Adeline's body from afar, landing on her ass clad in tight little cycling shorts, and his teeth press into his lip so hard he almost breaks skin. He watches on as Adeline and Norah fool around balancing on logs and the childlike giggle that fills the air makes Billy's expression go from one extreme to the other; soft eyes and a fond little smile of adoration.

"Oh man, you're in trouble," Gabe says.

"What?"

"B, you should see yourself right now. That girl has you looking like a puppy dog. One of those chocolate labradors, all adorably dopey and shit."

Billy checks himself and clears his throat but he knows it's true. Adeline possesses some kind of magic that strikes him dumb, his stomach flips and twists like a rollercoaster every time he's in her presence.

"I'm gonna take that as a compliment," he counters and Gabe just shakes his head, jogging to catch up with Norah.

His eyes fall back to Adeline as she waits for him, hand held out for him to take and that gorgeous beaming smile, and Billy very suddenly realises that he would take a thousand sleepless nights counting the freckles on Adeline's back while she snores softly beside him if it means he never has to sleep alone again.

ADELINE
March 8th, 1975

"ADDIE, THIS IS INSANE!" STAN IS DANCING TOWARDS HER, on his third or fourth drink already despite only being an hour into the party, and his dance moves are *highly* questionable. Adeline eyes him warily as he stumbles over his own feet and hands her the Harvey Wallbanger she asked for twenty minutes ago. He clearly got distracted at some point in his journey to the bar but she'll let it slide.

"Thank you, Stanley," she replies, beaming up at him, both for the drink and the compliment on her party planning efforts.

"Where's the birthday boy?" Stan asks as he moves to stand beside her. Adeline has claimed a spot by the back wall with the perfect vantage point to people-watch so she finds Billy immediately, talking enthusiastically with his parents. He catches Adeline's eye briefly, face breaking out into a bright grin complete with that endearing little nose scrunch of his as she points him out to Stan.

"He looks happy," he says and Adeline nods. All she wants is for Billy to be happy; this is his night, after all. She's watched him greet friends and mingle, catching him at the exact moment he meets her eye across the room. It reminds her of before, when they were just on the edge of each other's circles. When he would work the room at NASCAR events with that infectious smile on his face and it would soften the moment he saw her. Her whole world shifted every time. She never did work up the courage to speak to him at those things but his smile wouldn't leave her mind for days after and she would look out for him on race days. The Hard Strike garage was always the furthest away though, and by that point, she was actively avoiding Rex.

"Addie?"

"Rosie, hi!" Billy's younger sister, with that same infectious smile and sparkle in her blue eyes, throws her arms around Adeline, hugging her like they've known each other for forever. Which isn't surprising when their initial phone call – once Adeline mustered up the courage to actually make it – quickly went from discussing Billy's party to mooning over Mick Jagger and neither of them remembering how they made it onto that topic.

"Thank you for doing this for him," Rosie says, glancing back at her brother who spots her and pulls a face, tongue dangling out of his mouth and eyes crossed until his mother swats him on the arm. "Even if he is a dork."

Adeline laughs softly, "He's worth it, and I love planning stuff like this."

She glances back in Billy's direction just as he blows her a kiss across the room and she catches it, holding her hand to her heart.

"He's so smitten with you."

"The feeling is very mutual."

"Have you met our parents yet?" Rosie asks and Adeline's gaze slides to George and Eleanor Brooks. In the moment she'd looked away Billy moved, he's standing with *her* dad now and she prays they're not talking about her.

"Just in passing yesterday," she replies, "I want to, but the thought of it is so nerve wracking, like suddenly everything with Billy will shift up a notch and I'm not sure I've come to terms with that happening yet."

Billy is the first person Adeline's had a *big girl* relationship with. The first time she's felt so much for one person that it scares her. She's not even confided in Norah about this, but Rosie is very much like Billy, she has an open face that just makes it easy to talk.

"Well, meeting our mom will happen soon if she has anything to say about it. The woman is literally in love with you already," Rosie tells her, "Billy calls her gushing about you and then *she* calls *me* gushing about Billy gushing about you. It's a whole thing." Adeline blushes. She doesn't feel like she's gush worthy in the slightest.

"Billy hasn't pushed it but I'm sure I'll meet them before the weekend is out." She goes to say something else when she spots Tobias wandering over, an arm slung around the shoulders of a young guy she doesn't recognise. She doesn't fail to notice the chequered pants, black roll-neck sweater and leather jacket he's in though. Adeline thought Billy had dressed sharply tonight but this guy is on another level. She shoots at look at Rosie, whose eyes are locked on him, her cheeks flushed pink.

"Addie, I don't think you've met Peters yet, have you? Peters, this is Adeline, Michael's daughter," Tobias shouts over the music, words slurred. Rosie salutes Adeline goodbye, taking the chance to escape tipsy Tobias, a wise choice.

"Patrick. You can call me Patrick, or Paddy," the newcomer says, his gaze following Rosie as she walks away. Adeline notices, of course, a knowing smile playing on her lips. They'd look cute together.

"Ah, Queens, right?" Adeline realises, "it's nice to meet you. My dad told me you're the next Billy Brooks," she teases, chuckling when Patrick's eyes go wide.

"Oh. I– uh... I'm not *that* good. I mean– the guy's on his way to becoming a legend. I, uh. Yeah. No, definitely not," he stammers. It's endearing and Adeline feels a soft spot forming for the young driver already.

"Well, that's what I heard. Have you been introduced yet?"

Billy must have felt his ears burning because he suddenly

appears beside her. He snakes an arm around her waist, pulling her flush to his side and settling his hand on her ass.

"Hey, sweet girl. Who's this?"

Adeline looks up at him as she goes to answer but then Billy's lips are on hers before she even has the chance to open her mouth. It's a soft, gentle kiss but he drags it out the moment she melts into him and pulls away with a smirk, his eyes on Patrick. Adeline rolls her eyes despite the butterflies swarming in her stomach.

"This is Patrick Peters. He's the next you, apparently."

Billy quirks an eyebrow and then narrows his eyes as he looks Patrick up and down. He jerks his jaw back and forth, pouting his lips.

"Is that so?" He's being a menace and poor Patrick doesn't know where to look.

"Uh– I..."

"I'm just messin' with ya, kid! You want a drink? You look like you could use a drink!" Billy grins, "I'll be back, Tinkerbell." He presses a kiss to Adeline's temple and taps her ass before gripping Patrick by the shoulders and leading him to the bar. Jumping to the music as they push through the party, Billy turns back as if he knows she's watching and winks before they get lost in the crowd.

"How old is he?' Adeline asks Tobias.

"Twenty-one, Adeline. He can drink anything here in this great state of North Carolina." He flaps his hands around like some Shakespearean actor. "I would have instructed Billy to only buy him beer if he wasn't. I'm respon– sib... responsible," he hiccups.

"Sure," Adeline laughs and then she's beckoned to the dance floor by Norah. She smiles at Tobias and chugs back the rest of her drink, abandoning the empty glass on a table as she makes her way over to her best friend.

"Are you having fun?" Norah asks as she takes Adeline's hand and twirls her around. "Because it looks like you've just been doing a whole lot of standing around."

"I've just been observing," Adeline shouts with a shrug, "people watching."

"*Billy* watching," Norah corrects her.

"Let me live!"

"Where is he now?"

"At the bar with that new driver, Patrick," Adeline replies without missing a beat and Norah just raises an eyebrow. So what if her eyes have been locked on Billy over Norah's shoulder this whole time? She likes to look at him.

"Disgusting," Norah says with a smile. Adeline pokes her tongue out in retaliation and keeps dancing. The lights and reflections from the disco ball blur around her as she spins, arms in the air. She definitely hasn't had enough to drink to let loose properly, but she welcomes the pleasant dizzying feeling as the beat of the music pulses through her limbs.

The euphoria flooding her senses comes to a grinding halt when her eyes land on Billy again, shaking hands with Rex, and Adeline's blood runs cold. She knows Billy only tolerates him but the sight of them interacting like friends makes her stomach churn.

"What the fuck is he doing here?" Norah hisses as she instinctively shields Adeline from his view but she can still see his narrowed eyes scour over the crowd when Billy's attention is elsewhere.

"My dad extended the invitation to any teams still in Carolina," Adeline says through gritted teeth. "Should have known he would show up."

Norah pulls her to the edge of the dance floor. "Adeline, you look like you've seen a ghost. What did he say to you? In Richmond," she presses and Adeline swallows thickly, her eyes glossing over.

"Um... he said he wasn't done with me," she mumbles. The words get lost with the music but Norah hears them well enough.

"That fucker! You need to tell Billy what he did, Addie. The guy was creepily persistent with you for years and took advantage the moment he got the opportunity. Billy would never associate himself with that piece of shit if he knew that."

"Not the easiest thing to say out loud, Red," Adeline sighs. Norah only found out by practically forcing the words out of her and all

Tobias knows is that Rex has a history of bothering her, nothing more.

"Just... think about it. I wouldn't put it past Rex to tell Billy himself just to taunt him."

Adeline nods. The worry in her stomach feels like a tangled ball of yarn. Each time she tries to work through it, she pulls on the wrong thread and creates a new knot. She doesn't want to think about any of this right now. She wants to drink and dance and celebrate her boyfriend's birthday.

"Come on, let's get you another drink. Rex is gone," Norah says softly and Adeline searches the bar, checking her words are true. Norah tugs on her arm as they weave their way through the crowd, only stopping halfway when they bump into Gabe and Stan. "We're getting a drink, you guys coming?"

The men follow and Gabe latches onto Norah, kissing her so passionately it makes Adeline blush just to see it. She pulls Stan to the bar and they squeeze in next to Billy. He's deep in conversation with a driver from Apex. They're a good team, give Shaw & Gold a run for their money when it comes to the calibre of their drivers. Billy must sense Adeline beside him because his hand grazes over her minidress, settling on the small of her back. She leans over, pressing a kiss to his shoulder just as the bartender stops in front of them. With their drinks ordered and conversation over, Billy and Adeline split off from the rest of them and they end up near the back of the room, hidden in a small alcove.

"I missed you," Billy murmurs. He has Adeline backed against the wall, his fingers playing with the small tendrils of hair that perfectly frame her face.

"I've been around," she giggles, "anyway, it's *your* party. You *should* be mingling."

Billy dips his head and kisses her. Adeline notes the taste of cigarettes and rum on his tongue as she runs it along the sensitive skin just inside her bottom lip. Trailing his mouth away from hers, he takes Adeline's jaw in his hand, fingers gently pressing into the back of her neck as she tilts her head back and covers her skin in soft, barely-there kisses. Adeline's stomach swoops as Billy pulls her earlobe into his mouth. He sucks and flicks it with his tongue, a quiet moan vibrating through her as his hands settles on her breast. With his thumb tracing around and over her nipple through the fabric of her dress, the dizzying feeling from earlier intensifies and Adeline whimpers, only for Billy to pull away. He smirks, lips curling into a cheeky grin as he darts his tongue across to the corner of his mouth.

"Fucking tease," Adeline pouts, chasing his lips. Billy backs up and takes her in, devouring her slowly as he follows the curves of her body with dark eyes.

"This is cute," he says as his hand skims down her side. He toys with the royal blue velvet of her dress until he reaches the hem and his warm fingers brush against her bare thigh as he tugs at the material gently. Billy glances over his shoulder before leaving a series of hot, lingering kisses across Adeline's jaw. Her breath hitches when his stubbled cheek tickles, deliciously rough over her skin, and he speaks soft and low in her ear. "I can't wait to take this off you later, watch the way it falls from your body. I wanna reveal every perfect part of you, bit... by... bit." Billy kisses her between each word, nips at her bottom lip before he whispers, "You gonna let me sweet girl?"

Adeline nods.

"Say it, Tinkerbell."

"Yes, I'll let you." She bites her lip. She curls her ponytail around her finger, playing his game.

"*Fuck.* Good girl," he rumbles and Adeline nearly chokes. She doesn't know where this version of Billy has come from tonight but *holy shit,* does she want him to stay. Her heart pounds as she clenches her thighs together. Billy notices.

"Oh, you like that?" He chuckles, low and gravelly in her ear and Adeline swats at his chest.

"You need to stop."

"Or wha–"

Adeline cuts him off as she feels something in the front pocket of his shirt. "What's this?"

"Huh?" Billy frowns and Adeline dips her hand into the pocket and pulls out two joints. Her eyes widen as she cocks her head.

"Is this pot?! Where the fuck did you get this?"

Billy looks confused and then bursts out laughing.

"Oh, shit! Yeah. Birthday present from that Peters kid!" He grins, eyes lit up with excitement. "You wanna go–"

"Um, yes." Adeline downs her drink for the second time in the last hour. There's a door marked 'staff only' to the left of where they're standing and Billy guides her towards it. They quickly sneak through, giggling and stumbling over themselves before pausing on the other side to determine their next move.

"Stairs." Adeline points out a fire exit stairwell. "Probably leads to the roof?"

"Perfect. I wanna show you somethin'." Billy takes a hold of her hand and they run. Only they have to stop halfway when neither of them anticipate how many floors they would have to climb. In the end, Billy goes ahead and stands waiting for Adeline at the top of the stairs with his foot jammed in the door while he searches for something to hold it open. She makes it to him, eventually. Her black knee-high boots stick to her clammy skin as she falls into his arms.

"Fuck. I need to work on my stamina," she huffs.

"I can help you with that later if you want," Billy grins, wiggling his eyebrows as he pulls her out into the night. They find a ledge to perch on, facing the small sliver of the moon that's illuminated above them. The rest of the sky is pretty clear, stars still visible through the light pollution. Adeline sighs as she stares up at the darkness. Stargazing makes her miss Georgia. It's usually so dark on the ranch you can see the Milky Way and she'll lie in the bed of a truck for hours letting her eyes drift over the sky, spotting something new each time.

Billy nudges her gently, holding out a joint and she takes it between her fingers while he finishes his lighter from his back pocket. It's gold plated, engraved with his initials and the date of his first NASCAR win; a gift from his dad. Whenever Adeline borrows it, she runs her thumb over the engraving as she smokes, a sort of two for one coping mechanism. She watches Billy's hands as he flicks the top of the lighter and shields the joint from the breeze as he lights it. They're as strong and large as they are soft and nimble and Adeline's lost count of how many times she loses herself in thoughts of them on her; dancing over her skin, gripping her hips. It drives her insane.

"Ladies first," he whispers. Adeline brings the joint to her lips and Billy's eyes follow. She inhales slowly, feeling it seep into her lungs before she exhales and the air around her fills with the grassy scent. She hands it to Billy who does the same and they work their way through it in comfortable silence.

"Okay, so I definitely forgot what this feels like," she chuckles after her third hit. "It's been a while."

"You good, Tinkerbell?" Billy asks. He's staring at her, eyes flicking over her features.

"Just dandy."

Billy giggles, the word really tickling him. "*Dandy.*"

"I'm gonna look at the stars now," Adeline announces after a moment and she lies back until just her feet dangle over the ledge. "Oh, *WOW!*"

"What?!"

"They're... *so* bright," she murmurs, her arms stretched to the sky as she splays her fingers out over each tiny speck they can reach. Suddenly, the butt of the joint is shoved in her face.

"You want the last hit?"

Adeline shakes her head, "You should have it, birthday boy."

"Well, if you insist." Billy takes one last drag, stubbing out the end before he lies down beside her. Adeline's whole body is relaxed, her mind feels still apart from the tune of the last song she heard downstairs going round and round in her head. She hums it quietly and senses Billy turn his head to look at her.

"Can I help you?" She asks, her manicured finger tapping him lightly on the nose. Billy gives her a heart-stopping smile. The blue of his eyes is gone and the black pools of his pupils bore into her soul. It feels like a lifetime as they lie there staring at each other, quietly studying freckles and dimples, fingers tracing over lips and cheeks. Everything about Billy is heightened in her mind right now. His tanned skin feels baby soft under the pads of her fingers, his eyes, though dark, are sparkling, and his eyelashes are so, so long. He's fucking beautiful, and he's all hers. Adeline giggles at the thought, the infectious sound catching when Billy joins in and their quietly delirious laughter fill the moments around soft kisses and lingering touches. Adeline feels euphoric; a slow, magical happiness bubbling through her veins.

"Are you cold?" Billy whispers. Their faces are so close, Adeline feels his lips tickling faintly across her cheek as he speaks. "You're shivering, Tinkerbell."

"A little," she replies. She hadn't even noticed how cold it was outside, too wrapped up in Billy and the mellow feeling of her high. Now he's mentioned it, she does feel a chill wrapping itself around her bare arms. Billy climbs to his feet and helps her up, winding his arms around her tightly as they head back across the roof.

"Let's go back in. Do you have the room key?"

Adeline feels around her dress and then realises she left her clutch in the ballroom.

"Shit. Purse is at the party," she laughs, "we're gonna have to sneak in... wait! Weren't you gonna show me something?" She remembers as they slip back through the door.

"I think it was a consol– no, uh *con-stell-a-tion*," Billy says slowly. "I'm not gonna lie though, Tinkerbell, I can't remember which one and everything is definitely a little blurry right now."

He grips onto Adeline's waist, fingers pressing into her softness as they very slowly make their way back down the stairwell. She feels like her feet have weights tied to them with every step she takes and every time she stumbles, Billy nearly tackles her to the floor with how hellbent he is on keeping her upright. It's a wonder they make it to the first floor in one piece.

They creep back into the ballroom unnoticed. Billy darts to the entrance while Adeline searches for her purse. She could have sworn she left it where she'd been standing for most of the evening but she can't see it. *Maybe someone put it on the floor,* she thinks and she knocks over a chair as she practically crumbles to the polished parquet flooring. She's never been good at being subtle but her depth perception has gone to absolute shit; it seems she may as well be blind. It doesn't help that she can't focus on one spot for very long without needing to rapidly blink. The wood feels surprisingly comfortable though, spongey almost, as she sits in a heap for a moment. Then something shiny catches her eye and she inches forward until she's nearly under the table. *False alarm, damn it.* When she pokes her head up, fast and wired like a meerkat, Billy is flapping his arms around by the door telling her to hurry up.

"I can't find it!" She mouths to him. At least, she thinks she mouths it but by the looks she just received from those around her, she's starting to think that maybe she just screamed it across the room.

"Looking for this?" Norah appears behind her, the little black purse is hanging from her finger, the sequins glittering under the disco lights. The lights bounce off of it like shards of glass and she tilts her head, momentarily mesmerised. Norah's eyebrow is raised as she takes in Adeline's state and then she shifts her gaze to Billy who looks just as equally spaced out. "Are you guys high?!"

"No!" Adeline snaps. She's trying really hard to stay straight-faced but her lips keep betraying her, like they're attached to puppet strings and the puppet master is a shithead. She smacks her hand over her mouth as a loud laugh erupts.

"Jesus Christ." Norah shakes her head as she pulls Adeline up from the floor. She marches her over to Billy and pushes her bag securely into her hands.

"Shh, Nor. You can't tell anyone!"

"*You. Billy Brooks,* are a fucking bad influence," Norah hisses, poking him in the chest.

"Ow! Norah! *Quit it!*"

"Hey!" Adeline scrunches her nose in an attempt to look threatening as she jabs back at Norah. "Stop. Poking. My. Boyfriend." Billy wraps his arms around her from behind and rests his chin on her shoulder, squeezing her gently as he peppers her cheek with messy kisses.

"You could have at least invited the rest of us to your little stoner party, Brooks. Where'd you get this shit anyway." Adeline looks around and sees Patrick leaning against the bar.

"Him." She points and as soon as Norah turns to look, she and Billy make a run for it. Adeline laughs hysterically as Billy presses the elevator button at lightning speed until it finally chimes and the doors slide open. She doesn't stop laughing until they crash into their hotel room, falling over each other as Billy refuses to let her go.

She drops her bag to the ground as soon as the door slams behind them and Billy leaps onto the bed. He moans as he sinks into the duvet, the luxurious sheets still messed up from that morning.

"Baby, you gotta get up here. Feels like a fuckin' marshmallow." He reaches for her, beckoning her over and then flops onto his back, his head hanging over the foot of the bed. Adeline climbs up and flops down beside him. He's right. It feels like she's floating. She drops her head over the edge with his and glances at him, giggling as the blood rushes to her brain.

"What do you want?" Billy asks quietly.

"Right now?"

"No, like... in life?"

Adeline turns to the ceiling as she thinks about it. She's not really sure, when it boils down to it. All she's known is NASCAR. Travelling, road trips, hotel rooms and oil-slicked garages raging with testosterone. She was homeschooled because of it. She never had a guidance counsellor or college admissions rep asking her the big questions so she never really answered them. She's pretty happy with what she's got right now, though. Billy, and her friends who may as well be family. Settling down sounds good, nice, but she's only twenty-five; that's a future she sees years down the line. She looks back at Billy, waiting for her answer with large, doe-like eyes, as he gnaws on his bottom lip.

"I just want to be happy and play piano more... I don't know," she laughs.

"Lame."

"Hey!" She grumbles, slapping blindly in his direction. Billy catches her hand and brings it to his lips. "Your turn. What do you want?"

"I want you. Always. I'll keep racing, obviously. I'm gonna be the greatest NASCAR driver of all time with the most gorgeous woman by my side," he sighs as he plays with her hand and kisses each knuckle softly. Adeline's cheeks warm, the blush creeping up until her ears are burning.

"And then what?"

"And then, we're gonna get married and have so many babies. Little Billys and Adelines runnin' around. *Fuck.* We're gonna be living the life, sweet girl."

Adeline's a little blindsided by his admission but she'd be lying if she said she didn't want it; that life with him.

"Fuckin' Delilah ruined that dream for me," Billy continues, "but you, *you*, Adeline Gold. You've brought it back to life. I look at you and I see it all." He turns onto his stomach and slinks further towards the carpeted floor. "You're it. You're the lo– why is there a dick smiling at me?"

Adeline's eyebrows pinch in confusion before she remembers she hasn't wrapped the sweater yet. Billy pulls it out from under the bed and sits up, holding it against his body.

"Uh. Happy birthday?" Adeline says, chuckling through an awkward smile.

"This is for me?" Billy asks breathlessly through his own laughter.

"I found it in the thrift store, thought maybe you would find it funny–"

"Hey, there's even a little bit that looks like a birthmark right where– Addie, did you make this look like my dick?!" Adeline nods, her cheeks blazing but Billy is giggling hysterically, laughing so hard, a tear trickles its way down his cheek and he licks it up with his tongue as it hits his lip.

"I fuckin' love it," he beams, swooping forward and crashing his lips to hers. Adeline falls back as he attacks her face with kisses. His lips are warm and wet against her skin and she squeals as he licks from her jaw up to her temple.

The words are on the tip of her tongue. It would be so easy for her to say it right now, to tell him how utterly fucking in love with him she is. Billy pulls back, his nose brushing against hers softly, a blur of his handsome face blocking out the light. Then he's sitting back up, the palpable tension gone.

"Are you hungry? Because I feel like I haven't eaten in daaaays," he drawls. Adeline agrees. She's craving something sweet. Something rich and gooey that's probably going to make her feel sick but will be *so* worth it.

"There's cake downstairs!"

"What kind?" Billy asks sceptically.

"Chocolate, obviously."

That gets a groan out of him and he takes her cheeks in his hands, smushing her face gently as he plants a messy kiss on her lips.

"Chocolate cake and girl of my fuckin' dreams? Happy fuckin' birthday to me!"

The world is too bright when Adeline opens her eyes the next morning. She squints until she can see enough to work out that she's lying sideways across the bed and Billy is clinging to her. His face is snuggled into her stomach and her hand is buried in his hair.

The sun streams in through the window and she closes her eyes again. Her head is pounding, like someone is chipping away with an axe at her frontal lobe. When she opens her eyes a second time, she takes in more of her surroundings. Billy's birthday cake is on the bedside table surrounded by empty glasses, chunks are taken out of it like they ate it with their hands. She can't remember bringing it up to the room. The last thing she *does* remember is Billy's face extremely close to hers and the sensation of his tongue swiping across her cheek.

Billy mumbles something, stirring out of sleep. It takes Adeline a second to realise that he's in the sweater and nothing else and she chuckles as the memories of the night slowly come back to her.

"Mornin', sweet girl," he rumbles, squeezing her closer. He turns his head, one eye closed still as he smiles at her sleepily and untangles himself from her body, smoothing out her dress from where it had bunched up around her middle.

She feels disgusting, like she needs to clean her teeth a dozen times and shower for an hour. But Billy is looking at her, eyes sparkling with something she can't quite read, she just knows it makes her heart thump and her skin tingle. There's a beat of silence before Billy parts his dry lips to speak.

"I don't know if I said it last night," he says, his voice thick with sleep, low and quiet as he comes face to face with her. "But if I did, I wanna say it again sober. So you know I mean it with every single speck of fuckin' stardust you and I are made of." Adeline waits, her eyes on his mouth as he wets his lips and exhales a shaky breath. "I love you, Addie."

sixteen

ADELINE

ADELINE KNOWS BILLY LOVES HER. IT'S EVIDENT IN THE little things. The mini hotel room breakfast buffets he puts together while she's sound asleep and the way he washes her hair in the shower; almost too softly, afraid he'll accidentally pull it and hurt her. He tells her with the way he kisses her; the slow, deliberate kisses that take her breath away and he tells her with the way he literally cannot say no whenever she pulls out the pout and puppy dog eyes.

But hearing him *say* it...

Hearing the words fall from his lips, pink and plump after sleep, and they roll off his tongue in such a sweet, sleepy tone; Adeline wants his voice to sound like that every time he says it. Billy says it so confidently too, so sure of his love, and the moment the words are in the air, Adeline's world grinds to a halt. Time is suspended and her throat runs so dry, it's a struggle to say anything even if she wants to.

Billy blinks at her with his big, brilliant blue eyes, his hair fluffy and dishevelled, and everything around her falls away. It's just her and Billy. Almost thirty-year-old Billy who's in nothing but a sweater with a stupid smiley penis on it, which is such a ridiculous notion but somehow seems *so* right. It's an ode to the playful, immature side of their relationship that peeks out between the quiet moments and serious conversation. Adeline used to think relationships like theirs were impossible to maintain; that each person needs to be the polar opposite to balance the other out. Yet, she and Billy just *work*. So fucking well that it scares her sometimes.

It's been a hot minute since Billy spoke. He looks so gentle and boyish as he waits, gulping in a way that sends his Adam's apple bobbing in his throat. Adeline realises they've been sitting in silence for an awkwardly long time while she rattles off her monologue in her head. She's overthinking it, she knows. Wondering how to say the words back, of all things, which is stupid but her brain can't stop ticking back and forth. Does she just say '*I love you too*'? Or does she tell him she's *in* love with him? She's never done this before, never wanted to until Billy. She gnaws at her bottom lip feeling like she's eaten too much candy. The moment is so sweet and delicious but she can feel the sugar rush that leads to the inevitable crash, the nausea swirling around in her belly.

"I'm gonna need you to say something, Tinkerbell," Billy finally says, breaking the silence. Adeline takes a deep breath and quickly talks herself out of just kissing him. When the words tumble out her mouth, it's all on the out-breath. They bleed into one another like watercolours.

"Iloveyoutoo!"

And the world resumes.

"Sorry, what was that?" Billy asks with a soft chuckle.

"I *said*, Iloveyoutoo," Adeline says again, just as fast and with her eyes shut tight.

"Sorry, one more time but slower. I'm almost thirty, sweet girl, my hearin' ain't what it used to be." He grins, lips parted to reveal the brightest smile Adeline has ever seen grace his face. Adeline laughs, crawling across the bed to where Billy is sitting. Nose to nose, she pecks a fleeting kiss to his lips.

"I love you, Billy Brooks," she whispers.

"Yeah?"

"Mhmm." Adeline catches her bottom lip under her teeth and backs up slightly. She lets out a dreamy sigh that she just can't help as she looks at him and flings the back of her hand against her forehead dramatically. "My heart beats for you, Billy! I'm dizzy with it! I'm so stupidly and ridiculously in love with you–"

"Okay, okay. I get it, you love me," Billy laughs and his nose scrunches, the apples of his cheeks rising with it. "Wanna show me how much?" His lips are so incredibly close to hers but he holds back, teasing her. "I never did get to take this dress off you last night, did I?"

He crawls towards her. His gaze darkens as it flits from Adeline's mouth to her eyes and back again. Adeline shakes her head as Billy presses a kiss to the corner of her mouth and follows it with three small pecks across her jaw and back again; light lips ghosting over hers but never touching. She huffs out an impatient sigh.

"What are you waiting for, William?"

"Oh we're using our government names now are we, Adeline?"

Adeline scowls but it quickly turns into a giggle as Billy attacks her face with kisses until she falls back onto the bed. With his hands flat to the mattress on either side of her head, he hovers over her, blocking the light in a way that creates a halo around his shadowed face. His lips land softly over her forehead and cheeks in quick succession, week-old stubble scratching deliciously across her skin. She wants to feel it against her thighs more than anything and her belly floods with anticipation just thinking about it, but Billy is clearly in the mood to tease. He puckers his lips playfully and makes over the top kissy noises that mix with Adeline's squeals and laughter. His lips tickle her face, big smacking kisses and some so soft she barely feels them.

When he stops, it's like a switch flips. The world around them slows down again as Billy traces his finger down the small curve of her nose and over her lips and he holds her chin softly, his thumb brushing over the faded scar just below her mouth. As he rests the tip of it on her bottom lip, Adeline takes it into her mouth and sucks gently. Billy's eyes stay fixed on her and he clears his throat. The action cements her decision to play with him, swirling her tongue around the pad of his thumb and hums. She pulls away with pop and Billy swipes over her lips, wetting them and mirroring the action with his tongue across his own.

"I love you. My sweet, sweet Addie," he utters, voice so soft and quiet that if he wasn't inches from her face, Adeline doesn't think she would have heard him. Billy pulls her up so they're kneeling, chest to chest, and he flashes her a smile that would make her panties drop if she was actually wearing any. She spots them on the floor, thrown during whatever antics they got up to last night. Billy's sweater quickly joins them as he pulls it off and throws it behind him. He kisses Adeline softly as his hands wander to the back of her dress.

He starts with the zip, fingers cold against her bare skin as he pulls it down the stretch of her spine. It stops halfway down her back, the fabric loose at her shoulder. Adeline usually prides herself on being patient but Billy is taking his sweet time and it's killing her. He wasn't lying when he said he wanted to reveal her bit by bit. Pulling down one shoulder of velvet, his lips immediately find the exposed skin and his tongue trails a wet path down her arm in hot, open-mouthed kisses as he gently pulls it from the sleeve.

It's agonising and she whimpers quietly as Billy's cock, hard and hot between them presses against her stomach. Not that he seems even a tiny bit phased, he's completely lost in the task of removing Adeline's dress. His eyes flick up to meet hers every so often but otherwise he's kissing her, hands caressing over whichever part of her body he's just revealed. He moves onto the next sleeve, lips trailing across the base of her neck on his way to her other shoulder.

"You taste so fucking sweet, Tinkerbell," Billy mumbles as his nose brushes along the sharpness of her collarbone, inhaling the remnants of her perfume and moisturiser. "Like honey and vanilla," he groans, eyes rolling back as he involuntarily bucks his hips.

With both arms free from her dress, Adeline assumes Billy is just going to let it fall from her body. Instead, he rolls it down her torso, the cool air of the hotel room prickling her skin with goosebumps with each part of her he exposes.

"You're really committed to this whole revealing me bit by bit thing, aren't you?"

"Gotta savour you, sweet girl. Can't rush these things."

"*Billy*," she whines, "I just want your mouth on me."

He stops what he's doing and looks at her with a tilt of his head and a clench of his jaw. His eyes darken as she gently takes hold of her chin, forcing her to meet his gaze.

"Do I need to teach you a lesson about patience, Adeline?" Adeline stares him down but the moment he narrows his eyes and bites his lip, she's done for.

"Would it involve your mouth on me?" She replies anyway, her tone clipped.

Two can play at this game.

Billy doesn't warrant that with an answer and instead, he gets back to work. Mouth trailing across her chest, he dips his head and takes her pebbled nipple between his teeth, tugging gently before rolling his tongue over it.

"Is this what you wanted, Tinkerbell?" His voice is light as she smirks and keeps going, hands caressing up and under her dress, palming at her breasts. When he finally, *finally*, pulls the royal blue velvet from her body, Adeline is aching.

Billy walks his fingers down her sides slowly, palms landing on her ass and squeezing. With his lips attached to her jaw, he sucks on the spot just below her ear and Adeline breathes out a moan as his fluffy hair tickles softly over her skin. The faint musk of his cologne fills her nose and her touch receptors are working in overdrive with each brush of his fingers – her senses are shot and she loves it.

Lower and lower, Billy's mouth travels her body. He explores every dip and curve of her belly and hips until eventually he lies her back on the bed and settles between her legs. He wets his lips and Adeline follows the movement of his tongue, sure her own pupils are blown just as wide and just as dark as Billy's as he eyes her hungrily.

"Oh, *Addie*. You're so fuckin' wet for me, sweet girl." He glides a finger through her folds with a satisfied smile and sucks it clean of slick, groaning like she's the sweetest thing he's ever tasted. The sound rumbles deep in his throat and Adeline whines desperately. Her fingernails scratch through his hair and it draws a softer moan from Billy as he dips his head and swipes his tongue up to her clit. Frenzied butterflies fill her belly; she's already so close to coming undone, writing against the bed as her legs tense around Billy's head.

"Stay still, Adeline." His large hands clamp around her thighs, holding her down.

She does as she's told but the commanding authority of his tone combined with the way his nose nudges her clit as he works her effortlessly causes her to clench her thighs again. Pulling his mouth away, he fixes her with a hard stare and Adeline forces her body to still. Billy's eyes soften as he looks up through his ridiculously long lashes, a devilish grin on his dewy lips.

"Good girl."

Fuck. He remembered.

She can feel Billy laugh, a cocky chuckle vibrating through her body as he flattens his tongue, lapping at her pussy. It's enough to trigger her descent, tumbling into a back-arching, toe-curling orgasm.

"Oh my *GOD*. Billy!" Adeline's chest heaves. Her cheeks are flushed pink, skin coated with a glistening sheen of sweat as the fiery whirlwind in her belly slowly calms to a low simmer. Billy is still buried between her legs as he leaves gentle kitten licks over her throbbing bud, taking it between his lips, coaxing her through it. When his mouth leaves her, it's not for long. His teeth nip at the inside of her thighs, tongue swiping hotly over the faint bite marks he leaves behind and a long whimper of a moan slips past Adeline's lips at the glorious sensation of pain and warm wetness on her skin.

Billy nips and licks his way back up her body and captures her mouth in a heavy kiss. His tongue teases hers before he tugs gently on her bottom lip. His fingers tangle in her hair and he draws away from her slightly to stroke his fist lazily over his length before lining himself up with her entrance.

"Okay?" He asks, gentle now as he leans forward to peck her lips sweetly.

"Yeah," she breathes, "I love you."

"I love you too," he whispers as he sinks into her, slowly and then all at once as he bottoms out with a low and guttural moan. His forearms, strong and tense, support his weight as he begins to fuck her languidly. With each gentle roll of his hips, Billy huffs out a soft grunt with his face buried in the crook of Adeline's neck and his breath warm on her skin. She can feel every ridge and twitch of his cock as he pushes into and pulls out nearly all the way. It's fucking incredible and she needs more. Harder, faster.

"Billy, *please*," she whimpers, her brain in too much of a muddled sex haze to say anything more. Fingers dancing over his chest, she wraps her arms under his and around his shoulders, her nails pressing moon-shaped indents into his skin as she clings to him. Billy's back muscles ripples under Adeline's palms as she grapples for stability. She commits the feeling to memory as he thrusts a little harder, pushes deeper as he fills her to the hilt every time. She's unravelling beneath him as he kisses her roughly, all tongue and teeth, messy and raw.

"Tell me you're mine." The words are a deep rumble, words broken with stilted breaths as he snaps his hips faster.

"I'm yours, Billy," Adeline chokes out. She digs her heels into his back, trying to pull him deeper, wanting to feel every part of her body against his hard form as he slams into her. Billy trails his hands along Adeline's arms and he lifts them from his body until they're stretched over her head. With her wrists bound in one large hand, his other skims down her side and over her breasts. He rests it on her chest and Adeline knows he can feel her heart race, the erratic pattern of her breaths as he owns her completely. She brings her hips to meet his, chasing the feeling of euphoria that so often floods her body when she climaxes.

The room echoes with the sound of soft gasps and raspy moans as Billy fucks her into the mattress. She's pretty sure she'll have bruises, his hips slam against her thighs with each thrust but he counteracts the forceful motion with tender brushes of his lips over her neck and shoulders. His hand comes down between them, finger circling steadily over her pulsing clit and Adeline *feels* it. Feels the way she flutters around the hot drag of his cock and her toes curl again as the coil of pleasure in the depths of her belly tightens.

"*Fuck.* Billy, I'm almost– don't stop! *Please,*" she begs as her nails scratch down his back and he fucks into her again and again. Adeline's vision whites out as she comes, Billy's name tumbling from her lips in a whispered chant. It's pure bliss, adrenaline and ecstasy washing over her in waves. Billy's mouth covers hers, broken kisses between laboured breaths.

"Shit, Addie. You're something else, sweet girl," he whispers. His voice is hoarse as he babbles. "I love you. I love you so much." Adeline holds him, the pads of her fingers trace over his cheeks and lips as he tips over the edge and spills into her with soft groans. She kisses him lightly, Billy's thrusts staggered and out of rhythm until he slows to a stop and slowly collapses on top of her. They lie together, a mess of sweaty limbs, quiet and content. Adeline sighs and peers down at Billy as her fingers swim through his hair and she realises, in the afterglow, that she's never felt happiness like this before.

seventeen

BILLY
March 16th, 1975
Bristol International Speedway, Tennessee

BILLY JUMPS FROM FOOT TO FOOT TRYING TO EXPEL HIS PRE-race jitters. It's unusual, but since his loss in Carolina, his nerves have spiked. He wants this so badly. Racing is everything to him, it's the only thing he's good at. Until he met Adeline, the only time he's ever felt truly alive is behind the wheel of his car. He wants to do this for her too, he feels like he needs it to prove himself worthy of her.

He hates that he thinks this way; he's still learning to undo what Delilah did to him. She would never show up to a race but the moment she found out he didn't win, Billy would know how she felt about it, and it would usually come as a tidal wave of insults down the phone. What they had was never love, he knows that now.

"You ready, Brooks?" Michael appears beside him, done with his pep talk with Stan. It's one they've all heard a hundred times before but Michael has a way of making it feel new every time, and his words are always full of support and confidence. It's a glimpse into what kind of father he is too and Billy takes it as a reminder of how special Adeline is.

"Yeah," he says with a deep breath and a hint of a smile. It's such a piss-poor effort at being convincing that he almost laughs at himself.

"Remember the four A's and you'll be fine."

"Four A's?" Billy questions with a frown. "I thought it was Triple A?"

Michael grins, "It's four for you. Anticipation, acceleration, attitude..." he pauses, for dramatic effect Billy realises as his eyes shine. Clearly Michael thinks he's onto a real zinger. "And, *Adeline.*"

Billy shakes his head and chuckles softly. "Addie would hate that."

"I know, but I'm a dad. It's my job to embarrass her." Michael winks and claps Billy on the shoulder. "You'll get it when you have kids of your own."

Billy huffs out a nervous laugh and shoots Michael a sideways glance before his gaze roams across the garage. Everyone is getting ready to go. Stan is standing with his arms stretched out, his palms pressed against the top of his car and his eyes closed. He's breathing deeply. Billy counts seven seconds in and seven seconds out, Stan's lucky number. Norah is doing her weird NASCAR exorcism thing she always does, muttering under her breath as she circles her car.

Billy swallows thickly, acutely aware of how clammy his hands have become and the dampness of sweat that has graced his forehead. Why is he so nervous? He's done this a hundred times before.

Everything feels a little different now though.

When he raced with Hard Strike, he may as well have not been on their roster of drivers. No one cared where he placed or his lap times. Billy didn't really care either, he was a NASCAR driver and that's all he ever wanted. It often left him wondering why Christopher Lennox signed him in the first place when Rex Harlow was always the team's best asset. Now though, Billy has eyes on him. He gets written about, referred to as a NASCAR golden boy and painted in that 'can do no wrong' light whether he wins or loses. They air more races on television, and more people recognise him on the street. That one is rare, but it happens, and Billy isn't prepared for any of it.

He takes another breath and looks around, searching for blonde and listening for the familiar giggle that simultaneously makes his heart race and calms him, but Adeline has already left.

"She's with your sister. Next to the east side stands if you need a minute, Billy," Michael says and Billy realises his uneasiness is plastered all over his face. Michael obviously has a better read on him than he thought. Adeline is his good luck charm and with everyone else completing their pre-race rituals, it only feels right to see her once more before it all kicks off.

"Thanks, Michael. I won't be long," he breathes with a smile as he starts to make his way through to the stand entrance.

"Billy!" Michael calls after him and Billy spins, nearly losing his balance. "I should be thanking you. I've not seen my daughter this happy in a very long time."

Billy nods, fighting off the prickle of emotion he's been trying to keep at bay for the past hour. With a salute to Michael, he breaks back out into a jog and goes in search of Adeline.

The sheer noise of the crowd almost knocks him for six as he steps out into the stands. There's a low humdrum of chatter amongst shouts and music, tinny through the speakers as everyone waits for the race to start. It's not long before he finds Adeline and Rosie. They're standing to the side, hidden from everyone else but with a perfect view of the track. His sister is clutching a beer while Adeline sips on a Gatorade stolen from the team's supply,

Billy takes a moment, watching them from afar as they laugh about something. Adeline's nose scrunches and he can hear that little snort in his head as she throws her head back. He loves her *so* much.

The past three months have been some of the best of his life. Adeline makes him feel something he hasn't in a very long time. Hope trickles through his limbs whenever he's near her, from his fingers to his toes, he brims with it. She's the sun and the moon and

Billy lives for it; the quiet intimacy and loud spontaneity that blooms so naturally wherever Adeline is planted.

He steps up behind the two women and hovers, not wanting to interrupt, but Rosie senses him immediately and abruptly pauses her conversation as she looks at him with a raised eyebrow.

"Mind if I steal Addie away for a minute, Ro?" He asks tentatively. Rosie goes to grumble but Adeline's face lights up the moment she sees him and it doesn't go amiss by his sister as she reluctantly ushers them away. Billy gets deja vu as he leads her to the secluded tunnel he just came from. He stops once they're far enough away from the loud chaos of the track.

"Hey, what's up? Shouldn't you be heading to the starting grid?" Adeline asks. Her eyes are wide with concern, a small frown on her lips as she stares up at him.

"Nothing's up. Can't I just come see my girl one more time before the race?"

"*Billy.*" She looks at him pointedly, not buying his words for a second.

"I'm just a bit jittery," he replies, unable to meet her eye. "I don't know why."

"Hey, look at me. Baby, look at me." Her voice is soft as Billy feels her fingers under his chin. He shaved this morning and it always takes him a while to get used to feeling her hands against smooth skin as opposed to scratching over his stubble. She tilts his head, and as he finally meets her gaze, she's smiling at him.

Brilliant and bright.

"You're the best fucking driver out there," she says, "don't tell Norah and Stan I said that, but it's true."

"I dunno–"

"Billy, listen to me. You were made for this. The control and power you have behind that wheel are second to none. What is it my dad always says? The three A's or something?"

"Triple A," Billy replies and his lips curl into a smirk. "Although it's four for me apparently."

Adeline rolls her eyes, "Ugh, he's so embarrassing!"

"Yeah, I felt embarrassed for you," he chuckles softly. His arms wind around her waist and he hugs her tight, anchoring himself to her body.

"You *can* think of me if it helps," Adeline mumbles into his chest. She peers up at him just as he pulls away from kissing the crown of her head and Billy dips his head to capture her lips. He kisses her slowly, savouring the taste of her. Strawberry lip balm and lemon-lime Gatorade infiltrate his tongue. There's a shift in the mood as Adeline runs her hands through his hair and Billy has to force himself to stop. He breaks the kiss and she giggles, beaming up at him.

"You gotta go be a big-time race car driver now."

"I do. We'll continue this later, sweet girl."

Adeline sighs and shrugs her shoulders dramatically.

"*Fine.* I guess I can wait."

Billy steps back, linking their fingers as they begin to part ways. He stretches his arm out until he has no choice but to let go, his fingers travelling the length of Adeline's until they fall from the tips. When he turns to leave, she calls his name and Billy rolls his head around, taking a small step back to look at her as he awaits her parting words.

"What are you made of?" She asks, lifting her chin as she narrows her eyes and scrunches her nose. Billy tilts his head to the side, a smile blooming across his face and he feels his eyes crinkle at the corners; the reality of ageing, yet with Adeline, Billy has never felt so young.

"Fuckin' stardust, Tinkerbell," he laughs.

"Damn *right* you are!" Adeline grins, walking backwards. "I love you, Billy Brooks! Go show them what you're fucking made of!"

"I love you!" Billy calls back, dopey smile and all.

He shakes himself off as he wanders back to his car, loosening his shoulders and cracking his knuckles. There's adrenaline pumping through him now, oxytocin seeping into his bloodstream from seeing Adeline. His nerves are being evicted with each step he takes and he knows that from the moment he sits in the driver's seat, it's muscle memory. As fucking ridiculous as it sounds, he becomes one with the car; his legs an extension of the pedals, hands locked to the steering wheel.

Back in the pit, he glances down the lane. Bristol Speedway is built differently from others he's been in. Smaller, so there are two separate pits and no garage. Slow starters are relegated to pit stalls along the back stretch so, as Billy peers along the row of cars behind his, he sees Stan, Norah and Rex parked up in front of two Apex drivers and another ten from various teams. Everyone else is over on the far side of the track.

He nods to Stan, a silent good luck as the other driver pulls his helmet on and Billy is about to do the same when something catches his eye. A flash of red hair; an up do styled to perfection that he would recognise anywhere. She's moving quickly through the drivers and for a split second, Billy thinks she's heading for him and he panics, a flighty feeling in his chest as he tries to keep his cool. He never knows what kind of mood she's going to be in or how to handle any of them, not really. It's the last thing he needs. But she doesn't even see him, doesn't once look in his direction and he watches on as she throws herself at Rex of all people.

What the fuck is she doing?

Billy doesn't have time to dwell on it but he can't look away. It's the sort of thing she would do and he should have known she would play this game. In fact, he's surprised she didn't do it sooner. Fraternising with the enemy is Delilah's M.O. Always has been, always will be. Even back in high school, when they were so blissfully unaware of how sour their relationship would eventually turn, Delilah would flirt with everyone – but her favourite was always the opposing football team, or baseball team, or any team that wasn't theirs, really. She always claimed she did it to get the Brooklyn Bulldogs riled up, to help them win. Maybe that's what she's doing now, and if it is, Billy hates that it's working.

With a low growl, frustration fuels him as he pushes his helmet over his head and pulls his gloves on.

He will not let her get to him.

Not today.

LAP 1

Billy's gaze is trained on the green flag. His heartbeat is a steady rhythm in his ears as he waits for it to be lifted, waved high. He's revving gently, his car sufficiently warmed up. With his foot on the clutch, he lets the pedal rise a nickel depth at a time as the flag is raised and readies his other foot on the gas.

He can see Rex's car in his peripherals, can hear the thunderous roar of 42 engines as the flag is finally held high and brought down in once large swoop. Rubber burns as they take off and something in Billy shifts. His jaw tenses, his hands tightening around the steering wheel until his knuckles ache.

He pictures Adeline's perfect face.

He's got this.

LAP 78

He's stayed in a steady second place so far, tailing Rex who shot out into front at the start. Billy isn't worried though. He speeds up a little, listening closely to the revs so he can change gear smoothly. Waiting until he rounds the next bend onto the back stretch, he accelerates and changes gear without moving his feet an inch. Then it happens in slow motion, a moment that would be right at home in a Three Stooges cartoon. Billy overtakes Rex's car as it judders and bunny hops along the track.

He allows himself a second to revel in it but stops himself from celebrating prematurely. Rex may be his biggest competition, but the race isn't over.

He pictures Adeline's perfect face.

He's got this.

LAP 184

Halfway. Everything is a blur and Billy's mind is working on a system of gear changes and careful turns of the steering wheel. His hands are clammy in his gloves and sweat beads on his nose.

So far, he's only had to come in for two tyre changes. His Dodge is playing ball today, no overheated engine or random rattling. Not yet, anyway. His energy is high as he soars past the crowds. Rex never rejoined the race and Billy doesn't know who's behind him. Rubber to asphalt, he accelerates a little more, keeping the distance.

He pictures Adeline's perfect face.

He's got this.

LAP 300

Cramp. More specifically, cramp in his thigh. In his nervous stupor, he forgot to stretch and now each time his foot moves on the gas pedal, his muscle contracts painfully.

Fucking fuck.

He has no choice but to work through it. The end is so close and he's not backing down now. Maybe he can take a second to stretch his leg out when he goes in for his next refuel and tyre change. His prayers are answered when his in-car radio crackles to life and Gabe's voice calls him in.

Billy rounds the last bend and glides smoothly into the pit. If they're quick enough, he won't lose much distance and will easily maintain his lead. This time, he doesn't need to picture Adeline's perfect face because she's standing right there. Her mouth is curled into the cheesiest grin as she gives him two thumbs up, and the last thing he sees as he takes off again is her plucking Gabe's radio headset from him. His radio sparks back to life as he pulls back out in front and prepares for the next sixty-seven laps.

"I love you." Her voice is crackly and faint, but it's enough.

He's got this.

LAP 367

Final lap. Billy is both exhausted and completely wired at the same time. He's on autopilot now as the chequered flag comes into view out of the final bend.

Fuck it, he thinks and floors it. Whizzing over the finish line, an almost maniacal laugh bursts from his lips as the flag is brought down behind him. He slows his car down gradually and drives around the track once more, tempted to call this his victory lap and be done with it. His cramp is back and more than anything, he just wants to see his girl.

He does a quick scout for Delilah and Rex as he climbs out of his car but they're nowhere to be seen. That's one less thing to worry about at least. Freeing himself from his helmet, his hair is damp with sweat. Someone hands him a gatorade and he chugs it back as he concentrates on battling his way through the cheers and congratulations. Billy smiles, thanks everyone politely while he slowly works his way through the crowd.

She's waiting for him at the end and he fixes his gaze on her as he finally falls free. Hastily, he removes his gloves and reaches his hand out to touch her, to feel her under his fingertips before he tastes her.

The moment he does, everything clicks into place. Billy Brooks' life is good. No, his life is fucking great and it's going to take more than some pre-race jitters and an appearance from Delilah to knock him off his stride.

BILLY

March 25th, 1975

Atlanta Hartsfield International Airport, en route to LAX

"BILLY, YOU'RE NOT BREATHING."

The sound of Adeline's voice brings Billy out of his trance and he exhales heavily beside her. He's been staring at the embroidered Delta logo on the seat in front of him since he sat down, trying to calm down and ignore the thumping pulse he can feel behind his eyeballs. Billy has a cigarette tucked between the index and middle fingers of his right hand, his pinky and ring finger tapping away on the armrest.

When he glances to his left, Adeline is looking at him with the big doe eyes that usually make him cave into her every want, although this time, there's concern glistening in the green and gold flecks of her irises. Billy tenses his left hand, not realising he's gripping Adeline so tightly with it that his knuckles are white and hers are very, very squished. She may have to ice them when they get back to Malibu.

All this and the plane hasn't even started moving yet.

Billy hates flying, always has. He hates that he's not in control, he hates that the air hostesses are overly friendly as if they're trying to make up for something and, more than anything, he hates the tickling, nauseous feeling he gets in his stomach every time the plane does that weird little dippy motion during turbulence.

Despite the anxiety that's been following him around like a shadow in the lead up to this flight, Billy *has* had a pretty great week. He came first in the Atlanta 500; the smoothest race he's driven so far this season, and he came away from talking to the press afterwards feeling on top of the world. He and Adeline celebrated by staying in bed the whole day after. They ordered everything on the room service menu and took two bubble baths, snacking and bathing between napping and sex. Billy is pretty sure he died and went to heaven.

Now he's in hell. Hell disguised as Delta flight DL355.

"I don't get it, you were fine when we flew to New York?" Adeline questions him softly.

Billy turns to her with a pained smile, cheeks burning with embarrassment.

"I was putting on a brave face," he confesses as he feels the heat work its way down his neck and up to his ears.

"Why the fuck would you do that?"

"We'd only just started seeing each other, I was still trying to impress you," he says sheepishly. He'll never tell her the three trips he made to the bathroom that flight were to throw up or that leaving his seat to do so was a feat in itself.

Adeline rolls her eyes.

"You're such an idiot."

"Gee, thanks, Tinkerbell," Billy scoffs. He frowns at her but the way his lips twitch into a smile is involuntary when she laughs. Taking one last drag of his cigarette, he stubs it out aggressively in the ashtray on his armrest, pressing it into the metal until it's a crumpled pile of filter and ash as he prays the nicotine eases his nerves.

"I'm just saying, you didn't need to impress me," Adeline replies, leaning in closer. She traces her finger over his cheekbone and around his mouth to the dimple in his chin, the gentle sensation making his skin tingle. Billy swears she has a magic touch, and if he could have her small, soft hands on him all the damn time, he would. "You had me from the moment you shook my hand back in December."

"Oh, I know. Had to make sure though, didn't I?" Billy says, grinning as he leans in to kiss her. He loses himself in it for a moment, everything melting away as he concentrates on the softness of Adeline's lips, slow and languid against his own.

Adeline looks dazed when he pulls back. Her baby pink lips glisten, so inviting that he kisses her again. He nips at her bottom lip, relishes the way she gasps at the bite. Kissing is a great distraction. Maybe he should just keep kissing her and then–

Stan kicks the back of Billy's chair, as if it wasn't uncomfortable enough. He clears his throat obnoxiously and Billy reluctantly tears his lips away from Adeline's and turns to glare at him through the gap in the seats.

"What?" He snaps.

"Are you gonna be making out the whole flight?"

"Well, now we are. Hope you enjoy the show, Stanley." He throws a subtle wink in Stan's direction and turns back around, his mouth finding Adeline's again just to spite him.

"Stop teasing him," Adeline whispers against his lips and swats him lightly across the chest.

"Hey! It's not my fault he can't get himself a girl. Why should I let him stop me from kissing mine?" Billy grumbles.

"I heard that, asshole. I'm perfectly capable of gettin' a girl."

"Oh, I'm sorry. Is she here right now?" Billy quips. He peers out into the aisle and rises out of his seat as best he can to look further down the plane.

"Billy!" Adeline swats him again and, okay, maybe he deserved that one. She twists around in her seat to flash Stan an apologetic smile. "Sorry about him, Stan. I think he's using his fear of flying as an excuse to be rude."

Stan huffs out a snide laugh.

"Don't apologise for him, Goldilocks. He's a big boy."

Billy shamelessly raises his eyebrows at Adeline who shakes her head.

"We'll be good, Reynolds," he says, "enjoy the flight." He turns back around and nuzzles his face against Adeline's neck, letting out a little whine. "Seriously though, how are you so calm right now?" His voice is muffled as he covers whatever exposed skin he can get to with kisses.

"Because I've been flying since I was three-years-old," Adeline replies. "I love being in the clouds. It's peaceful."

Billy pulls back and looks at her like she's crazy. He flew for the first time at twenty-two for a kart meet on the other side of the country he was determined to get to no matter what. There were rumours of scouts for professional racing attending and he would have been stupid to miss that opportunity. Billy remembers being absolutely fine until about thirty minutes into the flight when the plane hit such bad turbulence that he was convinced they were going to crash, that his life would be over before it had ever really started. He thought flying with Adeline might ease his nerves but if anything, it only added to the anxiety. If they crash, he could lose her too.

Billy jumps when the pilot's voice sounds over the plane's tannoy system and the air hostesses take their position in the aisle to give a safety demonstration. How to prepare for impending doom, just what he needs.

"You want me to help you relax?" Adeline asks, a soft murmur in his ear. Her hand has moved to the back of his head, playing with his hair and gently massaging his scalp in the way Billy loves. The barely-there scratches of her nails through his hair send a shiver down his spine and he cocks his head to the side as the tension in his shoulders slowly shifts.

"What are you gonna do, Tinkerbell? Sing to me?" Billy jokes, lips curling into a small smile as he breathes out a shaky chuckle. Adeline brings her lips closer to his ear, her tongue flicking out over his earlobe before she whispers back.

"I was thinking more along the lines of a hand job, but I can sing to you instead if you want?" She shrugs, nonchalant and teasing. Her eyes sparkle with it and Billy feels excitement simmering though him. "I can be discreet. And you can be quiet... can't you, baby?" Adeline asks, tucking a finger under his chin and guiding his mouth to hers. She tugs on his bottom lips and Billy groans quietly.

She's daring him and Billy isn't one to shy away from a challenge. That, and he's already established that he can't say no to her when she's looking at him like she is right now. His cock twitches to life at the thought of her hand around him as she fists his length, all soft hands and slow strokes. He's about to reply, some babble about how he can be so quiet, so good for her, when the plane rumbles to life and he gasps as he sits up in his seat; back straight, body tense. Adeline unpacks the blanket from the seat pocket in front of her and drapes it over their laps. Billy watches her, slightly bewildered, and then sucks in a breath when she slips her hand under the dark blue fleece as he realises they're actually going to do this. Warm and light with her touch, Adeline palms him over the corduroy of his trousers and glances upwards as she presses the call button above them.

"What are you doing?!"

"You wanna sit with cum drying on your pants for five hours?"

"Uh–" Billy blinks.

"That's what I thought. I'm gonna ask for a cup," she whispers quickly as a hostess approaches them.

"Are we all okay back here?" The brunette, with bright red lips and beehived hair, asks cheerfully as Adeline presses the heel of her palm down beneath the blanket. Billy has to clear his throat and squeeze his eyes shut as he grows harder, his burgeoning erection straining painfully in the confines of his underwear.

"Hi, I was just wondering if we could get a cup of water before take-off? My boyfriend is feeling a little nauseous," Adeline says sweetly and Billy opens his eyes, squinting a little just as the hostess glances his way. She pouts at him like he's a child.

"Oh, of course! Poor thing. I'll be right back."

"I love that you're thinkin' ahead, Tinkerbell, but what the fuck are you– *uh–* are you gonna do with the cup when we're done?" He stutters out, his words morphing into a moan that he tries to conceal as Adeline strokes over his clothed cock.

"Sick bag," she replies casually. "I figured a cup would be easier for y'know... and then we'll put the cup in the bag and dump it all in the trash when they come round next."

"God, I love you," he breathes. Billy will admit he's impressed with her thinking but he's also acutely aware that Stan is sitting right behind them and there are strangers on the other side of the aisle. Billy's in the window seat so Adeline hides him a little, but the thrill is very much clouded by apprehension.

"This is kinda exciting, huh?"Adeline giggles, keeping her voice soft and low. She captures his lips in a heavy kiss and Billy mumbles into her mouth in agreement as Stan sighs loudly. They break apart just as the hostess returns with their water.

"Thank you so much," Adeline says as she removes her hand from under the blanket. She cradles the plastic cup of water as she takes it and Billy nods at the hostess in thanks, willing her to walk away. He's so hard now it hurts.

"You kids let me know if you need anything else." As she leaves, Adeline passes him the cup.

"Drink that and unzip your pants, hot stuff."

"You're enjoying this too much," he says, knocking back the water. He didn't realise quite how dry his mouth was, the cold liquid immediately wetting his gums as he runs his tongue over his teeth.

"Maybe I am," Adeline whispers. She leans over and he feels the warm wetness of her tongue licking up to his ear before she takes his lobe between her lips. Billy chokes on his breath, groaning softly, grateful for the hum of the plane as it drowns out the small sounds of pleasure Adeline's drawing out of him.

He pulls the blanket up a little further and fumbles with the button and zipper of his pants. He isn't really concentrating, mind too preoccupied with Adeline's featherlight whispering and finger-tips to match, dragging up and down his thigh as she tells him she can't wait to wrap her hand around his cock, how much she loves him and the pretty sounds he makes when he comes. Billy's really struggling to keep it together and he's really regretting wearing these trousers too. The zipper is shit, probably busted in another high speed clothing removal that means he now has to spend five minutes forcing it to move whenever he decides to wear them. In a situation like this though, he's pretty sure it's not budging out of spite. Finally, *finally*, it scrapes open and Billy huffs out a sigh of relief.

"Fuck. Okay, got it," he mutters and Adeline moves closer. She subtly spits into her hand as she turns her body towards him, then peppers the softest of kisses along his jaw before tugging down his underwear just enough to free his throbbing length. Billy's breath hitches in his throat as Adeline strokes her thumb over the tip and slowly drags her hand down, coating his cock in a slick combination of spit and pre-cum. She's taking her time with it and Billy whimpers quietly.

"Kiss me," Adeline says, "you can moan into my mouth."

Billy doesn't need to be told twice, he crashes his lips to hers hungrily, no care for what Stan or anyone else thinks anymore. Beneath the blanket, Adeline trails a teasing finger down the underside of his shaft, around his balls before taking them in her hand and squeezing gently. Billy squeaks, embarrassingly, warmth dribbling from his slit, and Adeline giggles softly as she drags her fist up the length of his cock again to collect it.

"Oh, *fuck–mmm*," Billy hums, licking into Adeline's mouth to suppress the guttural groan he can feel sitting in the depths of his chest. There's a bead of sweat trickling down from his hairline and he's trying so hard to be quiet but Adeline is hitting every nerve as she begins working over his cock with what Billy can only describe as gusto, adding just the right amount of pressure that makes his eyes roll back as his head hits the seat. "Just like that– *oh shit*, keep going, baby."

The plane is in the air now, Billy too far gone to have even noticed it gaining speed and hurtling down the runway. He does notice Adeline shift in her seat a little though, and his cock gives a little twitch of interest.

"Is this turning you on, sweet girl?" He breathes out. The words lose coherence towards the end, fading to a raspy whisper as Adeline picks up the pace, and Billy has to hold himself back. There's a very real possibility that if he tries to say anything else, it's going to turn into a compromising sound against his will.

"God, yes. So much," Adeline replies, kissing him hurriedly on the corner of his mouth. "You're doing so good, Billy. Staying quiet for me." Her tone is so sweet, her breath tickling his ear and it's the beginning of the end. He only just remembers the cup and makes sure he has a tight hold before–

"*Fuck*– Jesus, Adeline," he grunts. His voice is strained and he whines a little as he buried his face in the curve of Adeline's neck. His lips latch onto her skin, nipping and sucking, and it's all he can do to stop himself from making noise as Adeline keeps pumping her fist over his length in a steady rhythm. His stomach muscles contract, thighs and back tensing, as she swipes her thumb over the tip once more and Billy is so sensitive that it's his undoing. His cock flexes in her hand and he groans softly, his eyes squeezing shut as he concentrates on the hickey he's leaving on Adeline's shoulder.

As Billy comes, the seatbelt sign turns off and they're cruising at 37,000 feet.

nineteen

ADELINE
Los Angeles, California

"Come on, Tinkerbell. You know the rules, feet off the dash!"

Adeline flips Billy off through the window and blinks over at him irreverently as he climbs into the driver's seat, tempted to push her luck. He knocks her feet down anyway, unimpressed. They're a mile out of LAX, stopped for gas and a snack for the hour and a half drive to the beach house.

"Hey!" Adeline pouts at him as he throws a bag of her favourite chips into her lap and starts up the engine. She's been in a playful mood since they left the airport, teasing out the side of Billy she doesn't see very often but fucking loves. He has a lightness about him ninety percent of the time but now he's gaining his confidence back in the bedroom, that other ten percent–

"I already told you once," he says, stern and gravelly. Adeline slowly lifts her legs back up and smiles at him sweetly, pushing his buttons. "*Adeline.*"

"Yes, Billy?"

"Do I need to teach you a lesson, sweet girl?"

His gaze tracks over her legs and Adeline stretches, making sure every muscle is tensed, tight and toned as he devours her with hungry eyes. She grins when Billy groans in frustration and turns the key in the ignition. He doesn't say another word as he drives out of the gas station and Adeline hums, pleased, as Billy tenses his jaw and shifts in his seat, suitably riled up.

Windows down, sun on her skin; the moment she stepped foot on Californian soil, she wondered why she ever leaves. Yeah, she loves the chillier states, but Malibu is where her soul thrives and she's been ready for these two weeks back home since she caught a glimpse of the sea in Daytona.

She keeps her eyes out the window but can sense every glance Billy sends her way. They hit a stop light a few minutes later, slowing until the car sits at a low rumble, and suddenly his fingers are in her hair, grasping at it as he pulls her into a rough kiss. Adeline gasps, lips parting in the perfect offering as Billy teases his tongue along the slip of sensitive skin just inside her mouth. It tickles but the feeling doesn't last long, replaced with the dull bite of his teeth instead.

A car horn beeps somewhere behind them and Billy rips his mouth away. Revving the engine, he pulls away, wheels squealing on the asphalt and he glances at Adeline with a devilish little glint in his eye. He swipes his tongue across his bottom lip and rests it in the corner of his mouth, just a sneaky peek of pink, taunting her.

Billy drives fast, so fast Adeline has to cling on as he takes sharp turns and chances stop lights before they turn red. Before she knows it, Billy's foot presses on the gas pedal a little heavier and they're speeding down the PCH. She cranks the window open, stretching her arm out and letting the wind rush over her skin. Her fingers dance over the horizon where the sun reflects off the ocean in shades of orange and yellow. The sea air is revitalising and Adeline relishes the feel of it entering her lungs as she breathes in deeply; clean and peaceful.

The peace lasts until the air is filled with the sound of sirens. Blue lights, just about visible under the brightness of the sun, flash in the rearview mirror and Adeline sighs as Billy pulls over, cursing quietly when Officer Valance steps out of his cruiser.

Tommy and his porn-stache – still going strong, still creepy as fuck – saunters over to the Lamborghini and Billy winds his window down further before rummaging in his glove compartment.

"Licence and registration please, sir," Tommy says without sparing Billy a second glance.

Adeline huffs and leans right over Billy until she's practically in his lap and then she peers out the window with the most innocent of smiles.

"Hi, Tommy."

Tommy peeks in through the window then does a double take. "Addie! I didn't realise it was you in there. Are your speeding habits rubbing off on..." he glances at Billy's drivers licence. "Oh, Mr Brooks. You're... you're– you know what, never mind. I actually just read up on your last race this morning... my God, what a win!"

"Uh, thank you?" Billy says, a little taken aback by his enthusiasm.

"No problem. I've been following Shaw & Gold's success for years now, big NASCAR fan, never managed to get down to a race myself though," he muses, finger and thumb rubbing over his moustache.

Adeline pokes her head out the window again. "Hey, Tommy. We're in a rush. How about you let us get on our way and I'll make sure my dad gets you to the next race. April 6th if you're free?"

"Well, shit! Really, Addie? You'd do that?"

"Yep. I'll call him as soon as we're home."

"I knew I always liked you," Tommy beams. His crooked teeth have somehow gotten whiter. "Drive safe, Mr Brooks. You make sure you look after Addie here, she's one of a kind."

"Don't I know it," Billy says as Adeline falls back into the passenger seat. Tommy nods, taps the car as usual and walks away. Billy turns to her with a raised eyebrow. "The real question is, do I wanna know how you're on a first name basis with the local law enforcement?"

"I like to drive fast too," Adeline shrugs as Billy pulls back out onto the road, bottom lip pulled under his teeth and a lethal grip on the steering wheel. His right hand lands on Adeline's thigh, resting over the denim of her shorts as his fingers curl under the hem and she wonders if he can tell just how turned on she is, if he can feel her muscles tensing under his touch.

Billy parks his car next to Adeline's Corvette on the driveway and the familiar sound of the stones crunching under the tyres brings a smile to her face.

"Leave the bags, Tinkerbell," Billy says as Adeline goes to haul them out of the car. "I'll get them later." His voice is raspy, that contradicting rough softness that more often than not gets her worked up when it's used to whisper sweet nothings in her ear as he fucks her stupid.

Adeline meets his gaze and her stomach flips. He's looking at her over the top of the car with his signature Billy Brooks bedroom eyes. Heat swells in her body, pulsating through her as she blushes. Adeline's body reacts to Billy in ways she didn't even know were possible; no one has ever made her feel more alive.

"C'mere," he rumbles and the anticipation urges Adeline forward.

She stops in front of him and he brings the back of his hand to her cheek. Billy's touch is tender. He caresses her like she's a delicate flower, fingers soft as they trace over her eyebrows, down the length of her nose and across her lips. It tickles and Adeline giggles, scrunching her nose. As Billy's hand comes to a stop on her chin, a switch flips and he grips her jaw, tilting her face up to his. He's still incredibly gentle, but there's a new intensity behind the action and it takes Adeline a moment to comprehend the change.

"Are you gonna be a good girl?"

His warm breath fans over her lips as he speaks, so close to her face he's nothing but a blur of moving features. Adeline nods. Her body is on fire, flames of adrenaline and arousal flickering bright.

"Words, Addie."

"Yes. I'll be good," she breathes, unable to look away from his eyes and the soft blue irises that are nothing but a highlight in the dark. Billy hums, satisfied as she unlocks the door.

As soon as they're over the threshold, Billy lifts Adeline and carries her through to the house with large, determined strides. He kisses her hard, mouth heavy and tongue deliberate, and drops her onto the kitchen table with a soft thud. Wedged between her legs, Adeline tugs him in as close as he can get, her ankles crossed just below his ass. When he draws back she chases his lips but Billy holds her still, cradling her cheeks with fingertips light as anything. He studies her, eyes flitting across her face, lingering for a split second longer on her lips before he sways forward to kiss her again. It's dizzying. She sucks in a breath the moment she gets a chance but Billy seems hellbent on kissing the life out of her while his hands explore her body like it's uncharted territory.

When he finally lets her go, he stumbles back looking utterly ruined already and drinks her in. Adeline feels exposed even though she's fully dressed. She tries to control her heaving breaths and waits for Billy to make his next move.

"Take off your shorts, baby." He motions to the denim barely covering her thighs and pulls out a chair, plopping into it like he's settling in for a show. Legs spread wide, he rests his hand on his crotch and squeezes gently as he watches her clamber to her knees up on the table. Adeline takes her time, peeling the shorts down her legs little by little before dropping them to the floor. Sitting back on her heels, she revels in the way Billy can't take her eyes off her; she feels so seen.

Adored.

"Fuck, look at you," Billy murmurs, barely a whisper his voice is so soft. "Open your legs for me, sweetheart."

His eyes wander south, hungry and alight with lust, as Adeline shuffles back on the table and does as he says. Her heart is hammering against her ribcage, anticipation and pure want knocking impatiently as she watches Billy palms himself through the material of his pants. He scoots his chair forward, tongue sitting pretty in the corner of his lips as he smirks up at her and drags her slowly to the edge of the table, settling her legs over his shoulders. Adeline sighs through soft kisses to the insides of her thighs, a whisper of his lips that turns wet and hot the closer he gets to her pussy.

"You're drippin', sweet girl," Billy says, a hint of surprise in his voice as he raises an eyebrow and brushes his finger over her soaked silk panties. "Did I do this?"

"Well it wasn't Stan, was it?" Adeline retorts, rolling her eyes.

"Watch your tone, Tinkerbell." He hooks his finger under the lilac silk and grazes his knuckle over her clit. "Or you won't get what you want."

Just that small touch has her crumbling; she's not sure how long she's going to last once he touches her properly. And she doesn't get to find out either. The doorbell rings just as Billy ducks his head back between her legs.

"*Seriously?!*"

"Ignore it," Billy murmurs, too busy licking a warm trail along Adeline's thigh.

"It'll be the others," she sighs, gasping when he nips her skin with his teeth, the sharp pain giving way to warmth as his lips press over the same spot with a kiss.

"So? They can work out that we're *busy* and come back later. Like they were supposed to."

"They have keys, Billy. They'll just let themselves in." She starts to shimmy away from him reluctantly as he groans, frustrated. "We'll pick this up later," she promises.

Billy sorts himself out before he helps Adeline back into her shorts and smooths her hair down, leaving her with one more electric kiss. They pad through the living room to the door just in time to see Gabe follow Norah through it, key in hand just like Adeline said. She crosses her arms and raises an eyebrow.

"Hey, guys," Gabe grins.

"I thought we said three o'clock?" Adeline says. Billy stops behind her, arms wrapped around her shoulders and a scowl on his face.

"Sorry, Ads. We repacked and then got bored so we thought we'd just come over. I should have called." Norah winces as her gaze lands on Billy. "Did, uh… did we interrupt something? Because Billy has the face of someone who didn't get to come."

"I also didn't get to come," Adeline replies as she frees herself from Billy's hold.

"We got take out?" Norah says by way of apology. "And alcohol."

"You're forgiven." Adeline takes the bags and Billy stares at her bewildered. "Come on, hot stuff. You can help me while Norah gives Gabe a tour."

"All it takes is food and alcohol and you're over it?" Billy asks but he follows like a lost puppy, stopping behind her and kissing her shoulder as she begins unpacking the containers of Chinese food onto the kitchen counter. It takes longer than it should, the pair of them are easily distracted given their previous state, and they end up making out against the refrigerator.

By the time Stan arrives a little later – at the time they all agreed on, Adeline points out – they're all out in the back yard. It's warm for late March and the mid afternoon sun radiates across Adeline's skin gorgeously as she lounges on the side of the pool. Her feet kick and swirl the cool water around her legs and she sips happily on an ice cold glass of vodka and orange juice.

In the pool, Billy and Gabe are competing to see who can hold their breath for the longest like a couple of big kids. Gabe keeps dunking Billy's head under when he least expects it and he shoots up from the water spluttering while Gabe laughs hysterically. It's entertaining enough that Adeline puts her book down, heckling them through giggles. When Stan finally joins them out on the deck, he's in his swim shorts and nursing a cup of coffee.

"Did you not see the copious amounts of alcohol we so graciously provided, Reynolds?" Norah asks. She lowers her sunglasses on her nose and peers at him over the rim.

"Hard to miss. What did you do, rob a liquor store?" Adeline chuckles and Stan glares. "Nope. No. I don't wanna hear your cute little giggle, Gold. I'm only drinkin' this because I couldn't sleep on the plane thanks to you and Billy joining the fuckin' mile high club."

"Oh, don't be such a prude, Stanley. It was only a hand job," Billy laughs, wiggling his eyebrows suggestively.

"You did what now?!" Gabe looks between Adeline and Billy and then back to Adeline, his mouth hanging open as he points at her. "But you're so... I though– Addie, that's–"

"I know, Gabe. Billy is such a bad influence on me."

"It was *your* idea, Tinkerbell!" Billy butts in. He shakes his head, giving her a look that says *just you wait*. Adeline grins at him.

"Anyway," Gabe says, drawing out the word as he swiftly changes the subject. "Anyone wanna play a game? Norah, my angel, come get on my shoulders." Norah raises an eyebrow at him but obliges.

Adeline looks at Stan. "Do you wanna climb Billy like a tree, or should I?"

"Just get in the pool, Goldilocks. I'll referee and jump in next round."

"Oh, Stan! Can you film it? My camera is over by the towels!" Billy shouts, his voice half drowned out by the sound of Adeline squealing and splashing as she launches herself at him.

Stan ambles over to the table where Billy's Super 8 sits in its case. He uses it a lot, taking it on hikes and down to the speedway where Adeline will film him driving. But he mostly just films Adeline when she's not looking or they mess around with it when they're in silly moods, stuck in another hotel somewhere.

"No cheating," Gabe warns, two fingers aimed at Billy and Adeline as he glares with narrowed eyes. Billy holds his hands up in acquiescence just as Adeline leans down from her perch on his shoulders so her mouth is level with his ear.

"Do not let go of me whatever you do," she murmurs, flashing him a sweet grin.

"Never," Billy replies softly. Adeline kisses his cheek and sits back, resting her hands on the top of his head.

"Okay. Get closer," Stan says.

Gabe and Billy wade into the middle of the pool and Adeline

reaches her hand out for Norah to shake. She may be competitive as hell but she learnt good sportsmanship like most toddlers learn their ABCs. Stan turns the camera over in his hands. "B, how do I...?"

"Button on the side, Stan."

Stan fiddles with the camera a little more and then it whirs into life.

"Okay, got it. Play fair," he warns with a stern glance at them all. "Three, two, one...GO!"

Adeline is quick to grapple Norah, she leans her whole weight against the back of Billy's head and all but flings herself forward. Billy is sturdy; he holds his ground in the water but Gabe is broad and a wall of muscle. It doesn't matter how much Adeline tussles with Norah, the redhead isn't going anywhere.

"Addie, I'm gonna run at them," Billy yells and as he backs up a little, Adeline holds on. His grip on her thighs tightens, fingers digging into her hard enough to leave a mark but she doesn't care. "Throw all your weight at her, Tinkerbell. I've got you."

"You're really competitive aren't you?" Adeline giggles, leaning forward to kiss him.

"You're only just working that out?" Billy quips, ducking to the left. "Concentrate, sweetheart."

But it's too late. In the time it takes for Adeline to sit back up, Gabe has launched himself and Norah forward and with one forceful push, Adeline is knocked off her balance. Billy clings to her for as long as he can but she topples backwards off his shoulders. Her back stings as she hits the water with a splash and she goes under. The cries of victory from Norah and Gabe become muffled as she's submerged but not even a second later, she's hauled up by a strong arm around her waist. Adeline flips her wet hair out of her eyes before clambering straight back onto Billy's shoulders.

"Again! Best of three," she declares before her lips skim over Billy's ear. "Baby, don't you dare drop me."

✦

The empty food containers sit half buried in sand beside bottles of beer long gone warm. Adeline leans back against Billy as she watches the fire, her vision blurring with the glow. She's almost asleep, the flicker of the flames, gentle waves and soft, rhythmic thud of Billy's heartbeat lulling her into a cosy security.

She feels content and happy and she hopes the feeling stays. The others are playing a game where one of them hums a song and everyone else has to guess the title. Adeline gave up playing five songs ago and now she has Billy humming in her ear, a soft melody just between them.

"Do you want to go to bed, sweet girl?" He whispers and Adeline nods, eyelids half closed. The amalgamation of travelling, sun and alcohol has finally caught up with her. Sitting forward, she waits for Billy to stand then lets him gently pull her to her feet.

"We're gonna call it a night. Addie's fallin' asleep on me."

Their game is paused while they say goodnight, bone crushing hugs and tipsy tumbles onto the sand as if Billy and Adeline aren't just going up to bed. Back inside, Billy guides a very sleepy Adeline up the stairs and into her bedroom.

"You've never slept in here before," she comments as she plops down on the end of her bed.

"I haven't," he agrees, "it's cute. Very you, Tinkerbell."

"Thank you." She beams and settles in to watch him longingly as he kicks off his swim shorts and switches them out for a pair of white briefs. When he pulls his t-shirt from his body, Adeline lets her gaze linger and drag slowly over his form with little shame. He's so beautiful, all taut muscles and tanned skin, and that familiar knot in her belly loops around and around in anticipation of being pulled tight. She watches his ass as he wanders out to the bathroom. "I don't want to sleep yet."

"What was that, sweet girl?" He reappears, toothbrush in hand.

"I don't wanna sleep yet, wanna finish what we started earlier. *Kinda* want you to make good on that lesson you were gonna teach me," she says sweetly, batting her eyelashes even as her eyelids threaten to droop.

"Are you sure?" Billy questions, words mumbled as he cleans his teeth. Adeline answers by pulling her bikini bottoms down to her feet and kicking them to the floor before shuffling back and spreading her legs. Billy almost chokes on the foamy toothpaste in his mouth.

"Please," she whispers and he disappears again, returning sans toothbrush and moving to the bed. Without a word, he sinks to his knees and drags her slowly to the edge. He cradles her face in his hands and Adeline smiles, the apples of her cheeks rising and with them, the pads of Billy's thumbs as he brushes them over her skin. His touch is soft and tender but his kiss is hot and hungry when he covers her mouth, tongue sliding along her bottom lip and slipping inside to push against hers. Adeline breathes heavily, gasping as her fingers thread into Billy's hair.

"Are you gonna be good, baby?"

"So good for you, Billy," she replies, kissing him again before pulling him closer so she can mouth at his jaw and down to his clavicle. His skin is salty, earthy and fresh from the sea and the sand. Adeline gets two, maybe three soft pink bruises on him before Billy nudges her and tells her to lie back. He pulls her legs up to his shoulders, runs his tongue languidly along her skin.

"You're so beautiful," he murmurs, breath tickling.

Adeline isn't listening, she's too lost in the heavenly feeling of his stubble on her skin as his nose nudges her clit. Billy sighs, a little dreamily and his eyes flit up to her face with a certain sparkle. Impatience takes over and Adeline stares at him until he dips his head and offers sweet little kitten licks right where she wants him, *needs* him. As she shuts her eyes, her whole body tingles with anticipation and the slow build of pleasure– and then Billy pulls away, attention back on her trembling thighs. Adeline groans in frustration. Maybe she *is* too tired for this.

"You okay?" Billy asks, but it's not out of concern. His lips twist into a cheeky smirk, amused.

"Never been better," she responds through gritted teeth. Billy chuckles before he flattens his tongue and licks heavily through her folds.

Adeline squirms, soft whimpers leaving her lips as she falls, breathy moans of Billy's name fill the room as he wraps his lips around her clit and hums. Head fuzzy, her toes curl as she throbs, body thrumming with it. Billy laps it up, moaning and humming, tongue penetrating her. And then he comes up for air, lips dewy and chin covered in her arousal.

Adeline flings herself up from the sheets. "No!"

Billy grins, wiping his mouth with the back of his hands before he moves up her body to kiss her. "Does your dad still have any of that good whiskey we drank at Christmas?"

"Are you fucking kidding me right now?"

"What?" He looks at her with wide, innocent eyes. "I'm thirsty."

Adeline could throttle him but she asked for this. "In the living room cabinet."

"Thanks, sweetheart." He kisses her, quick pecks to the corner of her mouth before he climbs to his feet and heads for the door, turning around at the last moment. "Don't touch yourself while I'm gone, I'll know. And I'm not letting you come if you do. Got it?" Adeline nods. "Good girl."

The wait for Billy is agonising. She aches, body begging for some kind of release. Her fingertips tap out a tune on her belly, keeping herself preoccupied until he saunters back into the room. He sips casually on a tumbler of rich amber liquid, as if he wasn't just in the middle of eating her out, and lowers back to his knees at the foot of the bed.

"You want some?" He offers Adeline the glass and she shakes her head.

"I want to come," she whines.

"Well that all depends on whether you did as you were told, Tinkerbell."

"I did. Please, baby. I was so good."

Billy places the tumbler carefully on the floor and surges forward to kiss her. It's hot and slow, whiskey and her on his tongue. His mouth travels down her body, between her breasts and over her belly until he's back where she craves him. Head buried between her thighs, he places a soft kiss to her clit and Adeline mewls. Her pussy flutters at the delicate touch but she needs more. Billy glances up at her as he wets his lips, flashes her a wolfish grin, and then gets back to it. He works magic with his mouth, driving Adeline to a panting, whimpering mess above him. Her legs tense around his head, back arching off the bed as she makes it right to the edge of climax once more before–

"Billy!"

He peers up at her, looking a little wrecked himself but with a mirthful hint of a smile. At that moment, Adeline hates him just a little bit.

"I love you?" He laughs, nose scrunching as he attempts to be cute.

Adeline huffs, staring him down until he concedes and finally, *finally,* lets her come. Her orgasm is intense; she's tightly wound and overstimulated, her body tired. It's a free fall into overwhelming pleasure and Billy is there to catch her as she cries out, legs shaking. He presses a delicate kiss to her stomach as he climbs up the bed, flopping down beside her.

"Was that okay?"

"Yeah, Billy. Yeah, that was– *fuck,*" she giggles, giddy.

"It's all you, sweet girl. You bring it out of me," he whispers and pulls her into his embrace.

Adeline sighs. Her overtired brain is suddenly in overdrive as she lies in his arms. She tries to let Billy's steady breaths, the dull thud of his heart, soothe her into rest but the quiet is too much and her mind drifts. A spiral that starts with how in love with him she is and ends with '*I need to tell him about Rex.*' It's been eating at her since her run-in with him in Richmond, and even more so after seeing him at Billy's party acting like he didn't do what he did and shaking Billy's hand. She sees a future with Billy that she's never imagined with anyone else and that feels like even more reason to open up.

And Adeline's stupid overtired, overactive brain says to do it right now, before she loses her nerve.

twenty

ADELINE

"I NEED TO SHOWER," SHE SAYS QUIETLY. HER BRAIN FEELS off kilter, the tail end of her orgasm just wearing off as darker thoughts of Rex keep seeping in, filling the gaps like ink around wax.

She slides out from the bed. Billy lets her go and if he notices her change in demeanour he doesn't say anything. He just flops onto his back and tucks a hand under his head, watching Adeline as she gathers a clean towel from her closet and a fresh set of pyjamas.

She just needs a minute.

A minute to work out what she's going to say, write the script in her head even though she's bound to lose control of her mouth and blurt it out anyway. Either way, she doesn't want the words sitting on in her chest anymore, heavy and nauseating.

The last time she said it out loud was to Norah and even then it was a ramble of stuttering sentences and broken words that had to be gently coaxed out of her. Norah eventually managed to work out what she was trying to say while Adeline just nodded and sniffled, having someone else know simultaneously lifted the weight from her shoulders and brought the reality of it all crashing down.

She's by the door when Billy calls out to her. When she turns around, he's beckoning her back over to him with outstretched arms, grabbing at the air. Adeline doesn't think twice about shuffling to the bed. She perches on the edge and lets Billy wrap his arms around her; lets him kiss her sweetly. He's so gentle with it, lips slow and a little unsure as if he can tell there's something on Adeline's mind.

"I'll be here," he says, leaving a whisper of another kiss on her lips.

"I know."

In the bathroom, Adeline strips silently and looks at herself in the mirror. She rests her hands on her hips, squeezing the soft skin, and she feels the ghost of Rex. Of callused hands, rough and hurried. Her eyes are drawn to the steady, even rise and fall of her chest where her breasts are covered by her hair. She clutches it, pulls a little just to feel something. It's matted and tangled from sand and salt and Billy's hands.

Billy.

Billy has soft hands, she thinks. Always gentle even when he tries to be rough. He never tries to push past her limits and Adeline never has to tell him to stop. Sometimes she thinks he has a sixth sense, picking up on the subtleties of her body like that; the way her breath hitches silently in her throat or her skin breaks out in goosebumps, too sensitive to be touched.

As Adeline runs her palms over her stomach, she replaces the scalding burn of Rex with the tender touch of Billy and heaves out a sigh. Of relief, or of trepidation for what she's about to do, she isn't sure. But she knows she's safe now, in Billy's hands.

The bathroom window is open ajar and the soft voices of Stan and Norah filter in from outside. The beach gets chilly this late but they keep a wood burner and blankets on the porch and Adeline wouldn't be surprised if the two of them retreated not long after she and Billy left. She wonders briefly where Gabe is but then there's a creak on the stairs and a door down the hall closes softly.

Everyone accounted for.

Adeline cocks her head to the side as she brings her attention back to her reflection. The remnants of what little make-up she had on before their flight this morning litters her face in tiny specks. It's mostly mascara, dried and flaking after being smudged by the pool water. Combine that with her hair and the tired, paleness of her skin and she looks a mess.

With a sigh, Adeline turns to flip the shower lever and the sound of water raining down into the bathtub drowns out Stan and Norah. The shower takes a while to heat up, the pipes rattle and creak as it does, but the sound is familiar, almost relaxing with the way it momentarily eases the tension gripping Adeline's muscles like a vise. She lowers the lid of the toilet and sits while she waits, wincing as her bare skin hits the cold porcelain. The room steadily fills with steam and Adeline's thoughts circle back around to Billy.

She loves Billy more than anything. More than she *ever* thought she could love someone. He's the only man she's ever known, other than her father, who sees her worth and shows it. Billy can make her feel like the most beautiful woman in the world with just one look. Even when her hair is knotted and her make-up is ruined.

He's kind and he's gentle, but even Adeline doesn't know how he's going to react to what she's about to tell him. She's seen him lose to Rex; seen the quiet rage Billy controls and files away in a neat little brain box until he uses it to fuel his next race.

But this? This is a lot more than a lost race.

Adeline moves to the bathtub and holds her hand under the torrent of the shower. It's hot now, blistering almost. Probably too hot but she doesn't care, she just wants to feel clean. The hot water cascades over her skin, just on the comfortable side of burning and tingeing her shoulders pink. She washes her hair with the rose and hibiscus shampoo she knows Billy loves the scent of, and conditions it, combing out the knots as she thinks. She doesn't keep track of how long she stands there, fingers running through her hair, but it's long enough for the room to overheat. Lightheaded and nauseous, Adeline's stomach drops as she yanks back the shower curtain, retching.

"Fuck, fuck, fuck."

Adeline only just manages to flip up the lid of the toilet in time to throw up, her body bent uncomfortably over the side of the tub. She slides to the floor, her skin instantly clammy, hot and cold all at once as she removes herself from the sauna-like conditions of the shower. There are footsteps out in the hall and then Billy on the other side of the door. The bathroom shares a wall with her bedroom so there's no doubt that he heard her.

"Addie?"

"I'm fine!" Adeline calls back hurriedly. Her voice croaks and goes up two octaves and she sounds unconvincingly cheery.

"Addie, let me in," he says, keeping his voice gentle despite the demand of his words.

"I said I'm fine, Billy. I just had the shower a little too hot and I got lightheaded... I'm okay."

Billy sighs, heavy and shakily, and the doorknob jiggles.

"Baby, just... just unlock the door so I can see for myself. Please?"

Adeline huffs and heaves herself up just enough to crawl to the door and flip the latch. It swings open and Billy tumbles into the bathroom. He's trying not to show his panic but Adeline can see it all over his face as he peers down at her.

"Jesus, Addie."

"I'm fine."

She *does* feel better for emptying her stomach and the cold floor tiles are working wonders at cooling her body down. She moves to rest her cheek on it while Billy opens the window wider and turns the shower off, tutting at how far the temperature dial has been turned.

"It wasn't *that* hot," she grumbles.

"It's nearly at one-ten, Adeline." He has his serious voice on, low and rumbly as he sinks to the floor beside her and they both lean back against the bathtub.

She shouldn't be surprised that Billy sounds so worried. Adeline tolerates the slightly cooler water whenever she showers with him but when she showers alone she cranks it right up and makes sure to dial it back down again when she's done. Nine times out of ten, she's fine. A little overheated maybe, but she'll just lie in her towel for ten minutes afterwards waiting for the thumping of her heart to return to normal. But sometimes, she ends up like this, on the verge of passing out and throwing her guts up. She knows it isn't healthy but once it became a habit, nothing but scalding hot water makes her feel clean.

Billy reaches up and pulls Adeline's towel from the rail, wrapping it around her tentatively. Adeline tugs it around her body and mumbles out a weary thank you, scooting closer to him and resting her head on his shoulder. He moves, chin brushing over her wet hair, and when Adeline looks up, she's met with tender eyes. Bright, glistening blue irises painted with concern for her.

"What's going on, sweet girl?"

Adeline tips her head back against the edge of the bath and closes her eyes, teeth gnawing at her bottom lip. Her head is spinning and she's frustrated, both with herself and how difficult it is to just open her mouth and let the words tumble out.

"I'm going to tell you something and I need you to just listen," she says, her words slow and measured. Adeline doesn't open her eyes but she can imagine the confused expression on Billy's face – brows pinched and lips pouty – as he inevitably cycles through every possible thing she could say.

"Okay," he whispers.

She doesn't want to do this. But if Norah was right about what she said at Billy's birthday party, if he figures out Billy doesn't know, Rex is only going to use it against them. As leverage, or blackmail, or to get into Billy's head.

Adeline takes a deep breath and psyches herself up. There's a lump in her throat already and dread weighing down her limbs but she shifts uncomfortably on the bathroom floor and looks at Billy. Really looks at him, because if she's seeking comfort, she can always find it in his face. His soft features and kind eyes staring back at her are enough to at least start talking.

"Um... okay, so about three years ago," she begins, her voice already breaking. She swallows the lump in her throat and continues. "Three years ago, I was at a NASCAR party with Nor and, uh... and Rex– Rex Harlow was there because well, obviously it was a NASCAR party," she rambles. This is what she was afraid of, her brain's inability to form coherent sentences under this much pressure.

Billy is breathing heavily through his nose and his jaw ticks at the mention of Rex. He looks angry already, his right eye twitches as his eyes flick over her face and she hasn't even gotten to the worst part yet.

"Anyway," she says, "he had been flirty with me for months, trying to... you know. I think he was well aware of my uh, my reputation." Adeline winces. The word flirty is wrong, she knows that now. It was borderline harassment.

"Reputation," Billy repeats, there's an edge to his words even though his face remains stoic.

"Yeah, I um–"

"I get it, Addie," he says, "ain't nothing wrong with it, sweetheart."

Billy's voice is soft but his eyes harden. He's holding something back, unwarranted jealousy maybe, as he clears his throat as he takes one of her hands in his, gesturing for her to continue. Adeline gulps, distracted by the soothing feeling of Billy drawing tiny figures of eight around her knuckles with his thumb.

"I always avoided Rex at these things and Norah had warned me of him *way* before he ever tried coming onto me. But the later it got, the more I had to drink and–"

The words get stuck as Adeline's voice throat becomes hoarse. Her mouth feels like sandpaper and she runs her tongue over her gums and teeth but the dryness never goes away. Instead, she just gets the taste of residual vomit and that makes her gag reflex kick into high gear.

Just breathe, Addie.

Billy keeps up the gentle strokes over the back of Adeline's hand

and cups her cheek. He presses his lips to her forehead, quick but comforting.

"I'm here and I'm listening, Tinkerbell. Take your time."

Adeline nods. Her eyes glaze over, heavy tears sitting in the corners just waiting for her to blink and then it's game over.

"Ugh... um. So, I drank quite a lot, lost Norah and stumbled across Rex at the bar. He was being really nice, not the gross flirting he would usually try but like, genuine. And to *beyond* drunk Addie I guess he looked really–" she pauses, glancing at Billy who chuckles softly.

"You can say it," he teases, a small reprieve from the heavy tension.

"He looked really good," Adeline says with a pained smile and a squeamish shiver. "And so after a few more drinks, I ended up going back to his hotel room with him."

Adeline can tell by the look on Billy's face that he knows what's coming but it doesn't stop the plunge her heart takes when his brow knits together and he struggles to meet her gaze. She sniffles and squeezes her eyes shut, the waiting tears spilling over and clinging to her eyelashes.

"At first it was great. He was really gentle and made sure I was comfortable and– uh, he basically lulled me into a false sense of security because then something changed and he became rough with me and–"

She can't say it.

"Addie–"

"I told him no. I– I told him to stop," she stutters.

Billy pulls her into his lap, wrapping his arms around her, loose but secure, as her breathing picks up. She melts into him, erratic sobs muffled against the worn cotton of his t-shirt. Billy's chest heaves beneath her cheek, his anger radiating off of him in hot, furious waves.

"I told him to stop and he wouldn't." She digs her fingers into the front of Billy's shirt, twisting the fabric and Billy soothes her with small whispers, large, kind hands stroking her back and her hair.

"I've got you, sweet girl. I'm here."

They sit like that for what feels like hours. Billy holds her like she'll disappear if he lets go and Adeline's mind continues to reel. She's amazed she managed to get through any of that without completely crumbling.

What happened after Rex refused to stop is a complete blur, she probably couldn't even recall it if she tried; it's been blocked out by her brain, survival instinct of the best kind. She just knows that when she woke up the next morning, alone and naked, she had been violated.

At first, she blamed herself.

If only she hadn't had so much to drink.

If only she hadn't ignored Norah's warnings.

'If only' will kill you if you're not careful.

Adeline sat with that mentality for months and for over a year afterwards, she only ever felt Rex when another man touched her. Then Norah cornered her after she flinched as Rex walked by them. It took some convincing but slowly Adeline believed that Rex's actions weren't her fault and her self-blame turned into a quiet rage of her own.

'If only she hadn't done that' became 'how *dare* he?'

Three years down the line, Adeline can just about look at him without feeling the violent urge to punch him. She's moved on as much as she can but that doesn't mean dredging up the past hurt any less. She realises that now as she regulates her breathing. Her eyes sting from crying and her head hurts, a dull throb that feels like someone is swinging a mallet from one temple to the other.

She looks up at Billy, squinting slightly through the pain, to find him already watching her. Gingerly, he holds Adeline's face in his hands and brings his lips to the round apple of her cheek, kissing the last of her tears away.

"I love you," he murmurs as he moves to the other cheek and Adeline nearly falls apart all over again.

"Thank you for listening, Billy."

"Thank you for telling me."

Adeline rubs at her eyes and cards her fingers through her hair, grimacing. The strands are stuck together in thick chunks thanks to it being half dry and still covered in conditioner. She's going to need another shower.

"You okay?" Billy asks as Adeline stands from his lap. He quickly joins her on his feet, hands hovering at her sides like she'll topple over at any given moment.

"I still have conditioner in my hair," she giggles wetly, wiping her hand on the towel hanging by the sink.

"Oh. Here, I'll do it."

Billy lifts her into the tub, taking the towel as she unwraps it from her body. He flips on the shower, making a show of turning the temperature down and Adeline rolls her eyes playfully. She feels better. Lighter. She can tell Billy is holding in his emotions for her sake, but for now, she'll accept the quiet love he's exuding.

"Sit down, sweet girl," he says as he detaches the shower head and perches on the side of the bath. Softly, and with care, Billy runs his fingers through Adeline's hair as the water trickles over her. Just warm enough to get rid of the chill from the open window. Adeline allows her body to relax under Billy's touch as he rinses the conditioner, being overly gentle, even more cautious than he usually is when he washes her hair.

She lucked out with him; she won the boyfriend jackpot and then some.

Billy turns off the shower and Adeline leans into his touch as he squeezes the excess water from her hair. She climbs out of the tub, warm and safe, wrapped in a new towel and Billy's arms.

"Hey," she murmurs, cuddling in close, "thank you for taking care of me."

"Anytime, Adeline. I know you'd do the same for me."

Adeline presses up onto her toes and kisses him, sleepy and indulgent.

"In a heartbeat."

BILLY

Fucking Rex Harlow.

Billy prides himself on being level-headed. He's a lover, not a fighter, but right now he feels like he needs to punch something.

They've been lying in bed for an hour, neither of them able to sleep. Adeline has been drifting in and out, waking each time Billy tries to get comfortable. In the end, he carefully removes Adeline's arm from around his middle and sits on the edge of the bed.

"I'm going for a drive," he says, toes tapping the floor. He's jumpy, too wired to even attempt to sleep.

"Billy, I'm sor–"

"I'm not mad at you. I could never be mad at you, sweetheart. I just– I need to clear my head before I do something stupid."

"Billy," Adeline starts again, scrambling to get out of bed.

Billy pulls on his jeans and shoes, grabs the first shirt he sees before snatching up his keys from Adeline's dresser. "Baby, it's really late. Why don't you sleep on it?"

"I just want some fresh air, Addie," Billy says, opening the bedroom door. Adeline's footsteps are light as she follows him down the stairs and when they stop at the bottom, she scoots around him, quick as anything and places her hands on his chest.

"I don't want you to drive right now, not when you're this angry."

"Adeline," Billy sighs, "it's not doing me any good just lying in the dark, I need to *do* something."

Adeline stares up at him with her big, earnest hazel eyes and her features morph from defiant to resigned as she grabs his hand.

"Please just be careful."

"I will." Billy kisses her forehead, lips lingering on her soft skin for just a moment before he draws back, his gaze dipping to her lips. They're pink, shiny and raw, where she's spent half the night nervously picking at them but irresistible all the same. Adeline's breath hitches and then she lets out a sigh against Billy's lips as his mouth meets hers. The kiss is messy, hurried, because he needs to get out of this damn house and into his car. Pulling away, he tucks a loose wave of hair behind Adeline's ear and cradles her jaw in his hand. "Get some sleep. I'll be back before you know it."

twenty-one

BILLY

Billy doesn't know where he's going, he just knows he's angry. It's bone-deep, rattling around inside him and he feels like his only outlet is to drive; to feel the cool night air and hope the anger goes with the wind as he flies down the road. Too fast, probably.

He's angry at Rex, and at himself for not seeing how much of a complete creep the man is before now, but he's mostly angry *for* Adeline; seething at the fact that someone would dare lay a hand on her like that. Billy's never liked the guy, he tolerates him at most. Rex has always walked around with a chip on his shoulder, secreting scumbag energy like a stink bug.

It's not just Adeline he's worried about either. After what he saw at the track in Tennessee, Billy knows Delilah is associating herself with Rex in some capacity and if it's one of her schemes, a plan to get back at him, Billy just hopes she knows what she's getting herself into. He would hate to see her become collateral damage, no matter how badly their relationship ended.

Billy drives for what feels like hours as he tries to come up with a plan, a way to hurt Rex, but Billy isn't that kind of man. Every scenario he envisions dissolves the moment he inflicts violence and he ends up whimpering out a cry, screaming at nothing as he drives. By the time he pulls back up to the beach house the sky is a gorgeous blue hue as the sun rises over the horizon. In comparison, Billy feels like a zombie. Bones heavy, feet barely moving like he's being weighed down by a ball and chain as he shuffles to the front door. Unsurprisingly, his eyes feel tender and dry, no doubt blood-shot from another sleepless night.

He's a step away from the door when it swings open before he can even knock and he stumbles back as Adeline throws herself at him, palm smacking flat against his chest. Billy stiffens, preparing himself for more hits – he wouldn't blame her – but they don't come. Adeline's body softens and she melds herself to him, clinging to the back of his jacket and grasping desperately when it slips not once, but twice from her fingers.

"Where the hell have you been?!" Her voice is muffled against his chest, breath catching between words with gentle sobs. Billy lets out a heavy breath and closes his eyes briefly. *She's not Delilah*, he reminds himself.

"I told you I was going for a drive," he says, keeping his tone calm.

"For five hours, Billy? I thought something had– I haven't.... *fuck*. I was so worried!"

Guilt swirls inside him. It laps up to his chest like waves then drops, heavy and sickening back down to his stomach. He cradles Adeline to his body, his hands smoothing over her hair as he kisses the crown of her head.

"I'm sorry, sweet girl. I'm so sorry."

Adeline steps back and Billy holds her by her shoulders. She looks tired, skin pale and eyes red, and he realises she hasn't slept either. He knew she would try to fight it but he assumed she would drift off eventually. Billy pulls her close again, anchoring her to himself, and doesn't let go for a long time. It's only when Adeline starts to shiver in the early morning chill that he pulls back and takes in the rest of her for the first time, only half covered by the thin satin of her pyjamas. He reluctantly ushers her back inside to where the others are sitting around the living room, awake for some time too if the coffee cradled in their hands is anything to go by. Billy runs an anxious hand through his hair and prepares for Norah to rip him a new asshole for running off last night.

"Feel better?" The redhead asks. Billy can tell she's trying to hide how irked she is but Norah's never been great at that. Her temper simmers on low constantly, the burner never fully turned off.

"Norah, I–"

"It's fine, Nor." Adeline pipes up from where she's glued to Billy's side, her arms wrapped tightly around his middle. "Everything is fine."

Norah sighs. If she had anything else to say, it fizzles out before it can make it past her lips.

"You guys should get some sleep," Stan says.

Neither he nor Gabe have a clue what's going on and, despite being the biggest wind-up merchant going, Stan slips into peace-keeper mode easily. Billy can do nothing but nod in response, his body begging for sleep or at least to lie down.

"What are your plans for today?" Adeline asks before they leave.

"Uh, I think we're gonna head into Los Angeles. Gabe wants to go for a hike in the hills, see the Hollywood sign," Norah replies. "We can wait for you if you want?"

"No, you guys go ahead. No offence Gabe, but you scare me when we go on hikes. You go all boy scout on us," she chuckles. As she smiles, Billy catches the faint damp patches of drying tears under her eyes.

Gabe scowls playfully as he grumbles, "that's not true. I just like nature. And safety."

"Keep telling yourself that, Gabriel! But that is exactly how I would describe a boy scout," Adeline calls back as she drags Billy up the stairs. Her shoulders slump the moment they're out of view and the guilt stirs again.

"Addie," Billy starts but Adeline ignores him as they continue to her room. "Look, I'm sorry, Tinkerbell. I just–"

The bedroom door slams closed behind them and Billy's words die on his tongue as Adeline crashes her mouth to his. It's brash and frantic, choked out words and stealing breaths where they can get them. Adeline nips at Billy's lip so hard he tastes blood and he goes to protest but she stops him with a harsh press of her mouth and a mumble into his own. Her hands slip under the shoulders of his jacket, pushing it back until it slides from his body and hits the floor with a dull thud.

"Addie–"

"Billy, please. I just want to be with you."

"Addie, sweetheart, we need to talk about this."

Adeline's arms drop to her sides as she exhales a shaky breath and Billy is quick to cradle her cheeks in his hands, lifting her face until she meets his gaze. She's so beautiful, even with the tired eyes and the small frown she's wearing, the corners of her mouth tilted downwards just the tiniest bit. Billy stares at her for a moment, studying the softness of her features, before he tenderly kisses the frown off her lips.

"Billy..." Adeline whines when he pulls away.

"Can we sit?" He says, guiding her to the bed with a light touch. Adeline sits back against the headboard, her knees tucked under her chin. "I'm sorry I was gone for so long, I just needed to clear my head. I... Tinkerbell–" Billy pauses, cheeks rounding as he puffs out a sigh, thinking over his next words. "I love you, so fuckin' much, Adeline. Last night, when you told me what he did to you... baby, it broke my heart. And then I couldn't stop thinking about it and I just felt so *angry*."

"Are you still angry?" Adeline asks. She sounds so innocent, looking at him over her knees as she speaks. Billy's heart breaks all over again.

"Fuming. He's the worst kind of man, Addie. And I want– I want to kill him for what he did to you. I want to hurt him, like he hurt you–" His voice breaks and he hangs his head. He's exhausted, the adrenaline that had him so keyed up at 2am is seeping from his body slowly, leaving him drained.

"That's not you, Billy."

"I know, but–"

"Billy. That's *not you*," Adeline reiterates.

"I saw Delilah with him," Billy says.

"What? When?"

"At the track in Tennessee. She threw herself at him before the race... I don't know what to make of it, Addie, what if he does to her what he did to you?"

"You think he will?" Adeline asks quietly. "Maybe she's just trying to get to you, like how you told me she did before? Trying to rile you up."

"Honestly, I don't know. I wouldn't put it past her to scheme with him, she knows he's always been my biggest competition, but if he hurts her too..."

"You'll feel guilty that you didn't do something about it," Adeline finishes and Billy nods, dropping his head to his hands and rubbing at his eyes with the heel of his palm. "Do you trust her?"

Billy looks up at Adeline, his brow pinched as he mulls over her question. The truth? No, he doesn't trust Delilah as far as he could throw her, he hasn't for years.

"No," he answers honestly. "But there are two sides to this, Addie. I don't trust her, but I don't want her to get so caught up in Rex that she falls into his trap. Nobody deserves that."

"Me neither, I wouldn't wish it upon anyone," Adeline replies. "But she broke you, Billy, and then still thought she deserved to be with you. It's understandable to be on the fence about her. Maybe just... play it by ear? Or call her, if you're that worried."

Billy hums in response. "Yeah, maybe I will."

They leave it at that as Adeline moves on the bed, the mattress dipping as she comes to kneel behind him. Her lips fall to the skin just below his ear, dry and chapped from anxiously picking at them but Billy sighs all the same. The simple gesture of her kiss telling his body that it's okay to relax. Cold fingers graze his waist as Adeline skims her hands under the hem of his shirt and tugs the fabric over his torso.

"Arms up, hot stuff," she whispers. He aids her in removing his shirt and she throws it to the floor where his jacket still lies. Rolling his shoulders, Billy pushes his chest forward to stretch. Adeline's lips find the dip between his shoulder blades, three kisses planted down the length of his spine so softly they make Billy shudder under her touch. Everything she's doing is tender and gentle now, her hands and mouth trailing over his back and arms acting like a sedative. It's almost hypnotic the way his eyelids droop in response.

He feels the bed dip again but when he opens his eyes, Adeline is on the floor in front of him. She tugs at the laces of his sneakers, the neat bows undoing in one swift pull. Billy watches, dazed, as she continues to undress him. Adeline moves slowly, kissing and caressing, revealing his body gradually.

"C'mere, baby," Adeline murmurs as she pulls back the bed covers. The sheets underneath are wrinkled from their sleeplessness and Billy can only imagine how much Adeline tossed and turned, waiting for him to come home. He feels terrible, knowing how it feels to be waiting, unknowing. Gentle fingers wrap around his wrist as Adeline pulls him to the mattress and settles herself behind him. She holds him, her warm, steady breaths fanning across his neck as she snuggles in as close to him as she can get.

"I love you."

Billy peers over his shoulder. Adeline's lips have settled into a cute pout, wet and shiny from her tongue licking over them. He cranes his neck, stretching around to kiss her softly.

"I love you too, Adeline."

"Promise me you won't do something stupid," she whispers and Billy turns over fully, until they're nose to nose.

"I promise, sweet girl."

He kisses her again, just the lightest press of his lips to hers, but it's not enough to convey just how much he loves her, how far he'd go for her if she only asked. Billy needs to feel her under his hands, taste her on his tongue. He's wary as his mouth moves across hers, hesitant and slow with it, and taking his time to feel her out. Pulling her bottom lip between his, he sucks gently, eliciting a soft whine from Adeline that sends his blood pumping. Except he doesn't want to push her now, not after such a raw conversation and sleepless night. He pulls back a little, lips parted as his eyes flit over Adeline's face. She's so lovely like this, laid out in the messy sheets with her hair curling across the pillow in one direction and tucked under her chin in the other.

"Billy?"

"Are we," he pauses, letting out a breath before he asks, "are we okay?"

"Of course we are," Adeline replies, hushed as she reaches for his own face. "We are *so* okay, Billy."

"Good, okay... yeah. I just didn't want to, y'know..." He gestures vaguely at their bodies, curled together and warm under the bedsheets.

"Hey. Baby, I trust you. I know you won't hurt me."

Billy gulps, convinced his heart just leapt up to his throat with how hard it's beating. Delicately, he traces a single fingertip over the sweet apple of Adeline's cheek and drops cloud-soft kisses in its wake.

"I love you so much," he murmurs, "can I show you?"

He looks Adeline in the eye. Her irises are nothing but a thin halo of hazel around her pupils and when she speaks, her voice is barely there, her raspy whisper of '*please*' only just audible between them.

"Yeah?"

"Mhmm," Adeline giggles as Billy kisses her nose. All he ever wants is to see her smiling like this, toothy and bright with that special little shimmer in her eye. The one she saves just for him. He presses his mouth to that smile, hums happily into it as he kisses her gently.

Billy keeps everything slow, enjoying the change of pace as he trails his mouth over her jaw, dips his head to her neck and sucks until pink marks the shape of his lips bloom across her soft skin.

His.

His, to love and protect.

Adeline moans, light and breathy into his hair. There's a pleasant weight sitting in Billy's chest, counteracting the light flutters in his belly, and he almost laughs, giddy as he remembers that he gets *this*, to love her in this all being capacity. To hold her and kiss her and be privy to the sheer array of gorgeous sounds that leave her mouth. He tells her such and gets a bashful laugh in return.

Lowering his head, he kisses her thoroughly, sliding his tongue against hers and savouring it as he tastes the remnants of minty toothpaste and too sweet coffee. From her mouth, Billy moves lower, ducking under the bedcovers as he works his way down her prone form. He pushes her pyjama top up as he goes, lips and tongue meandering lazily down her stomach as he cups her breast, thumb flicking over her nipple. Adeline's breath hitches through a chuckle, her belly shuddering under his mouth, and Billy brushes his cheek over her navel, earning a louder, sweeter laugh when his stubble tickles her skin.

Just as he gets to the waistband of her little shorts and he bites back a groan just looking at the way they hug her hips, Adeline's fingers weave into his hair and she lightly tugs to get his attention. Billy whines but pops his head out from under the covers.

"Yes?" He asks with a devilish smile, the one he knows makes her weak.

"You're being an awful tease under there," she says coyly, "get to it, lover boy."

Billy rolls his eyes, nipping at the soft flesh on the underside of her boob and making Adeline squeal before he disappears again. His heart thumps distractingly hard against his ribcage, breathing shallow with ardent anticipation as he works quickly to rid her of her pyjama shorts and panties. He shoves them to the side, losing them in the bed somewhere, and runs his hands up her thighs. The pads of his fingers dance over the soft ridges and dimples he's so familiar with, up to her hips and back down again as he spreads her legs.

He wastes no time in attaching his mouth to her, licking up through her arousal and moaning around her clit. Adeline pulls at his hair again, nails scratching hard along his scalp and Billy whimpers, his cock twitching in response. He's painfully hard now, no choice but to dip his hand beneath the white fabric of his boxer shorts and give himself a few rough tugs to ease the growing pressure.

Further up the bed, Adeline whimpers, legs shaking as Billy laps his tongue up through her heat.

"*OH... oh, fuck...*" she rasps and Billy chuckles lowly at the reaction, humming just to get another. Adeline writhes beneath him as he sucks and licks teasingly and holds her still. He pulls away every few seconds, catching his breath as he presses hot, wet kisses along the insides of her thighs. Billy doesn't know how much longer he can hold out without feeling her around him or seeing her face as he fucks her nice and slow. "Don't stop, Billy! *Please... oh!*"

"You keep makin' those pretty sounds and I'm not gonna last much longer down here, Tinkerbell," Billy murmurs. "Do you want that? Want me to just fuck you instead?"

"Please!" Adeline chokes.

"Alright, I'm comin' up." Billy heaves a sigh like it's such a hardship and slinks out from under the sheets, kissing his way up Adeline's body; over her stomach and chest that sink and heave with each breath she takes. When he comes face to face with her again, her cheeks are softly flushed and glittering tears have gathered along her waterline, tacking her eyelashes together. Billy kisses her, letting her taste herself on his tongue, and gently brushes his thumbs under her eyes. "You doing okay?"

"Yeah," Adeline whispers, "yeah... just a lot, you know. I'm good, we can keep going."

"Okay. You'll tell me if you want to stop. I know you said–"

"*Billy*," she iterates, "keep going. I want you. I want you like this, please."

"Love you."

"Love you too. Now, *please* keep going."

"Since you asked so nicely," Billy grins as he steals away Adeline's sweet, tired giggles with another kiss and dips his hand back beneath the covers to finish what he started. It doesn't take long, quick fingers dipping and curling until Adeline gasps and cries out. Her fingers cling to his biceps, small half moon indents from her nails appearing on his skin. Billy glances down at the red curves, a small smirk of a smile on his lips. Adeline could mark him up from toes to nose for all he cares, he'd wear every single one of them proudly.

He removes his hand and brings it to Adeline's lips, watching through rapt eyes as she flicks her tongue out over the two fingers that just had her trembling with euphoria until they're clean and shiny with her spit instead. As she catches her breath, Billy stands to kick off his underwear. His cock springs free, hard and dribbling, and he closes his fist around his length, stuttering out a breath as he strokes himself slowly and wanders back towards the bed with his eyes on Adeline. With tangled hair across the pillow, pyjama top rolled up to her breasts revealing glistening skin tinged a little pink from being worked up, she slowly blinks up at him in a daze. Billy sighs, lost in the sight of her until she clears her throat with a soft giggle.

"Are you gonna stop staring and get over here?" She asks, holding her hand out. As soon as his fingers curl around hers, she pulls him down to the bed, mouth on his like she needs it to breathe. "I want you to fuck me now," she hums between kisses.

Billy's hand is still wrapped around his cock and he lifts up a little to line himself up with her entrance. Lips on her neck, he peppers her skin with kisses and whispered sweet nothings as he slides in, inch by inch, until he bottoms out with a gentle grunt. Adeline breathes softly in his ear, a quiet whine as her body adjusts to being full. Billy swipes her hair away from her eyes and kisses her as he moves. His thrusts are slow, deliberate drags of his cock as he curls himself around her, and he lets out a long, low moan. It's deep and gruff, right from the depths of his chest.

Adeline grips onto his back, raising her hips to meet his with each languid roll. She mouths words into his shoulder, muffled between gasps and whimpers and heartbreaking sobs that leave his skin damp. It almost becomes too much, this sweeping realisation that he's never felt so attached to another person like he does with Adeline.

By the time they're each on the brink of coming undone, both of them are crying. Billy's whole body is tingling, adrenaline and endorphins coursing through his veins as he spills into her with a quiet groan. Too tired and wrung out to do anything but kiss her, mouth hot and lazy, as she comes too and her legs tense around him, shifting him deeper and sending a wave of aftershocks through his body. Adeline clings to him, even after he's pulled out and lowered himself down over her. They're both sticky with sweat, limbs a tangled mess as they cuddle in the quiet aftermath.

Billy stews in his thoughts, warm and sated and sleepy. He sighs after a while and lifts his head from Adeline's chest. She's asleep, gentle snores and even breaths, and the sight of her so peaceful only confirms how in love with her he is. He's not sure what he would do if anything happened to her; feel lost and untethered, he expects. His heart aches just thinking about it so he doesn't entertain it for long. Instead, he presses the most delicate of kisses to Adeline's clavicle and makes himself comfortable and lets sleep slowly consume him.

"I'll always protect you, sweet girl," he mumbles, and it's a promise to them both.

twenty-two

ADELINE
April 6th, 1975

TIME AT HOME FEELS LIKE A SERIES OF SNAPSHOTS WHEN they're on the road. Moments that happen in quick succession, memories snapped and stored in her head like the world's most unorganised photo album. This time around, it's filled with hikes and day trips into L.A, an overnight stay in San Francisco and afternoons lazing by the pool or on the beach.

After that first weekend, Norah and Gabe leave them to it but Stan sticks around, disappearing and reappearing every now and again to give Billy and Adeline time alone. Their days always start out the same; in bed until late, waking each other up with hands and mouths, and then breakfast on the porch. Adeline could get used to this kind of life. Her mind feels at ease for the first time in weeks and she knows it won't last but she'll take it, and the constant stream of love and patience from Billy too.

Between the soft smiles and sweet kisses he leaves her heart pounding, drawing out carefree giggles that turn into whimpers and broken moans. Making out in the sea becomes fucking in the sea and Adeline declares they're never doing that again when they're in the shower afterwards, washing sand and seaweed from places sand and seaweed shouldn't be. Billy keeps her on her toes, brings out a side of her she knows she's always had but has never had anyone to share with.

Now though, they're in North Carolina and everything is back to business as usual. Billy's parents and sister are in town, driving down from New York while Rosie is on spring break. Adeline is sitting with them in the stands, away from the garages and a potential run-in with Rex or Delilah. Billy tried calling her before they left Malibu but she never answered so all they can do is hope Rex has nothing sinister planned.

They steal a quiet moment while Adeline helps Billy get ready, then he escorts her to the stands. They get there first and Billy pulls Adeline into his lap, hand resting on her hip and his thumb tucked under the hem of her top as he rubs small, reassuring circles over her skin. He's clearly on edge as they wait, face like thunder unless he's looking at her. His eyes soften then but Adeline still reaches out, brushing her fingertip over the little lingering indent between his eyebrows.

"Here they are," Billy murmurs, looking past Adeline as his eyes light up.

The Brookses shuffle along the row of seats, Eleanor with her arms outstretched and ready to embrace them both. She practically skips the last metre or so before Adeline gets the wind taken out of her. Billy chuckles, slipping his hands out from between his mom and Adeline so he can wrap his arms around them both in an Addie sandwich.

"Hi, Mrs Brooks," she giggles as she gets squished against her boyfriend.

"Lovely Adeline, I have told you how many times now? Call me Eleanor please. Mrs Brooks is my mother-in-law."

"Hi, Mom," Billy beams, leaning around Adeline to kiss his mother on the cheek. Adeline squeezes out of their hold, moving to greet Rosie and George.

She's grown fond of Billy's family. They're a unit, loving and supporting, and both Billy and Rosie are a real testament to that. Adeline feels lucky to have been embraced by all of them, finally feeling like the honorary Brooks they keep telling her she is, even though they haven't actually seen his family since the morning after Billy's birthday party. Neither she, nor Billy, were overly talkative, more concerned with easing their thumping heads, filling their stomachs with a greasy hotel buffet breakfast and sharing secret smiles.

Eleanor did steal Adeline away later in the day though, for pie and coffee at a little bakery down the street. She felt so overwhelmed she almost cried, a maternal figure actually wanting something to do with her was a new but very welcomed feeling.

As Billy greets the rest of his family, Adeline looks around the speedway, at the last minute preparations as the drivers limber up by their cars. She knows Billy has to go soon but she really doesn't want him to. She clings to his arm until the very last moment and once his parents have wished him luck and said a small prayer, he pulls her with him to the side.

"If Rex tries anything..." She breathes, restless and worried as she chews on her lip and peers up at him with wide eyes.

"I'm not gonna retaliate, Tinkerbell. I'm here to drive and win." Billy flashes one of his heart-stopping smiles, the kind that's a little lopsided and brightens up his whole face. "If I'm gonna deal with Rex, it'll be off the track," he rumbles, voice low and serious. His eyes are sparkling though, and his lips are still curled into a smile as if he's trying to play it off as a joke.

Adeline forces a smile onto her own face and kisses him until she's breathless.

"What are you made of, hot stuff?"

"Fuckin' stardust, and so are you." He kisses her again, quick small pecks of his lips as he reluctantly breaks away from her. Adeline watches him take four steps in the other direction before he turns abruptly and takes two long strides towards her, pulling her into his arms. He captures her mouth in a searing kiss and Adeline's whole body fizzles, happiness zipping from her head down to her toes.

"Go! You'll be late!" She giggles, swatting him away.

"I love you. Be good!" Billy calls behind him, pointing at her as he walks away.

Adeline waits until she can't see him anymore then joins his family. Eleanor is looking at her like she just watched the pair of them walk down the aisle, her eyes glistening and hands clasped against her chest. Adeline sits down beside her and Eleanor leans in close, cupping Adeline's cheek tenderly.

"You're good for him," she whispers, as if it's a secret. "Thank you for making my boy happy, Addie."

All Adeline can do is nod as she gives Eleanor a teary smile. Taking her hand, they sit together like that for the whole race. Both of them willing Billy to win and be safe until he crosses the finish line in first place.

For the first time all season, they skip the post-race party in the hotel bar. Instead, Billy takes them out to dinner at a restaurant in town. Just them and Adeline crowded round a little table in a family-run restaurant. Adeline sits between Billy and Rosie, the siblings bickering around her while George and Eleanor shake their heads fondly like it's just another Sunday evening in the Brooks household and they've missed this just as much as Adeline loves it.

"So, Addie," George says and Adeline snaps her head up from inspecting her last bite of cheesecake. "Billy tells us you play the piano."

She shoots Billy a look and he just shrugs. "I talk about you all the time, I can't remember *everything* I tell them about you."

Adeline rolls her eyes, her cheeks flushing warm as she smiles at George and she replies, "yeah, a little."

She really doesn't want to make a big deal out of it. She plays for fun, not because she has some big dream of being a musician. Billy looks around the restaurant and she peers over her shoulder, clocking the piano in the corner just as he does. She quickly shakes her head, raising her eyebrows in silent protest. Billy either doesn't notice or chooses to ignore her.

"Play something for us, Tinkerbell. Show them how amazing you are."

"Billy, I- I don't..."

Billy's hand slides along her thigh under the table and he sticks his bottom lip out, making his eyes as big as he can. He knows how much of a sucker she is for the big eyes.

"For me, sweet girl?"

Adeline narrows her eyes in a playful scowl in response to his dirty persuasion tactics but resigns. Billy's face breaks out into a grin, the corners of his eyes crinkling into the laughter lines she loves so much. Now that Adeline has spent time around them both, she realises he gets his smile from George.

She knocks back her glass of wine and pours herself another from the bottle before sliding out of her chair. She's going to need all the liquid courage she can get for this, the last time she played in front of anyone who wasn't Billy, Norah or her dad was at a Christmas party when she was fifteen. She got halfway through a song and blanked, her fingers hitting several wrong notes before she quietly stopped playing and hid in the bathroom for twenty minutes hoping nobody noticed.

As she makes her way across the restaurant, Adeline stops a waiter to make sure it's okay for her to play their piano and he nods, encouraging it.

There goes my way out of this, she thinks as she sets her glass down on the lid of the old grand and pulls out the stool. She glances around the restaurant nervously as she sits down but the only people paying attention to her are Billy and his family. They're all sitting with hopeful, expectant expressions as they wait for her to play and she realises she doesn't even know what to play. Maybe she'll just go hide in the bathroom again.

Dropping her shoulders as she takes a big, deep breath then a sip of her wine, she locks eyes with Billy and forces everything else out of her vision. He grins at her and mouths *I love you* before biting gently on his bottom lip and scrunching his nose in a way that makes her insides flutter hopelessly every time.

Fingers cracked and poised, she still doesn't have a song in mind. She starts playing anyway, quietly feeling out the keys in a twinkly little pattern that gets others looking up. Slowly, the random notes give way to *Loving You* by Minnie Riperton. She thinks about Billy as she plays, hears him whistle through his fingers.

"Told you she can play anything, she's incredible!" His voice carries excitedly across the restaurant and Adeline laughs, tipping her head back. She doesn't know what she did to deserve this gem of a man, but she's never letting him go.

twenty-three

ADELINE
May 10th, 1975
Nashville Speedway, Tennessee

Something doesn't sit right with her as they step out into the speedway grounds. They've managed to avoid Rex for the past month and there's been no sign of Delilah since Billy saw her back in March but Adeline still feels the prickle of uneasiness on her skin.

At each race through April, Adeline has sat in the stands, accompanied by either George and Eleanor, Rosie, or Patrick if he's around. She feels like her freedom has been stripped from her through fear of confrontation. It's not been much better for Billy either. He broke his winning streak after North Carolina, coming second and fourth in the Rebel 500 and Virgina 500, and he only just won last week in Alabama by the skin of his teeth. They're both stuck in their heads and constantly on edge.

Adeline knows jealousy is at the root of Rex's sick agenda, whatever it is. Before she and Billy began dating, he would at least leave her alone to some extent. Sure, there would be the odd passing comment and grossly lingering looks but Adeline could deal with that, ignore it for the most part. Something clearly changed the moment he realised, somewhere in that twisted brain of his, that he'd lost her to Billy and his last threat echoes in the forefront of her mind every time she finds herself alone, even for a second.

"*I'm not done with you, Adeline.*" He had spat out the words, punctuated them with a vindictive, sadistic snarl and now Adeline has a bad feeling deep in her gut. A twisty, strangling hold on her intuition that won't ease up no matter how much Billy tries his best to reassure her. It's like Rex is trying to lull her into a false sense of security all over again and sometimes she slips, falls for the calm before she sees something out of the corner of her eye that forces her guard up again.

It's exhausting. Even now as they stand in the sun just outside the Shaw & Gold garage, Adeline feels her body shrink with the heaviness of it all. Her back is against the wall, her small frame shielded by Billy as they share a cigarette. She's in a world of her own as they smoke, Billy is saying something but it's just muted noise like she's underwater. The only thing she's truly aware of is the soft figure of eight he's stroking around her knuckles of her right hand in an attempt to keep her calm and grounded. Her other hand opens and closes methodically, her nails digging indents into her palm while she waits for Billy to pass the cigarette back to her.

"Sweet girl? Tinkerbell…" Billy's voice is faint until a loud ring of her name snaps her out of it, her eyes refocusing as she meets Billy's gaze.

"Huh? What?"

"Thought I was gonna have to call you every name under the sun then, sweetheart," he chuckles gently as he offers her the last drag of the cigarette. As soon as his hand is free, he brings it to her face, his fingers tracing delicately over her cheekbone. "Where were you?"

"Anywhere but here," she replies lightly. Her cheeks hollow as she inhales, holding the smoke for as long as she can before she breathes out to the side. Billy watches her closely, carefully.

"You're gonna watch with your dad today, right?" He's checking because none of his family could make it to Nashville and Patrick has a karting race down in Miami.

"Yeah." Adeline looks up and smiles at Billy but the pained expression on his face makes her falter. "I'm going to film some of the race from the sidelines but I'll be in the garage the rest of the time. I'll be okay, promise." The words are said with weak conviction, as if she's trying to trick her own brain into believing them too. Once they're all on the track, she'll have nothing to worry about. Everything will be fine.

"Have you thought any more about what we said?" Billy asks tentatively and Adeline sighs, chucking the butt of their cigarette to the floor. She stamps on it, channelling all of her frustration into the sole of her Converse.

"He'll know it was me," she mumbles, her eyes still trained on her shoe as she grinds the butt to ashes.

"He needs to be punished, Addie. Racing is Rex's life, you take that away..."

"They won't believe me," Adeline pauses and exhales a shaky breath. "NASCAR, this world... It's a man's world, Billy. It's run by rich, middle aged men who spend their downtime in strip clubs and brothels treating women like things instead of people. Men like that won't even bat an eyelid if I tell them one of their best drivers assaulted me. Rex will deny it, we both know that. And all they'll do is ask why now? They'll think I'm making it up for attention."

"But it *happened*, Tinkerbell. He *hurt you*," Billy says, his voice thick and lip trembling, and he swallows, clearing his throat. He's trying to stay strong for her but Adeline knows it's breaking his heart just as much. He takes a step closer and Adeline rests her hands on his chest, her fingers tracing the vertical ribbing of his white tank. "These men have mothers, wives, daughters, sisters – how would they feel if it was them that this happened to? And right under their noses? I know you don't want to tell your dad but he has leverage, Addie. Shaw, too."

"I don't know, Billy. It'll break my dad's heart and he's been through so much already. Even if I do tell him, what if we go to the top and they still don't do anything?"

"Then we cross that bridge when we get to it, sweetheart. Just say you'll seriously consider it? And if you do decide you want to, I'll be there right beside you. And Norah, too. Hell, even Stan and Gabe would back you up and they don't know shit!"

Adeline breathes out a giggle as she whispers, "thank you."

"For what, sweet girl?" Billy asks. His voice has settled, his tone so smooth, the words ooze from his lips like caramel as he tilts his head and his mouth curls into the softest smile Adeline has ever seen.

"Loving me, being in my corner... all of it," she chokes out with a quiet whimper, her eyelashes suddenly dewy with tears.

"Hey, hey... baby." Billy holds her face in his hands, forcing her to look at him as he talks in a hushed murmur. "You are the fuckin' love of my life, Adeline Gold. I will *always* be in your corner. Forever."

He sways forward, closing the minuscule gap between them as his lips meet hers. It's so delicate at first, sweet, small kisses until Adeline tugs Billy closer by the fabric of his shirt. He opens his mouth, enveloping her top lip between his as he licks into her mouth. Every move he makes is slow and deliberate as he cups Adeline's cheeks in his large hands and his thumbs tenderly caress her skin. She feels *so* safe with Billy, the way he holds her sometimes makes her heart feel like it's being wrapped in the softest of blankets, warm and secure. Adeline melts into him, falling further and further away from reality with each gentle swipe of Billy's tongue, gratefully so. When he draws back, with heavy breaths and a flushed face, she whines at the departure of his mouth from hers and Billy huffs out a laugh.

"So needy, Adeline," he teases sweetly.

Adeline pouts and chases Billy's lips for another kiss but he dips his head out of the way playfully, darting left and right as she tries to catch him. By the time she manages to kiss him, she's giggling against his mouth; Billy's plan all along, she assumes as she feels his grin across her lips. He holds her close, swaying their bodies back and forth.

"I love you."

"I love you too, Tinkerbell."

"You know what?"Adeline says, an idea sparking as her smile widens with excitement. "We should go out tonight."

"Celebrate my inevitable win?" Billy's blue eyes sparkle with the easy cockiness he pulls off so well. They're still swaying, wrapped around one another as their feet lift and drop back to the ground with soft thuds each time they swing from left to right.

"Find a bar with live music, drink a little whiskey, try our hand at line dancing... what do you say?"

"I say when in Nashville, baby!" Billy grins, the words fall from his lips with a giddy shout.

Adeline shakes her head at his silliness and checks her watch as she weaves her fingers though Billy's, squeezing softly.

"Wanna help me set up?" She asks with a sweet smile.

Time has gotten away from them. The speedway opens soon and she's allowed herself to be distracted by Billy for long enough. He agrees, albeit a little less enthusiastically, and spends the next hour following Adeline across the venue as she runs through her usual pre-race checklist. He carries the heavy crates of Gatorade and helps her set up the refreshment tent, stealing snacks and kisses along the way.

By the time they're done, Adeline is sweltering. The thin floaty sleeves of her top stick to her arms and the flyaways of her hair are damp, slick against her forehead. The Nashville heat is no joke, even in early May.

"I'm gonna go freshen up," she says, lifting up onto her toes to press a kiss to Billy's cheek. "You should probably start getting ready."

Her lips trail along Billy's skin until she reaches his ear and pulls his earlobe between her teeth, flicking it with her tongue. Billy groans, rearing back as he shoots her a look and snakes his hand around to her hip to pull her closer.

"Don't start something we don't have time to finish, sweet girl," he warns quietly and Adeline just grins, sneaking back in to run her tongue up to the spot just below Billy's ear and covers it with a warm, wet kiss. Just to feel him squirm.

"I'm gonna go to the bathroom now," she murmurs.

"I want Norah to go with you, where is she?" Billy says suddenly, scouring the garage for her.

"I'll be fine, it's literally down the hall. And I really need to pee!" Adeline attempts to wriggle out his grasp but Billy holds on.

"Oh, you do, do you?" He chuckles, eyes shining with mischief. She squeals as he hugs her closer, squeezing her body against his.

"Billy! I *really* do need to pee!" She giggles, "it's in your best interest to let me go."

"*Fine*. But I'm finding Norah and sending her in after you," he whispers, kissing her softly.

"Okay. I love you."

"Love you too," Billy calls as Adeline hurries out the door to the bathroom with a plan of pee, freshen up, and head back to the garage as quickly as she can. As much as she told Billy she'd be fine, that unease creeps its way into her chest again as she practically skips down the deserted hallway to the women's bathroom.

It's always quiet at this time and Adeline checks that no one followed her before she pushes the door open. The paranoia forces her to check each stall too, kicking each door warily, holding her breath until she's completely sure she's in there alone. She locks herself in the stall closest to the door and does quite possibly the quickest pee of her life. The main door creaks open just as she's pulling up her pants and she sighs.

"I'm nearly done, Nor. Billy didn't have to send you," she calls before she flushes the toilet. There's no response and she waits, breaths slow and silent. She straightens herself out and places her hand on the lock, turning it slowly.

It's probably nothing. Just another woman doing exactly the same as I am, Adeline thinks but her own thoughts don't even sound convincing and her gut is telling her to be smart about this. She stands to the side so she'll be hidden from view and pulls the door open the tiniest amount, begging the hinges to not creak.

All it takes is one quick peek to see that it's not Norah waiting for her on the other side of the door, and the thick, calloused fingers that wrap around the wood as she tries to slam it closed again.

No, no, no. Please, no.

"Hello, Adeline. Miss me?"

The door is pushed open violently to reveal Rex standing there, tall and menacing in the small frame. He leers down at her with a predatory smile, eyes raking over her body.

Adeline's insides turn. Her heartbeat pulses through her limbs, a quick and heavy thud as she stares up at him. She's already gasping for air. Fear sinks its claws in, dragging chills down the length of her spine.

This can't be happening.

She's frozen as Rex reaches out, rough skin on her cheek as he trails his index finger over her face and down the side of her neck. It's crooked from an accident he had as a child. He told her that when he was trying to sweet-talk her last time. He told her a lot of things, though now, she isn't sure how much of it was true.

His hand continues its journey until he rests his palm on the top of her arm and the warm touch is like a shock to her system. Something awakens inside her and she pulls her shoulder back harshly, an attempt to free herself from his grip.

"I told you, Adeline. I wasn't done with you," Rex snarls darkly. He squeezes her arm hard and his fingers dig into her flesh. She winces when he adds more pressure, turning her skin red and he hauls her towards him, wrapping his other arm tightly around her middle and holds her back flush to his chest. Rex's breath fans, warm and rancid, over the back of Adeline's neck and she kicks against the wall of the toilet cubicle in an attempt to knock him off balance. Instead, he growls angrily and drags her away from the stall before shoving her hard against the row of sinks.

"Rex, please! You're– you're hurting me," Adeline stammers, her breaths stilted as panic sets in. Her vision blurs when Rex sidles up close again, ghosting his mouth so close to her ear she feels the dry skin of his lips and scratch of his stubble against her skin as he speaks.

"If you would just fucking stay still, you little brat."

Adeline looks around for something, anything, to defend herself with but comes up short. Rex moves to turn her around and in the short moment when she's not backed up against the solid porcelain, she drops her weight to the ground and screams at the top of her lungs.

"BILLY! *BIL–*"

"Shut up! He's not coming for you, *Tinkerbell.* That's what he calls you isn't it?" He taunts.

"Fuck *off!*" Adeline sobs. Rex tries to pull her back up to her feet but she's using all her strength to stay down and edge towards the door, fighting against the weight of him.

"I've missed you, Adeline, that's all. I just wanna show you how much, gorgeous. Why won't you let me show you?"

Rex crouches before her and she feels like she's going to be sick. Sharp, acidic bile rises and falls, burning her throat and leaving a bitter taste in her mouth. Her arm hurts and her head is pounding as hard as her heart as she sucks in a deep breath, screams herself raw and hopes it's enough.

twenty-four

BILLY

BILLY KEEPS HIS EYE ON HER CLOSELY AS SHE LEAVES FOR the bathroom. He hates this. Hates the feeling of not being in control. He feels like no matter what he does, it's never going to be enough to protect her.

His eyes scan the busy room as he quickly starts looking for Norah, maybe he can get her to follow Adeline to the bathroom, just– just in case. He spots Stan first, in the corner with Tobias, talking to a reporter Billy recognises from a racing magazine. Everyone else is standing in clusters and the sound of chattering mixes with the revs of engines and tinkering of machinery. Billy turns on the spot just as Gabe passes by in a hurry, a car part in his greased up hands.

"Hey, Gabe! Have you seen Norah?" He asks, jogging to keep up with him as he weaves his way back through to the pit.

"Can't say I have," Gabe replies before adding, "not since our little rendezvous earlier," with a wiggle of his eyebrows.

"Didn't need to know that, but thank you."

"Try outside?" Gabe suggests. He tilts his head in the direction of the door, nods, and disappears.

Billy keeps looking on his way to the exit, darting between drivers and execs as they mingle before the race.

"Where the fuck is she?" He's about to look outside when he sees red hair bouncing above the crowd, heading straight for him. "Oh, thank– Delilah?"

"William! Fucking hell, I've been looking for you everywhere."

"Wha– what are you doing here? Why didn't you call me back–"

"You need to find your girlfriend."

"What? She's in the bathroom, I don't–"

"Billy, I'm so sorry. I'm so sorry I was such a bitch to you. I– shit, you just need to get to Adeline. *Now.* Rex–"

Billy doesn't need to hear anything more, he's already fighting his way back through the crowd with Delilah hot on his heels. The second he's out into the hall, he breaks out into a run, his feet carrying him on autopilot as Adeline's shouts meets his ears. He glances at Delilah as they reach the bathroom door.

"Stay out here."

She nods, biting anxiously on her cherry-red nails as Billy pushes the door open. The whines, the wood swinging and smacking against the wall with a bang. Adeline's head snaps up at the sound and her eyes meet his, red with tears and silently begging for help. Billy's heart hammers, thundering in his ears as Rex peers around with irritation and strengthens his hold on Adeline as he stands to full height.

"Let me guess, Delilah couldn't keep her mouth shut? They're all the fuckin' sa–" Billy grabs him by the shoulder, hauling him around and swinging at him in one swift movement. He clocks him right in the jaw. The sickening crunch of bone from the impact of Billy's knuckles makes Rex drop his hand from Adeline, cradling his cheek as blood seeps from his mouth and he cries out in pain.

Adrenaline rushes through Billy. Sweat beads on his brow as his blood pumps ferociously through his limbs, throbbing in his hand. He shakes it out, reeling back for another hit as Adeline scrambles up from the floor. This time, Billy's fist connects with Rex's nose and he staggers backwards, more blood trickling down into his mouth as Adeline stares in equal parts horror and relief.

Fuck.

She quickly stumbles behind Billy. As she grabs his arm, he can feel just how much she's shaking; how absolutely overrun with fear she is. Rage crackles through him and right now, his love for Adeline outweighs all his morals. Billy tugs on Rex's shirt, pulling him up until they're toe to toe. Eye to eye.

"Adeline, wait outside," he says, voice calm as he reaches back to squeeze her hand once before letting go. He waits until the door closes before he continues, hauling Rex closer knuckles turning white as he tightens his grip.

"You listen to me you fucking son of a bitch," he grits out through heaving breaths. "Don't look at Adeline, don't *think* about Adeline, don't even so much as *breathe* in Adeline's direction. If I see you near her again, if I see you lay your dirty *fucking* hands on her again, I will make sure you never know what it's like to look at *anything* as beautiful as her for the rest of your fuckin' life. Do you understand me?" Billy is seething. He jabs Rex in the chest with his index finger, punctuating each word. "I said, do you *fucking understand* me, Harlow?"

Rex says nothing. Instead, he spits on Billy's shoe. Blood and saliva splatters and drips onto the linoleum floor.

"You're gonna wish you never came in here, Brooks."

Billy punches him again, catching Rex's lip as blood smears across the back of his hand.

"I mean it, Rex. You come *anywhere* near my girl again and you won't see the fuckin' end of it."

He pushes Rex to the ground, blood boiling, but the other man shows no remorse. His lips curl up at the edges, eyes leering.

"You better watch your back," he croaks but Billy's done listening. He's already walking out the door.

✦

ADELINE

She's still shaking as Billy guides her away from the bathroom. The true horror of what just happened, what *could* have happened if Billy hadn't shown up, suddenly hits her like a ton of bricks.

She doesn't think she would have survived it. Not again and certainly not awake.

Billy ushers her into a quiet room, a large empty store cupboard, and sinks to the floor with his back against the wall. Adeline goes with the gentle tug on her arm, landing in his lap and Billy wraps her up in his arms, solid and secure and soft all at once as she bursts into tears.

"I got you. I got you, sweetheart," he says, over and over as she cries.

"I'm sorry," she mumbles through her tears, sniffling as her nose runs. "I shouldn't have gone in there alone."

"Woah, no. None of this is your fault, sweet girl. You should be able to go to the fucking bathroom on your own," Billy reassures her. Her hair has fallen out of her messy up-do in the struggle with Rex and he brushes loose tendrils from her face, holding her cheeks in his hands as he presses a kiss to her forehead, lips lingering. "He's sick in the head, Adeline. How nobody else sees it, I don't know."

The room falls quiet, just Adeline's hitched sobs and the muffled sound of the speedway beyond the door. Time seems to slow down as she sits cradled in Billy's arms. His lips land over her face and knuckles as he hums softly under his breath. She listens to the low vibrations in his chest, using them and the steady beat of his heart to calm herself.

"Thank you," she says wetly, wiping her snotty nose with the sleeve of her shirt. Gross, but necessary.

"You don't need to thank me, Adeline. I told you, I'm always gonna be in your corner," Billy says, offering a tentative smile. He strokes his fingers over her cheek again, staring at her as if he's looking for something in particular. "Did he hurt you? Before I came in there?"

209

Adeline nods and Billy's jaw ticks, sharp lines and angry features as he tenses and his eyes blaze with fury.

"Only my arm," Adeline hastens to add, "and my back when he shoved me against the sinks–"

"I'm gonna kill 'im," Billy growls.

"Billy, I'm okay. I'm okay now. He gripped me pretty tight, and wouldn't let go when I dropped to the floor trying to get him off me so it pulled at my shoulder a lot, but he didn't *touch* me, not this time."

Billy sweeps her hair to the side, fingers delicate as they move over the joint of her shoulder. He pushes the fabric of her top to the side and presses his lips to her skin. She sags under his touch, convinced the warmth of his mouth eases the pain.

"I promise you, I'm never gonna let him hurt you again. I'm sorry I didn't do enough this time."

"Don't, Billy. You can't put this on yourself either," Adeline argues, fingers grazing over the soft stubble on his jaw. She catches his lips with hers in the gentlest of kisses and sighs against his mouth. The sound of the crowd filters in from outside, the distant echo of a booming voice over the speakers followed by cheering and hollering. "What time is it?"

"Uh…" Billy glances at his watch, "ten-thirty."

Adeline jumps. "Billy, you gotta go!" She makes a move to climb out of his lap but Billy holds her still.

"I'm not racing."

"What do you mean you're not racing? You have to race, we can't hide in here all day."

"I'm not leaving you, Addie… I can't," he says, the words tumbling from his lips. "Not now."

"*Billy,*" she sighs imploringly.

"*Adeline.*"

"You're on your way to winning the cup, you can't just throw that all away. I won't let you give up on that, Billy. This is your life."

"It's just one race, sweet girl." Billy smiles as he replies but it's hollow, eyes glistening sadly.

"No." Adeline clambers to her feet and holds her hand out. Her whole body aches but she ignores it. "You're racing. Get up."

"Tinkerbell."

"Don't *Tinkerbell* me, Billy. Get up."

Billy sighs but lets her pull him to his feet. He takes the entirety of his own weight, humouring her as he stands with a huff.

"Fine. But I'm only doing this for you. Because I love you. A lot."

"That's all I ask," she says with a proud little smile. She's all cried out, temporarily content and distracted. "I love you too, by the way, just in case I don't say it enough."

Back in the garage, she helps Billy get ready in record time. Despite her insistence for him to drive, she's reluctant as she leaves him at his car, kissing him through the window one last time before she goes in search of her father. With Billy's camera in hand, she finds Michael in the owner's hub at the side of the track closest to the finish line and huddles close to him anxiously as they watch the cars head to the starting grid.

Her heart is out there, revving his engine in pole position, and Adeline whispers a prayer as the green flag flies. She chews on her lip anxiously as she watches the early laps, filming snippets for Billy to watch back later. By the halfway point, he's in first place with Stan on his tail, a usual occurrence for the pair of them. It's Rex that Adeline has her eye on though. His lap time is sitting at around twenty-five seconds behind Billy, a pretty large distance, but he's driving inconsistently. He's darting between cars and then slowing right back down again and it's giving Adeline a headache.

The stomach-dropping bad feeling is still persistently present, a monotonous ticking of a bomb in her head like she knows it's there but can do nothing but helplessly wait for the explosion. The joy she usually experiences when watching Billy drive is overshadowed by an ominous sense of anticipation.

For the whole race, her heart is in her mouth. She has a death grip on her dad's hand as the first cars cross the line into the last lap. It's almost over, just one more lap and Adeline can breathe. Billy will win, hurry through his podium duties so he can find her like he always does. Kiss her like he always does. He whizzes around the track, so in control despite the shit show of a day it's been so far, and Adeline bounces on her feet, jittery with apprehension and pride as she tracks his car into the back stretch with his camera, probably shaky, unviewable footage but she wants to capture him crossing the finish line.

That's when she notices it.

Rex's car gains speed. It's too much for the condition of the track, still not completely dry from a downpour the night before, and he pulls up alongside Stan's car until he's wheel to wheel with Billy, forcing the front end of his car into the rear end of the Dodge.

"What the fuck is he doing?!" Adeline screeches in panic, dropping the camera and ripping her father's radio from his hands, bringing the microphone to her mouth. He looks at her bewildered and Adeline flaps her hand around in the general direction of Billy and Rex.

"Billy! Billy, you need to speed up. Rex is too close, I think he's gonna try something!"

Her heart is racing, eyes darting between the track and her father as she waits for Billy to reply.

"Addie, I'm gonna track down an official," Michael says but his voice is distant.

"Fuck. Please, Billy, say something."

The silence in her ear is agonising.

"I'm on it, Tinkerbell."

Adeline breathes a sigh at the crackly sound of his voice and spots him immediately trying to create some distance between his car and Rex's. But it doesn't work, Rex matches his speed, bumper to rear all the way down the back of the track until–

It happens in slow motion. Rex catches the back of Billy's car with more force than before, ricocheting off the metal and skidding himself across the grass in the centre of the track. At the same time, Billy's car flips and it feels like all the air is being sucked from Adeline's lungs. The sound of screeching rubber and crunching metal fills the speedway as the Dodge hits the outside barrier and comes to a stop, upside down and smoking.

An eerie silence follows and then the only thing Adeline can hear is the sound of her own scream as she runs towards the love of her life.

twenty-five

ADELINE

THE WAIL THAT LEAVES ADELINE'S BODY IS INHUMAN.

She's somewhat aware of her father and Tobias already crossing the track as she runs, sprinting onto the asphalt with fire in her veins, adrenaline kicking her into high gear. The smell of burning rubber becomes more pungent the closer she gets and from her new vantage point she can see the crumpled hood of the Dodge, metal twisted and torn like it's paper. One door has been ripped off its hinges and there's shattered glass everywhere. And somewhere, amongst the mess, is her Billy.

Faint calls of her name filter across the noise, distant compared to the one thing running through Adeline's head like a news ticker; just get to Billy, she *has* to get to Billy. She pays no attention to the hands that wrap around her arms and tug her back as she screams his name over and over, begging and praying to see him leave the wreck unscathed.

It doesn't happen.

Instead, the lights of the speedway's onsite ambulance flash in her peripherals as Adeline's eyes stay fixed on Billy's car. She can't drag her gaze away and the sound of his name leaving her lips becomes incoherent, a babble morphing into heaving sobs that feel like they're simultaneously taking all the air from her lungs and squeezing her heart.

"...Adeline." She blinks at the sound of her name and suddenly her cheeks are wet, hot tears dripping from her chin.

"D-dad," she hiccups, her breathing too erratic to get any other words out.

"Shh, it's okay. You don't need to talk, sunshine. I just wanted to make sure you were still with me."

Adeline meets Michael's gaze, finally looking away from where Billy is. His face is blurry through her tears but she can tell he's crying too, and Michael Gold is not an emotional man. He looks at her with his soft eyes, heartbreak and love all in one look, and it hits Adeline suddenly that at any point in her life, this could have been him. These men and women she loves so much aren't as invincible as she once thought and she berates herself for ever thinking they were. She clings onto her father a little tighter, face buried in his broad chest, and she's four-years-old again as his hand moves across her back in the familiar pattern of strokes that used to send her off to sleep.

"Mr Gold?" An EMT approaches them and when Adeline peers up at them, the solemn look on their face makes Adeline hold her breath.

Please, no.

"Yes?" Michael says, clearing his throat.

"My colleagues are attempting to extricate Mr Brooks from the car now so they can assess his condition. Mr Shaw has informed us that his next of kin aren't present and, legally, you're listed as the second for all your drivers. Are you happy to travel with him to the hospital if needed?"

In her hysterics, Adeline hadn't even noticed Tobias leave their side and take charge of the situation. He's right in with the ambulance crew, sleeves rolled up and holding a stretcher ready for when they get Billy out and transfer him to the gurney.

"I'll go," Adeline says.

"Addie–"

"I wanna go with him."

"Miss, I'm not sure–" the EMT tries to interject, eyeing Adeline warily.

"I'm his *girlfriend* and I want to go with him," she repeats. Michael sighs and holds her by her shoulders.

"Are you sure?"

Adeline nods though she's not sure at all. She has no idea if she'll be able to handle seeing Billy in the state the crash has left him in, all she knows is that she needs to be with him. She lets her gaze track over the speedway to the scene that's unfolding. The crowd immediately above his car are watching with intrigue as the crews work to get Billy out and Adeline feels like she's going to throw up. Hot bile rises uneasily up to her throat as she thinks about the possibility of them pulling his dead body from the wreckage and *all these* people are watching like it's prime time entertainment.

"Why has no one evacuated the crowd?"

"What, sunshine?"

"The crowd, Dad. They're all just watching it happen. What if–" Adeline pauses as a strained sob catches in her throat. She doesn't even want to keep thinking about her next words, let alone say them. "What if they can't save him? I don't want him to go with a fucking audience." Michael closes his eyes and exhales a shaky breath through his nose. Adeline watches as her father's heart breaks for her all over again.

"I'll get them moved along," he says adamantly. "Let's find someone to stay with you until the ambulance is ready to go."

It's Gabe who ends up joining her. He wraps her in his arms and she breaths in the strangely comforting scent of motor oil and exhaust fumes that clings to his navy overalls.

"He's gonna be okay, Addie," he whispers into her hair. "It's Billy."

It's Billy. Gabe states it so simply. Like it's obvious, like he *knows* Billy is going to survive this because he's Billy. Strong, resilient Billy. Adeline takes that thought and runs with it as the mechanic keeps her distracted, long enough that she doesn't even realise they've transported Billy from the wreck and into the back of the ambulance until the same EMT from before appears in front of them again.

"We're all set, miss."

"Where are you taking him?" Gabe asks.

"We've called it into Vanderbilt University Medical Centre." Gabe nods but he doesn't let go of Adeline just yet.

"Thanks, we'll be right behind you. Addie, you gonna be okay?"

"Yeah. Thanks, Gabe."

He hugs her tight, squeezing her gently one last time before she's escorted to the ambulance. It's small in the back. Adeline can't see much except for another EMT inside, Billy's still body on the gurney, and the oxygen mask attached to his face. She freezes before she even steps inside, eyes glued to him, scared that if she looks away, he'll stop breathing.

"We gotta go, sweetheart. Are you coming?"

"Yeah. It's just–"

"It probably looks worse than it is. Come on, up you get. You can sit on his right here, look," the EMT says, her tone kind and gentle. Adeline tentatively takes a seat on the plank of wood that pulls down to make a chair. It's uncomfortable, digging against every disc of her spine one by one as she attempts to sit back.

And then she looks at Billy; *properly* looks at him. It's worse than anything she could imagine. The oxygen mask hides most of his face but she can still see the blood. There's so much blood; congealed in gashes on his pale skin from smashed glass and seeping through a bandage on his head. The cream gauze is soaked through, as is what remains of his racing suit down his left side. There's a tourniquet wrapped tightly around his bicep and Adeline can see bone. She wretches, dry heaving at the sight of his mangled limb.

She shouldn't be able to see bone.

If she couldn't see the slow but gentle rise and fall of Billy's chest, Adeline would think he was dead. That thought is the one that triggers the anxiety attack. The what-ifs run through her brain on auto, a constant stream of worst-case scenario possibilities. Her breathing becomes heavy fast, inhaling quick gulps of air as she tries not to cry. It doesn't work, a strangled sob catches the attention of the lovely EMT who's busy filling out paperwork.

"Hey, honey. I'm gonna need you to breathe for me. Can't have you hyperventilating and passin' out on us, we only got a certain number o'hands," she says in her sweet, southern drawl. Adeline attempts to nod but her whole body is cast in stone. The EMT, whose forest green jacket is embroidered with the name Lucille, notices and places a reassuring hand on Adeline's arm. "What's gonna happen is we're gonna get your boyfriend here where he needs to go, okay. And then I'm gonna get you a big ol' cup of tea, sweetheart. You just gotta hang tight for a little longer, let us get William here to the hospital nice and safe." Adeline manages a nod this time.

"Yeah, okay," she croaks before her breath hitches in her throat again. Her chest is tight, a compress of dead weight right on her sternum.

"Here, why don't you hold his hand." Adeline lets Lucille guide her hand to Billy's. There's dried blood on his fingers too but his hand is relaxed by his side as she slips it into her own. He's warm, which is a nice thing to know, and as she watches them monitor his heart rate, she listens to the steady beeps of the portable machine and begins to calm down. "That's it, let him know you're here, honey. He's gonna need that, he's gonna want to know his strong girl is with him." Lucille's kind words just make Adeline sob again and the EMT rubs her back soothingly while Adeline strokes her thumb over Billy's skin, the familiar figure of eight around his knuckles.

The journey feels like it takes forever, each minute slipping by so slowly that Adeline curses every car that takes its sweet ass time to move out of their way, as if the blue lights and two tones of the siren mean absolutely nothing. She doesn't let go of Billy's hand even when they *do* finally make it to the hospital, not until she physically has to. She clings to him as if her touch is the one thing keeping him alive.

"I'm afraid you can't come any further," an orderly tells her as they wheel Billy from the ambulance and into the E.R. "You'll have to wait down the hall until his next of kin arrives."

Adeline is about ready to pitch a fit. She waits outside the doors, hoping to catch Lucille when she comes back from briefing the E.R team. Unable to stand still, her shoes squeak as she paces, the noise high pitched and echoing in the silent corridor. Lucille pushes back through the doors a lifetime later. Her face looks drawn but she finds a soft smile for Adeline as she makes her way over.

"If I could, I'd get you back there with him," she says, "but he's in good hands, honey."

"When will I be allowed to see him?"

"Not until his next of kin are here. I know it's hard, sweetheart, but if you're not legally his spouse, there's not much else you can do but wait."

"Yeah," is all Adeline says in response.

"Come on, let's get you that tea."

She follows Lucille to the waiting area where the quiet shifts to a buzz of activity. Doctors, nurses and EMTs buzz around and patients mill about in seats. Adeline feels dizzy watching them all, the world moving around her still when hers stopped the moment Billy's car overturned. She somehow finds herself in a seat and the swimmy feeling in her head settles as she focuses on her hands in her lap.

"I'll be right back," Lucille says, leaving Adeline with a gentle pat on the shoulder. Adeline glances up and musters a small smile, her gaze falling again as Lucille sets off in search of tea. Left on her own, Adeline zones out. She traces the figure of eight on her own hand, imagining it's Billy's soft fingertips and if she tries hard enough, she can hear his voice telling her everything is going to be okay, with or without him. She knows she can't let herself think that way but it's hard not to when Billy's life is possibly hanging by a thread.

The worst part is not knowing. Adeline has never been the patient kind but this time, the waiting feels like it's slowly chipping away at her soul; a tiny piece of stardust floating from her with each second that ticks by.

She accepts the first cup of tea gratefully when Lucille returns.

She's made it super milky and sweet and Adeline takes comfort in both the taste and how the warmth of it seeps through the polystyrene to her shaky hands. As she sips, she keeps her eyes trained on the door, waiting and hoping for a familiar face to walk through. Lucille offers to stay with her but another call comes through almost immediately, leaving Adeline alone in the waiting room with rapidly cooling tea and a jumpy leg. A distraction would be nice but she can't bring herself to pick up a magazine from the stack beside her, too afraid she'll miss something; a hushed whisper about a crash victim between doctors and nurses or Billy's name uttered in passing.

Thirty minutes later, Adeline has never been so relieved so see the five people that greet her when she next glances to the E.R. entrance. They all look exhausted; eyes red and skin pale. She can't imagine she looks much better. Her dad and Tobias walk in ahead of the others but as soon as Norah spots her, they're all fighting through. Stan reaches her first. He envelops her in his arms and Adeline breaks. Her whole body shakes, great, heaving sobs soaking Stan's shirt but he doesn't seem to mind. Not when he's crying into her hair too, stroking her back as if it'll somehow soothe them both.

"Do you know what's happening?" Norah asks. She takes a seat beside Adeline and pulls a pack of cigarettes out of her bag. Adeline takes one when offered. She left her bag at the speedway and, now her tea is gone, she's been craving something to occupy her fidgety hands.

"They won't tell me anything until George and Eleanor get here."

"They're on their way, sunshine," Michael says, "Rosie too. Tobias put them on the first available flight out of JFK. Eleanor asked how you were doing."

"Of course she did," Adeline sniffles, allowing the faintest smile onto her lips as she wraps them around her cigarette. She's beginning to love Eleanor Brooks as if she were her own mother.

It's a few minutes before her father stands with a heavy breath, brushing a hand over Adeline's hair.

"I'm gonna see if they'll tell me anything. Hold tight, kiddos." It's a long shot. Michael stands his ground at the nurses desk, but now they know the Brooks family are on their way, Adeline can tell that the staff aren't going to give anything away by the defiant shake of their head despite their sorry eyes.

Billy could be dead and all Adeline can do is wait.

twenty-six

ADELINE

GABE AND STAN ARE SNORING. THEY'RE SLUMPED AGAINST each other in the uncomfortable waiting room chairs, their mouths open and their faces serene. Adeline wishes she could sleep but she's still too keyed up, her feet bouncing on the carpeted floor as she stares at them enviously. Her mouth feels dry but she's too stubborn to leave her seat to get a drink from the vending machine, instead swilling saliva around her gums as if it'll help.

"You wanna go get another–"

"I don't want another fucking cup of tea, Norah!" Adeline doesn't mean to snap, for her tone to be sharp in a way that makes her best friend physically recoil beside her, but if one more person mollycoddles her she's going to explode far beyond a testy snipe. Her outburst wakes Stan and Gabe, who stretch and glance over with concern.

"Okay," Norah sighs, crossing her arms as she settles back into her seat. "Just trying to help."

"I know, I'm sorry... I just–" Adeline breathes deeply, running her hand over her tired features. Her skin still feels tight with tears, eyes heavy and exhausted despite it only being the middle of the afternoon. "I just want to know that he's going to be okay."

"He'll be okay," Gabe says, gentle with his words and his smile as he kicks a leg out and nudges her foot across the gap between their seats. It's not enough, not really, but it might just calm the rough ebb and flow of panic in her gut.

By the time Billy's family arrive, it's 5pm and they look just as withdrawn and weary as Adeline feels.

"Do you know anything?" Eleanor asks, and it's deja vu as Adeline shakes her head and hugs her tight. "Why don't you go get some fresh air while we try to find out what's going on? Bet you've been cooped up in here for hours, sweetheart, it'll be good to stretch your legs for a few minutes." She says it softly, but there's that underlying motherly authority that makes Adeline nod without thinking even though her whole body is screaming to stay put.

"Come on, Addie. We'll come with you," Norah says and before Adeline knows it she's being hauled outside by Stan and Gabe, who probably would have carried her if they had to but she's not up for that kind of humiliation today.

It is better, outside, she'll admit. Adeline takes a moment, takes a breath of air that isn't pungent with the scent of antiseptic.

"What, um... what happened after I left?" She asks, kicking up a stone that's come loose from the decorative shingle and overgrown flower beds by the doors.

"Toby dealt with Rex," Norah replies. She wraps her thin jacket tighter around her body and Adeline only just notices that she's still in her race suit. Stan too. "He was angry, lashing out at anyone who came near him so he called in the speedway security."

"Angry is an understatement," Stan mutters, "the dude looked like he was fuckin' foaming at the mouth." He's been pretty quiet since they arrived, subdued in a way Adeline's never seen him before. Now he's back on his feet, he hasn't stopped pacing, hands grasping and running through his hair so fast he's going to end up with a fistful of knotted strands.

Norah steps in close, her voice hushed as she asks, "Addie, did something happen before the race? Billy was running late and–"

"I don't wanna talk about it. I can't– not now." Her brain is doing a great job at dealing with one trauma at a time and she can't dredge it all up when she's still so worried about Billy.

"Addie–"

"I said not now, Nor. Please, just give me some time."

Norah holds her hands up in easy acquiescence and changes the subject, something about an upcoming car show that Adeline zones out on. She focuses instead on the door they wheeled Billy through five hours ago and she can't help but think of him, lying in a strange room, surrounded by strange people he doesn't know. Her vision blurs with the image of him waking up alone, the hospital door and the light of the waiting room beyond dappling like a Monet painting.

A smudge of white enters the frame and it takes Adeline a moment to realise it's a doctor approaching George and Eleanor. Ignoring Norah's calls, she hurries back inside. Her stomach dips and her heartbeat falters as she tries to work out what the slight frown on the doctor's face could mean.

"Mr and Mrs Brooks? I'm Dr. Roberts, I'll be your son's attending physician. Why don't we have a seat and I can talk you through everything?"

Eleanor refuses to sit and as soon as she spots Adeline lingering, she reaches out to wrap a tight arm around her. They're a solid unit, the Brookses. Rosie is tucked into her mother's other side and George stands behind them both, a supportive hand on his family's shoulders.

"Please, what's happening with my Billy?"

"William is stable and we're about to move him to the ICU," Dr. Roberts says, "Although he was wearing his helmet, he took quite a nasty knock to the head so we're keeping him sedated for the time being. I'm confident it's only a minor head injury, but I want to keep monitoring it just to be on the safe side. He also has a fractured ankle and bruising on his ribs and back." He pauses and something tells Adeline that isn't the worst of it. "His left arm– ma'am are you sure you don't want to sit?"

"Just say it," Eleanor says, her tone short even as her voice shakes.

"His left arm was crushed on impact. He's going to need surgery and, from the initial x-rays, it seems the best course of action would be to insert metal plates into his arm to help heal the bone that is still intact. We'll be operating as soon as a theatre becomes free but for now we've made him comfortable. I'll make sure a nurse keeps you updated as to when he's due to go into theatre so you can see him beforehand."

"But he's going to be okay?" Adeline croaks.

"It's going to be a long and hard road to recovery," Dr. Roberts says softly, "his body has gone through a lot and we'll only really know the extent of it after we've operated. He's not completely out of the woods yet but none of his injuries appear to be life threatening. It could have been a lot worse."

"Thank you, Doctor," George murmurs, and Adeline feels the comforting squeeze of his hand on her shoulder as her knees buckle. It's like someone finally let go of a balloon that was threatening to pop as she collapses to the floor in relief.

Billy is alive. He's alive and he's going to be okay.

They don't get to see him before he goes into surgery twenty minutes later.

Every wait they endure feels like Father Time is personally stretching the clock, the seconds dragging out into minutes that never end. It's agonising. There's a small reprieve when Michael and Gabe run out to the nearest fast food joint to stock up on quarter-pounders and fries. It's not until Adeline takes a bite of her cheese-burger that she realises how hungry she is and she eats two more and a portion of fries before she feels full.

"Do you feel better?" Norah asks as Adeline slurps up the last of her Coke.

"Yeah. I'm sorry about earlier, Red. I didn't mean to snap."

"I know. Don't worry about it."

The next wave of relief doesn't come for another hour, when Dr. Roberts appears with a smile on his face.

"The surgery went well. We've moved William into a private room. It'll take a couple more hours for the anaesthesia to wear off but you're welcome to see him now. Two at a time if you don't mind, just while we carry out his post-op observations."

"Let's go see our boy, hmm?" Eleanor says, pulling Adeline up from her chair.

The corridor to Billy's room is long and Adeline feels like she has to creep through the door once they get there. It's plush, a suite more than a standard room. Unsurprising when Tobias admitted to making sure they put him in the best private room the hospital has.

"Oh," Adeline breathes as her gaze lands on Billy.

"He looks so young," Eleanor whispers as she takes a seat by the bed.

Adeline can't stop staring at him. Billy has been cleaned up, a new bandage wrapped around his head and the deep cuts she remembers from the ambulance neatly sutured. His arm is in a cast and held up in an elevated sling and his chest rises and falls with the steady beep of the heart monitor.

"I'm so sorry, Eleanor," Adeline utters quietly. She takes a seat and slips her hand into Billy's.

Still warm.

"None of this is your fault, Addie."

Adeline takes a breath. "I feel like it is."

"This is not your fault," Eleanor repeats unreservedly. "I know guilt is an awful, *awful* feeling. It has a way of latching onto us, manipulating us even when we're not guilty. But this, *all* of this, is down to Rex Harlow. Not you, lovely Adeline." Adeline looks up then, wiping her damp face with her sleeve. "Billy told me," Eleanor confesses, "he was so worried about you and he always comes to me over his father, a complete mama's boy."

"Oh."

"I promised Billy I wouldn't tell a soul, and I promise you too. I hold no judgement, it's a disgusting crime what happened to you, my sweet. And if you need a hand to hold, when the time is right, I'm here. We all are. You've got a good group of people around you, Addie."

"I have," she agrees, letting her head fall to Eleanor's shoulder. "Thank you."

Time works a little differently in the room with Billy, no minute feels too long as they talk to him in hushed voices, watch as his eyelids twitch when they laugh softly through more tears. Eventually, there's a quiet knock on the door and Norah pokes her head around the corner with a smile.

"Stan and Gabe are itching to come see him and you need a break from this place," she says in a tone that means business. "There's a bar down the street, let's go get a drink."

There's no use arguing so Adeline leans over to press a kiss to the corner of Billy's mouth, brushing her fingers tenderly over his washed out skin.

"I'll be back soon, baby," she says as she tears herself away from his side, a difficult feat now she has him back but Norah's right. "If he wakes up…"

"I'll send someone down to tell you, I promise," Eleanor says, and Eleanor Brooks never breaks a promise.

The bar is rowdy. There's a band playing and every available space is filled with patrons dancing in place and singing along to the country setlist. Norah fights and flirts her way to the bar, grabbing them a couple of beers before they head back outside to the small tables that line the porch. Music filters out every time someone opens the door but otherwise it's quiet and Adeline glances up into the night sky. The plethora of stars above brings her a little peace before the conversation she knows is coming.

"Addie, what happened?"

"Rex cornered me in the bathroom," she says. The words come out a little easier after her conversation with Eleanor, and she knows she can tell Norah anything.

"The fucking–"

"Nothing happened. He– um, he threw me around a little but Billy came in before he could do anything worse. Delilah was outside, when Billy told me to leave, I think maybe she knew Rex was planning something and warned him." She takes a swig of her beer, the bubbles fizzing in her ears as she holds it in her mouth before she swallows. "I still don't know what the deal is with her, but if she hadn't said anything..."

"There's probably gonna be an investigation," Norah says, "Toby knows what happened was more than an accident and your dad's not stupid."

"I know. But I have no idea what happened between Billy and Rex in the bathroom, he wouldn't tell me. Whatever was said obviously triggered Rex to do what he did."

Norah sighs and chugs back the rest of her beer. "They're gonna want to hear your side of the story."

Adeline's been trying not to think about that, about the fact that she's going to have to pull the cork on everything she's kept bottled up for so long. But it's the only option if they want Rex to face any kind of consequences.

"And I'll tell it, if it means I never have to see Rex again."

"I'm so proud of you, Addie. You know that, right? You've been dealt some shit but–"

"Are you trying to make me cry again?" Adeline laughs wetly, "because I think I'm all out of tears."

"Sorry, sorry... I'll save my emotional speech for another day."

"You do that." Adeline drains her bottle and places it beside Norah's. "Can we go back now. Billy's obviously not awake yet and I want to be there. And I miss him."

"Sickening," Norah teases.

"Shut up! You and Gabe are worse." The beer has obviously had its desired effect, she feels lighter than she has all afternoon as she stands up.

"You wouldn't be saying that if you could experience being in a room with you and Billy from my perspective, but we'll agree to disagree." Norah throws her arm around Adeline's shoulders and plants a loving kiss to her temple. "Come on, sweet Adeline. Let's get you back to your lover boy."

As they approach the hospital, just as busy as it had been earlier in the day, Stan meets them by the doors.

"Hey, I was just coming to get you. He woke up about five minutes ago, he's still a bit out of it but he's been asking for you."

"He is? I'm gonna–" she gestures inside with her thumb, barely containing her happiness, and Norah chuckles.

"Go, Addie. Better not leave him waiting any longer."

Billy's sitting up in the bed when she walks in and the moment he sees her, his whole face lights up.

"Baby! Oh, you're a sight for sore eyes," he rasps, reaching for her with his good arm, fingers wiggling. The goofy, familiar smile on his face is enough to make Adeline weak at the knees as she makes her way over to him.

"Hey, hot stuff. How're you feeling?'

"Like I've been hit by a bus," Billy slurs. "Better now you're here though." He reels her in as soon as she's close enough and she leans down to softly kiss him, careful of the small cut on his bottom lip. She savours the feeling of his mouth on hers, chapped but warm and eager as his tongue slides past her lips. It's overwhelming, to be kissing him like this when mere hours ago she thought she never would again. "Lie with me?"

"Hmm?" Adeline hums, cradling his jaw as she kisses him again.

"C'mere, I wanna lie with you."

"There's not enough room, Billy."

"We'll make room," he huffs, raising his eyebrow as he flings back the thin hospital sheet and attempts to move over. He doesn't make it very far. "Get in here, Tinkerbell."

Adeline rolls her eyes but kicks off her shoes and settles beside him. The bed is definitely not big enough, proven when she accidentally nudges his fractured ankle and Billy winces, his face contorting into a pained grimace.

"I told you. There's not enough room for the both of us." She makes a move to leave the bed but Billy grabs her wrist and clumsily hauls her back.

"Shut up and cuddle with me."

This time, Adeline keeps her feet off the bed. Sighing, she settles in as close as she can and listens to the steady beat of Billy's heart as he presses a kiss into her hair.

"I thought I'd lost you today," she whispers into the quiet, dimly lit room. She doesn't think Billy hears at first, the words linger in the air for a beat too long.

"You know I'd never leave you, Adeline." His voice breaks as he says it and his arm shifts from around her. Adeline peers up to see Billy wiping a couple of stray tears from his cheeks and she cranes her neck to kiss him, tasting the saltiness of a drop that he missed and settled on his lips.

"I love you," she murmurs. "Every speck of stardust in you."

Billy breathes out a soft laugh and it turns into a yawn, his eyes falling heavy. They must have given him some of the good stuff before she arrived because he mumbles his response with a sleepy thickness.

"I love you too, sweet girl."

twenty-seven

BILLY

BILLY FEELS BROKEN. BEATEN, BATTERED AND BRUISED IN more ways than one as he turns his head stiffly on the pillow. Adeline is dozing in the chair by his bed. Her hair hangs over her face but Billy can't move to brush it back, tuck it behind her ear like he usually would. He's been trying to stay strong for her but the longer he has to stay here, in this white room with scratchy sheets and the monotonous beep of the machines, the more he's struggling to hold it together.

She's by his side constantly. It's only when someone convinces her to leave for a while, to shower and get some fresh air, that he breaks down. Stan is usually there then, silently soothing Billy as best he can with a manly rub on the back and once he's finally calmed down, Billy makes his best friend promise not to tell Adeline or his mother how weak and unstable he feels.

She stirs in the chair beside him as he reads. He has to lie the book flat on his chest every time he wants to turn the page. It's so fucking tedious and has taken him an hour to get through one chapter but he can't sleep and there is literally nothing else to do while Adeline naps. He watches her fondly as she wakes, her nose twitching thanks to that one strand of hair Billy couldn't move.

"Hey, sleepyhead," he murmurs. He closes his book, not bothering to save the page. Adeline glances over at him, bleary-eyed and frowning.

"Hi. *Ugh*. I'm sorry, baby. I don't know why I'm so tired," she mumbles, scooting closer to his side.

Billy shakes his head, a soft chuckle slipping from his lips as he moves his book to the side of the bed and attempts to stretch his good arm across his body. He groans a little at the strain on his bruised ribs but keeps going until he can brush Adeline's hair from her face. There's dried drool in the corner of her lips and an imprint on her cheek from the criss-cross fabric of the chair and yet, even slipping back into consciousness, she's never not beautiful.

"Maybe it's because you refuse to sleep at the hotel. In a bed," Billy replies, his head tilted to the side as he levels her with a pointed stare.

"I'm not leaving you here alone."

"Adeline."

"No. We're not having this argument again, Billy. I'm staying here until you're discharged."

"Tinkerbell, you need to look after yourself too. I'm not goin' anywhere in this place and you need a full night's sleep."

"I *do* slee–"

"In an actual bed, Addie."

"He's not wrong." Tobias stands in the door with Eleanor and a woman Billy doesn't recognise. His mom bustles into the room first, brushing the back of her hand over his forehead like he's some sick Victorian child. Billy's dad and sister went back to New York a few days after his surgery, once they knew he was out of the woods. Rosie has finals, and she's already taken so much time out of studying to follow her big brother across the country, it was time she got back to it. That, and Billy has an inkling she's been spending time with Patrick whenever he's back in the city. He'd say something about young love but who's he to talk?

232

Stan, Norah and Gabe are all prepping for the next race in Delaware. The world may have stopped spinning for Billy, but it keeps turning for everyone else. He's trying not to think about it. His friends promised to visit again before he leaves the hospital and goes wherever he'll be going to recover. It hasn't been discussed yet but he knows wherever he ends up, Adeline is going with him.

"This is Wren," Tobias says as the two of them enter the room and Wren closes the door softly behind them. "She's a physical therapist, the best in her field."

The long bell sleeves of her dress sway with each step Wren takes into the room, cork wedges heavy on the hospital's outdated linoleum. Billy eyes her dubiously. She looks nothing like the physical therapists he's encountered before. She shakes Billy's good hand as Tobias pulls two chairs up to the bed.

"I know we haven't discussed this at length, Billy," Tobias starts, "but we need to talk about the chances of you making a full recovery."

"Right," Billy sighs and closes his eyes, nostrils flaring as he breathes out heavily. Adeline reaches out and runs a hand through his hair and Billy whimpers quietly.

They *have* talked about this, albeit briefly. Adeline always starts the conversation but they never get far, not when Billy can't even handle the thought of never holding her with that arm again let alone never being able to drive professionally. So, he chooses not to think or talk about it, opting to kiss her or change the subject instead and hoping the conversation never comes up again. It drives Adeline insane but it seems his active avoidance has come to a screeching halt as Tobias completely ignores Billy's distressed reaction and launches back into his speech.

"Wren will work with you on the rehabilitation of your arm and ankle. She's worked with football players, dancers, rodeo cowboys, you name it. She'll do an initial assessment when the doctors feel it's safe for you to move your arm and then she'll go from there working on your mobility."

Billy looks at Eleanor like a child waiting for their mother's approval, his gaze unwavering until she tells him that all of this is okay.

"All of this is in your best interest, Billy. You know that." His mom perches on the edge of his bed as she cups his cheek delicately. "I know you're scared, sweetheart – I know how your brain works – but ignoring the fact isn't going to help. Everyone here wants you to be happy and we'll be with you every step of the way, and if you don't end up driving again, it's not the end of the world."

Billy feels like it is. His whole world is crumbling one wall at a time, each bad thought knocking into another like a shitty set of dominoes.

I won't ever drive again.

I'll be a deadbeat, a washed-up loser.

Addie won't want me if I'm a loser.

"I would love to see you back out on the track one day. All of us want to see that more than anything, Billy, but we have to be realistic," Tobias says softly, dragging Billy out of his head and right back into the room. He's not sure where it's worse. "There's a real possibility your arm won't fully heal and Wren here is your best chance at changing that."

Billy nods, "Okay. What about... I don't know where I'll be. We haven't decided," he says, looking at Adeline. "We might be in California? Or New York?"

"I'll come to you, wherever you are," Wren replies. "Once we've worked out a rehabilitation program, I'll schedule regular visits and give you exercises to keep up with in between. This all works around you, William."

"You can call me Billy," he says and Wren smiles warmly.

"Do you know where you want to go, sweetheart?" Eleanor asks but there's a knock on the door before Billy can answer, the room growing smaller again as Michael walks in.

"Hey, Addie. It's getting late, you wanna go grab some dinner, sunshine?" Billy hears the quiet rumble of Adeline's stomach at the sheer mention of food as she nods happily.

"We're pretty much done here," Tobias says as Eleanor presses a soft kiss to Billy's forehead and gathers herself to leave.

"I'll speak to your doctor about your arm this week, Billy," Wren adds as she places her own chair back against the wall, "we'll focus on your ankle until then." As both women head towards the door, Adeline pushes her chair back slowly.

"You want me to bring you anything, hot stuff?" She asks, leaning forward to gently run her fingertips over the grown-out stubble on Billy's cheeks. It tickles and his features relax into a dopey smile as she moves to card her hand through his fluffy hair, freshly washed by his nurse this morning. When Adeline reaches the nape of his neck, she twirls the soft strands around her fingers and scratches at his scalp. Billy tilts his head back like a cat, holding in the moan that's sitting at the base of his throat. He feels so fucking starved of Adeline's touch that he'll take anything at this point. The most delicate stroke of her finger over his arm almost makes him hard at times and he cannot wait to get out of the hospital, to be able to just *be* with her.

"Surprise me," he whispers, craning his neck up to meet her mouth, lips sliding against hers in a tender kiss. He tugs on her bottom lip and suckles gently before letting it go with a soft pop. Adeline's eyes flutter open as she pulls back, her cheeks flushed a pretty berry pink.

"You got it," she murmurs. "I love you."

"I love you too, Tinkerbell." Billy chases her lips for one more sweet, chaste kiss and then she's gone, filtering out after his mother and Wren. Tobias stands and carefully squeezes Billy's good shoulder before he moves to head out too.

"Get some rest, Brooks."

"Actually, Toby, can I talk to you?" Billy shuffles up the bed as best he can as Tobias nods and closes the door again. He takes the seat Adeline just vacated, the wooden legs scraping across the floor as he scoots it closer.

"What's up?" Billy's eyes dart to the door. Through the glass panel, he can see Adeline retreating down the corridor with Michael and he waits until they disappear out of sight before he sighs heavily.

"What's happening with Rex? Addie said you escorted him off the track but no one has told us anything else."

"He's been suspended from racing for the time being."

"Just like that?"

"As much as he tried to make it look like an accident, it was painfully obvious from where we were standing that he was targeting your car, Billy. There will be an official investigation but the redhead I've seen around, your ex, right?"

"Yeah...uh, her name's Delilah," Billy replies.

"Well, *Delilah* was very eager to give a statement and as much as I don't know exactly what happened before the race, I am aware that Rex has been bothering our Adeline for some time now. If there's more to it, you're both going to have to give statements. When you're ready, of course."

Billy's glad something is actually being done about it. For Adeline more than anything. He's known men his whole life who go around thinking it's okay to treat women as they please, uncaring of the fact that what they're actually doing is harassing and assaulting them. All through high school and his karting days he bore witness to it, listening as Delilah's friends confessed to her that their dates snuck a hand up their skirts. Looking back, there's more he should have done; things he should have said. It shouldn't have taken it going this far for him to realise he needs to do more, that he can't pretend he's doing good just because he doesn't agree with the behaviour of other men.

"Will he be charged?" Billy asks.

"For the crash or..." Tobias trails off and Billy nods, his eyes shifting in a way he hopes conveys there's more to it without revealing too much. He told his mom Adeline's story because he trusts her, he's confided in her his whole life and knows she won't breathe it to another soul. But to anyone else, it's not his to tell.

"It depends. We'll talk about it more once you're healed up. I can assure you none of this will be swept under the rug, Billy. Both you and Adeline have my word." Billy breathes out, relief flooding his body. He doesn't want any of this to be taken lightly, not when Rex has been getting away with it for so long.

"You should speak to Addie," he says suddenly as Tobias stands to finally leave. "She was filming the race, the footage might be helpful?"

"I'll do that," Tobias replies. "You know where I am if you need anything else."

"Thanks, Toby." The door clicks shut and Billy is alone again.

He settles down for a nap, one that's long overdue. Sleep has been evading him since everything happened, not that he slept great before anyway, but he knows his body needs it more than ever. Every time he closes his eyes he sees the blur of the world as his car overturned, remembers how everything went dark suddenly like a fuse tripped in his brain. In the darkness he always sees Adeline. No one has told him what happened in the moments after the crash, but he has no doubt that she would have made a run for him and his mind likes to torture him with the image of her heartbreak. It plays like a movie; the world turning, the darkness, Adeline's scream. Out of them all, he knows that one is going to haunt him for the rest of his life.

May 23rd, 1975

It's another week of monitoring before Wren is able to start working on a program for Billy's arm. They've been working on his ankle in the meantime, making sure the joint doesn't seize up. It's nice to be out of bed, moving around even if just a little. Adeline comes in to help and Wren teaches her the exercises too for the days between appointments.

On the first day of therapy for his arm, the cavalry arrives. Stan, Norah and Gabe bundle into his hospital room excitedly, Adeline clinging to Stan's back like a little koala. She has the biggest smile on her face and Billy's heart bursts at the sight of it. It's the happiest he's seen her in days.

"There he is!" Gabe bounds over to the bed. "How're you doing, man?"

"He's doing great. Aren't you, baby?" Adeline beams, hopping down to the floor.

"I'm doing a lot better. Thank you, Gabe," Billy chuckles as he pulls Adeline to his side and she lands with a soft bounce on the bed.

"Wren's on her way up, by the way, we passed her signing in at the nurse's station."

"Who's Wren?" Stan asks. He and Norah pull chairs around while Gabe wanders the room, reading the new Get Well Soon cards Billy received since they last visited.

"She's my physical therapist. I have a session today."

"You should have said, *Adeline*," Norah scolds. "We'll get out of your hair for a while."

"You guys can stay!" Billy replies, "the room's big enough and you can all see me stumble around like Bambi."

"Hell yeah," Gabe says at the same time as Norah's gentle, "if you're sure?"

A soft knock at the door interrupts them both and Adeline beckons Wren in with a wave of her hand. She stops in the doorway, clearly not expecting to see so many people in the room as she attempts to hide the shocked little rise of her eyebrows with a polite smile.

"Uh, hi. I'm not interrupting am I?"

"Nope, come on in Wren," Adeline replies, pointing to each of their friends in turn as she continues, "this is Norah, Gabe and Stan. They're just visiting before their next race."

"Oh, you're all drivers?" Wren asks, her eyes flitting from Norah to Gabe before they land on Stan, and Billy watches as she visibly does a double-take. Her gaze wanders over his best friend's broad body appreciatively and even Billy can see why. He dressed nice today, brown corduroy pants and a patterned shirt with a wide collar and cuffs. Billy didn't even realise Stan owned clothes that weren't grey sweats and his racing uniform. Stan runs his hand through his beard, looking flustered by the subtle attention he's receiving from a pretty girl.

"Oh, uh....yeah. Actually no, that's not right. Norah and I are," he stammers out, "Gabe is Billy's crew chief."

Everyone else in the room shares a look, their lips curled into coy smirks as Stan stumbles over his words. Billy sends a wink to Adeline who looks like she's just won the lottery. In fairness, she *had* predicted this happening and Billy had shot down the idea instantly. He was convinced he knew Stan better than anyone and Wren just wasn't his type. Turns out Billy should probably listen to his girl more often.

"Should we get started?" He asks, the tension between Wren and Stan dissipating as their weird staring match comes to an end.

"Oh! Yes. Sorry, Billy." Her cheeks are a shade of red Billy can only describe as beetroot as she quickly hurries to the bed. She finds what she's looking for in her case folder and then gets Adeline's help to shift Billy into a sitting position before they pivot him around to sit on the edge of the bed. "We'll start with some of the ankle exercises that I hope you've been working on with Addie." Wren glances across at Adeline.

"Twice a day," she confirms.

"Great. You ready, Billy?"

"As I'll ever be," he breathes out as they begin with joint rotations and gentle stretches. Adeline has been strict with him and he's thankful, each movement feels a lot easier now than when he first started. Once his ankle is suitably warmed up, Wren and Adeline help him stand and he hobbles over to the bar attached to the wall. He limps back and forth, putting a little more weight down with each turn.

"You're doing great, bud," Stan encourages from across the room and Billy lets go of the rail briefly to flip him off. "Hey, I'm trying to be supportive!"

Wren laughs, glancing at Stan over Billy's shoulder. When he turns for another lap, he shoots his best friend a knowing, shit-eating grin – *silver linings.*

For the next hour, they work through his core strength and lead up to some very gentle exercises for his arm. The others talk quietly amongst themselves, watching every so often when Wren makes Billy do something new. It's the first time in while Billy can say he's had fun, having his friends there with their laughter and words of encouragement. Despite that, he's exhausted by the time Wren packs up. Billy yawns, feeling bad that everyone made the effort to spend time with him and all he wants to do now is sleep.

"We're here until tomorrow evening, Billy. We'll hang out when you're feeling more awake," Norah smiles, brushing her lips to his hair as the others wait by the door. "Make sure he sleeps," she says to Adeline.

"I try but he's bratty," she responds with a grin and Billy glares at her, anticipating the nose scrunch he gets in return. "I wanna hear everything Stan says about Wren by the way."

"Yes, ma'am." Norah salutes lazily on her way out and the room falls into a sleepy silence.

Billy sighs, pulling Adeline down to the bed and kissing her soundly before she settles against his side. He nuzzles his nose into the curve of her neck and takes a deep breath in, hoping sleep will come easier for a change.

twenty-eight

ADELINE
May 31st, 1975

THE HOSPITAL CAFETERIA IS A GHOST TOWN. IT'S 11PM AND Billy is sleeping, finally, after hours of restless dozing in fits and starts. Michael all but dragged Adeline away for a snack and a coffee and while a kind nurse agreed to keep an eye on her boyfriend, easing Adeline's anxieties over Billy a little, her mind is very much still on him.

"Your mom called," Michael says, pushing a sugar packet towards her.

"Dare I ask why?"

"She saw the story in the sports pages. She just wanted to make sure you're okay."

The sugar packet in Adeline's hand looks *super* interesting all of a sudden. She doesn't bother looking up as she stirs the white granules into her murky looking coffee, not that she would expect anything less from a hospital cafeteria in the middle of the night.

"Of course she did."

"Addie–"

"No, Dad. She abandoned me. She abandoned *us*. She doesn't get to suddenly care just because she read my name in a fucking newspaper article," Adeline hisses. She doesn't often get angry at her father but she detests how much of a hold her mother still has on him. Just one phone call and *oh*, Adeline should care about what the woman who upped and left them twenty-two years ago thinks.

"She's just worried."

"No, she's not."

"She wants to see you."

"Oh, fucking hell," Adeline breathes, rolling her eyes.

"She's still your mother, Adeline."

"Don't. Don't play that card. Eleanor Brooks is more of a mother to me than that woman. I have spent so long trying to avoid her, scared I'm going to bump into her every time I'm in New York. She's manipulative, Dad. And you fall into her trap every time." Adeline lets out a long breath, her hands shaking as she meets Michael's gaze. She expects him to look angry, upset even, at her outburst but there's nothing but love and pride reflected on his face.

"I've been beside you for twenty-six years but I seem to have missed the part where you turned into this strong, independent woman," he says, almost incredulous as he stares at her in awe. "I'm sorry, sunshine."

"Dad," Adeline sighs, "it's not your fault but you've gotta stop trying to force a relationship between us. If she asks you about me again, I'd appreciate it if you didn't tell her anything. Please?" Michael nods and reaches across the table to squeeze her hand in slow, steady pulses. It stills her shaking fingers, calming her down almost as much as Billy's figure of eight trick. "I'm thinking of taking him to Georgia," she says after a beat.

She hasn't been to the ranch in a long time, it feels like the perfect reason to go back.

"I think that's a good idea."

"Really?"

"It's a place of healing. You and I know that better than anyone."

"Is Myles still there?"

"Yeah, he pretty much runs the place now. He'll be happy to see you."

"I've missed him," Adeline admits quietly. "And the horses."

Myles Farley, her best friend for each and every summer she spent on the ranch, was like the big brother she never had growing up. He taught her how to ride a bike and a horse and then at sixteen, Michael took him on as a ranch hand.

"I'll find you a car," Michael says, "I can't imagine Billy will want to fly and the drive shouldn't take you any longer than a day."

"Okay... okay, yeah. Thanks Dad. Billy's being discharged tomorrow so..."

"You holdin' up okay? With everything?"

"I'll be alright," Adeline smiles. She's got heavy, tired eyes and a crick in her neck but for once, she almost believes it.

It's been a hot minute since Adeline was last behind the wheel of a car but she settles in for the drive from Nashville into Georgia like it was only yesterday. Billy takes up the passenger seat, all long legs and fidgeting until he gets comfy and finally ends up napping beside her. A breeze blows through the cracked window, messing through his fluffy hair. It's grown out a lot, as has his stubble; the dark hair curling along his jaw. He looks entirely too sexy with it. Older too, but so does his whole face right now with everything taking its toll on him. Adeline is happy that he's finally able to rest, the low hum of the car engine lulling him to sleep as they speed along the highway.

They're not far now. Without Billy reading the map, she's able to follow road signs and what she recognises of their surroundings until they pull off onto a smaller country lane and the familiar gates come into view, open and waiting for them. Nothing has changed, not really, as she drives along the bumpy track that leads to the house. It looks smaller now she's grown but it still has the same old, blue window shutters and chipped painted wood. The porch swing catches her eye too, and the awful floral fabric Adeline picked out when she was five.

Michael must have called ahead because Myles sits on the steps, muddy jeans and a goofy grin she would recognise anywhere. Billy stirs as she parks up and gently stretches his good arm out across the car.

"Are we here?"

"Yeah. Did you have a good nap?"

"Slept like a baby," Billy grins sleepily as he leans over to kiss her.

Myles jogs down towards them, his boots crunching on the grit of the path as he approaches the car. Adeline climbs out and skips over to him, shielding her eyes from the low sun.

"Little Adeline Gold, as I live and breathe!"

"Hey, Myles!" She throws her arms wide as he engulfs her in a bear hug and spins her around, kicking up dust from his boots as she murmurs, "got someone I want you to meet."

Billy manages to swivel himself around so he's half in and half out of the car and Adeline drags Myles around by his wrist, giddy to introduce the two. "Myles, this is my boyfriend Billy. Billy, this is Myles. Known him nearly my whole life."

Myles laughs and offers Billy his hand. Adeline doesn't miss the way Billy eyes him as he shakes it and she nudges his good foot, glaring at him when he glances her way.

"Nice to meet you, Billy. I've seen you race on TV a couple'a times. You're one hell of a driver."

Billy smiles weakly. "Thanks, man. Not so much at the moment."

"Shit, yeah. I read about that. I'm sure Addie here will have you back on your feet in no time."

"I'm sure she will," Billy grins and Adeline clears her throat.

"Anyway, key's in the door," Myles says. "I gotta go bring in the horses. I'll uh, I'll see you around. I'm in the coach house just down the way if you need anything."

"Thanks, Myles. It's good to see you."

"You too, Addie." Myles heads towards the paddock and Adeline turns to Billy, arching an eyebrow.

"What the hell was that, Brooks?"

"What was what?" His voice is laced with innocence and he's wearing a smile to match.

"I didn't realise you were the jealous type."

"I'm not... jealous. He was just... friendlier than I was expecting."

"You have nothing to worry about, hot stuff. I'm always gonna be yours."

Adeline bends down and brushes her hands over Billy's jaw until her fingers intertwine at the back of his neck. He's eager to meet her lips as she kisses him; soft and slow but his tongue is quick to explore her mouth. He drags it across her lips and over her teeth until she moans, keening into his touch.

"We should go inside, baby," she whispers, parting from him with a soft sigh and lingering fingers on his cheek. Billy groans, grasping for her as she steps back. "I'll help you in and then come back for everything else."

"We're continuing this later," Billy rumbles, tugging her forward for one last kiss before he reluctantly agrees, letting her take some of his weight as they head inside.

After two journeys back and forth, Adeline dumps the last of their bags in her old bedroom; they'll get settled in this evening and everything else can wait until tomorrow. She quickly changes into a loose sundress, her body begging for clothes that don't stick to her in the heat, and then helps Billy out of his jeans so he's more comfortable. Evening approaches by the time they're both back downstairs, Billy sitting comfortably at the table while Adeline whips up something from the pantry for dinner. It's just pasta and a jar of tomato sauce only just under its expiration date, enough to fill their bellies until Adeline can get into town to stock up.

She barely cooks when they're on the road so she relishes the simple act of it now as she throws in herbs from the little pots on the porch, still going strong even as the temperatures rise. She tastes the sauce and dances to the radio, feeling Billy's eyes on her between pages of the book he's pretending to read.

He moves to the couch once they're done with dinner, sinking down into it while Adeline cleans up. The old furniture is worn and she knows for a fact that the springs dig in if you even attempt to get comfortable, but Billy seems happy enough to wait there for her. He watches her every move, following her with unmistakable bedroom eyes, dark and intense and hot on her back as she flits around the kitchen. She's just about done when he clears his throat roughly and beckons her over.

"C'mere, sweet girl." Billy leans back in his seat, the thick outline of his cock prominent through his boxer shorts. He palms at his length, pre-cum dampening the grey material, and a small whimper slips past Adeline's lips as she watches him from the other room. Legs open, splayed wide just waiting for her, Billy already looks wrecked. He whines under his breath as he continues to pleasure himself and as Adeline gets closer, he stops and pulls his underwear down as best he can with one arm, freeing his dick. It springs up against his stomach, heavy and weeping.

"Gonna be a good girl and sit on my cock, Tinkerbell?" Adeline clenches her thighs, panties slick with her own arousal at the sight of him, red and leaking over his soft abs. She nods, hurrying over to him. "You want this, baby? Wanna feel me fill you up, stretch you out. It's been a while hasn't it?"

Billy groans and spits into his palm. He swipes his thumb over his tip, saliva and pre-cum mixing over his shaft as he begins to stroke himself. Adeline nods again, unable to do much else.

"Gotta tell me, Addie. Tell me how much you've missed my cock."

"Missed it so much, Billy," she whines, straddling his thigh gently because he's still sore, bruises healing slowly and she doesn't want to hurt him.

Already, she's dripping, her pussy clenching around nothing as she slowly starts to grind down over the firm muscle of his thigh. Sighing in sweet relief, she moves slowly, slick soaking through the silk of her underwear as she throws her head back and breathes out Billy's name in a soft moan. Billy hums lazy and indulgent with the way he pumps his fist over his length.

"*Fuckin' hell.* You're so gorgeous, Adeline. Gonna show me how much you missed this? How much you missed my cock."

Adeline lifts up a little and dips her hand beneath her sundress, dragging two fingers through her folds. She holds them up for Billy to see, for him to realise just how wet she is; though the shiny patch of her arousal on his thigh gives it away just as much.

"*Shit,*" he hisses and his eyes darken as he watches her slick drip, stretching between her fingers as she parts them, then he takes her hand in his and sucks her fingers into his mouth.

Billy groans, pressing his tongue up against her fingertips and his eyes flutter closed as he tastes her. Hand to his chest, Adeline feels the low vibrations of the downright pornographic sounds he's making, the rumbling bass to the erratic hammering of his heartbeat.

She slides her hand down his torso until she reaches his cock, brushing over the tip with her thumb ever so lightly. Billy's whole body shudders beneath her. He swirls his tongue, humming around her digits when she finally wraps her free hand around him. With slow, even strokes, she slides her fist over his length rhythmically. Billy hisses, his hips jerking as Adeline traces her fingertip over the prominent, sensitive vein that she knows drives him crazy.

"*Jesus*, Addie," he whimpers, fingers curling over the edge of the arm rest, digging into the outdated fabric of the couch. "Please, sweetheart."

"Want me to sit on your cock now?"

"Please. *Please*, sweet girl. Need t'be inside you," Billy's rasps through a moan as he begs. "Missed feelin' you around me."

"I know, baby, I know," Adeline soothes as she lifts her hips and pushes her panties to the side while Billy holds the base of his cock. She lifts her leg, straddling him completely and Billy brushes the tip through her folds, nudging her clit and sending a spark of pleasure through her. It's been too long. Billy lines himself up and she sinks down, a deep, dirty moan leaving her lips as she revels in the stretch, each vein and ridge of his length dragging against her walls as he buries himself in her to the hilt.

"*Oh, fuuuuck.* That's my good girl," Billy drawls.

"Jesus Christ," Adeline blushes. He's pulsing inside her and she's desperate for it; needs him to fuck her with everything he has.

"You like that, huh? Like it when I call you a good girl. When I tell you how fuckin' perfect your pussy is. All warm and tight and just for me."

"You know I do," Adeline whispers as she cards her fingers through Billy's hair, pulling on the chestnut strands until he whines. Dropping his head to her shoulder, he pushes the strap of her sundress down and licks across her skin. "Can I move, Billy?"

"Not yet. Just wanna enjoy you squeezin' me," Billy mumbles. He brushes his nose up the column of her neck until he reaches her ear, suckling gently on the lobe as he groans in a way that shouldn't be so adorable. The rough graze of his beard over her sensitive skin makes Adeline gasp and Billy chuckles, rubbing his cheek across her chest and nuzzling into her breasts. She's absolutely ready to explode. With slick dripping around Billy's cock, she grinds her hips just a little until her clit hits his pubic bone. It feels so fucking good but she aches for more, whining weakly.

"That's not good girl behaviour, Adeline," Billy murmurs into her skin.

"Baby, *please*."

Without warning, Billy grips her jaw in his fingers and crashes his lips to hers with a bite. It's messy; all tongue and teeth as he begins to rut up into her with quick, small thrusts. Adeline moans softly, short huffs of breath as she rolls her hips to match Billy's pace.

"This what you wanted, Tinkerbell?" He whispers with a grunt against her mouth.

"Yes, Billy! Thank you–" she chokes out. "Oh my–*fuck.*"

Adeline lifts herself up, bouncing carefully on Billy's cock and driving him deeper each time. She grips the back of the couch instead of his shoulder, trying her best to be gentle even though they're both pushing for something more.

Billy lifts Adeline's dress with his right hand. He struggles to get it any further than past her belly one-handed so she helps, pulling it over her head and tossing it across the room. It lands somewhere in the kitchen, draped into the bucket of water from when she mopped the floor earlier and soaking up the bubbles.

"Look at you," Billy mumbles in awe, mouth already lowered to her bare chest and taking a nipple between his lips. He takes his time with each one, grazing them with his teeth and flicking over them with his tongue, warm and wet, until they're firm and pebbled in the cool air. His mouth moves across her breast, covering it with hot-open mouthed kisses, and then he bites down on the fullest part and Adeline's soft whimpers turn into a gasp. Billy chuckles breathlessly against her supple flesh.

"I'm gonna come, Billy," she whispers as he mouths his way back up to her lips, marking her skin.

Adeline picks up her pace, moving one hand to run through Billy's hair and her fingers tangle as she kisses him fiercely. His hand trails down her belly, fingers finding her clit and he rubs small circles over the sensitive bud as Adeline continues to ride him. The room fills with hitched breaths and deep groans and the echoing slap of skin on skin. Billy curses as Adeline clenches around his cock and her body is taken over by the familiar warmth, the tight coil of her oncoming orgasm tugs impossibly tighter.

"Come on, Addie. Wanna feel you come on my cock. Let go, sweet girl," Billy commands, his voice rasping against her cheek as he thrusts up into her.

"*Oh, God!* Billy, fuck–"

The coil snaps and the pleasure is loose and light like silk ribbon unravelling through her body. Her eyes squeeze shut, her vision whiting out as she comes.

"*That's* it, sweetheart," Billy purrs. He kisses her, wet and warm and lazy. His tongue slides against hers, as slow as the rhythm of his hips as he keeps fucking her, chasing his own climax. It's intoxicating. Adeline's heartbeat thrums just beneath her skin, her body tingling and glistening with sweat.

Billy's movements grow sloppy as he tires himself out and Adeline picks up the slack, lifting herself up nearly all the way off his cock before she sinks back down and Billy lets out the most guttural groan.

"Fuck," he hisses as he brings his hand to Adeline's waist, fingers pressing into her softness as he controls her pace. Another orgasm is creeping up on her, her pussy fluttering deliciously around Billy's length. "*Uh–* oh fuck, Addie, that feels incredible– don't, don't hold back, baby. Be a good girl and touch yourself, make yourself come."

Adeline does as he says and her second orgasm immediately crashes over her like a tidal wave. Her toes curl and her blood rushes in her ears. Billy's hips falter beneath her; he grunts with each final thrust. Once, twice, three times hard and deep until he spills inside her with a shuddering groan. Hot breaths from parted lips breeze over her skin as he collapses against her, slick with sweat and beyond sated. Adeline feels warm and full; content for the first time in weeks. Her lips trail over Billy's neck, sucking gently on the sensitive spot just below his ear and humming at the salty taste of his glistening skin.

"I love you," she whispers.

"I need another nap," Billy replies as his head lolls back and Adeline almost chokes as she splutters out a laugh. "And I love you, obviously."

"I did say we should wait a little while until we fuck," she giggles, lifting herself from his softening cock and settling back on his thighs. "Your body was definitely not ready for that."

"Don't even, Adeline–" Billy starts but Adeline swallows his words with a soft kiss, running her fingers through his hair.

"I won't deprive you of sex, hot stuff, don't worry."

"Good. Let's just... do it on a bed next time, huh? My back is killing me."

twenty-nine

ADELINE
July 6th, 1975
Gold Family Ranch, Georgia

THE SOUND OF SOMETHING METAL HITTING THE KITCHEN
floor wakes Adeline from the first night of good sleep she's had in
weeks. She's finally comfortable enough to sleep without the fear of
accidentally rolling over into Billy in the night. Their first night in
the ranch house hadn't gone quite as well. Billy had claimed he was
fine, that it didn't hurt *that* much when Adeline had star-fished out,
flopping an arm across him and landing on his bad side as she
curled herself into him without thinking. The pained grimace on his
face had said otherwise.

The thunderous clash that echoes through the house stirs her
almost instantly. She doesn't know what time it is but sunlight
streams through the crack in the old gingham curtains, a small sliver
of warmth on her skin. It could be 5am or it could be midday, the
sun means nothing in July.

What Adeline does know is that she's alone in bed. The sheets
that should be wrapped around Billy are cold, the pillow free of
creases from where his cheek should be squished into the fabric.

Adeline scrambles to her feet. The old wooden crutch she found in the attic is gone; Billy's been hobbling around on it for the past few weeks but he still needs Adeline's help on the stairs. Which is why she pulls on the first item of clothing she sees and hurries down to the kitchen, taking the stairs two at a time.

Through sleepy eyes she sees Billy standing by the stove with his back to the door and his head hung low. The crutch is leaning against the counter as he holds onto the edge of the oak top for balance. Adeline's gaze is drawn to his hair, sticking up at all angles. It's longer than it was before the accident; the soft tendrils tickle the nape of his neck and curl around his temples. She loves it and she has a feeling Billy does too despite how often he complains about it getting in his eyes. The lazy smile that blooms across his face when she washes his hair for him or runs her hands through it, teasing the curls and twisting them around her fingers as he falls asleep, gives him away.

A pan, the one Adeline assumed woke her, lies on the tiled floor upside down near the kitchen table. Billy must have kicked it away in frustration. She notes a broken egg on the counter top too, crushed to pieces with yolk oozing out amongst the shards of shell.

"Fuckin arm. For fuck– can't fuckin' do anything anym–" Billy mutters to himself.

"Billy? Baby?"

Billy whips his head around. He rubs his eyes with the heel of his hand, the delicate skin around them red and puffy.

"Tinkerbell, hey. I was just... um, I wanted to–" he chokes on the words before his eyes screw shut and a small sob works its way up from his throat. "I was– wanted to– scrambled egg," he manages and then he crumbles. His eyes glisten, threatening tears as he lets out a strangled cry.

Adeline is by his side in seconds, her hands cupping his cheeks as she gently wipes the salty drops away.

"*Baby,*" she murmurs, wrapping her arms around him tightly. Her heart is in her throat as Billy buries his face in the curve of her neck, his soft sobs muffled by her pyjama top.

Sometimes, Adeline feels like she's not the right person to comfort others like this. The strong will she often sees in Norah, the ability to push aside her own feelings to deal with someone else's – she doesn't have that.

So Adeline does what she knows.

With one hand massaging through Billy's hair, she softly drags her nails over his back. Down the length of his spine, around the sides of his waist, over his shoulder blades. It's what she does when he can't sleep or when he wakes up sweating and groaning through a nightmare. Her fingers hit those spots that tickle just right and lull him into a state of drowsiness.

Adeline doesn't push him to talk about his dreams. She thinks he should, at least if not with her then with someone else, but he tells her if he wants to and that's all she can ask of him right now. Most of the time, he tells her it's just a replay of the crash. That he can feel the sensation of the car flipping, his stomach dips and he hears himself screaming. It rings in his ears until it morphs into a higher pitched, female cry; her. That's when he wakes in a panic. From the way he startles awake some nights, though, Adeline knows he's had worse dreams. Those are the ones he refuses to tell her about.

"I'm sorry," Billy mumbles, "I just wanted to do something for you – by myself – but then I couldn't even fuckin' crack an egg with one hand and then the pan fell and my balance is so shit, Addie. I couldn't bend down to pick it back up again. I just feel so fucking useless."

"You're not useless, Billy. You managed the stairs today," she says softly, adding a little cheer to her voice. Billy pulls back, wiping his eyes and sniffling.

"Ended up on my ass halfway down," he huffs. He's pouting adorably and his nose is a little red. It makes Adeline want to wrap him in blankets and feed him soup. "Went the rest of the way down like that, like I did when I was a kid."

"You could have woken me, you know."

"Didn't want to," Billy says sulkily, "you were finally sleeping and

I need to start doing things for myself. I *want* to start doing things for myself."

"I know, I'm just worried you're gonna hurt yourself. I don't mind you waking me if you have to, baby. I want to help you."

Billy slides his good hand down into Adeline's, letting out a quiet sigh as he gives her fingers a gentle squeeze.

"Adeline, sweet girl. I love you..." he starts as he moves out of her embrace and Adeline stares up at him, waiting.

"But?" She pushes.

"But, I'm not a child. You don't gotta chaperone me everywhere I go.'

"Oh."

"Which isn't very fuckin' far right now, anyway," Billy mutters as he ambles over to the coffee maker. Two coffee mugs are waiting on the counter, creamer already poured into Adeline's favourite cup – a slightly grubby cream ceramic with orange and brown flowers and a chipped handle. Billy fills them with a shaky hand as he leans his hip against the counter for support. He slides Adeline's across to her once he's done and lifts his own, gingerly placing his left foot on the floor as he turns. The movement is slow and measured as he gradually adds weight to his bound ankle, wincing as his heel hits the tile before he has to revert back to the ball of his foot. He's improving every day but Adeline still hates watching him struggle.

"Here, let me," she offers, reaching for the coffee in his hand. Billy swats her away flippantly.

"It's fine, baby. I can carry it." He smiles but it's weak, not quite meeting his bloodshot, glazed eyes. Adeline places a gentle hand on his shoulder instead, half expecting him to shrug her off.

"Go sit down, I'll bring it over," she says.

"You don't need to, Addie. I can do it."

Billy moves the mug out of her reach, limping a couple of steps towards the kitchen table while Adeline watches him like a hawk. She follows closely behind him with a hand shadowing his, just in case. She's glad she did when Billy momentarily loses his balance halfway. He leans into her to steady himself but the jolt still dislodges his fingers from the cup handle. He manages to keep a hold of it and is just close enough to the table to reach out and attempt to place it down, albeit a little haphazardly. As he shuffles himself closer, Adeline sighs and swoops in to help.

"Billy, just– you're gonna drop it."

"I'm almost there, just let me do it," Billy replies, sharp with frustration. His teeth are clenched, jaw tight, as he actively moves the mug away from Adeline again.

"Surely it's easier to let me help, Billy. I don't see why you're so–"

Billy puts the coffee down and pivots to face her.

"*Adeline!*" He yells and she flinches as his hand slams down on the table. The wonky wooden tabletop shakes with the impact and the coffee ripples in the cup like waves before it sloshes over the edge. "I said I could do it. Just back off... *please.*"

Adeline does as he asks, moving to the sink and quietly soaking a cloth to clean up the spillage. She couldn't respond to Billy's outburst even if she wanted to, any words she tries to summon wouldn't make it out. She swallows, trying to dislodge the sudden lump in her throat. Her stomach is in knots. Not once in the seven months they've been together has Billy raised his voice at her. In fact, they've hardly argued past ridiculous bickering, usually over something so stupid they end up laughing about it not even an hour later.

But this is different.

Billy makes no attempt to speak again and when Adeline finally brings herself to look at him, his head is in his hand and he's grasping his hair so tightly it has to be painful.

She silently wipes down the table, lifting the coffee mug to clean underneath it. One step back towards the sink and Billy's fingers wrap gently around her wrist.

"Addie..." he starts, softly now.

"I'm going outside," she replies, shaking her hand free. She rolls her shoulders back, straightening up. "Don't follow me."

Adeline glances over her shoulder as she heads out, wishing she hadn't as she meets Billy's gaze across the room. His eyes are crystals, bright blue and shiny wet with tears, and Adeline has to turn away before she breaks her resolve and rushes back to him. Instead, she leaves out the back door and into the large garden that occupies the side of the ranch house, leaving Billy alone in the kitchen.

Adeline surveys the space once she's outside. They grew their own produce when Michael first bought the place, her mother adamant they would eat organic, home grown food whenever they visited. Now, it's just overgrown grass and patches of dry dirt, but the brambles around the perimeter still produce blackberries twice a year.

She finds a couple of empty milk crates and an upturned plastic punnet by the old wooden gate. The punnet is faded pink and cracking from being left in the southern Georgia sun for too long, but it'll do to collect the few ripe berries she's spotted. Adeline wallows for a few minutes while she inspects the fruit, crouched in front of the hedgerow in her pyjamas with sore eyes, bed hair, and no shoes. She must look ridiculous and the last thing she needs is the sound of horseshoes echoing across the ranch, getting closer until Myles appears sitting atop Meadow, the Appaloosa mare he's owned since he was a teen.

"Hey, Butternut," Myles calls as he brings Meadow to a stop just inside the garden gate.

"I thought we agreed you weren't gonna call me that anymore?" Adeline replies, disgruntled, as she stands and makes her way over to the horse. She strokes gently over Meadow's muzzle, murmuring a soft hello as she offers up a handful of blackberries and treasuring the simple reply of a huff of air and nuzzle against her palm.

"And forget the best moment at a county fair I've ever witnessed? I don't think so." Myles grins and Adeline groans at the memory.

When she was seven, her father took her along to the county fair for the first time. Filled with enough corn dogs and funnel cake to feed a grown man, Adeline was buzzing and most likely on the verge of a sugar crash when they announced the winner of the giant vegetable competition. A state renowned farmer had grown the biggest butternut squash Adeline had ever seen so when the kids were invited up to take a photo with it, obviously she was first in line. The squash was heavy, covering half of her little body as she shook under its weight. She remembers someone stood beside her waiting to take it back once the photo had been taken but her arms gave out before she could hand it back and the vegetable crashed to the ground, splitting open over her feet. She had been mortified, bursting into tears on the spot as everyone in the crowd gasped and the other children waiting started to wail too.

"Don't," Adeline warns with a shiver. "I still have nightmares. I haven't eaten butternut squash since."

"I won't offer you some of my Ma's spicy butternut soup next time she brings me a batch then."

"I'd appreciate it," Adeline chuckles, turning back to the blackberry bush.

"I actually stopped by to let you know that I saw a car pulling in through the gates a minute ago. Are you expecting visitors?"

Adeline frowns. No one had said anything about visiting soon and Wren isn't due again for another week or so. As if on cue, Stan's red, white, and blue monstrosity pulls up in front of the house. Meadow huffs, shaking her head at the loud engine.

"Racing friends," she informs Myles, "sorry about the noise." Adeline takes a deep breath. She would be happy to see them on literally any other day; it's like a cruel joke from the universe that they decided to show up right now.

"Speaking of," Myles says as he calms Meadow with gentle strokes. "Have you told Billy about the practice track yet?"

"No. And I don't intend to until he's ready to get back out there. Is my dad's old car still in the garage?"

Myles nods, distracted, as Stan, Norah and Gabe climb out of the car and walk the short distance to the garden. With Gabe here, it might be a good opportunity to get the car looked over. If – *when,* Adeline reminds herself – it gets to the point where Billy feels like he can get behind the wheel again, she wants it to be ready.

"Aren't you a sight for sore eyes!" Stan barrels towards her, crushing her against his broad frame as soon as he's close enough. If she didn't feel like she needed the hug so much, she would have shoved him off in jest with a sarcastic comment. Instead, she lets herself melt into him, squeezing the big oaf tightly.

"Hi," she says quietly, her face smushed against his chest. When she finally lets go, she greets Gabe and Norah with equally bone crushing hugs and introduces them to Myles before she goes back to picking blackberries. Conversation flows for a little while and then Stan looks towards the house, his brow pinched.

"Where's Billy?"

Adeline sighs but doesn't look up from the hedgerow. She keeps plucking fruit on autopilot as though the world will come crashing down if she stops.

"I don't know. I left him in the kitchen," she replies with a shrug. "He's probably still there." She ignores the nervous glances thrown around between her friends, almost breaking when she feels Stan's heavy hand on her shoulder for a brief moment.

"We'll go find him," he says, pushing a reluctant Gabe towards the back door.

Myles ushers Meadow backwards and, with a tip of his hat, leaves the garden too. Norah joins Adeline on the ground, clearly not caring if her jeans grow muddy as she busies herself sampling black-berries. Adeline swats her hand away. She wants to make jam and after sacrificing a few berries for Meadow she won't have enough if Norah eats them all too.

"Okay, spill," the redhead says after the silence between them lingers for a little too long. "What's going on?"

"Nothing, I'm just getting some fresh air. Harvesting," Adeline replies indignantly, gesturing to the punnet in her hand.

"In your pyjamas and with bare feet?"

"I wanted to be at one with nature."

"You are the worst liar I have ever met, Addie. Tell me."

Adeline drops the punnet and falls to her knees.

"I'm just trying to look after him," she croaks, wiping her face with grubby hands as quick tears trickle their way down her cheeks.

"I thought I'd lost him, Nor. I thought he was gone and I'm scared that if I stay away from him for too long he's going to disappear. I want to be there for him but he's getting sick of me."

"For starters," Norah says sternly, "I'm pretty sure it's impossible for Billy to ever get sick of you. You are *everything* to him. And secondly, I get that you're scared but have you taken a moment to look at it from his perspective?"

Adeline glances at her friend, confused. "What do you mean?"

"Delilah pretty much suffocated him, Addie. Told him how to stand, where to go and what to do. She was constantly on his back and I know everything you're doing is because you love him, but maybe he's just finding it all a little too much. Plus, he's injured with a slow recovery process. He's gonna be frustrated."

Adeline immediately feels terrible. The stubborn, pessimistic streak she tries so hard to squash down has reared its ugly head and she's suddenly very appreciative of the fact that her best friend is here to talk some sense into her.

"Has he left the house?" Norah asks.

"He sits on the porch."

That earns her an exasperated sigh.

"Adeline, you have a *car*. Drive the poor man up to the stables, take him into town with you. Even if he just sits in a diner while you run errands it's gotta be better than sitting on the fucking porch. He's probably got fucking cabin fever."

"He hasn't said–"

"You ever thought that maybe he doesn't want to disturb the peace?"

"Too late for that," Adeline mutters. She can still hear the utter despair in Billy's voice as he shouted her name. Norah quirks a questioning eyebrow and Adeline wets her lips nervously.. "I think I pushed him too far. I was just trying to help but he exploded at me so I came out here."

Norah hums, a sad little noise, as she pulls Adeline into a hug.

"Maybe it would be a good idea to give him some space. Let him gain some independence back, attempt things on his own and wait for him to come to you when he needs the help," she suggests tentatively and Adeline nods. That's all Billy asked for and instead of supporting him, she was overbearing; stuck in a repetitive argument that could have been easily avoided if she had just listened. At least she gets that now. "He knows you care, Addie. And if I know Billy, he's probably killing himself in there over the fact that he lost his temper."

Adeline sniffles through a chuckle as she wipes the last of her tears away. "Who made you so wise?"

Norah presses a soft kiss into Adeline's hair, wrapping both arms around her.

"You're wise too, Addie," she assures her, "you've lived through too much shit not to be."

BILLY

HE CAN'T DO THIS.

It's been a month since he was discharged from the hospital and the slow, painful progress he's making is beginning to take its toll. He can't straighten his arm and his muscles and tendons are too weak to even attempt to wiggle his fingers even a little bit.

He's tired of sitting on the couch watching television or reading out on the rickety old porch swing. The ranch is lovely – quiet and serene – but Billy is slowly losing his mind. He feels useless and the cracks are starting to show; sharp replies to Adeline's simple questions, a roll of his eyes when she insists on helping him dress every morning. He's regretted all of it from the moment he broke. The second he raised his voice and made her flinch away from him he wanted the ground to open up and swallow him whole.

Adeline has been nothing but attentive. She's kept him smiling most days and he knows everything she's doing is out of love but he's so sick of being mollycoddled. If it isn't Adeline, it's his mom calling the ranch house every day and making sure he's eating and sleeping, and if it isn't his mom it's his sister. Wren's visit last week was a welcome reprieve. Billy insisted Adeline get out of the house and go tend to the horses or something, *anything*, while Wren worked.

He loves Adeline, more than he's ever loved anyone and, as he watches her walk out the back door with quick steps and a sullen glance in his direction, his heart breaks.

"Fuck."

Billy stumbles out of the chair and hops over to where his crutch still rests against the kitchen counter. His ankle is nearly healed, the moon boot he was supplied with is long gone and now the joint is wrapped tightly in gauze. He *should* be able to put weight on it and he did in his last session with Wren, but then he tried to do it alone two weeks ago and nearly fell down the stairs. He'd been reluctant to try again until this morning.

The want to follow Adeline outside pulls at Billy's gut, puppet strings tugging him towards her. He limps across the kitchen, fighting the urge to crash outside and apologise, as much as it goes against everything his body is telling him to do, and he stops just short of the door. Close enough to hear what's going on out there, to hear Adeline pottering around and the sound of horse hooves – oh so familiar to his ears now.

Adeline laughs about something with Myles, the sweet sound makes Billy falter but it's the rumble of a car engine, Stan's car engine, that makes him sigh, pinching the bridge of his nose and screwing his eyes shut. More voices filter in from outside and he tries to will himself to move before his friends inevitably see him lurking, but it's too late. He's met with the startled faces of Stan and Gabe as the door swings open, whining on its hinges.

"Hey, man. You all good?" Gabe asks, looking at him like it won't matter what the hell Billy says, he won't believe him anyway.

"Uh. Yeah. Hey," Billy says, words stilted as he makes the effort to move out of the way. "Come in, I'll make more coffee."

He feels spaced out, watching the scene unfold instead of living it. He wasn't expecting guests or for the very obvious tension to be so thick and stifling; the look his friends share as they shuffle in behind him and take a seat at the table doesn't go unnoticed. Still, they let him get on with it, even if it does take him a little longer, and they accept the coffee with gracious smiles when he finally sets the mugs down on the table one by one.

Stan takes a sip of his drink and fixes Billy with a concerned look, his lips pushed into a pout as he contemplates the conversation ahead. In the end he settles for, "So, what happened?"

"I yelled at her," Billy whispers. He hates himself even more now he's said it out loud. They try not to make it obvious but disappointment washes over Stan and Gabe's faces regardless.

"Wanna tell us why?"

Billy nods. He keeps a watchful eye on the door, sucks in a deep breath, and starts from the beginning.

He doesn't see Adeline for the rest of the day, just a blur of her as she comes inside and heads straight upstairs. Norah appears in the living room doorway a few moments later, glancing at the three men with a look of displeasure as she informs them she's taking Adeline out. Out where, Billy doesn't know, but he figures Adeline could do with the break from him. Billy wouldn't mind a break from himself too.

Instead, he gets to watch a rerun of an old baseball game, talking shit about the teams playing until he somehow ends up being the topic of conversation again and, once he starts, he finds that he can't stop. He tells Stan and Gabe everything; about the nightmares, his anxieties and frustrations, the fact that Adeline has been so, *so* patient and loving with him and yet it all just feels too much sometimes. It all comes spilling out; his guts laid bare for his friends to see.

"B," Stan murmurs softly, his coffee cup long discarded, half empty and cold when he'd turned his body to focus on Billy's ramblings. "How long have you been holding all that in for, bud?"

"Too long," Billy whispers, his voice is hoarse but he feels lighter for it. Gabe leans across from the armchair and gently squeezes Billy's good shoulder.

He doesn't ask about Rex. But when Gabe gets up to use the bathroom, Stan tells him all he knows in a hushed voice. Then when

Adeline appears in the doorway later in the afternoon, the three of them are back to joking, the TV volume turned down low and the coffee table full of empty beer bottles instead of coffee cups. The sheepish smile on Adeline's face and the way her hazel eyes are sparkling when Billy's own meet them across the room makes something physically shift. There's no longer a dark cloud lingering over his head, no longer a tonne weight on his back.

"Hey, guys. Do you mind if I steal Billy away for a while?"

Stan and Gabe both smile, their heads bobbing in eager, synchronised nods before they place a hand on either side of his back and push him up from his spot on the couch. Billy stumbles to his foot, reaching for the crutch that Stan holds out for him. Adeline looks like she's about to step forward to help, her eyes flickering to his feet and up again, the internal battle playing out before them. She doesn't move, just offers him a soft smile instead and waits for him to meet her by the door.

"Where are we going?" Billy asks as she leads him outside and to the car.

"Just get in, hot stuff."

The sun is still shining high overhead, painting everything in a bright glow as they head further into the ranch. It's not the direction Billy thought they'd be going in but he watches out the window as they pass parts of his new home that he hasn't seen yet. The paddocks and stretches of field that eventually lead to the lake. They're in the car for all of two minutes before Adeline shuts off the engine, reaches into the back seat for a Tupperware container and climbs out. Billy does the same, leaning with his arms folded on the roof as his gaze sweeps up to the large wooden stables. He can hear the gentle huffs of the horses from where he's standing. Adeline looks back at him with a grin on her face and Billy's heartbeat falters at the sight.

"You coming?" She calls over her shoulder. Her voice bounces with a cheekiness he hasn't seen in her for a while as she starts walking off without him. Billy nods and follows her dumbly, much like that first night at the beach house.

Inside, Adeline stops by the first stable in a row of five. In her hands is the tub from the back seat, full of roughly chopped carrots Billy now realises, and a box of sugar cubes.

"This is Maple," she says as the chestnut brown horse stretches her neck over the gate to greet them. Adeline holds a piece of carrot out and Maple laps it out of her palm. "I've had her since I was twelve."

"Pleasure to meet you, Maple," Billy says softly and the sound of Adeline's giggle that follows is like the first sight of water after days in the desert.

"I was thinking, once you feel up to it, we could come down here more regularly and you could help with them?"

"Really?"

"Yeah, I think it'll be good and–" Adeline stops midway to the next stable and turns to face him. Her brows are pinched into a small frown and Billy has the urge to reach out and gently brush his thumb over the tiny wrinkles that appear above her nose. "Fuck. I'm so sorry, Billy. I didn't mean to be overbearing. I just– I was scared you would somehow end up hurt again and I feel like I have this responsibility to look after you, like it's partly my fault this even happened and I have to make up for that somehow."

"Well, that's bullshit, Addie," Billy replies as he limps a little closer to her. Tentatively, he leans his forehead to rest against hers, watching the blurry shape of her eyes fluttering closed. "I get it, sweetheart, but you don't gotta apologise for carin'. This is on me, too. I got so pissed off with the fuckin' eggs, it just– I think all this anger and frustration has been sitting dormant in me for so long and it just took one small thing... but I shouldn't have shouted, not like that. I'm sorry, Adeline."

He lets out a sigh as Adeline places a hand on his chest, fingers drumming slowly over his heart.

"We're okay," she breathes, drawing back and scrunching her nose. "Just don't do it again."

"Yes, ma'am."

Adeline's small hands cup his cheeks just like they had done this morning. The same love seeps from her fingertips and Billy doesn't know how the fuck he could lose his temper with the sweet, gorgeous woman who adores him so much.

"I think this is the part where you kiss me," Adeline whispers and Billy breathes out, relief exuding from his lungs as he drops his crutch to the ground and pulls her towards him with his good arm.

"I love you."

"I love you too, Billy. If you need me to back off, at any point, please tell me. I don't wanna fight with you again."

"I will, promise. We'll be alright, sweet girl."

Adeline gives a small nod of agreement before nosing along Billy's cheek. The cool tip of her nose tickles over his skin as slow, soft breaths are exchanged between them until Billy encases her top lip between his own, his tongue immediately sliding along the seam of her lips and into her mouth. He takes his time, there's no rush as he feels her out and savours the sweet taste of her after the bitter pill he swallowed earlier.

From there, the kiss becomes an array of soft touches and small whispers. Adeline chuckles against his lips as she bites down gently and Billy gasps, pinching her waist in teasing retaliation. She presses another kiss against the corner of his mouth, trailing her lips along his jaw, and Billy's about to slip his hand down to her ass and tug her harder to his body when she pulls away breathlessly with flushed cheeks and a coy smile, her bottom lip caught under her teeth. When she casually passes him a carrot and gestures for him to feed the horse like they weren't just making out a second ago, Billy can't help but bark out a laugh.

As they work to feed the horses chunks of carrot, the stable grows quiet; just soft huffs and the odd clop of hooves on the ground as each horse moves to greet them in turn. At the last stall in the row, Billy watches Adeline stroke down the length of the horse's nose, this one white and speckled grey with eyes that seem to bore into Billy's soul, and he takes a breath as he prepares to bring up the one subject they've been actively avoiding for the last month.

"Stan told me Rex is still coming to the tracks," he says and when

Adeline only responds with a quick glance in his direction he continues. "He gets turned away, hauled out if he refuses to leave but he's not ashamed to show his face. He's been questioned by the committee too but apparently he's not admitted to anything."

"Doesn't surprise me," Adeline replies like it's the outcome she was expecting anyway, no matter the damage Rex caused. Billy sighs and feeds the last carrot in the tub to the horse, who snuffles and turns away as soon as the food is gone.

"We'll be ready," he says, "when the time comes and we have to face the music. I won't let him get away with it, Adeline."

"I know." She loops her arm through his and leans her head on his shoulder. "You wanna see some more of the ranch?"

Billy is about to reply when something rustles in the far corner of the stables, behind bales of hay and bags of feed. He doesn't think anything of it at first, and Adeline hasn't even noticed, but then he hears the tiniest, muffled cry and Adeline's head shoots up too.

"Did you hear that?"

Billy nods slowly. "Sounded like it came from over there."

Hesitantly, Adeline makes her way over to the back of the stables, quiet as a mouse so they don't lose the soft whine sound to her footsteps across the straw-covered floor. Billy can't do much else but watch on.

"Can you see anything?" He asks as he hobbles forward a little so he can get a better look. Just as Adeline shakes her head, another pops out from behind a hay bale. Ginger fur, the lightest parts tinged with dirt, and the roundest eyes Billy's ever seen appear before them.

"*Oh.*" The cat is tiny, shaking as it stares them both down. "Hi, little one."

Adeline crouches down, practically on her hands and knees as she slowly approaches the kitten.

"Careful, baby. Don't scare it," Billy whispers and Adeline glares at him over her shoulder until her lips involuntarily curl into a smile and her shoulders shake as she huffs out a quiet laugh. The cat watches their interaction curiously.

"Come on," Adeline coos, "we're not gonna hurt you. Where did you come from, huh?"

"Do you reckon it got separated from the rest of the litter?"

"Most likely."

With a tilt of its head, the orange fur ball takes an unsure step forward, yowling as it goes. Adeline reaches a hand out, tapping lightly on the ground until the kitten gains enough confidence to launch forward and swat its paw at her wiggling fingers. Billy's heart bursts as Adeline plays with the tiny animal, her whole face lit up with something so pure and unadulterated. In this small moment, he sees his whole future with her; a picture perfect image of where they'll be in five years time. Their own house, a baby or two. Everything. Billy wants it all with her.

He's pulled out of his reverie by Adeline giggling, refocusing to find her with bright eyes and a beaming smile, the kitten now carefully cradled in her arms.

"So," she says, giddy as anything. "I guess we have a cat now."

thirty-one

ADELINE
August 4th, 1975

ADELINE WATCHES WREN MANIPULATE BILLY'S ARM FROM her spot in the corner, curled up in the tatty armchair with a book sitting open on her lap. She hasn't taken in a single word in the last hour, instead, she's been silently observing and wincing every time Billy does.

"How's that? Wren asks, gently stretching Billy's arm upwards.

"Kinda hurts in my shoulder," he replies quietly, his eyes screwed shut. His hand rises no further than the top of his head and his arm remains bent at the elbow. Wren presses gently on the spot just above his bicep.

"There?"

"Yep, right on the money, Wren. You can let go now," Billy rushes out and Wren laughs as she lowers his arm back to his side. Adeline tracks the movement. The weakness of Billy's left arm is glaringly obvious compared to his right; skinny and slow still despite the weeks of physical therapy.

"What about your elbow? I noticed you're struggling to

straighten it," Wren says, her nimble fingers quick to massage the joint.

Billy exhales a long and heavy breath as she works her way up to his bicep and eventually his shoulder, easing the muscle around the metal plates in his arm. He has three; one up towards his shoulder where the most damage was caused, one just below his elbow and a small one in his wrist. Billy's body has adapted well to them so far and he's making progress as quickly as anyone expects him to be, quicker even, despite the aches and stiffness. Adeline massages his arm most nights, but there's no denying Wren has a certain knack for releasing the tension from his limb.

Adeline wishes she could do more. The guilt she harbours always forces itself to the forefront of her mind whenever she sees the struggle of his recovery. It doesn't matter how many times Billy tells her the crash wasn't her fault, that even if Rex didn't hold some kind of vendetta against them, he was still a reckless driver. It was only a matter of time before he caused an accident.

"Elbow's fine but the muscle just above it aches if I try to straighten it any further," Billy tells Wren as she fishes out her little tube of miracle pain relief gel from her bag.

"You're gonna need to work on that," she replies, squeezing out a little gel and warming it in her hands before she rubs it liberally over Billy's arm. "I'll give you some new stretches and hopefully the muscle will become a little more malleable in time."

"In time," Billy repeats with a grouchy, heavy sigh. "It's already been three months."

Adeline has lost count of how many times she's heard him ask Wren whether she knows when he'll be cleared to drive again. Today is no different. Usually, he'll then mope around for an hour after the session when she tells him she's not qualified to make that call. Adeline will find him down in the stables, lying in the hay with the cat – who they've affectionately named Pancake – on his chest pawing at him like she's kneading dough. Actually, she finds him down in the stables most days, walking in to him grumbling at the little ball of ginger fur as if she understands everything he's saying. It's cute. Billy grumbles when Adeline tells him that too.

"You have a hospital appointment soon, Billy. They'll x-ray your arm again and have a better idea of how it's healing than I do," Wren says kindly as she begins packing up her things.

"Alright," Billy responds, agreeable despite the frown still etched onto his face. "Thanks, Wren. I do appreciate everything you're doing– driving out here, putting up with my grumpy ass."

Wren laughs, settling her hand gently on Billy's good arm. "It's easy to put up with when you're making such good progress," she says. "You're determined, not all my clients are."

"And you get to see Stan when he's here," he teases and Wren's cheeks flush pink.

"And I get to see Stan. Speaking of, is he down at–" Billy coughs obnoxiously, cutting her off as his gaze darts to Adeline and back.

Weird, Adeline thinks as her eyes fall back to the words she's read twenty times over already.

"Thanks again, Wren," Billy says pointedly.

"See you next time, Addie. Make sure he keeps up with the new exercises please!" Wren calls as she's effectively pushed out into the hall. Pancake leaps from her spot lounging in the sun at the sudden movement, following after Billy. With the room quiet again, Adeline manages to read for a few minutes before he reappears. She watches him over the pages of her book as he hooks his sling back over his shoulder and securely adjusts it to his arm, still shirtless from his session and allowing her to see just how good the Georgia sun has been to him. The work he's doing on the ranch shows too, in his good arm – and the rest of him. Adeline catches her lip under her teeth as she shamelessly gawks at him.

Billy's oblivious to her stare as he potters around the living room, humming to himself. He straightens out the cushions on the couch and collects Wren's used glass from the side table, muttering under his breath as he uses his thumb to wipe away the damp watermark it leaves on the wood. A soft pout forms on Adeline's lips as she admires him. For all his flaws, of which there are few (although he claims to have a list as long as his arm), Billy Brooks is a one-of-a-kind love; a rarity amongst men in this day and age. How Adeline got so lucky she'll never know but her love for him fills her heart and then some, bursting over the edges and keeping her alive.

Billy ambles into the kitchen, still humming, still completely unaware that Adeline is watching his every move. She only tears her eyes away when she can't see him anymore, the words of her book blurring in her vision as she listens to the water running in the sink and the quiet squeak of the dish sponge against the glass.

"You okay over there, Tinkerbell?" Billy appears in the doorway, cheek dimpled under his ever-growing beard as he sports a lazy smile. His hair is even longer now too, at a length where soft tendrils fall in his face every so often and Adeline has the pleasure of tucking them back behind his ears.

"Hmm?" She hums as she closes her book and slides it onto the coffee table before making her way over to him.

"You looked like you were about to cry," Billy replies, his tone hushed.

"Just thinking about how much I love you." Adeline leans into Billy's touch as his fingers glide over her jaw and he cradles her cheek. He kisses her softly, plush lips enveloping hers with a gentle hum of satisfaction. He pulls back slowly, leaving a series of lingering kisses until he ends up looking down at her with a certain fondness that his gaze often carries for her. Wrapping his arm around her middle, Billy holds her close and rests his chin on the crown of her head.

"How are you feeling about everything?" Adeline mumbles into his chest. He's clammy from the heat but she doesn't mind as her cheek sticks to his skin, her senses overcome with the light saltiness and fresh scent that is so uniquely Billy.

He presses his lips into her hair as he murmurs, "Never better."

"*Billy.*"

"I'm coping, sweet girl. Do I wish I was the epitome of good health? Sure. But I'm coming to terms with the fact that I'm not, I know I won't be for a while and that's okay."

"You know you can tell me anything, right? I won't hate you if you say you're sick of this place. Or if you'd rather go back to New York, we can do that."

"I'm happy being wherever you are. You're all I need." Charming no matter the circumstances, Billy always seems to know what to say and Adeline relents with a beaming smile.

"Okay, if you say so."

"I know so," Billy retorts, "in fact, I have a feeling I'm gonna be happy for the rest of my life."

"You seem pretty confident about that."

"Well, I figured you weren't planning on getting rid of me anytime soon."

"Not at least for another few years," Adeline says. She tilts her head back to look up at him, pouting, and Billy indulges her with another kiss.

"Good to know," he says, "I love you."

"Eh. You're okay, I guess," she shrugs with a grin, yelping and giggling when Billy pinches her on the hip. They fall quiet after that; Adeline's cheek presses to Billy's chest again, his good arm holding her tightly. She shivers as his fingers dip under the hem of her shirt and tickle over the soft curves of her waist. Minutes stretch by as they stand in the doorway to the living room, until they're interrupted by Pancake, bored in the hall and slinking her way between their legs. The little belled collar they bought for her jingles as she moves and Billy chuckles warmly, letting Adeline go in favour of the little cat. "Oh, I see how it is."

"Can't have this lil girl missin' out on the love, Tinkerbell," Billy grins before he directs his cooing to Pancake instead, "can we, cutie?"

The orange tabby purrs in response, nudging Billy's jaw with her head. Adeline has always thought that she'll be well into her thirties before she ever decides to settle down but watching Billy with Pancake makes her think she could get used to living like this. The pause in their hectic lives, the chance to stay in one place for a prolonged period of time, she hasn't had that in a while. But she knows Billy is restless, itching to resume life on the road.

Pancake's affection for Billy is short-lived. She wriggles free and finds her spot in the sun again, stretching all the way out in the strip of light so the rays make her marmalade fur glow.

"Yeah, I'd rather lie in the sun too," Adeline says, scrunching her nose when Billy narrows his eyes. The sparkle that's ever-present shines in the blues of his irises and eventually, his mouth twitches into a smile he can't hold back. "Lunch?"

"Lunch," he agrees, hot on her heels as they step into the kitchen. Adeline opens the pantry door and stares at the shelves, hoping the grocery shopping she's been meaning to do has miraculously done itself.

"Any ideas?" She says over her shoulder as she moves to the other side of the kitchen and reaches up into the snack cupboard. No response comes but then she feels Billy presses himself to her back, every ounce of his sharpness and softness pushed up against her. He moves her hair to the side and nuzzles into the curve of her neck. Nose brushing up and over the sensitive skin just below her ear as he breathes her in, Billy groans, so deep and rumbly in his chest that it reverberates through her.

"Somethin' sweet," he hums and his teeth graze over her shoulder, her shirt dulling the bite as he nips over the cotton. "You maybe?"

His mouth is hot over her neck as he drags his teeth over her thudding pulse, teasing and sucking before he covers the mark he's surely left behind with a wet slide of his tongue. Adeline giggles, low and breathless, as Billy skims his hand down her side and bunches up her shirt. He squeezes her waist before dipping his hand under the waistband of her shorts and Adeline is quick to help him out as she tugs the other side down over her hips and ass and shimmies out of them, kicking them to the side. She turns to face him, her back against the kitchen counter as he cages her in. The very tips of her fingers dance over the tanned, firm planes of his stomach and Billy sucks in a breath. Adeline will never get over the way he reacts to her touch, the gentlest of grazes over his skin eliciting sounds from him that makes her dizzy, makes it hard to believe *she's* the one who does that to him.

Billy wedges his thigh between hers and gently kicks them apart. He smirks as he draws a line down her side with two fingers, over her hip and over her panties. The gentle caress sends a soft fizz through Adeline's belly.

"So wet already, baby," Billy whispers like it's a secret, stroking over the damp silk of her underwear.

"Billy," Adeline whines, drawing out his name as she pulls him closer, chests flush, and kisses him. Slow and warm, her tongue explores his mouth, the taste of his morning coffee and cinnamon toast still lingering. Billy fills the kiss with small sighs and uttered words that get lost with each swipe of tongue and nip of teeth.

When they get a breath, Adeline hovers her lips over his, not wanting to stray too far. A kiss to the edge of his mouth, up to his cheeks as her fingernails rake through his beard. Adeline whimpers quietly, impatient to feel the way it scratches her thighs up.

"Take me upstairs?" She asks, breathless and frowning when Billy shakes his head.

"I think right here will do," he says, nonchalant as he draws back to look at her with wide, dark pupils and an appraising sweep of his eyes over her body. "Yeah, right here will work. Turn around, sweetheart."

Adeline spins, anticipation thrumming through her as Billy presses in close until she can feel the hard line of his cock against her ass. His hand slides around to her front, slipping into her panties with a fervent determination and no preamble. Slick and hot, his fingers tease at her entrance and skim over her clit. Billy flicks the swollen bud gently and Adeline's whole body jolts.

"*Oh!*"

A chuckle rumbles out of Billy behind her, his breath warm on her neck. He mouths at the skin, wet kisses and biting teeth that leave Adeline's head in a spin. He slips his hand out of her underwear, too soon for Adeline's liking, sliding his palm up her body. Her shirt bunches up, cool air hitting her belly as Billy squeezes the soft flesh of her breasts with firm fingers.

"Fuck, I wanna get my mouth on you properly," he murmurs, "hop up on the counter, Tinkerbell."

He steps back to give her room. Their movements feel rushed, overly eager, as Adeline lifts herself up onto the worktop, ungracefully pushing things out of the way as she shuffles back. In front of her, Billy deftly unbuttons his pants with one hand, shuffling them down his thighs and kicking them off haphazardly. Adeline takes that as her cue to strip too. Their clothes are lost to the kitchen, strewn over chairs and lying in doorways until they're both giggling, giddy and naked. Billy is fully hard, cock resting against his belly and already, a pearl of pre-cum sits pretty on the tip. Adeline wastes no time, reaching for it, wrapping her hand around his heavy shaft.

"Uh-uh," Billy chides, his voice breaking as Adeline strokes him slowly. "Hands off, Tinkerbell. I'm starved."

He pries her hand from him, linking their fingers together instead. His eyes travel the length of her as if he's trying to work out where to start. There's so much love and desire in his gaze, her cheeks grow hot, no doubt pink down to her chest where her heartbeat thunders. When he makes up his mind, Billy crashes his mouth to hers, slanting so perfectly over each other as he takes her top lip between his. All hot breaths and slick tongues, Adeline's mouth opens up to let him in, deepening the kiss with a guttural moan. She sighs, taking in a deep breath as Billy works his way down the swell of her breasts, teeth and tongue marking their territory across her skin. It feels like heaven and Adeline's back arches as he wraps his lips around her pebbling nipples, catching them between his teeth and tugging gently.

"Fuck. *Billy...*" His name comes out as a breathy whimper and her hand finds his hair, long enough now to grip tightly, pulling the strands and pushing his head lower. Billy groans loudly and peers up with a wolfish grin from where he's busy drawing shapes with his tongue across her sternum.

"So impatient, sweet girl. Tell me where you want me." She

pushes him down again and Billy takes the chance to drag his tongue slowly over her soft belly. He lets out a delighted hum like she's the best thing he's ever tasted. "Words, Addie," he reminds her as he leaves a warm kiss over her belly button.

"Just fuckin eat me out, Billy," she says, exasperated, before she smiles and adds a sweet little, "please."

Billy laughs, the kind that lights up his whole face. His eyes always go a little fond when she's the one who made him laugh and Adeline's insides turn to goop. He doesn't leave her in anticipation any longer, hand leaving hers to grip her hip, holding her still as he presses open mouthed kisses to the crease where her thigh meets her hip. The roughness of his beard is delicious against her skin, leaving a dull burn and a prickling tingle in its wake until the hot breaths over her cunt become a hot mouth, devouring her like she's his last meal. Lips wrapped around her clit, the hums and moans growling in his throat reverberate through her body.

Adeline's grip on his hair tightens and Billy tenses his tongue, fucking her with it. Shaking and legs tense, she's dizzy with the intensity of it all. Ears filled with her own soft gasps and quiet curses that mingle with the wet sounds of Billy's mouth on her.

"So fuckin' sweet. Really hittin' the spot, baby," he murmurs, mouth tugged into a boyish smirk when he comes up for air.

Billy's fingers join his mouth and Adeline becomes lost in her state of euphoria. The beginnings of her climax slowly surge through her, a gentle tingle of warmth that grows stronger with each controlled flick of Billy's tongue and a hum of pleasure over her clit. When she comes, loud and unabashedly, he has two fingers knuckle deep in her pussy and his mouth latched onto her sensitive bud as he works her through it. Billy curls his fingers, hitting her sweet spot and he drags it out for so long, Adeline is convinced he's trying to coax two orgasms out of her. It's a welcome relief when he backs up, happily licking his lips.

"Holy shit," she breathes, chest heaving as Billy crawls back up over her. His beard is glossy with saliva and her slick, lips pink and swollen as he lowers his mouth to hers.

"See how sweet you are?" He whispers, "I'm the luckiest man in the world."

"Shut up," Adeline giggles. If her skin wasn't already pink and hot to the touch, she'd be blushing even more. Kissing him again, she reaches for his cock. "How about I help you with this, and then we make some real food?"

Billy hums against her lips, eyes bright and blurred in her vision.

"Luckiest. Man," he reiterates, kissing the exasperated groan right out of Adeline's mouth.

thirty-two

BILLY

BILLY IS A TERRIBLE LIAR. HIS EYELID TWITCHES AND HE sweats like he's just run five miles. He's amazed he's gotten away with this for so many weeks, but when Adeline thinks he's been hiding out in the stables for hours on end, he's actually been sneaking down to see Myles for secret meetings about Adeline's birthday. He usually takes Pancake with him because she's weirdly obsessed with the goofy ranch hand and, so far, Adeline is none the wiser. She's quite content spending her days sunbathing in the yard, baking and tending to the horses out in the paddock.

When Billy knocks on Myles' door and lets himself in today he's greeted by everyone but Myles. He's a little late to the party having kept Adeline *occupied* while Myles and Wren directed cars through the ranch to the coach house, and now Adeline is showering and napping before dinner so everything is going to plan.

"Hey, B!" Gabe calls from Myles' kitchen where he's tag-teaming the sandwich making with Norah.

"Hey," Billy replies as he lingers in the doorway. Pancake leaps from his arms and runs straight to where the goods are, brushing herself against Gabe's legs and purring in hopes of a piece of lunch meat.

"Little flirt," Gabe mutters but his voice goes up an octave and he coos his next words at the cat. "You know it works too, don't you? Here you go, cutie." Beside him, Norah rolls her eyes as Gabe crouches down with a piece of ham bigger than Pancake's face. Billy leaves them to it and goes back to find Stan in the living room.

"Congrats on the win, Stanley," he grins, ruffling Stan's hair. He earns a groan in response but Stan is on a winning streak so Billy really doesn't care if he embarrasses his friend, he's proud of him. "Where's Myles?"

"He went into town to pick up the cake and any last minute supplies," Stan informs him. He's stringing paper bunting on to twine, each triangle of construction paper adorned with a different letter to spell out 'HAPPY BIRTHDAY ADDIE' in Billy's neatest writing. Wren is beside him, making sure the twine doesn't tangle and stealing kisses every so often. Billy's never seen Stan happier.

"Okay, good. Michael gets in early tomorrow morning, right?" Billy checks, running a hand through his hair. Planning a surprise birthday picnic is stressful. Even more so when it's for the woman he loves and he feels like he's got some big shoes to fill on the birthday celebration front.

"Yep. Patrick and Toby are arriving this evening and–"

"My family are flying in midmorning tomorrow," Billy finishes. With food being prepared and decorations being made, he realises he only has one more thing he needs to figure out as he runs through the to-do list in his head. He's positive Norah can read his mind as she abandons her place at the sandwich-making station and pulls him gently into the corner of the room.

"Have you decided when you're gonna do it yet?" Her perfectly shaped eyebrows furrow with uncertainty, the same looks she gave him when he told her his plans three weeks ago and she had cornered him like a mama bear in response. It didn't take a lot to convince her that Billy had never been more sure about anything in his life, and he had made his intentions clear to Michael, anyway. He just needed Norah's help choosing the ring.

Everything they've been through – the crash, the stuff with Rex – all it's done is confirm what Billy knew all along. Adeline is *it* for him. He wants her in his life forever, until they're old and grey and sitting on their porch reminiscing about their lives now, a few kids and a lifetime of love behind them.

"Nope," he says in answer to Norah's question, and then after a beat, "I'm not rushing into this am I?"

"You're the love of her life, Billy. And I *know* you – more intimately than I'd like to be honest–"

"Hey, you said I was the best sex you'd ever had!" Billy pouts.

"And then I met Gabe." Billy crinkles his nose at that. "But that's not the point," Norah continues, "my point is, you were miserable with Delilah, and you were miserable to be around most of the time–"

"Nor, if this is your idea of a pep talk, you might wanna get some practice in," Billy interjects.

"Will you let me finish?" Norah admonishes him and Billy nods sheepishly. "Thank you. As I was saying, you were miserable. And now, despite everything, I've never seen you happier, and I've never seen Addie happier either. I think you're soulmates, as fucking cheesy as that is."

"You really think that?"

"I think," Norah says, reaching to give Billy's arm a gentle squeeze, "that you were drawn to her from the moment you saw her. I think she set something alight in you that made you see that you deserved better. And Billy, you *do* deserve this. I know how your brain works. You're worthy of her and of whatever life you end up building together." Billy feels his cheeks burn. He forgot how sincere Norah can be.

"So I should propose?" He asks, tone light as his lips lift into a smirk that makes Norah poke him.

"Maybe let me warn Addie about how fucking obtuse you can be first. Yes, Billy. You should propose."

Billy nods. *Good. Okay, well that's that then,* he thinks as he huffs out a long, apprehensive breath, cheeks rounded like a chipmunk. He's never been so nervous in his life. Where sleepless nights used to be spent running through racetracks in his head, he now replays various ways in which he proposes to Adeline and all the ways it can go wrong. In his head, her saying no is the least of his worries, especially when he gets to the scenario where he falls off a cliff before she can answer. He'd never propose on the edge of a cliff anyway, stupid brain.

"Just don't break her heart, Brooks," Norah warns but it's warm, playfully light as she kisses him on the cheek and goes back to Gabe.

"Wasn't planning on it," Billy whispers to the empty air. Luckily, he's distracted for the next couple of hours, getting stuck in with birthday prep. Myles returns with the cake, more food and supplies. He dumps bags of chips, balloons, cookies and ice cream – which he says are specifically for making ice cream sandwiches – onto the kitchen counter. Nobody has the heart to tell him that they'll probably melt before they get eaten in the 86-degree heat.

Patrick and Tobias arrive earlier than planned, settling in for the tight squeeze at Myles' little coach house with everyone else. No one seems to mind though. Already there are piles of blankets and pillows strewn about the living room and the biggest pot of chilli is sitting on the burner, simmering slowly as the afternoon wears on. It's just before Billy sets off for the stables with Pancake, who has been overfed and loved-on all afternoon, that Tobias pulls him out into the yard with Patrick.

"I have a proposition for you, for both of you," he says and Billy's eyes slide to Patrick who shrugs, clearly just as in the dark. "I want you to mentor Peters."

"Holy shit, are you serious?!" Patrick all but yells, beaming. Billy on the other hand–

"You want me to... mentor him?"

"Yes, Brooks. You're the best we have and I know you're out of commission right now but Patrick is on track to race next year and I think you could really help steer him in the right direction."

Billy raises an eyebrow. There's a sliver of envy snaking its way through him as his gaze lands on Patrick again, the gut-wrenching feeling of being replaced by a newer, younger model.

"So you want me to train my replacement."

Tobias sighs. "Look, no one is replacing you, Billy. I expect you back in the race as soon as you're ready but we don't know when that'll be. I've spoken to Adeline, there's a practice track here and Michael's old car. Gabe fixed it up, it's good to go."

Of course there is, Billy thinks, there's a reason Michael was the best driver of his generation.

"I..."

"Listen, I've not seen you for two months and even I can tell you're getting restless so I'm offering you a temporary solution." Tobias pats Billy's cheek affectionately. "The choice is yours."

"Can I think about it? No offence, Peters."

"None taken," the young driver laughs and Billy watches his eyes carefully before determining that Patrick is definitely high. Billy hopes he bought more to share.

"You can think about it," Tobias says and then adds quietly, "I have an update on the Rex situation too, but we'll leave that until after the birthday celebrations, shall we?"

Billy nods in agreement, "thanks, Toby."

He wakes early the next morning, leaving Adeline to sleep as he showers, shaves and dresses in a loose shirt and light wash jeans. He places the bouquet of flowers he'd bought two days ago, and miraculously kept alive, on top of the dresser and makes sure the card tucked inside is visible. It's brimming with soft pink roses and lilacs among the greenest leaves and baby's breath, all flowers that screamed Adeline when he took a trip to the florist in town with Myles.

The sun is already bright in the sky when he chances a quick peek behind their bedroom curtain, casting everything in that soft morning glow that he loves so much. Billy takes slow, cautious steps back across the room and plucks Pancake from the indent on his pillow that she occupied the moment he got out of bed. She lets out a quiet yowl in protest but quickly settles in his arms and Billy glances back at Adeline once he's at the door. The thin sheets drape over every dip and curve of her body like she's a Grecian statue, and her hair fans out over both pillows as she snores softly.

It takes everything in him not to strip down and slide back beneath the sheets. If his plan didn't involve Adeline getting the sleep she so desperately needs, he would wake her up slowly with his mouth, kiss his way down the softness of her belly, and skim his hand down her gorgeous frame until he could only peer up through his eyelashes to watch the way her lips part and her eyes flutter open. He can hear the quiet little gasp, the soft *oh* of pleasure that would escape her. Instead, he lingers a moment longer as she turns over in bed and then slips out of the house and heads down to the empty barn across the ranch with Pancake tucked into the front of his shirt.

Already, the air is stiflingly hot. The paddock is empty and Billy isn't surprised by Myles' decision to keep the horses inside today, it's only going to get hotter. The shade of the barn is welcome, dark and cool, the only warmth comes from the broken streams of sunlight that filters through the cracks in the old wood roof. Stan and Gabe are already setting up the pasting tables and covering them with red and white chequered table cloths he borrowed from his parents, the edges lined with a lace trim his mom sewed on herself. Later, they'll carry down the food and drink in coolers but for now, he helps blow up balloons and hang the bunting across the walls as best he can with one hand until the place resembles the kitsch little park picnic of Adeline's dreams. Just outside, Billy throws blankets down onto the dry grass and allocates a clashing parasol to each one before he checks his watch and figures it's probably about time to head to the stable.

That's where Adeline finds him just twenty minutes later, with Pancake on his good shoulder as he feeds Maple slices of apple. He grins as her light footsteps approach, crunching on the dusty track before she appears in the doorway.

"Good afternoon, sleepyhead."

"Hey, golden boy," she beams as she reaches him, rising up onto her tiptoes to kiss him softly. Her fingers brush over his cheeks and Billy can feel the small frown appear on her face as she realises he's gone from a thick beard to neatly shadowed stubble.

"It'll grow back," Billy chuckles, "I was too hot."

"Yeah you were," Adeline flirts, humming as she kisses him again and murmurs nonsense against his lips.

"Did you have a good sleep?"

"Mmm, the best," she replies as a sleepy little smile blooms over her lips as she reaches up to give Pancake a scratch. Billy knows he's looking at her like she hangs the stars and the moon every night just for him. He thinks about the box hidden in the duffel bag under their bed, thinks about going back to get it before they head down to the barn but the moment doesn't feel quite right and something tells him he'll know when it does.

"I'm almost done here," he says, holding out another piece of apple in the palm of his hand for Maple to take. "You wanna go for a walk before lunch?"

There's a look in Adeline's eye that suggests she knows he's up to something, a little glint that's daring him to crack, but Billy holds steadfast and smiles back with a cheeky little rise of his eyebrows. Adeline sighs, accepting that she'll have to wait a little longer with a nod as she reaches for a handful of apple.

When they're nearly there, just coming over the crest of the hill in the smallest field as the barn comes into view, Billy glances down at Adeline. She's tucked under his right arm and watching their feet as they walk, oblivious.

"You might wanna look up, sweet girl," he murmurs and Adeline draws her gaze to the scene in front of her – to their friends and family gathered in front of the ramshackle little barn. The softest of gasps escapes her lips and *this* is what Billy has been looking forward to. All the planning, all the sneaking away to craft decorations and run into town with Myles, all the coordinating to get everyone to the ranch; it all boils down to the look on Adeline's face right now. Her lips part, surprise and joy and wonder etched in her smile and the laugh that rushes out of her mouth.

"*Billy!*" Her voice wobbles a little, eyes creasing at the corners as she blinks up at him then squeezes them shut in disbelief.

"Happy birthday, Addie," he whispers, closing the gap to kiss her. Soft and sweet. "Come on, everyone's been waiting for you to wake up."

Adeline heads straight for her dad then Billy watches her bounce from picnic blanket to picnic blanket to greet everyone. He edges closer, gratefully taking a beer from Stan as Pancake wriggles free from his shirt and pads straight to Rosie and Patrick. They're engrossed in each other completely until the little ginger cat steals their attention by clambering into Rosie's lap.

"You're all very sneaky," Adeline says to Norah as they settle on the blanket. "When did you get here?"

"Yesterday. We all stayed with Myles."

"*All* of you?"

"Well, the Brooks gang and your dad got here this morning, but everyone else had a big sleepover," Norah responds before popping a chip in her mouth.

"I bet that was fun," Adeline laughs and Billy snorts when the glare Norah shoots them both in return says that it was not fun at all.

"Toby snores. Loudly."

The rest of the afternoon passes by in a haze. At some point the sun gets too much and everyone relocates into the barn. Someone sets up a wireless radio and a makeshift dance floor and Billy spends forever twirling Adeline around, stopping only for giggle-filled kisses and sips from ice cold bottles of lemonade, dripping wet from the cooler. Patrick sidles up to them on their hundredth spin of the dance floor – someone switched to an old school radio station and they've been attempting to swing dance and Lindy Hop around the barn – and he slips Adeline two perfectly rolled joints as a birthday present. She tucks them into her bra and kisses him softly on the cheek. Billy chuckles as Patrick leaves them, rosy from his neck to his ears.

"You're trouble, Tinkerbell."

"I did warn you I might be, you're the one who stuck around to find out." Adeline grins and then her smile softens as the swing band playing on the radio transitions into something slower, a little more intimate. She steps in closer, pressing herself against his front, mindful of his arm in its sling . "Thank you, baby. I can't remember the last time I had a birthday like this."

"It was nothing," Billy shrugs as they sway languidly to the music. Adeline's lips find his jaw, mouth meandering and leaving soft kisses until her head fits perfectly into the curve of his neck. "I'd do all this and more for you Addie, you know that."

It's 3am when they're finally curled up together, happy but exhausted. That's when Billy gets the feeling in his gut. It's when his palms clam up but in a good way and his heart pounds with excitement instead of nerves, when he presses a kiss into Adeline's hair and pries himself away from her hold for just a moment to reach under the bed to this duffel bag.

"What're you doing?" Adeline mumbles sleepily, her hands pawing for him. Billy feels the content sigh that breezes through her parted lips when he falls back onto the bed and she clings to him once again.

"Asking you to marry me," he replies in a whisper.

"What?"

Billy flicks the ring box open with his thumb and he hears Adeline's breath catch in the darkness, he feels her heart matching the pounding of his against his side.

"Marry me, sweet girl?"

thirty-three

ADELINE
August 5th, 1975

BILLY'S EYES HAVE NEVER LOOKED MORE BLUE THAN THEY do flitting nervously over Adeline's face. His Adam's apple bobs as he gulps, loud in the heavy silence of the bedroom and her gaze falls from his eyes to his throat to the ring box in his hand. For once, all she feels is peace; never more safe or more loved than she does with Billy.

He's the one thing in her life that always makes sense when everything else is so up in the air. He made sense when they didn't even know each other but somehow her gaze always found his across a crowded room. He made sense when he turned up on her doorstep all those months ago and something between them shifted, clicked into place. Billy Brooks is her future, that much she's sure of, that much she's known since the beginning. Their souls are tied together in ways she didn't even realise were possible.

And so, it's the easiest decision she's ever had to make.

"Yes."

"Y-yes?"

"Yes, Billy. I'll marry y–" Adeline's words are lost as Billy's lips crash to hers in a bruising kiss, slightly chapped and still tasting of beer and birthday cake. He nips and sucks between sweet pecks and slow sweeps of his tongue as if he doesn't quite know how he wants to kiss her, but as long as he is then that's just fine. The ring is discarded somewhere on the bed as he cradles her jaw in his right hand and Adeline leans into him. She wants to be in his space, all-encompassing, as close as she can be to the man who looks at her like she's the eighth wonder of the world. Like she's the sun and the moon and the stars all at once.

Her fingers dance over Billy's bicep, up his neck and through his hair, and he shivers, groaning as she catches his bottom lip under her teeth. He whispers her name and '*my girl forever*' between kisses, so sweet and soft it makes Adeline's insides melt like butter. She wants to remember this feeling for the rest of her life.

"*Fuck*– wait! Shit," Billy mumbles suddenly, tearing his mouth away.

"What? What is it?" Adeline's eyes dart over his left arm as Billy runs his other hand through his hair, tugging at the ends.

"I was so excited I forgot to do my big speech."

"*Billy!*" She swats him on the thigh over the bedcovers.

"Hey! Ouch! What was that for?"

"I thought something was really wrong, you dumbass!"

"It is," Billy says, face deadpan as he shifts his body so his weight is all on his right arm and he ends up hovering over her. He's trained his features to be hard, stoic but clearly struggling to keep it that way as his lips twitch and his eyes sparkle. "My fiancée keeps–"

"Say it again."

"My *fiancée*–" Adeline kisses him, hands back in his soft hair, tufts sticking up at all angles. Wild bed head to match his sleepy eyes but he's never looked so handsome. She pulls him towards her until he falls, landing across her body with a soft grunt. "You gonna let me do my speech now, Tinkerbell? Let me tell you how much I love you?"

"I'd rather you showed me."

"Speech first," Billy says and his eyes glimmer to match the cheeky grin on his lips. "Then I'll make good, sweet love to you, baby." Adeline brings Billy's hand to her lips and kisses his palm, clutching his fingers with both hands.

"Okay," she whispers against his skin and Billy takes a deep breath and closes his eyes. He's thought about this, she can tell, probably written it down somewhere and memorised it. Adeline's heart thumps in anticipation.

"Adeline, we always tell each other we're made of stardust," Billy begins, "but sometimes I look at you and I think you're made of something more. You're made of things so cosmic, so far out in the universe that they're yet to be discovered.

"I've never had any doubts with you, Addie. I think I knew I could love you the moment I met you, and I knew I *did* love you after that first night in New York. That was the first time in a long time I didn't have to spend a sleepless night alone. The first time in a long time that I got to wake up to someone who was there because they wanted to be.

"I love you. I love you in the morning with puffy eyes and wild hair. I love you in the moments before a race with stolen kisses and... *other stuff*."

Adeline giggles. Her face is wet, tears streaming down her temples and onto her pillow and her jaw hurts from smiling so hard. Billy sits up, carefully straddling her legs, the sheets falling from his shoulders and pooling around his thighs. He wipes under Adeline's eyes with the pad of his thumb and leans forward to press a kiss to her sternum, mouth wandering a silky path up to her lips.

When he rises back up, his face is illuminated by the early morning sun that shines through a gap in the curtains. The dusting of new stubble over his cheeks, his straight nose and sharp jaw are all showcased around the glistening oceans that are his eyes. He looks older; the addition of lines and scars that weren't there when they met but in the glow surrounding him, he's still so gorgeous and ethereal. Billy presses his thumb gently to the centre of Adeline's bottom lip, tugging it down as he continues.

"I love you when you pout, when your lips turn down into that adorable frown, and I love you when you laugh. When your giggle is so infectious that it's the only thing I ever want to hear for the rest of my life. You've shown me what love really means and I don't think I would have survived any of this without you, sweet girl.

"I want you forever. I want you when you're angry and when you're hysterical. I want you when you're laughing and full of joy. I want you in the loud moments and the quiet moments for as long as you'll let me have you. Because you're magic, Adeline, and you've had me from day one."

He fumbles for the ring box amongst the sheets and holds it out in front of him. Adeline doesn't look down at it, doesn't even look away from his face. She's already said yes but she wants to memorise the way his lips move and his eyes look luminescent with tears in the golden morning light as he asks her again.

"So, Adeline Gold, will you be my forever girl? Will you marry me?" Adeline nods, cradles Billy's face and kisses him with everything she has. "Here, let me," Billy whispers against her lips, settling the ring box down beside him and pulling the gold band from its cushion. Adeline holds her left hand out and Billy slides the ring on in one smooth motion.

The perfect fit.

When Adeline kisses him again, it's a desperate collision of lips and tongues. Billy groans and shifts his weight forward above her as Adeline trails her fingers over the hard planes of his stomach. Her nails drag through the soft line of hair that leads to his cock, already hard and heavy against her thigh and tenting the white cotton of Billy's underwear.

"I can't believe I get to marry you," she murmurs softly as she traces the defined lines of his Adonis belt and the tips of her fingers dip just below his waistband to the base of his cock but never any further. Billy's breath catches every time; Adeline's touches are quick and light, barely brushing her fingers over his hot skin. He closes his eyes, wiggles his fingers as he blindly reaches out for her. When he finds her jaw, his palm is warm and clammy from nerves and how worked up he already is.

Adeline smiles sweetly, lip catching under her teeth. She sits up as best she can under Billy's weight, stretching to suckle and lick at the skin of his chest and along his jaw until he crowds her into the sheets and claims her mouth again. Carefully, she holds his waist and pushes him to the side. Billy slides off of her with a gentle '*oof*' breezing past his lips as he falls to the mattress.

"On your back, hot stuff."

"Yes, ma'am."

Billy scrambles to get comfortable, pillow propped up beneath his head and Adeline waits until he says he's ready before she throws a leg over him. The t-shirt of his that hangs loosely from her small frame is pulled off and thrown across the room. Billy whistles appreciatively and Adeline giggles, blushing as if it's the first time he's ever seen her like this.

"What the fuck did I do in a past life to end up here?" He mutters, half to himself. "Must've been somethin' pretty spectacular."

"Must've been," Adeline hums in agreement as she blinks down at him, lips pressed into a coy smile.

There's a moment of calm as they look at each other, flushed faces and adoring gazes. Billy winks and then his hand is on her skin, needy and hot to the touch as his palm caresses Adeline's thigh and rounds her hip to her ass, squeezing the supple flesh. She kisses him, biting and tugging as her own hands work between her and Billy to pull his boxer shorts down. Tearing away from his mouth with a breathless gasp, she shuffles backwards, and Billy grunts as his cock springs free, angry tip dripping pre-cum and bobbing against his stomach.

Adeline tenses, her stomach swooping at the sight of him. She leans down and laps across his torso with her tongue, teeth grazing over his skin and coaxing sharp breath from Billy's lips. Her name tumbles out after that, a whisper-cum-moan, as she brushes over his cock on her descent down his body. She loves how vocal he is now, unafraid to be vulnerable after years of being made to feel like his needs were unimportant. He's brazen with it as he writhes beneath her, no holding back.

"You're a fuckin' tease, Adeline," he groans out, "need your mouth on me, sweet girl. Wanna watch you suck my cock lookin' all pretty like that."

"Such a sweet talker, Brooks," Adeline laughs as she shimmies herself lower.

"Hey, don't *Brooks* me. You're gonna be a Brooks soon too!" Billy counters and the realisation of that sends a little thrill through Adeline as the early morning sun hits her back as it streams into the room, warm and reflective of the mood.

Pressing gentle kisses, just a skim of her mouth on his hips, she pulls the fabric of his boxer shorts over his knees until he kicks them off and buries his fingers in her hair. The sigh that leaves Billy's mouth when Adeline wraps her fingers around his length is one of relief. It starts as a hiss between clenched teeth and ends as a rough gasp of breath as she swallows the head of his cock, collecting the premature dribble of cum with an enthusiastic sweep of her tongue.

She moans at the taste of him, at the reflexive throb of his cock in her hand. Billy is so worked up, begging her to take him down her throat around whimpers of '*fuck me, sweet girl*' and '*I'm so in love with you*.' And Adeline, she's overflowing with it. Every little bit of Billy Brooks incites a rush of need and want and love. He can simultaneously excite her and calm her with a touch or a whisper and she adores him for it.

Adeline hums, contemplative, peering up at him through her eyelashes to see Billy's eyes squeezed shut. He's tense, anticipating her next move. She works from the base of his cock to the tip with sweet kitten licks, tiny drags of her tongue over his balls and up the bulging vein that runs along the underside. She gets the heady, clean scent of him as the tip of her nose brushes along the velvety skin. Billy whines, soft and under his breath, and Adeline decided to take him out of his misery, wrapping her lips around him again. She feels the stretch of her jaw as she takes him deeper. He's thick and long and she doesn't go down on him often enough for it to feel anywhere near natural.

Moaning around him, the vibrations tingle through her jaw and cheeks as she moves. Billy sweeps her hair up and clutches it in his hand, whimpering and mumbling incoherently. When she pushes further, swallowing his cock, his hips buck up involuntarily and Adeline splutters as he unexpectedly hits the back of her throat.

"Oh, fuck! Addie, I'm so sorry, I got carried away!" Billy's head pops up from the pillow, face flushed and his eyebrows drawn into a panicked frown. She pulls off of him with a wet pop.

"I'm okay," she pants, swallowing thickly. Billy moves to sit up but pushes him back down with a hand on his chest. "Billy, I'm fine. Just warn me next time."

"I'm sorry, sweet girl."

"Relax, baby," she whispers, scrunching her nose up as she smiles and drags her hand down to his stomach. Catching her breath, she strokes over his length and Billy's head drops back to the pillow. He lets out a shuddering moan, fingers clutching at the sheets.

"Okay, okay. Yeah, just like that, sweetheart. *Fuck* – you're such a good girl for me, Addie, so good to me–" his words cut off into a moan.

Adeline preens a little at the praise as Billy's abs tense under her palm and his cock flexes in her hand, hard and heavy. His sweet sounds and responsive touches have only fanned the flames of arousal already alight within her; body hot and panties almost see through with slick. She keeps fisting over the lower half of his cock and takes the rest of him into her mouth again, working him over until he's a babbling mess, trembling under her. It only takes a particularly languorous lap of Adeline's tongue and a gentle cup and squeeze of his balls before he comes, spilling hot and fast into her mouth with a guttural moan and a string of curse words.

"Fuck, Tinkerbell. You're a fuckin' wonder."

Adeline swallows; the salty, bitter taste lingering on her tongue as she runs it over her teeth without thinking. Giggling softly, she watches Billy trapped in his state of bliss, chest heaving and skin glistening with sweat. He takes a moment to recover, staring up at the ceiling with a sated, lopsided grin on his face, and then he reaches out his right hand to tug on Adeline's.

"Get up here, baby," he urges and Adeline doesn't have to be told twice as she falls forward, catching herself before crawling over him. Billy's fingers tangle in her hair as he pulls her down into a searing kiss. He takes his time, exploring her mouth and lapping up the taste of himself between giggles and whispers. "S'only fair that I get a taste of you now, right?"

Adeline sits up, resting her hands on his shoulders before she drags her nails down over his chest, faint pink lines appearing and disappearing over his dewy skin.

"Where d'you want me, hot stuff?"

Billy's eyes hold a mischievous glimmer, the cloudy-blue completely lost to his lust as he clenches his jaw and juts his chin out as if to say '*up here.*' Adeline's gaze goes wide.

"C'mere, sweetheart," he murmurs. It's deep and rumbly and Adeline feels the words reverberate through him to the palms of her hands.

"Billy– we haven't... you won't be able to breathe if I–" Billy fixes her with a *look.*

"I'll tap twice on your thigh if I need air, how's that sound?"

He looks so pretty lying beneath her, waiting. The more she thinks about it, about the warm, wet sensation of his mouth on her, the more she wants it, wants to give him the power and the pleasure of it. The utterly devilish grin on Billy's face as he watches the idea turn over in her head is what tips the scale, and the wink he throws her way tells Adeline he knows he's got her.

"That's my girl. Up you get."

Billy's hand slides up the inside of her thigh as she moves forward, gaze locked on the flimsy lace of her panties as he hooks them to the side when she settles over his chest.

"Two taps," she says.

"Two taps."

Adeline's stomach flips as Billy wets his lips with a swipe of his tongue and leaves it sitting idly in the corner of his mouth. Then he takes a firm hold of her waist and pulls her pussy to his face.

His mouth is hot, instantly on her like he hasn't eaten in days as he licks a long stripe through her folds and latches onto her clit. Adeline's legs feel weak already and she clenches her thighs as she presses her fingers into the headboard to keep herself upright.

"*Baby*– fuck, yes," she whines. Her back arches and Billy's hand slides up her side, cupping her breast and brushing the pad of his thumb over her nipple. His tongue is relentless, rigid and fast as his fucks her with it, groaning and mumbling into her heat until his hand leaves her chest and there's two quick taps on her thigh.

Adeline shifts her weight back, losing the sensation of his mouth.

"You taste so fuckin' sweet, Addie. Can't get enough of you," Billy babbles breathlessly. "Wanna save a bit of you for later." He rests his cheek on her thigh, grinning against her skin as Adeline's own cheeks burn hot. The cheeky grin turns into soft, warm kisses in the crevice of her thigh before Billy sucks in a breath, refilling his lungs before he dives back in.

Adeline loses herself in it this time, colours swirl behind her closed eyes as she focuses on the way she pulses against Billy's mouth. The skin between her thighs burns, the delectable scratch of his stubble over her soft flesh as her weight shifts and he drives his tongue deeper. With one hand on the headboard, her other finds its way into his hair, clutching at it to ground herself as the steady build up of her orgasm reaches its peak and comes crashing down ceremoniously.

"Billy, yes, *yes!*" She cries, "oh my–*GOD.*" Billy's name falls from her lips like a prayer as she shakes above him. She has to scramble backwards before she collapses and as she straddles his belly, Billy blinks up at her. His lips are shiny, all pink and dewy, as they curve up into a dopey smile, meeting his glazed, sleepy eyes like he's drunk on her.

"Woman of my dreams. I can't believe I get you like this," he breathes, laughing as she falls down beside him. Adeline beams back, happiness trickling through her like slow, sweet molasses.

"For the rest of our lives, baby," she whispers, capturing Billy's lips in a lazy kiss as she curls herself into his side.

When they wake up later after a much needed nap, Adeline drags herself to the kitchen to make them both coffee and happily slides back into the bed. She leans against Billy as they share a cigarette and enjoy the quiet, letting the caffeine do its job of easing them from their sleepy states. Billy tilts Adeline's face up towards him, kissing her soft and slow. Instead of beer and birthday cake, Adeline now tastes coffee, tobacco, and herself on his tongue.

They're startled out of their tangle of limbs and engagement bliss by the phone on the bedside table ringing, loud and obnoxious in the otherwise quiet room.

"Who the fuck is calling? Everyone is still here," Billy mumbles, rubbing the heel of his palm forcefully against his eyes and groaning through a yawn.

"Toby had to get a red-eye back to Cali, remember?"

"Well, if it's him, I'm telling him to fuck off. Who calls at 7am the day after a party?"

Adeline giggles and rolls her eyes, kissing Billy's cheek as she leans over him and takes the phone off the cradle. Billy sighs the moment the incessant ringing stops.

"Good morning, you've reached the Gold-Brooks residence," Adeline sings down the phone. She props her elbow up on Billy's chest, chin resting in her hand. Billy laughs and every time it's the sweetest sound she's ever heard. He crinkles his nose as Adeline holds a finger to his lips and he pulls it into his mouth, biting down gently.

"*Sweetheart–*" The soft hint of a French accent crackles down the phone and Adeline's stomach drops.

"Mom?"

Billy frowns, releasing Adeline's finger. Her hand drops to his chest, fingers curling around the strap of his sling. Suddenly, she feels like she's gasping for breath, mouth dry. When was the last time she spoke to her mother? Outside Macy's? Never on the phone, not once on the phone. Adeline doesn't even remember the last birthday they spent as a family, too young for those memories to stick.

"*Happy birthday, Addie.*"

"No."

"*Excuse me?*"

"No," Adeline breathes, lip trembling. "You don't get to do this."

Billy takes her hand, pressing a kiss to her palm. The warmth of his lips is like a balm. He keeps his mouth on her skin, another kiss to the heel, another on each tip of her fingers. His kisses cover the lines of her skin, mapping out his love, telling her he's there.

"*I'm trying to–*"

"You don't get to *try* to do anything, Stéphanie."

"*Adeline.*"

"How do you even know where I am?" Adeline demands. "I asked Dad not to tell you anything anymore."

"*Lucky guess. Adeline, I just want to talk. I just... I just want to know how you are.*"

"You don't deserve to know how I am."

"*Don't say that, sweetheart. Please. I know I've been a terrible mother, I was a terrible wife too. I know. But, please, let me make it up to you.*"

Adeline sighs out a heavy breath. This is her one chance to tell her mother what she's always wanted to say because she never wants to talk to the woman again after this. In fact, she never wants to think about the woman again. From here on out, her thoughts and the space they inhabit are off limits to her mother. Adeline wants to be able to go to New York, to a city she loves and that feels like home, without the lingering fear that the next face she may see as she steps off the subway is her mom.

"I'm not having this conversation. I'm not gonna suddenly welcome you into my life with open arms after twenty-three years and pretend that you didn't walk out on us. That's not how this works. If you must know, I'm great, Mom. Really fuckin' great. And I'm getting married. There's the life update you were so desperate for." Adeline's voice breaks on the last word and Billy's face becomes a blur of rosy cheeks and bright blue eyes as her own eyes fill with tears.

On the other end of the line Stéphanie sniffs, and Adeline wants to hang up. She wants to hang up and never talk to her mother again but a meek whisper stops her from launching the phone, cord and all, across the room.

"*Really?*"

"Yes. You're the first to know and I really fucking hate that. You don't deserve to be the first to know."

"*Congratulations, Addie.*"

"Thank you," she chokes. "I'm gonna be a great wife."

"Yeah you are, baby," Billy chimes in as he combs his fingers through Adeline's hair. His bottom lip is pushed out in a pout and his eyes are glistening.

"And I'm gonna be a fucking great mother when the time comes too. So thank you, I guess, for teaching me what not to do."

"*Adeline.*" Her name is a plea but Adeline's not listening.

"Bye, mom. Don't call me again."

Billy eases the phone from her death grip, all white knuckles and tense fingers, and places it down. Then he holds her as she folds against him, arms locked around him, legs tangled like he's the only thing keeping her together. Right now, he might just be. She seeks comfort in the gentle rise and fall of his chest and the steady beating of his heart beneath her ear. There's a knock at the door just as Adeline's eyes start to close. Billy's been humming for the past ten minutes, lulling her back into the state of calm she was so sure was lost for the day.

"I'll get it," she whispers.

Pushing herself up from the bed, she pulls on one of Billy's t-shirts and a pair of athletic shorts. She kisses him gently on the corner of his mouth and makes her way downstairs, heavy footsteps until she reaches the door and yanks it open. Her father greets her on the other side, hands tucked into the pockets of his jeans as he rocks back and forth on his feet.

"Morning, birthday girl," he beams, stepping into the hall as Adeline moves aside. She closes the door behind him and eyes him wearily. Adeline has a knack for being able to tell when her dad is hiding something, no surprise was a surprise for long when Adeline would call him out on his shifty behaviour and he would cave to her pout and puppy dog eyes. As matching hazel irises meet her own, she can't help but narrow her eyes at him.

"What does it feel like you're not just here to say happy birthday?"

Michael chuckles. "You got me. Toby called, said he couldn't get through to the ranch house."

"That'll be because I was on the phone to my mother," Adeline interjects.

"She called? I promise I didn't tell her you were here, Addie."

"I know. I know you wouldn't go against what I asked, Dad. Anyway, I handled it." She shrugs, a sad smile on her face. "What did Toby want?"

"Sunshine, the guys on the NASCAR board– well, it's the legal department, mostly – are getting impatient. They want you and Billy to make statements by next week or they're dropping everything. Rex Harlow has been a pain in their ass. He's showing up at tracks demanding to race. He picked a fight with Gabe in Nashville last month after they refused him again."

Adeline stares at him, alarmed, as white noise fills her ears and she stumbles back.

"Was Gabe okay? He never said anything about it."

"Rex was drunk. He threw a few punches; didn't land any of them. Gabe handled it how Gabe does."

Adeline sighs. Too many people have been fighting her battles recently. She hates to think how long it'll be before someone else she loves gets hurt.

"You said they want us there next week?"

"Yeah, Toby pushed for it. They'd have had you two in Daytona today if they had their way but he told them you needed more time and a week is all they would agree to. I'm sorry, sweetheart. I thought it best to tell you straight away."

"It's okay, I– it's fine," she lies. "I just–"

"He did it," Michael says suddenly.

"Huh?"

"Billy– he did it." Her father tips his head towards her left hand where it rests just below her clavicle. The pull on Adeline's lips is involuntary as she glances down.

"Oh! Yeah, this morning."

Michael grins, engulfing Adeline in a hug. Her whole body relaxes against his and she squeezes him back.

"Congratulations, sunshine," he murmurs softly into her hair, pressing a kiss to the crown of her head before letting her go.

"Thanks, Dad. Can you not tell anyone else just yet? Please?"

Michael nods. "My lips are sealed," he replies, throwing her an over the top wink. "I'm glad today has still given you something good, Addie."

"Me too," Adeline whispers.

"I'll see you at breakfast."

"Yeah. Thanks, Dad." She presses up onto her tiptoes, kissing him on the cheek as she says goodbye and closes the door. When she turns around, Billy is lingering at the bottom of the stairs. "They want us to make statements next week," she tells him.

And just like that, the world keeps turning. They've been in this bubble for weeks, months, even, and in the space of a few hours she's had to face her mother and now this.

Happy fuckin' birthday, Addie.

Adeline will be the first to admit that she goes through life with that ignorant ideal of out of sight, out of mind. Her loved ones cater to it. Knowingly or not, they protect her from the inevitable curse of over-thinking that she's so susceptible to. But she's not stupid, and she doesn't have the heart to just sit back and let her friends take the brunt of Rex's shitty behaviour.

She slumps against the wall, casting her gaze over to Billy.

They're both acutely aware that their stint of domesticity in Georgia is coming to an end. Billy's ankle is fully healed and his arm almost there, healing far better than anyone thought it would considering the slow progress of his physical therapy. At least they have a week. One week before everything gets regurgitated, heaved up just for Adeline to have to choke it back down all over again. She wants Rex to pay for what he did to them, justice for the pain he's caused and reassurance that no one will fall victim to him again. But what if she wants to stay in this little slice of heaven just a little bit more?

"You okay?" Billy murmurs, low and quiet. She's only just realised he's moved; beside her now and holding her up with his good arm.

"I will be," Adeline replies and her voice breaks. "I just want this to be over."

The rock on her ring finger catches her eye; shining and crystalline in the early morning light. The first sob breaks from her throat like the first drop of rain on a window, that one quiet patter of water before the heavens open and the glass is tearstained.

Bit by bit, reality starts to seep through the cracks Adeline has tried so hard to seal. She doesn't get to live this quiet life yet, a life she didn't even think she wanted until Billy fell into hers, and that's a harder pill to swallow than she realised.

"Okay, here's what we're gonna do, Tinkerbell," Billy says softly, taking charge as he guides her to the couch. He falls back with her and hugs her close. "We're gonna shower and put on our best clothes, everyone's gonna come here for breakfast before they have to leave and we're gonna surprise the shit out of them because I refuse to let today be anything but happy from here on out. How does that sound?"

"Good," Adeline whispers. The hairs on his bare chest tickle her nose as she presses her lips to his skin. He's warm, always so warm and soft, able to ease the tension in her bones just by being near.

"Your dad says we have a week, right? For that week, we're gonna forget about everything. We're just gonna be Billy and Adeline. We'll muck out the horses and go for walks and swim in the lake – well, I'll paddle but you can swim – and you can watch me lose my shit with Patrick."

Adeline giggles and peers up at him. "You're gonna mentor him?"

"Yeah," Billy says, running a hand through his hair. "I need to get back in a car or I'm gonna go insane, Addie."

"Good. Maybe you'll stop moping whenever Stan and Norah mention a race."

"I don't mope." Billy pouts, catching his finger under Adeline's chin as he gently lifts her lips to his in a delicate kiss. "And when we get to the hard stuff, I'm gonna be there, sweet girl. I'm gonna be there for all of it. You're the bravest woman I know, Adeline, but you don't have to face any of this alone."

thirty-four

BILLY

Rivulets of steaming hot water trickle their way down Adeline's chest, over every dip and curve of her body, until they hit the porcelain of the tub below. Her skin glistens faintly in the crappy bathroom light and Billy watches her, rapt, as she tilts her head back under the stream of the shower to wet her hair. As she reaches for the shampoo, Billy does too.

"Let me?" He murmurs, holding his palm out for Adeline to squeeze out a puddle of the pearlescent liquid. Billy washes her hair the best he can with one hand, fingers working extra to lather up the shampoo. Adeline hums softly as he massages her scalp then rinses the suds from her long tresses.

Adeline returns the favour, deft hands tangling in his own hair until the bubbles run down his skin, and when she's done, Billy loses himself in the gentleness of her body. The water runs cold as they waste glorious time kissing. Billy's hand traverses her body, caressing the soft peaks of her breasts while his mouth laves at her skin, damp and warm even under the cool spray of the shower.

He could stay here forever, worshipping Adeline like the goddess she is, but he feels her shiver and snuggle herself closer to him. He's not much warmer and his fingers are wrinkled so he shuts off the water and stretches around the shower curtain for a towel, draping it over Adeline's shoulders as she climbs out.

"Thank you, baby," she murmurs, tilting her head back for one last kiss before they dry off and dress, ready for breakfast. Adeline helps ease his arm through the hole of his white tank top, and then the sleeve of his shirt, her nimble fingers working at the buttons with ease. Carefully, she adjusts his sling and smooths out his collar. "You'll do," she teases, kissing him softly just as the doorbell rings.

With a quick glance over his shoulder, Billy leaves Adeline sitting at the vanity, towel-drying her hair before she begins to style it into the big, loose waves he's so used to seeing. She seems happy, content in a way she hasn't in a while and Billy is gonna do his damned hardest to keep it that way.

Everyone piles into the house when Billy opens the door, some looking a little more awake than others as he greets them all with one-armed hugs and kisses on cheeks. His sister and Patrick stumble through the door last, sleepy smiles of puppy love on their faces.

"Why must you summon us *this* early?" Rosie whines once they're in the kitchen. She leans back against Patrick, his arms wrapped around her middle and looking like trying not to fall asleep on her shoulder.

"Roseanne, it is 9am," Billy responds, sounding an awful lot like their mother.

"Exactly, William. *Early.*"

Billy rolls his eyes and pulls her out of Patrick's hold. He crushes his baby sister against his chest. He misses her when they're apart. They've grown closer as they've gotten older; now that Billy no longer has the urge to steal her Halloween candy or pull the head off her favourite Barbie doll.

"As much as I love this rare display of affection, I'm struggling to breathe, B," she garbles against his shirt. Billy laughs as he releases her, pressing a sloppy kiss to her forehead for good measure.

"Love you."

"Love you too, you big oaf."

Rosie joins Norah and Gabe at the kitchen table, the two of them huddled together on one chair and talking NASCAR with Patrick. As everyone mingles, Stan helps Billy make coffee, though Billy seems to be spending more time trying to get his mom to relax and she and Wren rummage through the fridge and cupboards in preparation for breakfast.

"Ma, I invited you here as a guest. Sit down." He glares playfully, pointing to the couch where his father has made himself comfortable with Michael and Myles. "You too, Wren."

His mother goes begrudgingly and Wren salutes, stealing a kiss from Stan before she happily joins the others. By the time Adeline eventually appears – to loud cheers of 'happy birthday' and hugs all around – Billy and Stan are in the swing of making breakfast. He catches her eye across the room, a secret smile between them. No one's spotted the ring on Adeline's finger yet, but their ogling doesn't go unnoticed.

"What's gotten into you two?" Rosie laughs when she crosses the room to make more coffee and intercepts Billy's fifth wink in a row. "You're usually disgustingly cute anyway, but whatever this is–" she gestures between them, "it's too much for a Monday morning."

"Oh, leave them alone," Eleanor scolds with a soft chuckle.

Billy glances her way and smiles. He called her this morning, when Adeline was downstairs with Michael, because try as he might, Billy has never been able to keep a secret from his mother.

"Yeah, leave us alone," Billy repeats, poking his tongue out at his sister.

Adeline grins at him as she helps set the table. She works slowly, with big, sweeping gestures so obvious she might as well be waving the thing in their faces. Billy is *this* close to blurting it out but it turns out he doesn't have to.

"Sweet Adeline, is that a *ring* on your finger?!"

Thank you, Gabe.

The most gorgeous laugh bursts out of Adeline as she nods and holds her hand out excitedly. The blue sapphire Billy hand picked sits perfectly surrounded by a cluster of diamonds, the ring catching the light when Adeline turns her hand this way and that. The room bursts into life as realisation dawns. Norah squeezes Adeline so tightly she squeals, giggling before she's pulled into the arms of Eleanor. Empty handed, Norah saunters over to Billy.

"So, you did it," she says, gently knocking his shoulder.

"Yep," Billy breathes as his eyes follow Adeline around the room.

"M'proud of you, Billy. You've come a long way since Tulsa."

"Thanks, Norah." He pulls her under his good arm, nose buried in her hair and he presses a soft kiss to her head. "Thanks for always looking out for Addie too, we're lucky to have you."

Norah leans into him and they observe the chaos from the outside for a little longer before they're pulled into the fray. By the time things have calmed down, the pancakes and bacon are cold.

"It's fine, sweetheart," Eleanor says when Billy huffs at the ruined breakfast. "We're all starving and I'm sure it'll taste wonderful still."

"Thanks, Ma," he murmurs, accepting a gentle ruffle of his hair that makes him feel seven again. When everyone is eating and in their own quiet conversations, Billy turns to Patrick and sets his fork down. "So, Peters, I was thinkin' about Toby's proposal."

"I get it if you don't wanna do it, Billy. I don't wanna step on your toes."

Billy shakes his head. "No, no. Patrick, I'll do it. I think I need to, and I wanna help you."

"Really?"

"Yeah, man."

"Thank you! Seriously, this is gonna be awesome!"

"You can stay here if you need, when we're training or coaching, whatever you wanna call it." Billy glances at Rosie. "You can too, I guess, until you're back at school. Just... no funny business."

Rosie giggles and Billy shoots a look between his sister and the young driver. Patrick nods, big dips of his head as his eyes go wide.

"Yes, sir."

"Great, we'll start this afternoon."

"C-cool. Yeah, thanks."

"You're a menace," Adeline whispers to him, her smile evident in her words, each one lifted with a soft lilt. Billy just shrugs, his nose scrunching as he closes the gap to land a soft kiss on her lips.

"I am," he replies; another kiss and an exasperated sigh from Rosie at their PDA. "But I'm yours."

Billy grips the handle on one of the garage doors, waiting for Patrick to grab the other before they pull them open to reveal Michael Gold's 1964 Ford Galaxie, the last car he ever raced in.

"Oh, shit," Patrick breathes as they both stand there, staring in awe. "This is so rad."

He races over, wasting no time, and runs his hand over the paintwork, slow and featherlight. It's still shining after Gabe fixed it up and cleaned it, and Billy lets out a whistle in appreciation. He loved his Dodge, grieved over the thing while he lay in his hospital bed, but *this* was his dream car when he was a teen on the karting tracks.

He's a little jealous that Patrick gets to drive it before him.

"Okay, kid. Let's fire her up." He tosses Patrick the keys but hesitates to get any closer to the car. His feet stay rooted to the ground, something whirring inside him like a gear willing him to move but instead he's frozen. He's been chomping at the bit to get back in the game, so why can't he fucking move? Billy closes his eyes and sees images of the crash flashing behind his eyelids in double time; blink and you'll miss it. He thought he was ready, he's *felt* ready for weeks.

His eyes flutter open again to the sight of Patrick finishing up his checks and adjusting the seat. There's the tell tale sound of the ignition and Billy flinches when the car roars to life. He jerks his left arm, pain ripping through him like shards of glass dragging along the seams of his scars and he goes somewhere else. Mind foggy, Billy's not sure how much time passes but faint calls of his name bring him back around. The garage falls silent again, just his own ragged breaths and Patrick's footsteps upon the concrete until the young driver stops beside him.

"Billy?"

"Yeah?" His own voice sounds distant, that's not right.

"Billy, you're shaking." Patrick wraps an arm around him awkwardly and slowly guides him to a wooden chair in the corner, next to the work bench and piles of scrap.

"I am?"

"Yeah. Just, uh... stay here. I'm gonna get Addie," Patrick blurts. The words go straight over Billy's head but he nods anyway. His chest feels tight and he's struggling to breathe let alone talk. He's felt like this before; after a nightmare and in the hospital. Adeline had helped but he can't remember what she did. Billy's eyes flit around the room, the only thing he *does* remember is Adeline getting him to tell her things he could see and anything is better than sitting help-lessly in his panic.

One by one, he begins to list things off in his head; the car, a tool-box, a pile of spare tyres. Outside, he sees the horses in the paddock across the ranch, just tiny specks in the distance. As he looks up, he fixes his gaze on a framed newspaper clipping on the wall ahead of him. It's a write up on Michael Gold's Championship win, the win that inspired Billy to start racing in the first place. He reads the headline over and over before the words blur into ink splotches and he begins the sob. Each wrack of his chest eases something in him and slowly, his breathing starts to even out.

As his thoughts clear, Billy realises one thing. He doesn't want the crash to define him. He doesn't want to be remembered as the driver whose racing career ended before it even really began.

He growls in frustration, jaw clenched and his right hand balled into a fist. His nails dig into his palm until he can't feel the pain of the indents being left behind when he unfurls his fingers.

And then he takes a deep breath.

Wiping the tears from his cheeks, Billy hauls himself up from the chair. He takes a step on wobbly legs and then another and another until he's beside the car and reaching for the window net.

Billy doesn't want to be remembered for his downfall. He wants to be remembered for his comeback, and that starts with getting back in the car.

thirty-five

ADELINE
August 14th, 1975
Daytona, Florida

ADELINE WISHES SHE WAS ANYWHERE BUT IN A CAR ON HER way to the NASCAR headquarters. Even flanked by Billy and Eleanor Brooks in the back seat, each with a comforting hand on her, flinging herself across her fiancé and leaping from the car seems to be a better option than facing whatever awaits them.

The short plane journey itself had been torture. An hour still felt like too much time to do nothing but think, and even with the armrest up and tucked in the secure hold of Billy, Adeline had felt restless. Then when they came through the arrival gates to see Eleanor waiting for them as promised, somehow Adeline's heart plummeted further. Her stomach is in knots, tightening with each minute they get closer to their destination, and her legs are trembling even though she's sitting. Billy must notice because he untangles his hand from hers and moves it to her thigh.

"You're okay, sweet girl." His voice is soft and it sounds distant despite him being right beside her. Billy gives her leg a gentle squeeze just above the hem of her dress, palm warm through the fabric, and he traces calming shapes on the skin just below. On her right, Eleanor has Adeline's hand clasped in her own.

It was a relief to see the Brooks matriarch; Adeline had collapsed into Eleanor's arms as soon as she was close enough, indulging herself in the kind of hug she imagined only a mother could give. Billy had stood by, soothing her with gentle whispers and a tender hand on her back.

"I don't know if I can do this, Billy."

"Addie, look at me," Billy murmurs as he carefully tilts her chin towards him. He brushes his lips delicately over hers, slightly chapped but soft in pressure. "You're *so* strong, Tinkerbell. You've always been so fucking strong and this is just one more thing that's going to make you stronger."

"He's right, sweetheart," Eleanor says quietly, "and I don't often get to say that."

"Hey!" Billy whines and Adeline breathes out a soft laugh as he pouts at his mother.

"Oh hush, you."

Adeline giggles again, grateful for the moment of light. They're almost there, she realises, recognising the streets as they blur past. She lets out a shaky breath, chest heaving with it. Billy takes her hand again. He draws that familiar figure of eight around her knuckles, grounding her as he speaks.

"Listen, sweet girl. We're both going to be right beside you. I spoke with Tobias and he said it'll just be us giving our side of the story. I promise you, Adeline– look at me, please," he murmurs when her eyes fall back to her lap. Adeline raises her head, swallowing down the lump in her throat. "I promise you, I will do everything in my power to make you feel safe in that room."

She doesn't think she's ever seen Billy's eyes so blue, his irises shining and almost translucent with emotion. Adeline's gaze drops to his throat, his Adam's apple heavy with a hard swallow as he silently begs her to trust him.

"I know you will," she whispers, "thank you."

"You need to get out of there, just say the word," Billy says and

Adeline follows his line of sight as he glances around her to Eleanor who nods in agreement.

The rest of the journey is quiet and contemplative. Billy hums to the radio, soft and low into Adeline's hair as she rests her head on his shoulder. When they finally pull up outside the building, it looks as unassuming as ever, the same as it's always been, and that settles something within Adeline as she follows Billy out of the car. Fingers entwined, they're facing this together.

"Ready?"

"No," she answers honestly. Billy brings their hands up between them, soft lips finding her wrist, travelling to her knuckles with peppered kisses until he grazes his thumb over the ring on her fourth finger.

"I'm here, Tinkerbell."

"Don't let go?" Adeline whispers.

"Never."

Inside, Billy takes the lead. He approaches the reception desk with the kind of confidence Adeline has missed seeing in him, all swagger and charm in his smile. He barely says hello to the young receptionist when a door opens abruptly and two men who couldn't look more different from each other enter the lobby.

Teddy Wilson, the newly appointed chairman of NASCAR, not that you'd be able to tell by this casual outfit of light wash jeans and what Adeline would call a 'dad shirt', greets them with a smile. He used to drive with Michael back in the day and seeing him always set her mind at ease. Beside him is Oliver Temple, head of the legal department. His long, jet black hair falls in a way that feathers around his face, immaculately framing his high cheekbones to match the perfection of his three-piece suit. He's intimidating as anything, always has been, and Adeline finds herself inching closer to Billy. Oliver's impatient glance at his watch and tap of his overly shiny shoe tells Adeline he was probably the one demanding their presence.

"Well, if it isn't William Brooks, up on two feet and looking mighty well."

"Mr Temple," Billy replies with a tight smile. "Good to see you."

"How many times do I have to tell you to call me Oliver, William?"

"Only the two times we've met before, sir."

Oliver laughs, fake and with a hint of impatience as he eyes narrow in on Adeline.

"Miss Gold, lovely to see you as always." Adeline nods, plastering on a polite smile. She's grateful when Teddy takes the reins of the conversation again.

"Thank you for travelling down," he says, "Tobias told me you guys are pretty settled up in Georgia, we're sorry to drag you away."

Eleanor clears her throat behind them. She's stayed quiet so far but Adeline has a feeling she'll speak up if needs be.

"We just want this dealt with as it should be, Teddy," Billy says before reaching back for his mom. "This is my mother, Eleanor."

Teddy flashes her a smile as he shakes her hand, "Pleasure to meet you, Mrs Brooks. Shall we head on back?" His gaze flits between the three of them. "We'll get you some coffee before we start, or maybe something a little stronger." He winks at Adeline, offering a gentle nod before he turns back to the door they came through, Oliver following closely behind.

"You go ahead, mom," Billy says, "tell Teddy we want the best scotch he's got."

Eleanor shakes her head fondly but agrees and brushes her hand over Billy's back reassuringly as she passes them. Billy waits until the door clicks closed and the receptionist makes herself look busy before he pulls Adeline flush to his body. A soft gasp breezes through Adeline's lips as she collides with his chest and he wraps his good arm around her waist.

"You okay, sweet girl?"

"Yep. The quicker we get this over with, the better," she replies as she messes with Billy's collar until it lays flat to his shirt; anything to keep her hands busy.

They both dressed smartly for the occasion. Adeline is in the most conservative dress she owns, the lightweight yellow fabric keeping the Florida sun from overheating her too much. Billy is in his favourite brown slacks and a baby blue shirt. He's pushed his hair back, loose strands tucked neatly behind his ears. He looks so handsome, Adeline has been distracting herself all morning with how he might look on their wedding day.

Billy dips his head, catching her eye, and a smile unfurls across his lips as he leans in to kiss her. It's deep and slow, his mouth slanting over hers so deliciously that she feels her knees buckle and her belly swoop. Adeline is immediately transported to every moment they spent losing themselves in each other over the past week. There's not a spot in that ranch house they haven't had sex in, and yet every kiss feels like the first.

"What are we made of, Tinkerbell?" Billy whispers, lips tickling hers as he speaks. Adeline huffs out a soft laugh and kisses him again before she replies.

"Fucking stardust."

"Fuck yeah we are," Billy grins, his nose scrunching as his whole face lights up. "I love you, Addie."

"I love you too," she breathes and Billy takes her hand as they prepare for what's to come.

Five minutes later, they're sitting opposite Teddy and Oliver at a large conference table. Adeline is already a glass of scotch down – an attempt to calm her nerves – and Teddy pours her another with no hesitation.

"This isn't an interrogation, Adeline." Teddy is softly spoken and Adeline is glad he's sitting in on this. She's never liked Oliver Temple much, not during any of their past interactions, and she definitely doesn't like the way he's looking at her now. "We just need to hear the events leading up to the accident between Billy and Rex Harlow from your perspective – and yours, Billy."

"It wasn't an accident," Adeline mutters, "Rex hit Billy deliberately. If you watch the footage I surrendered you would see that."

"We're aware of the accusations, Miss Gold," Oliver says, his jaw set harshly as he glances up at her from the papers in front of him. "Plus, we *have* reviewed the footage and we have several eyewitness accounts but we still need your side of the story. So please, if you could start from the beginning, when did you first meet Mr Harlow?"

"1970," she answers without missing a beat. "It was his first year racing with Hard Strike."

"And how did you meet?"

"Uh... some pre-race thing, I think. I was with my dad so it was probably just a brief introduction. I didn't interact with him all that regularly and then three years ago he sexually assaulted me." The words come out easily despite the shake in her voice and Billy sucks in a breath beside her.

"Addie–"

"It's okay, Billy. If they want my side of the story, they're going to hear it." On her other side, Eleanor squeezes her hand. "Rex Harlow took advantage of me," Adeline states. She's trying her hardest to keep her breathing steady but her legs are jumpy, tapping her toes nervously. With her hands encased in the unyielding hold of her family, she continues. "He knew I was drunk, lulled me into a false sense of safety and then ripped it away when I wasn't compliant. I told him I didn't want to have sex with him and yet he had sex with me anyway."

Teddy looks devastated as Adeline meets his eye across the table.

"I'm so sorry that happened to you, Adeline," he says softly, "if I had known–"

"My own father only found out this morning, Teddy."

Adeline had crumbled earlier this morning, telling Michael over the phone. It was easier to get it out that way, she's not sure she would have been able to look him in the eye if she had done it face to face. Michael had cried with her. He apologised as if Adeline being around Rex had been his fault and she had felt emotionally drained afterwards, her eyes sore and head heavy as she went through the motions of packing her overnight bag. Billy had hovered, aware and there if she needed him. Adeline doesn't think she'll ever be able to repay him for his attentiveness and unwavering care for her.

Oliver raises an eyebrow, clicking his pen in a way that is so obviously irritating that he must be doing it on purpose.

"And you believe this was the event that led to Mr Harlow and Mr Brooks crashing in Nashville?"

"That, and the fact that he cornered me in the women's bathroom before the race," Adeline replies shortly. "If Billy hadn't come in, I don't doubt that Rex would have tried to do more than just rough me up a little."

"I see," Oliver hums, his gaze passing between Adeline and Billy with an unbelieving weight and his lips pursed. "And what happened in the bathroom once Mr Brooks arrived? Where is the connection between Mr Harlow *assaulting* you and then deciding to deliberately crash his car?"

"I punched him," Billy says simply. "I told Addie to wait outside for me and warned Rex to stay the fuck away from her. He decided to threaten me; told me to watch my back and that I'd regret interfering."

"*Billy...*" Adeline and Eleanor are eerily in sync as their heads snap towards him. It's the first either of them is hearing of this and Adeline's heart constricts, her breath tight in her lungs.

"Sweetheart, he– he threatened you?" Eleanor stutters.

"I didn't think anything of it at the time, Ma. I just needed to get Addie away from him."

"I never liked him," Teddy comments, "and I'm sorry it took something like this happening for his behaviour to come to light. You understand it's going to take a while–" He's interrupted by a knock on the door, a mousy-looking secretary peering in once called.

"I'm sorry, sir, but there's a Delilah Jones in the lobby. She said it's imperative that she speaks to you."

Billy frowns, "Delilah?"

Teddy pushes back from the table and Adeline follows suit, tugging Billy up from his chair. If Delilah is here, she wants to see this.

"Why do you think she's here?" Adeline whispers, peering up at

Billy as he slides his hand into hers and they traipse behind Teddy and Oliver.

"Beats me."

In the lobby, Delilah sits on the orange velvet couch like she owns it. Her hair is styled to perfection, red nails tapping rhythmically on her knee as she waits. On the opposite couch, are three other women Adeline's never seen before.

"Oh, thank God you're here! You have no idea how hard it is to get information out of Tobias Shaw!" She hops up when she sees Billy and Adeline, hurrying over on her little kitten heels. Oliver pushes through their little group, a scowl on his hard face as he takes in the scene before him.

"May I ask what the hell is going on? Who is this?"

Billy sighs. "This is Delilah, my ex," he clarifies before turning back to the woman in question. "What are you doing here?"

"Can we all go somewhere more private?"

Confused, Adeline steps forward to say something but Billy stops her with a gentle squeeze of her hip and a nod. Teddy must catch it because he turns on his heel and beckons them back to the conference room, now full with people. He sags back in his chair and runs his hand over his face.

"Okay, Billy's ex–"

"Delilah."

"Sorry, Delilah. What can we do for you?"

"I want to help with the case against Rex Harlow."

"There is no case, this isn't an episode of The Rookies," Oliver says harshly, "we've heard both sides of the story and we'll take action accordingly."

Delilah glances at Billy, nodding to his untouched tumbler of scotch.

"Can I have that?"

"Sure," Billy shrugs, sliding it across the table. Adeline watches curiously as she drains the glass, meeting her gaze.

"What did he do to you?"

"No worse than what he did to you. I'm sorry, Adeline," Delilah replies and Adeline's surprised to see that she actually does look sorry, her expression earnest and disheartened. "If I'd realised how much he'd hurt you I never would have gone to him to get back at William. When I realised Rex had gone to find you that day, well, I couldn't have ever forgiven myself if I didn't do something, not after I learned what a bastard he is first hand."

"You told Billy Rex had followed me to the bathroom, that's why you were outside?"

"Yeah. After that, I couldn't let Rex hurt anyone else so I did some digging and well…" She gestures to the women sitting beside her. Adeline feels her stomach drop like a lead weight. She shouldn't feel surprised that a man like Rex is a serial offender, he oozes scumbag after all, but it's still a gut punch.

"Are you all willing to give statements?" Teddy asks. "With five women's claims against him, and the evidence we have that the crash with Billy was deliberate, that's more than enough for me to take to the rest of the board. He's looking at a ban, easily, maybe more. Plus, compensation for you, Billy, of course."

That's all it takes for the other women to agree, a mutual understanding that it's probably the most closure any of them are going to get, Adeline included.

"We'll be right back," Oliver says gruffly. He looks disgruntled, clearly annoyed that this process turned out more complicated than he hoped. When they leave, every emotion Adeline's been holding in floods out of her; relief, exhaustion, gratefulness. It all bubbles up to the surface as she breaks and collapses against Billy. She meets Delilah's eye as she wipes her own and mumbles out a quiet but sincere '*thank you*'.

"It was the least I could do. Rex deserves whatever he has coming to him," she replies and her eyes slide to Adeline's hand, the inkling of a smile crossing her face as she notices the ring. "And you two deserve to be able to move forward in peace."

"Thank you," Billy murmurs. His own voice is thick with emotion, the deep timbre reverberating through his chest. Mixed with the sound of his heartbeat in her ear, the low rumble soothes

Adeline as she relaxes against him. Billy presses a kiss to her crown and Eleanor tenderly brushes her hair from her face. For the first time since this all started, Adeline truly feels like everything is going to be okay.

Tobias Shaw may be a slightly egotistical hothead with more money than he knows what to do with, but Adeline can't say he doesn't look after his drivers, even if they are informed of things like follow-up hospital appointments a mere hour beforehand.

While Billy has an x-ray, Eleanor and Adeline sit side by side in a private room, the clinical feel of the hospital takes her right back to Nashville and she hates it.

"Have you thought much about the wedding?" Eleanor asks. The question fills the comfortable silence between them with something other than the distant beeping of machines and dripping from the tap in the corner.

"We've discussed it a little, both Billy and I would love it if you could help us out though. I know he wouldn't want to ask but neither of us really knows what we're doing," Adeline confesses, "we just know we want to spend the rest of our lives together."

"I would be honoured, sweetheart. You just tell me when you're ready and we'll get right on it." Now that things with Rex are behind them, she's chomping at the bit to have her life filled with happier moments.

"Thank you, Eleanor. Has, um… has Billy spoken to you much about driving?"

"That boy tells me everything, Addie, you know this," Eleanor says with a soft chuckle. "He called just the other day to tell me he got in the car without panicking for the first time all week."

Adeline beams. She'd been there when that happened. Billy had a megawatt smile on his face, nose crinkled with excitement as he sat behind the wheel for almost an hour, just getting the feel of it again.

"I'm so proud of him," Adeline sighs, "I don't think… I don't think he's thought about the possibility of not driving again though." It's been eating at her since Billy decided to help Patrick. He was happy to be back on the track, talking nonstop about how excited he is to drive once he's fully mobile again that Adeline can't bear to ruin the one thing that's brought him so much joy recently.

"He's thought about it, Adeline. Don't you worry," Eleanor soothes, taking Adeline's hand. "That boy has lived and breathed driving for as long as I can remember but he knows it's not the only thing life's worth living for, not anymore. Let's just take it one day at a time, see what the doctor has to say today, hmm?"

"Yeah, okay. Thanks, Eleanor. I don't know if either of us could have gotten through any of this without you."

"I just wish I could have done more, but with being in New York and workin–"

"You've done more than enough, honestly. Billy's so lucky to have you as a mom."

"I'm yours too now, sweet Addie. Don't you ever forget that."

Adeline's eyes itch with tears. She forgets how lucky she is some-times, to have this whole extra family that loves and cares about her. Not only the Brookses but Norah, Stan, and Gabe too.

"Seriously, Ma? I leave the room for twenty minutes and you make her cry?" Billy leans in the doorway, a soft, teasing smile on his lips. His arm is sans-sling but it's still resting against his chest out of habit as he steps aside to let the doctor into the room. Winking as he hops up onto the bed, Billy makes himself comfortable and they wait as the doctor flicks on the backlight on the wall and slots Billy's x-ray into place.

"It's good news," he starts and Billy flashes Adeline the brightest grin. "William's arm is in good working order and any fractures where the metal plates were not needed have healed nicely. Now it's just about getting the mobility back."

"Will that be to full functionality?" Eleanor asks.

"At least 90%, it all depends on William's commitment to his physiotherapy and ensuring he begins using the arm in everyday life. I can't see why he can't do everything he did before.

"You don't have to worry about that, doc!" Billy exclaims, "I am 100% committed."

Adeline closes her eyes briefly, chuckling to herself. Today has been crazy, her body doesn't know what's hit it but she knows her heart feels so much lighter than when she woke up this morning.

"So, I'd like you to keep up your sessions with Miss Hardy. She's the best in the business so you listen to her, and as you already know you can do without the sling now. Just take it easy at first, don't over exert the muscles," the doctor warns.

Billy sends him a lazy salute. "You got it."

"Mr Shaw has requested a copy of my medical report from today. Is it okay that I share it with him?"

"Go ahead," Billy replies.

"Great, I'll get that faxed over. You're free to go whenever you're ready. Can't wait to see you back out on the track, William."

"You and me both, doc. You and me both."

The doctor leaves and Eleanor hops up, tugging them both into a hug.

"What a day, my babies!" She laughs, planting a lipstick staining kiss on Billy's cheek and he cringes, ears pink.

"*Ma!*" He wipes his hand over the red mark on his skin.

"I'll wait outside," Eleanor says, rolling her eyes as she gathers her bag and ruffles Billy's hair. "Don't take too long." Billy waves her off, his face light as he laughs and his whole body shakes with joy. Big and beaming, his heartbreakingly handsome smile makes Adeline giddy and she leans into it as he kisses her, slow and tender, lips curved against each other as they giggle. Billy's voice is soft as his mouth travels up to brush across the shell of her ear with a whisper.

"Let's go home, sweet girl."

thirty-six

BILLY
August 15th, 1975
Gold Family Ranch, Georgia

BILLY'S GUARD DROPS AND HIS WHOLE BODY RELAXES THE moment they drive through the ranch gates the next day. They had ended up staying overnight in Daytona; invited to dinner with Teddy and then put up in the swankiest hotel, all on NASCAR's dime. As much as Billy couldn't wait to get back to Georgia, he wasn't about to say no to that. Their evening had ended quietly. Adeline was clearly exhausted from the day and she was asleep as soon as she made herself comfortable, sprawled over and wrapped around Billy like an octopus.

Billy drops his head back against the passenger seat and as he watches the vast fields pass by out the window, he can't help the slightly delirious chuckle that bursts out of him.

"Are you good over there?" Adeline asks and briefly shoots him a concerned look as she concentrates on driving down the bumpy track to the house.

"Never been better, my sweet girl. Never been *fuckin'* better."

Billy catches Adeline arching an eyebrow and he shrugs, unruffled by her questioning expression.

The truth is, arriving back at the ranch really does feel a lot like coming home. Billy has considered New York home his entire life; always a brownstone in Brooklyn. Always the same habit of swinging by one specific (and slightly questionable) hot dog cart on 32nd Street whenever he's in Manhattan and walking that bit further to the subway station that smells a little less like piss than the others. He loves the city, always will, but there's something about being out in the country – the quiet of it all. He thinks that's part of it anyway but he knows the reason this place feels so much like home now is because he shares it with Adeline.

"You wanna go get Pancake from Myles?" He suggests as they pull up outside the ranch house. "I'll open up, check Patrick hasn't wrecked the place while we've been gone."

"You want *me* to go get the cat even though you're her favourite?"

"That's not true, she loves you. She's always makin' her little biscuits on you," Billy counters. "I'm sure Myles probably wants you to check in anyway, let him know we got back safe."

"*Fiiiine,*" Adeline drawls, turning on her heel. She scuffs up dust from the road as she does.

"Hey, don't I get a kiss before you go?"

Adeline pulls a face as if she's really thinking about it, nose scrunched and squinting to the sky where the sun is setting.

"No, I don't think you do," she answers jovially, grinning at him. Billy admires the way her eyes sparkle playfully, youthful and happy again after so long. He levels her with an affectionate look, shaking his head as she starts down the dirt track that leads to Myles'. Adeline peers over her shoulder to call back to him, "I love you!"

"Yeah, yeah. I love you too, Tinkerbell," he shouts back. Billy waits for her to get so far down the road, zoning out a little as his eyes track the glorious sway of her hips. When he finally drags his eyes away and heads inside, he shucks off his sneakers by the door and dumps the one bag he managed to carry in from the car. He'll go back out for the other one later, but first, he needs to check in with Patrick.

"Peters? You here?"

"Living room!" Patrick's voice echoes through the house and Billy hurries down the hall with a skip in his step and anticipation bubbling up in his belly.

"Did it arri–" The words die on his lips as he stops short in the doorway and his eyes flick from Patrick's beaming smile to the baby grand piano that now sits neatly in the corner of the room, like it's always belonged there.

"The delivery guy showed up not even an hour after you guys left yesterday," Patrick says and Billy approaches the instrument as if it's a wild animal, tentatively reaching his hand out until he's close enough to run his palm over the glossy black finish. He's in awe of it, mind already flying away with itself as he pictures Adeline playing it, filling the house with music. And she deserves it, this little part of herself that she's gone so long without.

"It's beautiful," Billy breathes, "*fuck*. She's gonna love it."

The restored 1940s Steinway piano cost Billy a pretty penny but every single one will be worth it to see the look on Adeline's face. For so long he's had reservations about giving *too* much, only becoming aware of how much he gave and gave and gave over the course of his relationship with Delilah. A lot of the time he would willingly hand over money and time and parts of *himself* that he kept hidden for a reason. Being with Adeline has been so refreshing. She asks for nothing; just him, and his love, and for her he has that in abundance. So he's happy to treat her, to give her something he knows will only add to her happiness and because he wants to, not because he feels obligated.

"*I just want to be happy and play piano more...*" That's what Adeline had said when Billy asked her what she wanted in life all those months ago, as they lay together in a hotel room in North Carolina, high and upside down on the bed. Billy knew then that he was going to spend the rest of his life with her; knew then that they were too tangled up in each other's souls for it to go any other way.

He really does hope she likes the piano. There were only so many times he could catch the way Adeline's fingers twitched on his thigh when they curled up on the couch together, a tune played on invisible keys, for the idea to get stuck in Billy's head. He had called around music stores and piano specialists when he knew Adeline was busy tending to the horses and he took secret trips into the city with Patrick or Myles to see the pianos in person. When he found the Steinway, it just so happened that the scheduled delivery was today. After everything, the timing seemed almost too serendipitous.

Billy runs his fingers over the keys and plays through a scale, the notes gorgeously clean and light in the air.

"Sounds great!" Patrick's enthusiastic, his own hand coming down to bash out a few notes, just a little more haphazardly than Billy had. The younger driver lacks the delicacy, a thunderous series of *DUN DUN DUN* down the far end of the piano rather than a delicate scale a few octaves higher.

"Well, it did until you did that."

"We can't all be pretty *and* talented, Brooks," Patrick scoffs and Billy chuckles. He tinkers away at a few more keys as if he's testing they all work and then claps his hands because he can do that now, albeit gently.

"Where is Addie anyway?" Patrick asks then.

"I sent her to pick up Pancake from Myles, she'll probably be back in a minute so, uh–"

There's an awkward pause as Billy drums his fingers on the top of the piano.

"Oh...*Oh.*" Patrick jumps. "Yeah, I'll uh... I'll go. Good luck, I hope she loves it...well, I know she'll love it but, shit, you know what I mean."

Billy snorts, laughing softly as he places a hand, his left one, on Patrick's shoulder. His fingers curl, a grip on the other man's shirt that aches through his limb. It feels good to use it, though, to feel and express with it, despite the residual pain.

"Thanks for doin' this, Patrick."

"Anytime." Patrick smiles as he heads for the door. "I'll be down at the track if you need me, not that you will but y'know." Billy follows him out into the hall and waits for the door to click closed before he leaps into action.

He heads up to their bedroom, taking the stairs two at a time, to retrieve his Super 8 from the closet. The case is filled with processed film, reels of the stuff neatly labelled in Adeline's pretty cursive handwriting. He knows there's footage of him racing but he can't bring himself to watch that yet, he even managed to avoid seeing the tape Adeline handed over as evidence. A lot of the others he's seen though, mostly in what Adeline called his 'Recovery Slump'. It's all footage of them before the accident – goofing off in downtime between races, out on hikes and play fights in hotel rooms that quickly turned into heated make out sessions before one of them remembered to turn the camera off.

His reminiscing is interrupted by the telltale sound of Adeline's footsteps outside and Billy quickly locates a new film cartridge, loads into the camera and checks the batteries are still working to capture the moment. When he arrives back in the living room, he's only slightly out of breath as the front door opens and closes again.

"Myles says hi!" Adeline calls through the house and when she enters the living room she has Pancake in her arms, nuzzling into her soft, ginger fur. She doesn't notice Billy right away, her attention on the cat as if they'd been apart for longer than a little over 24 hours.

Billy observes Adeline quietly, keeping the camera trained on her as she whispers away to Pancake. She's become ridiculously maternal over the cat since they found her in the barn and Billy can't help but imagine what she's going to be like when they have an actual baby, a kid that's bound to inherit their mother's strong-willed nature; gorgeous and funny too.

When she finally looks up, Adeline almost drops Pancake, who leaps to the floor in an attempt to save herself and bounds over to Billy. He bends down to pet her, all while trying to keep the camera steady and focused on Adeline. Her hazel eyes glisten in the amber stream of sunlight that drenches the room and her chin wobbles, bottom lip trembling. Biting down in an attempt to stop it, her gaze flicks from Billy to the piano and back again.

"Billy..." It's almost a whisper, the quiet gasp of his name.

"Surprise, baby."

Adeline wanders further into the room, stopping before him with an adorable pout. Billy leans in and happily rids the pout with a kiss. The camera in his hand goes momentarily forgotten as he nips her bottom lip, soothing it with his tongue. Adeline smiles into the kiss, her lips soft and slow against his. Her fingers tangle in his hair as she licks inside his mouth, tasting him and Billy groans with the slide of her tongue. It's dizzying. The way she thanks him with quiet whimpers every time their lips part for just a moment makes Billy feel hazy, weightless on his feet. His cock stirs, heavy in his pants with the anticipation of this going further but just as he's about to pull Adeline closer she steps away, her flushed face remaining just inches from his.

"Thank you," she murmurs and Billy, with half-lidded eyes and swollen lips, sways in to steal another kiss. Adeline appeases him with a small, sweet peck before the warmth of her body leaves his vicinity and she moves to inspect the piano.

Billy is a fool in love; a fool in love who quickly remembers he's holding a running camera that's currently filming the floor.

"Billy, this is a Steinway," Adeline says breathlessly and Billy grins, pleased.

"Correct."

"Billy, these pianos are..." she pauses as she sits down on the bench with a wiggle and plays a few notes. Billy zooms in on her fingers, physically moving the camera closer, and Adeline giggles as she quickly hides her hands behind her back. "These things aren't cheap."

"Are you going to keep telling me things I already know or are you gonna keep playing?" He steadies the camera in his good hand and flashes her a lopsided grin. Adeline hits a single, solitary note and glances up at him with a raised eyebrow as if to ask, '*is that what you wanted?*'

"I regret buying you that camera," she states.

"No you don't. Keep going!"

Adeline huffs dramatically but keeps playing and Billy keeps filming. He sits down beside her on the piano bench and alternates between filming her hands on the keys and ridiculous close-ups of her face, capturing every time she scrunches her nose and pokes her tongue out in protest. Even then, she's the most gorgeous woman Billy's ever known.

The camera finally clicks, signifying the end of the film cartridge, and he places it down gently on the top of the piano. Adeline laughs, leaning into him as she lays her head on his shoulder and ends the piece of music she was playing with a childish bash of the keys, much like Patrick had earlier.

"Thank you for this, Billy."

"You're welcome, sweet girl." He twists to place a kiss into her hair and her whole body relaxes against him as she looks up to meet his lips in a sweet kiss.

Billy sighs, content in the moment and the realisation that he gets a lifetime of this? A lifetime of being beside Adeline, sometimes under her – or over her – and kissed by her. And he gets to *do* the kissing too?

"Hey, you wanna learn to play something?" Adeline asks suddenly, smiling up at him and radiating so much joy with her big, hazel eyes that he can't say anything but yes. She wiggles in her seat again and manoeuvres Billy's right hand into the correct position, his fingers splayed out on the keys.

"You have good piano fingers," she comments as she runs the pad of her forefinger over each of his, from nail to knuckle, and Billy shivers.

"Good for other things too," he smirks. Adeline doesn't give him the satisfaction of a response, but her cheeks turn a pretty shade of pink all the same.

"How's your left hand?" She says instead, "think you can play with it?"

"Probably. I mean, the pain isn't too bad today and it's just moving my fingers, right?"

Adeline nods and presses a soft kiss to each of his knuckles before she delicately places his fingers in the right place. The quiet '*I love you so much*' spills from Billy's mouth before he can even process his lips moving, but the tenderness with which Adeline handles him is too much sometimes.

"Not as much as I love you," Adeline responds simply.

"You better teach me something good," Billy says then, bunching up his nose as if it'll rid the lump in her throat.

"Do you doubt me?"

"Never. I just don't wanna be braggin' that the only thing I can play on the piano is some frumpy hymn most people learn to play in middle school."

"Don't ask for much, do you?" Adeline teases, "okay, you're just gonna play the single note with your left hand, less strain that way. Then the three notes of the chord with your right. It starts with a C, so your left hand plays this note." She adds a little pressure to his thumb so the crisp note plays out and Billy nods.

"C. Got it."

"And then alongside that, your right hand is going to play the C, E, and G up here all at the same time like–" she says, checking his fingers are on the right keys. When she nods, Billy plays the chord. "Perfect, baby."

"Fuck, I'm good at this," Billy grins, "what's next?"

"E. So it's just a shift up to this key on your left hand and then you right moves to these ones. You basically just go the same note an octave up and then put a finger on every other key for that chord."

"Like this?" Billy presses down gently, a new note echoing from the piano.

"Just like that." Adeline looks up at him with a fond smile and Billy dips his head to kiss her. He means for it to be quick, a small peck of gratitude, but he gets lost in it easily. His tongue slips along the seam of her lips, teeth nibbling at the plushness. "Billy – baby, concentrate," Adeline giggles between kisses, "you wanna brag, you gotta learn the whole song."

"I would apologise but I'm not sorry." He kisses her once more for good measure and then turns his attention back to the piano. "What now, sweet girl?"

"A minor now, back up this way a little." Billy plays it, and then returns to the first chord and plays them through, committing them to memory. It's the last note that gives the song away, leading him in to sing the next line with a soft gaze fixed on Adeline.

"...*take my whole life too...*"

Adeline carefully moves Billy's hands to the side and picks up the piano, playing the chords as Billy sings softly. He keeps his voice low, almost a whisper in her ear and ends it by taking her earlobe between his teeth. He flicks his tongue over the pink mark left behind as he lets go and mouths lazily as the skin just below her ear.

"I think this should be our song, Tinkerbell."

"Yeah?"

"Mhmm," Billy hums as he kisses down to her mouth, his tongue leading as his lips meet hers. "I think... we should dance to it at our wedding."

"The wedding we're still yet to plan?"

"Well, we just made one decision. What's a few more?" Billy grins and noses along Adeline's neck. He feels needy today, left arm no longer strapped down and he's itching to use it despite the dull, lingering pain. He wants to touch Adeline, feel her soft skin against the palm that's gone without for so long.

"I asked your mom to help," Adeline says quietly, "she's really excited about it."

Billy chuckles, "I bet she is. I'll fly her down to us next week, how does that sound?"

"Perfect."

They're quiet for a moment, just the soft tinkling of the piano before Billy slides off the bench and pads over to the shelf of vinyl records they keep in the corner. He knows he's seen it before, having made his way through most of Michael's record collection in one afternoon when he was first discharged from the hospital. He finds what he's looking for after a moment, the small EP hidden between larger albums. When the needle hits the vinyl, scratching softly, and Elvis begins to croon, Billy wraps his arms around Adeline from behind and rests his chin on her shoulder.

"Dance with me?"

Adeline tilts her head back, her face lit up as Billy pulls her up from the bench. He sways her slowly, holding her close. He's hardly a dancer, and it's usually not until he's a few drinks in that you'll find him on the dance floor, but he can take his girl for a spin around the living room. Billy closes his eyes, pretends it's their wedding day as he breathes in the delicate scent of Adeline's rose shampoo and indulges in the feeling of her body pressed to his just so.

"How does a December wedding sound?" He whispers into her hair, "a winter wedding?"

"I'd marry you at the courthouse tomorrow, Billy. You know that."

Billy laughs, "I would too, sweet girl, but I think my mom would kill us both if we did that. I wanna do it properly anyway; see you in a pretty dress with all our friends and family there."

"Then December sounds good," Adeline agrees as she tilts her head and her lips find his jaw. "Now we just need to decide where."

"Look at us, plannin' a wedding." Billy almost pinches himself, he half expects to wake up in New York alone.

The song ends, back to the warm crackle of vinyl before it stops spinning. But Billy doesn't stop. He hums the tune into Adeline's ear instead, keeping her wrapped in his arms. It's serene being in their own little bubble until Pancake darts across the room, spooked by something, and tangles up in their feet with a loud yowl.

Billy stumbles over her, tries and fails to save his own balance. As he goes down, he takes Adeline with him and they land ungracefully on the floor with a soft '*oof.*'

"Fuckin' cat."

"You love that cat," Adeline giggles as she sits up and runs her hands over him, checking for injuries.

"I'm alright, Tinkerbell," he says, "but, now we're down here..."

"Have we done it on the floor yet?"

"Not in this room," Billy laughs and pulls Adeline on top of him. "Hi," he whispers, mouth slanting over hers, warm and wet as he explores her with his tongue.

He toys with the hem of her shirt, fingers sliding under the fabric to dance across her belly and he finally feels her under his left hand. He also feels like he's one second away from crying.

"Gettin' to hold you with two hands..." he chokes out, "Addie. *Christ*– I didn't think..." It's sore, he can't quite caress her like he can with his right hand but *fuck*.

"Hey, you don't have to do anything with it if it's too much," Adeline says softly.

"Need t'know it's still good for somethin'," Billy murmurs, so quietly he doesn't think Adeline has heard and he's unsure if he actually wanted her to. The gentle hold she has on his wrist and the way she guides his hand out from under her shirt tells him otherwise. Her other hand finds his cheek, fingers trailing through the rough terrain of his stubble as she forces him to meet her gaze.

"Billy, your arm does not make you. If you'd lost it that day, you'd still be one hundred percent of the man I fell in love with. No less. Never less," she says and her breath catches in her throat as she brings his palm to her lips and kisses it. Billy sighs, unable to do anything but watch her show him the love she thinks he deserves. The love he's still learning to accept.

Adeline mouths at his hand and wrist until her lips land where his heart is, warm and tender over his pulse, and then she removes his shirt with cautious care and kisses her way up his arm. Loving on every scar, the tip of her nose brushes over the crevice of Billy's elbow and tickles across his weakened bicep until she's marking the golden skin of his clavicle. She's beaming by the time they're face to face again, lips curved against his as she whispers into his mouth.

"And I think we both know you're more than capable of making me come without it, but if you wanna see what it can do I'm not gonna stop you."

Billy kisses her then, crashes his lips to hers, and it's only now that he picks out the sweetness of chocolate in her mouth. A stolen cookie from Myles', no doubt, because God forbid Adeline Gold goes without sugar. Billy laps it up though, the chocolate hazelnut goodness and everything else that's so sweetly Adeline. They kiss on the floor of the living room like they have all the time in the world.

Billy goes back to making sure every inch of Adeline gets soft touches, squeezes and strokes. He frees her from her trousers and hugs her waist as he shifts her further under him; covers her body with his. Then he uses his left hand to take her apart and put her back together again, slow and languid with it. He builds her up and watches her fall, tumbling through bliss and back just for him to do it again and again. Her back arches off the floor and her lips part with a symphony of gorgeous moans and sighs of his name. Caught up in it, Billy thinks if he were to die right now, he wouldn't be so mad about it.

"You got another one in there for me, sweet girl? Just one more and then I'll make love to you real good."

Adeline opens her eyes after he's worked her through her third orgasm, staring up at him with a dazed smile. Billy cups her jaw and traces her bottom lip, all plump and pink and bitten raw, with the pad of his thumb. The sun, in its final glow of the day, settles on Adeline's face and lights her up like the angel she is. He kisses her again, wanting to bask in her halo.

"So good for me baby," he whispers and Adeline blinks then scrunches her nose with a playful smile and weaves her fingers through Billy's hair, pulling lightly as her lips meander up to his ear. Billy is already rock solid, his cock heavy and aching, and he whimpers pathetically. The warmth of Adeline's mouth, her grip on his hair – it's a lot.

"I think we can safely say your left hand still works a charm," she says after a moment of laving at the sweet spot below Billy's ear, so matter of fact that he can't help but burst out laughing.

His body shakes with it and his right arm finally gives out after holding himself up for so long. Billy lets himself fall, softly resting his weight on Adeline. She wraps her legs around his waist and Billy moans into their next kiss, grinding down just a little to relieve the building pressure and swallowing the breathless gasp it earns from his love.

"Well, we had to make sure," he manages a moment later.

"Oh, of course. And now we know..."

"Now we know," Billy repeats, letting his head fall against Adeline's shoulder with a soft chuckle. He grazes his teeth over her collar bone and follows it up with a swipe of his tongue and press of his lips. "I love you."

"I love you too," Adeline whispers. She brushes his hair back from his face and kisses his temple. "Can I show you how much?"

"Yes. *Fuck* – yes. Please," he whines, his kisses becoming more frantic. Between fervid passes of his tongue and his wandering hands, he's all over her. The world spins as Adeline rolls them over and he's suddenly underneath her, watching her pull her shirt over her head. Billy's jaw drops, never mind the fact that he sees her naked on a daily basis, and he doesn't even think about it before he surges up and wraps his lips around her nipple. He sucks, tongue flicking over the hardened bud, and he feels her chest expand with the sharp gasp that leaves her lips.

"Billy, oh– *oh God.*" Adeline's hand comes down between them, finding his cock, hot and straining beneath the thick denim of his jeans. She starts palming over his length with strokes so torturously slow, Billy almost whites out from that alone. His mouth falls slack and Adeline's chest pinkens from the way his rough stubble brushes over her soft skin.

"Shit. *Shit.* Tinkerbell, if you keep doin' that, I'm gonna come in my pants," he slurs.

"We can't have that," Adeline says, her lips curling into a smirk as she kisses him. Her mouth leaves his, travelling over his jaw and down the column of his neck as Billy tilts his head back against the rug. He closes his eyes and loses himself in the sensation of

Adeline's mouth and hands, so soft yet so determined as she kisses down his chest and licks over his hip bones.

He hears the soft jingle of Pancake's collar somewhere amongst the wet sounds of Adeline's mouth and the desperation leaving his own. Billy opens his eyes again just as Adeline shuffles back and unfastens the button of his jeans. *Finally,* he thinks, but the brush of his boxer shorts over his length as she shimmies everything down is sweet torture; what he needs and not enough all at once.

Adeline wraps her hand around him, her thumb collecting the pre-cum from his slit as she swipes over the head of his cock and then drags her hand down to the base. She repeats the motion, pumping over his length until he's so sure he's about to come. He's sure Adeline knows it too because she stops and peers at him through her eyelashes, acting all coy as she drops a kiss to his tip and takes him into her mouth, just between her lips, before letting go. The steady simmer within him becomes a rolling boil threatening to spill over and his cock throbs from the lack of orgasm, twitching against his stomach.

"*Baby,*" Billy gasps as he searches for a hold on Adeline and pulls her down into a messy kiss. Then he's bathing in her shadow as she sinks down onto his cock and he knows he's not going to last long. She's so hot and tight, sucking him in as she rolls her hips and keeps him buried deep. It's the slowest most intense fuck of his life.

"Addie... sweetheart, I gotta–" he grunts and she slows, letting him take over. Billy grips her hip with his right hand, his left palm resting on her thigh as he begins to rut up into her, deeper and harder with every thrust.

"*Billy.* Oh! *Oh my God!*" Adeline comes and Billy feels her squeezing the fuck out of his cock as she rides it out and falls against his chest, boneless. She kisses him. It's a chaotic clash of tongue and teeth as Billy pulls almost all the way out and he moans as the thick vein on the underside of his cock slides deliciously inside her. That's what does it. It leaves him shaking as he spills into her with a soft groan and a string of curses. Exhausted.

They're a tangle of limbs on the floor afterwards. Billy's jeans are still pulled down to his thighs as they trade lazy kisses. He's pretty sure Adeline dozes off on top of him a little while later, her steady breaths warm across his chest. They really should clean up and relocate Adeline to somewhere more comfortable than half on him and half on the floor but he's learning to live in moments like these and take them for what they are. So, instead, he lets her sleep and whispers all the plans he has for them as she snores softly into the curve of his neck.

Blocking his eyes from the early morning rays, Billy ambles down to the ranch gates. His t-shirt is askew on his shoulder and his hair must look like a bird's nest from the rough glide and pull of Adeline's fingers. At least the horses don't seem to mind his appearance as he passes the paddock on his way to the mailbox.

Knocking down the flag, he flips open the latch and reaches inside to pull out the thin stack of envelopes. Two bills, a letter from his mom and the morning newspaper. More than usual. Billy tucks the envelopes under his left arm and uses his right to flip the newspaper open to the sports pages, folding it back so he can read as he walks. He doesn't even make it two steps before the headline of the first page stops him in his tracks.

EARLY RETIREMENT FOR NASCAR STAR

"What the fuck?"

Billy reads on.

'*Hard Strike Motorsports says goodbye to Rex Harlow as the 1972 Winston Cup winner hangs up his racing suit.*'

He's back at the ranch house before he knows it, putting too much weight on his ankle as he slams the front door closed and hurries up stairs to where Adeline is still lounging in bed. As he swings into the bedroom, she's just hanging up the phone.

"That was my dad," she says as Billy throws the paper on the messed up sheets. Adeline skim-reads the headline. "What's that?"

"A crock of shit is what it is," Billy growls. "Bastard shouldn't get to keep his reputation with a fuckin' retirement story."

"He's been banned for life, that's what my dad just said." She reaches for Billy to come back to bed, unusually calm. "Let everyone think he chose it. *We* know he would have gone kicking and screaming and that's enough for me. Never seeing him again is enough for me."

"Maybe it'll all come out eventually?" Billy says, kissing her softly and squeezing her tight.

"Yeah, maybe. But right now it's over," she whispers and Billy realises that's all Adeline ever really wanted.

thirty-seven

ADELINE
November 4th, 1975

"Forty-six, fifty-two," Adeline calls, holding up the stopwatch as Patrick climbs out of the car. He pulls off his helmet, his brunet curls flat to his head, and makes his way over with slouched shoulders. Billy meets him halfway and claps him on the shoulder with an encouraging smile.

"Fuck," Patrick grunts, disheartened. "That's worse than the last one."

"The average lap at Daytona is forty-five seconds. You're nearly there, bud."

"Not close enough. I wanna qualify, Billy." He runs a hand through his hair and blows out a heavy sigh. "Can I go again?"

"Sure," Billy replies, "go through the starting line checks, I'll be right over."

Patrick trudges back to the car as Adeline threads her fingers through Billy's. He squeezes back gently and brings their hands to his mouth, pressing a warm kiss to Adeline's knuckles.

"You reckon he'll make it?"

"Kid's good," Billy responds with a shrug. "He's still braking on the bends a little too heavily, all the weight ends up on the front wheels and the back of the car pulls. That's what's slowing him down."

"He's got the drive though. Like you; he wants to qualify but won't take anything but first place."

"He'll qualify." Billy seems sure about it and honestly, Adeline can see why. Patrick's progressed in leaps and bounds over the past few months. He's cleaner, more precise with his driving decisions, and in clear control of the car. Watching him makes Adeline miss seeing Billy behind the wheel. It's only been six months but it feels like a lifetime since she last saw that beaming smile on his face. She misses the way it would light up even more once he found her after the podium and the way he would kiss her like it's the only thing he's thought about for the past two hundred laps.

"What about you? How are you doing?" She asks quietly and Billy wraps his arms around her. He uses both of them with so much ease now that Adeline' breath catches every time he does it, half expecting him to wince in pain. Instead, he takes a deep, even breath.

"I think I wanna try today. Just a lap, maybe two– just to see."

Adeline exhales. If he does even half a lap today, that's– that's the furthest Billy would have driven since May. Beyond sitting behind the wheel in the garage and getting the feel of it again.

"I'd be proud of you even if you only managed to start her up. You know that, right?"

"Yeah, sweetheart. I know," Billy says softly. "I can't wait to race again, but it's because of you that I'd be okay if I didn't. You gotta know that too, Addie."

The smile that blooms over Adeline's lips is so big her jaw aches and she ducks her head as her cheeks flush warm. She can sense Billy's gaze on her, unsurprised when she glances up to him looking at her with such adoration, such *love*. Sometimes she has to pinch herself as a reminder that they have this, and it's not until moments like this that she realises how much they've changed each other's lives just by being in them.

"I love you," she breathes, burying her face into the soft muscles of his chest. "I'm always gonna love you."

There's so much she could add to the end of that–

I'm always gonna love you even when we fight.

I'm always gonna love you even when you don't love yourself.

I'm always gonna love you even if everything were to fall apart tomorrow.

– but she leaves them unspoken. Billy knows.

"I love you more," Billy says. He punctuates it with a kiss, slow and lazy with it. Every ounce of added pressure and roll of his tongue against hers is deliberate, made to draw out small gasps and a breathless moan.

"You should go," Adeline sighs between kisses, reluctant to stop. Billy grins against her mouth and tugs teasingly on her bottom lip before letting go with a soft pop. Then he pouts – his go-to move to win her over – and she so nearly falls for it. She nearly shouts for Patrick to tell him practise is over for the day, but Billy promised him another lap at least, so she relents and gently pushes Billy away instead. "Go on, hot stuff."

Billy has other plans though and Adeline squeals as he picks her up and spins her around until she's dizzy and giggling. With her head thrown back, he kisses along her jaw, hot and open-mouthed until he finds her mouth. He places her down gently and presses his lips to her forehead, his growing beard wiry and scratchy but Adeline loves it. Loves the way it feels under her fingertips, deliciously rough over her sensitive skin.

"Okay, I'm goin'," Billy finally says, stepping back and taking his gorgeous lips and beard with him. Adeline most definitely does not whimper at the loss of them. "You should go call your dad."

Adeline grumbles but Billy is right. She and Michael agreed on calling weekly to catch up and she missed the last one for reasons Adeline is definitely not telling her father about.

"When I come back we'll do your lap," she says. "Do *not* drive without me here, Billy Brooks."

"Aye, aye, Cap'n." Billy gives a lazy two finger salute, grinning at her as he takes the stopwatch. His smile is bright but the apprehension is still heavy in his eyes and more than anything Adeline just wants to make everything good and okay for him. She brushes his hair from his eyes and cups his face.

"Love you."

"Love you too," Billy murmurs as he walks backwards towards the start line and Patrick, who's been waiting with the patience of a saint.

Once she's back in the house, Adeline makes herself comfortable by the phone with a cup of coffee and a handful of mini cookies from the pantry. Snacks are imperative when one missed call means Michael will have twice as much to catch her up on. He answers on the third ring and after their usual pleasantries – which is Adeline just repeating '*I miss you*' over and over until she feels like she's got it out of her system – Michael tells her about his time on the road and Adeline tells him all the Pancake related and dad-friendly stories she can think of.

"Oh, hey. I was thinking," Adeline says once they're onto the topic, "the next race is in Atlanta, right? Do you guys wanna come here after and then we can all travel to California for the final race together?"

She and Billy have spoken about going to that one. With Rex out of the NASCAR scene (and banned from stepping foot into any speedway or raceway across the country thanks to Teddy), they don't have to worry about running into him. Plus, Adeline *really* wants to see her friends race one last time before the new season begins in January.

"*You're gonna be there?*"

"Yeah we'll be there," she says with a smile, "and Thanksgiving too."

"*Good. I think it'll be nice to have everyone together after the year we've all had.*"

"Will you make your stuffing?" Adeline asks and Michael's warm laugh comes down the line. She can picture him shaking his head fondly, years of that expression ingrained into her brain.

"*Yes, sunshine. I'll make the stuffing.*"

"Cool. I told Billy it's the best part of Thanksgiving."

"*You flatter me, Addie. It's your grandma's recipe, she's the one you gotta thank.*"

"And I shall thank my dead grandmother profusely, she'll be top of my list," Adeline chuckles as her gaze lands on the clock. She's been on the phone for almost forty-five minutes, Billy's bound to be done with Patrick by now. "I gotta go, Pops. Billy's waiting for me down at the track. He's gonna drive today."

"*Well, ain't that somethin'. Let me know how it goes?*"

"I will. Love you, see you next week."

"*Love you, sunshine. Stay outta trouble.*"

"No promises," she sings before hanging up and hurrying back to Billy.

He beams when he sees her approaching, leaning casually against the car with driving gloves on ready and his helmet waiting on the hood.

"Have you been waiting long?" Adeline pants out, slowing to a stop in front of him.

"Nope," Billy says, popping the p. "Patrick just left. Said something about helping Myles for the rest of the afternoon. How's your dad?"

"Good, yeah. I asked him about everyone coming here after Atlanta and that we'll be at Thanksgiving too. Oh, maybe you can invite your parents and Rosie!"

"Sounds good, baby. Did you tell him we'll be at the last race too?"

"Of course."

"Good, I'm not missin' Stan win the cup." Adeline grins at him and gestures to the car.

"Are you ready?"

"Honestly? No," Billy laughs nervously," but now seems as good a time as any."

"I'll be right here, and if you change your mind, it's okay."

"No, I gotta do this."

There's the strong-willed, determined Billy she fell in love with. Adeline clutches at his driving suit and reels him in, kissing him furiously and longingly all at once. She draws back, breathless and Billy looks dazed, a big, dopey smile on his face. Adeline bounces on her feet as he pulls on his helmet and climbs into the driver's seat. Apprehension and pride accumulating as one giant ball of tension in her belly. Once Billy's strapped in, ready to go, he beams at her from beneath his visor and Adeline knows he's ready.

"What are you made of?"

Billy turns on the ignition and it's like a switch flips. His whole posture changes; arms and back and neck braced for the speed.

"Fuckin' stardust, Tinkerbell!" He shouts over the roar of the engine and then his foot leaves the clutch and Billy Brooks drives for the first time in six months.

thirty-eight

BILLY
November 12th, 1975
Ontario Motor Speedway, California

STAN WINS. HE CROSSES THE FINISH LINE IN FIRST PLACE and with it, he ends the race with enough points to tip him over the top and make him the 1975 Winston Cup champion. Billy and Adeline watch the race from Adeline's usual spot beside the stands, away from the crowds. They scream their way through the last lap, when it becomes obvious Stan has won, until their voices are hoarse and they're red in the face.

Being back in the chaos of race day is, well, it's something. Billy wasn't sure what to expect – six months away, six months of quiet and feeling detached from the whole thing – but once they'd arrived and he found himself amongst the grease and noise of the Shaw & Gold garage, it was like he'd never been away.

Stan is busy talking to the press when they reconvene with everyone before the podium ceremony and Billy and Adeline slip by unseen. They've been lucky, really, escaping to Georgia. No one knows where they've been except those who need to and Billy's grateful for it. Grateful to have avoided the press more than any other driver in his situation probably would have. He knows Tobias has been fielding calls to the office himself since May, giving them smart-ass responses as only Tobias would, but the demands for a statement from Billy have only increased since Rex's 'retirement'. The journalists aren't dumb.

"Does it feel weird being on the other side of it?" Adeline asks as they watch their friend work his charm; it's Stan being his usual goofy self but the press are lapping it up.

"A little," Billy admits, "kinda nice just being back though."

Adeline cuddles into his side, all warm and soft in his arms.

"You'll be up there again before you know it," she murmurs, pressing up onto her tiptoes to place a tender kiss to the underside of his jaw. Billy hums in response, he really hopes she's right but he's not about to set himself up with high expectations. Not when he's barely made it over 60mph doing a lap of the track at the ranch. He knows it'll take time, probably longer than he'd like, if he's ever going to get back to the confident, fearless driver he was.

Before he can dwell on it too much, Norah sidles up to them. Still in her racing suit and with her red hair a little all over the place from her helmet, she grins at them proudly.

"Hey, guys. It's about to start. D'you wanna come up front with me and Gabe?" Billy agrees enthusiastically and slides his hand into Adeline's. He lets himself be grounded by her soft palm and slight fingers locked with his as they follow Norah out to the crowd of drivers and crew waiting around the podium. The first thing he notices is how loud it is out amongst the fray. It's all background noise when he's up on the podium, when the blood is still rushing in his ears and they're ringing, the echo of roaring car engines still bouncing around in his head. Billy must squeeze Adeline's hand without realising because she's suddenly up on her tiptoes again, her mouth tickling over his ear.

"You okay?" She whispers and Billy nods with an easy smile. He presses a quick kiss to Adeline's lips and then nudges her in front of him when the announcer taps his microphone and Teddy, as chairman, takes his place to present the medals and championship cup.

Third place is a Hard Strike Motorsports driver, Marcus Foster. He used to keep Billy at arms length when he drove for the team, like he was some kind of outsider. Looking back, Billy can't believe he even signed a contract with them, but he was desperate to be in the big leagues and they held the door wide open.

With his arms around Adeline's shoulders, Billy cheers and whoops for Rick, the Apex driver who placed second. He's a decent guy and a beast on the track, good enough to have been Billy's strongest competition alongside Rex and Stan. Speaking of, he can see his best friend waiting at the edge of the podium. He's bouncing on his feet and rolling his shoulders like a boxer waiting to enter the ring. Billy can almost see the nerves rolling off of him; he remembers how that feels. As drivers, they're so used to hiding behind their helmets, in their cars and going at breakneck speeds around the track, that the moment they're thrust into the spotlight for actually being good at it is the moment they realise they're not prepared to be so *seen*. He catches Stan's eye and grins.

"You got this," he mouths, giving him two enthusiastic thumbs up and Stan's face lights up just as the announcer begins his introduction. He reels off Stan's series stats, really getting the crowd going and dragging it out as much as he can. Billy watches Stan suck in lungful of air and then–

"Ladies and gentlemen, your 1975 Winston Cup Champion, Stanley Reynolds!"

Stan runs up to the podium and the cheers become deafening. Billy whistles and screams for his best friend, gripping Adeline's shoulders and shaking her excitedly until her laughing and giggling melds with the celebration around them. Then Stan is the one to catch Billy's eye and he tilts his head, beckoning for Billy to go up there with him.

"No way!" Billy laughs. This is Stan's moment, the last thing he wants is to overshadow it.

"Billy Brooks, get your ass up here!" Stan shouts. His booming voice is loud enough over the din that it gains people's attention and well, now what? Billy shakes his head still but Stan hops down with a determined flick of his eyebrow and stalks towards him while Adeline pushes him forward despite his protests.

"Go, baby!" Adeline urges, "they wanna see you."

"Addie, wait– no, Stan." But it's too late, his feet, with a life of their own, carry him up the steps behind Stan, who tucks him under his arm once they're back on the middle podium. Cameras flash and somehow the noise doubles. It roars in his ears as people begin to realise who Stan has pulled up there with him.

"Really, pal?" Billy hisses as he plasters a smile on his face.

"People missed you, B."

And well, Billy would be lying if he said he hadn't missed this too. He glances down at the crowd and is met with Adeline beaming at him, all rosy-cheeked and proud. Billy knows he would be fine if he never raced again but that doesn't stop the want that courses through him. The want for the rush, the adrenaline – and to look down and see the love of his life looking at him like that?

Fuck.

There's no question about it.

Billy's gonna race again.

Billy *has* to race again.

Thanksgiving, 1975
Malibu, California

He emerges from Adeline's bedroom to the sound of music and chatter, and for a brief moment wonders just how long he was napping for. Billy blinks, bleary-eyed as he hops down the last few stairs and into the living room to find the house is far more crowded than when he disappeared upstairs for a pre-dinner snooze.

"*Baby!*" Adeline's voice carries above the noise, her eyes lighting up as she clocks him at the bottom of the stairs. She's dancing, twirling and giggly, with a cocktail shaker in her hand. Stan is beside her, holding a bottle of vodka in one hand and orange juice in the other, and Billy assumes they're in the process of making Harvey Wallbangers.

"How many of those have you had already?" He chuckles as he pads over to them. Adeline reaches out as soon as he's close enough, her small hand landing softly on his chest. Light fingers drum over his heart as she grins up at him, sheepish and playful, and then she cups the back of his neck and pulls him in for a kiss instead of answering his question. Billy kisses back; can't not give her what she wants even in a room full of people. He tries to keep it chaste, short and sweet, until Adeline slyly deepens the kiss. She tilts her head and bites down on his bottom lip just hard enough to elicit a gasp and for his lips to part so she can lick into his mouth. Billy tastes her then, all vodka and orange juice and whichever hor d'oeuvres have already been passed around.

Someone wolf whistles from across the room. Gabe, Billy guesses judging by the grumble of pain and pitiful '*hey*' he hears not even a second later – the result of him being scolded by Norah, no doubt.

"Okay, lovebirds. This is a family show, don't push it," Tobias says, his eye roll evident in his voice. Adeline pulls back, if only to serve Tobias a glare and a pout, before pressing one last kiss to the corner of Billy's mouth just for the sheer hell of it.

"Hi," she whispers, gifting him with the adorable scrunch of her nose that makes him melt every time. Billy grins back and nods to the cocktail shaker in Adeline's hand.

"Hi, Tinkerbell. You make enough of that to share?"

"Maybe. You'll have to fight Stan for it though."

Billy's gaze slides across the room to his best friend, cuddled on the couch with Wren and shrugs.

"I could take him," he says. Stan narrows his eyes, all serious as he points two fingers at himself then turns them at Billy before he falters and falls into a fit of tipsy giggles. Billy lifts one eyebrow incredulously.

"You need to work on your scare tactics, pal!" Billy calls and slings his arm around Adeline, planting a smacker of a kiss to the side of her head as he drags her with him to the kitchen. He's parched, and starved, and figures that's the best place to start in his search for a post-nap snack.

Whilst Adeline pours them both a drink and chats quietly to her father, Billy picks at what's left of the hor 'd'oeuvres – mostly the least favoured devilled eggs and cheese sticks – before joining Adeline and Michael, who appears to be making his famous stuffing. Just a peek at the stuff makes Billy begin to salivate. Fuck, he loves Thanksgiving. To make matters worse, the kitchen is filled with the smell of succulent turkey and herby, roasted vegetables. None of it helps his hunger as he peeks into the oven, opening the door just enough for the delicious scent to waft out in a billow of steam.

"Don't even think about it, William." His mother appears beside him, fussing him out of the way with a dish towel over her shoulder and Michael's '*kiss the cook*' apron double tied around her middle.

"I was just looking," he responds, feeling every bit like he's twelve years old again, caught with his hand in the cookie jar.

"That's not going to make it cook any quicker," Eleanor laughs. "Here, if you're that hungry, I saved you some of those canapés you like." Billy grins as his mom rummages in the refrigerator, producing a tray of cucumber slices with perfectly swirled smoked salmon mousse on top.

"I ever tell you how much I love you, Ma?"

"You're such a suck-up, Billy," Rosie taunts from somewhere behind them. Billy didn't even notice her sneaking into the kitchen. The card game she was playing with Patrick, Gabe and Norah looked like it was getting pretty heated when he and Adeline left the living room, so he assumes his sister lost. He's quick to swipe the tray from Eleanor's hands when Rosie reaches for one of *his* canapés – the audacity – and he twirls out of the way with the tray high above his head as he narrowly avoids falling into Adeline. She pushes a glass of Harvey Wallbanger towards him and in return, he offers her a slice of cucumber.

"Betrayal!" Rosie gasps dramatically and Eleanor sighs.

"Alright, kids. Out of the kitchen." Rosie flees and Billy fills a plate with as many cucumber slices as he can, leaving the empty tray behind with a kiss on the cheek for his mother.

"Come on, Tinkerbell. We linger any longer and she'll set the dish towel on our asses," he laughs as he leads Adeline out of the kitchen with a muffled *'thanks, Ma'* called over his shoulder around a mouthful of canapés. As they enter the living room, Billy stops to assess the scene in front of him. Thanksgiving for the Brooks family is usually a small affair. Just him, Rosie and their parents, a small turkey dinner and, if they're up for it, a trip over the river to watch the Macy's parade on the streets rather than on television. Right now though, he couldn't be more grateful for the extended family he has. Stan, Gabe and Norah, Patrick and Wren and Tobias – they've all contributed to his recovery some way or another.

He nudges Adeline gently towards the only free seat in the room, pulling her onto his lap, and they work their way through his plate of food as they watch the others play charades, heckling them and giggling when Gabe gets annoyed. The whole day has warmed Billy's insides with happiness; everything feels cosy and lovely like Thanksgiving should be, even in California. Stan keeps feeding them cocktails and Adeline goes quiet against Billy's chest, soft and sleepy as the afternoon wears on. He realises, as he strokes slow, methodical lines up and down Adeline's arm, that he wants *this* more than anything else. Holidays with a big family, ridiculous games and good food and– he stops the sentimental thought spiral before the hope of it all makes him cry. Adeline sighs, blinking out of her drowsiness when Billy tenderly noses into her hair and kisses her temple.

Charades ends and the music is turned up, filling the room with high energy once again. Billy taps Adeline on the thigh and she hops up, letting him tug her into his arms for a dance. They spin and twirl, switching partners and laughing breathlessly until they end up falling into – and onto – each other on the couch.

"If you kids are done working up an appetite," Eleanor chuckles as she ambles into the living room, "dinner is ready." Billy jumps to his feet, roping in the boys to help carry dishes from the kitchen whilst Adeline and Norah refill everyone's glasses, and then they're seated, all twelve of them squeezed around the Gold's dining table.

"Who wants to go first?" Michael asks, "Addie?"

"Sure," she replies as her fingers slide over Billy's thigh and he catches her smiling at him, all soft and adoring. "I'm thankful for Billy, and the family I've gained because of him. But more than anything, I'm thankful he's still here."

Billy swallows as the urge to cry creeps up his throat again, itching at the backs of his eyes. He can't look at his mom. If he does that, he won't be able to help the tears. Instead, he keeps his eyes down and sips at his drink as Michael gives his thanks and once he knows the attention is off of him and Adeline, he glances her way and whispers a hushed '*I love you*'.

They go around the table after that and Billy takes the time to compose himself further. Stan expresses his gratitude for Wren, Norah and Gabe, and his mom and dad keep theirs short and sweet, thankful for their babies and getting to watch them thrive. Patrick thanks Tobias and Michael for taking a chance on him and Billy for mentoring him. And then they're back to the start, and all eyes are on Billy.

He takes a long pull of his beer and raises his eyebrows as she rubs a hand through his overgrown beard. The earns some laughs, some levity to the fact that he's about to thank the heavens he's still alive.

"I guess, well..." he starts, "I'm thankful I'm still here too, obviously, and for everyone at this table– well, everyone except Rosie."

"Thanks, knucklehead," she quips and Billy flashes her a fond smile, because as much as they bicker and tease, Billy loves his little sister a whole lot.

"Most of all, I'm thankful for you, Tinkerbell." He turns to Adeline just as she bows her head, her cheeks flushing pink. Billy tucks a finger under her chin and when her watery eyes meet his, he continues. "Thankful to have you in my corner, thankful to be in *your* corner. Thankful that you seemed to come into my life right when I needed you. Uh, yeah. That's it. Happy Thanksgiving, everyone," he says, grinning, and then quieter, softly into Adeline's ear, "Happy Thanksgiving, baby."

Later, with full bellies and a tipsy warmth trickling through their veins, everyone migrates out to the beach. It's a mild late afternoon for November and the sun is just beginning to set, sparkling across the sea. They all settle on the sand and George and Michael start a fire, his dad looking oh so keen to show off his old boy scout skills.

People pair off, mingling with other families who have gathered further down the beach, and as Billy lies back beside Adeline, he feels a kind of settled happiness in his bones that he hasn't in a long time.

"I think this might be one of the best days of my life," he murmurs as he peers over at Adeline with one eye closed, the other scrunched against the setting sun.

"It's been pretty great, hasn't it?" Adeline hums in response as Billy pulls her against his side and they soak up the last of the day's warmth. Someone wanders closer just as he feels himself beginning to doze and he reluctantly opens an eye, expecting it to be Stan or Gabe, come to ruin the peace. Instead, Michael sits down next to them, knees bent up and beer in his hands.

It's time then.

"Hey, sunshines. Mind if I talk to you guys for a minute?"

Adeline sits up as Billy forces himself out of that weird phase of sleep where he's not sure if he's dreaming or not. He blinks himself awake as Michael catches his eye, the weight of their secret held in his smile.

"What's up?" Adeline questions, levelling her father with narrowed eyes as she tries to suss him out.

"Nothing bad, I just... Well, I was going to wait until next month but I want to give you something, an early wedding present, I guess." He shifts on the sand as he retrieves a folded envelope from his back pocket and holds it out to them. Adeline takes it tentatively, turning it in her hand before she begins to peel back the seal and pull the paper out. Billy peers across at it, his gaze tracking over the page as Adeline reads quietly under her breath.

"This property transfer deed, executed November 19th 1975 by grantor Michael Franklin Gold to the grantees Adeline Elizabeth Gold and William James Brooks... the property described as a 210-acre ranch– Dad, is this..."

Michael nods, reaching for Adeline's hand. "I know how much you love that place, Addie, and you two have made a home there over the last six months. So, it's yours; the perfect place to raise that dream family of yours that Billy won't shut up about," he chuckles. Adeline glances at Billy over her shoulder and he shrugs, his lips curling into a sly smile.

"What? We talk."

Poured my heart out, more like, Billy thinks as he remembers the long heart to heart he and Michael shared back when he'd asked permission to marry Adeline and Michael had countered his question with his own about transferring ownership of the ranch.

"Dad, you can't just... *give* us the ranch," Adeline says, flabbergasted.

"I can," Michael retorts with a laugh, "just did."

There's a beat; a moment where Adeline physically takes it in, her face going through several different emotions before she throws herself into her father's arms, sending them collapsing to the sand, and Billy can't tell if she's laughing or crying. He catches Michael's eye and murmurs a soft '*thank you.*'

"Thank you, Dad. Seriously, I can't– this is crazy!" Adeline mumbles into their embrace.

"You kids deserve it. You're gonna have a long and beautiful life together on that ranch," he says, "I just know it."

thirty-nine

BILLY
December 20th, 1975
Gold Brooks Family Ranch, Georgia

"I'm gonna puke."

"You're not gonna puke."

"I am. I'm gonna chuck up all those pastries Gabe force fed me this morning and my suit will be ruined and the wedding–"

Stan sighs and levels Billy with an exasperated glare. "Billy, you need to chill. You're marrying the woman who looks at you like you hung the fuckin' moon and stars in the sky just for her, you have no reason to be nervous."

"I would," Billy replies, running his clammy palms down the front of his suit jacket.

"Huh?"

"I would hang the moon and stars for her, y'know, if I could."

"I know you would, pal. But right now, all she wants is to see you at the end of that aisle when she walks through those doors." Billy glances at Stan – ever the voice of reason – as the weight of his best friend's hand comes down on his shoulder, giving it a comforting squeeze.

The wedding isn't due to start for another hour but Billy needs room to pace, somewhere to get out the nervous energy that's been pulsing under his skin since he said goodbye to Adeline last night. She was whisked off to some fancy hotel in the city with his mom and sister, Norah and Wren in tow, and Billy's been like a jumpy, skittish kitten ever since.

The doors to the barn creak open and Billy moves his head so fast he almost causes himself whiplash, but it's just Gabe and Patrick. They wander in with beers in their hands and concerned, slightly forced smiles on their faces. Patrick has Billy's camera case in his free hand, loaded up with film cartridges and under strict instruction to film the whole day.

"You good, man?" Gabe asks, handing a beer off to him. Billy takes it, chugs back half the bottle and belches.

"Yep."

"He's not good, is he?"

"Can't go a day without her," Stan jokes. "Hey, Billy. Does Adeline know what she's getting herself into?"

"Please," Gabe scoffs, "they're both as bad as each other."

"Are you guys done?" Billy snarks and gulps back more beer in hopes it sedates his jitters just a little. It's reminiscent of how he feels pre-race, too much adrenaline mixed with excitement and impatience to just get out there and do it.

"Yeah, we're done," Stan replies. Billy doesn't miss the way his gaze slides to Gabe in an almost cynical eye roll.

He keeps pacing, stopping at the front of the barn every few turns up and down the aisle to admire its makeover. They could have married in the little chapel down the road – or even in the hotel where Adeline is currently getting ready – but when it came down to it, marrying at the ranch just felt right, even in December.

The barn has stayed empty since Billy cleared it out for Adeline's birthday back in August, only today it has been kitted out with blankets on seats and space heaters plugged into portable generators in a bid to keep the chill out. The aisle is made up of an array of vintage rugs Adeline picked out from thrift stores, all layered over each other to cover the floor. Sheer navy fabric hangs draped over the slatted wooden walls and Billy's pretty sure they bought every hardware store out of Christmas festoon lights. They're strung across the roof to look like stars. It looks perfect and it's all down to Adeline.

Billy's lost count of how many times he would be called into the kitchen for his opinion over the past few months, walking in to his mom and Adeline sitting with several large pieces of card stock in front of them as they planned everything out together. Billy's also lost count of how many cups of coffee and slices of his mom's famous apple cake he supplied them with. It was all worth it though, for his heart to burst every time Adeline would tick something off the list, give him the most gorgeous smile and say '*one step closer*'. As if he needed the reminder that he's lucky enough to spend the rest of his life with the girl of his dreams when he's been counting down the days too.

"Oh, Norah called," Patrick says quickly, as if he'd only just remembered, and the sudden announcement draws Billy out of his head. "Well, no, actually Adeline called and then it was just thirty seconds of Norah trying to wrestle the phone from her. She said she misses you and can't wait to see how handsome you look– Addie said that, not Norah... obviously."

Billy smiles bashfully as the tension in his body melts away. The urge he's had to hop in the car and drive to see Adeline halted by just a few words. He knows it would have been 'bad luck' but he figured he's had his fair share of bad luck already this year, he would have taken his chances.

"Thanks, kid."

Patrick nods, flashing Billy an understanding smile just as Michael knocks in the door and peers in.

"People are starting to arrive," he says, "Myles is just showing them where to park. I can set them up with a pre-ceremony drinks thing if you guys need more time?" He's looking at Billy but it's Stan who speaks up.

"I think we're good. We'll get rid of these," he says, shaking his empty beer bottle. "Patrick can start seating people while we get freshened up back at the house."

Choosing Stan as his best man was no-brainer, and with Gabe, Patrick and Myles all groomsmen, Billy knows he has a good bunch to keep him in check today. He claimed Pancake too, even had a little bowtie made to match and it's probably the cutest thing he's ever seen – even if it did take twenty minutes for him to wrangle her into it. Gabe has offered to hold her during the ceremony and Billy feels bad telling him that she'll probably claw her way out of his arms before he and Adeline even get to their vows.

"Come on, B." Stan holds out his packet of Marlboro, a cigarette already between his lips and another pushed out of the packet, waiting for Billy to take it. He does, letting Stan light it for him once they're outside and they take a slow meander back to the house while Patrick hurries off to escort people to the barn. It helps, kinda. He doesn't smoke half as much as he used to but it does just enough to mellow him out a little more.

Back at the house, Billy cleans up and brushes his teeth before wandering through to the living room to sit at the piano. Pancake, right on cue, pounces up onto his lap and attempts to bury her paws into his pressed dress pants. As she curls up comfortably in his lap, her fur clings to the fabric immediately but Billy doesn't mind, not when the gentle vibrations of her purr soothe him more than the beer and cigarette ever could.

He savours the moment of quiet, the last he's going to get until he and Adeline get to sneak off for some alone time later. Stan and Gabe must sense his need for it because they hang back in the kitchen with Michael, so it's just a man and his cat sitting at a baby grand piano. Billy tinkers, sparse notes and an off-tune, until he absentmindedly finds himself playing *Can't Help Falling in Love*.

That's how Eleanor finds him.

"Oh, my sweet boy! Look at you, you look so handsome."

Billy chuckles, his gaze falling to his lap. He never could take compliments from his mom growing up. Turns out he still can't without turning into a bashful fool.

"Thanks, Ma. You look beautiful," he comments softly, taking in her dress. It's soft pink and frilly around the sleeves, and with the way she's styled her hair, Billy just knows she went through the trouble of sleeping in her curlers like she would have for church back in the 50s. He and Rosie used to help her take them out when they were kids. He's so caught up in admiring his mother and the sweet memory that it only just occurs to him that if she's here then– "Wait, is Addie here already?"

"No, not yet. Your father came to collect me first, I wanted to see you before the ceremony. Adeline looks gorgeous, honey. Glowing."

Billy smiles as he imagines Adeline all dolled up and he scoots along the piano bench, careful not to disturb Pancake, and Eleanor sits down beside him. She gives the cat a gentle scratch behind the ear before looking up at Billy with big, blue eyes that mirror his own and crinkle at the corners as she smiles.

"Is this the part where you give me a pep talk?" He asks jokingly and Eleanor cradles his jaw, her thumb brushing softly over the apples of his cheek.

"You don't need a pep talk, sweetheart. You've been ready to marry that girl for months. I just came to give you some love before you become a married man."

"Well, you know I'll always take that," Billy grins as he drops his head down onto his mother's shoulder. He's a mama's boy through and through and he'd never deny it.

"I'm so proud of you, William."

"I'm only gettin' married, Ma."

"Even for that," Eleanor says. "How many times would you come back from the Jones' complaining about Delilah's father trying to palm off his mother's ring? She was never the one for you, Billy, and I'm sorry we ever pushed that on you."

"It's how things were done back then, I don't blame you."

"Still, I'm proud of you for getting out. We hated seeing you so unhappy. Especially when you would tell anyone who'd listen how excited you were to get married and have a big family someday," she sighs. "I'm glad you're allowing yourself to have that dream again."

"It's all Adeline," Billy says wistfully. And it's true. He's sure that kind of life would have sat on the back burner for years otherwise, at least until he was ready to retire from racing, and who knows when that would have been.

Eleanor agrees with a soft hum as Billy goes back to playing the piano. Adeline has taught him a variety of songs since August, evenings at the piano becoming a regular thing as they wound down for the night. He plays around with them, his mom humming to the ones she recognises, and together they while away the minutes.

Not long now.

"We should probably head over," Gabe calls as the clock inches closer to 2pm. He pokes his head into the living room with a tender smile for Eleanor.

"Here goes nothing," Billy breathes, anticipation simmering low in his belly. He tucks Pancake into his jacket for the walk over, her little face poking out as she settles in against his chest. "Thanks for the pep talk, Ma."

"Wasn't a pep talk, Billy," Eleanor tuts softly as she links her arm through his. "Let's go get you married."

There's a hum of chatter when he enters the barn and everyone greets him with wide smiles and words of congratulations. They shake his hand or pat him on the back as he makes his way to the front. Once there, he hands a cosy and reluctant Pancake over to Gabe and takes a moment to prepare himself. A hand through his hair and a straighten up of his suit, and as he looks out to the doors, it hits him suddenly.

He's about to marry his best friend.

The barn is warmer now it's full of people and Billy is *sweating*. He's practically vibrating with adrenaline but with Stan beside him and his mom and dad in the front row, he doesn't have to look far for a reassuring, albeit teary, smile.

Then the doors open and the entrance music starts. Norah leads the way, smiling at Gabe before she sends a wink Billy's way as she takes her place opposite with his sister and Wren.

"Who knew you scrubbed up so nice?" Rosie whispers with a

shit-eating grin as she passes him. It earns her a chuckle and the gentle teasing from his sister feels like the slice of normality he needs to momentarily calm his nerves.

Until Adeline walks in.

Billy feels like he's been sucker-punched as the air is knocked from his lungs. His mouth is dry and the face-splitting smile is automatic as he meets Adeline's gaze. She is completely and utterly the most beautiful woman he's ever seen. Walking towards him, a vision in white, she has flowers in her wavy hair and a secret smile on her lips as she mouths a silent greeting across the barn.

Billy thanks his lucky stars. He thanks the parties they would circle with an eye on each other, thanks Michael and Tobias for signing him, and Delilah's father for hitting that last nerve that drove him to the Gold's beach house – to Adeline – on Christmas Day. He thanks the secret kisses and hidden moments in hotel rooms and everything else that brought them to this point right here, right now. Adeline comes to a stop beside him and Billy is acutely aware of the slight tremor in his hands and the way his heart rate picks up.

"Hi, sweet girl," he whispers, low and only for her. His breath catches and he swallows thickly, willing himself not to cry yet as he curls his fingers around Adeline's; painless now and with as much feeling as ever. As the strings fade out, they turn to Tobias.

"Alright folks, let's get this show on the road.

ADELINE

THE MOMENT IT SUDDENLY HITS ADELINE THAT SHE'S ABOUT to marry Billy happens just as she waits outside the barn. Norah fusses around her dress and her father stands beside her, patiently waiting for her to give the go ahead as they listen to the soft hum of voices filtering out from inside.

"How're you feeling, sunshine? Ready to do this thing?"

Adeline grins up at him. Honestly, she hasn't stopped grinning all morning. Not when Norah woke her up at the crack of dawn, or when she had to breathe in just a little more than usual to get her dress done up, or even when a rogue horse decided to stop and graze right in the middle of the road and almost made her late. As for being ready? Adeline has been ready to marry Billy since the moment he shook her hand a year ago. Every moment since just feels like it's been leading to today.

"I'm ready," she says, taking one last deep, calming breath as Michael nods and brushes his lips delicately against her hairline.

"I'm so proud of you, Addie."

"Don't say that, I can't cry yet!" Adeline laughs, "but thank you. Love you."

"Love you too, kiddo."

Then the doors are pulled open and Norah sends her a wink of good luck before she takes her first steps into the barn. The string quartet they hired springs into action, a smooth, seamless transition into *At Last* by Etta James.

She keeps her eyes on her feet at first, too scared she's going to trip on one of the rugs, but she forces herself to look up at Billy and she's sure her heart actually flutters the moment her eyes land on him. He's shaved; smooth cheeks making him look so baby-faced she almost giggles at the difference a beard makes. He looks so gorgeous still, of course, with the dimple in his chin and pink, full lips as he pouts nervously.

"*Hi*," Adeline mouths when he looks her way and he flashes her that heart-stopping lopsided grin of his. It takes everything in her to keep in time with the music and Michael's steps beside her when all she wants to do is run to Billy.

Halfway there, she takes a moment to glance around the barn. They kept it a small affair; just friends, family, the Shaw & Gold team and NASCAR executives who have known Adeline since she was a little girl. Although she's positive most of them only turned up to see Tobias officiate, because he's licensed to do that apparently, though she and Billy didn't ask questions when he offered.

There is a small part of her that wishes she had a better relationship with her mother; that she should be there. But one look at Eleanor Brooks, twisted around fully in her chair and dabbing her eyes with a handkerchief, puts that thought to rest. Adeline has everyone she needs in this room.

"Hi, sweet girl," Billy whispers once they're side by side and her hand is in his. The soft lilt of his voice eases something within her and as Billy's breath catches, she brushes her thumb over his knuckles. Then the music fades and Tobias begins.

Surprisingly, for Tobias Shaw, he keeps his introduction short and sweet. An anecdote about the two of them that gets a laugh, and a not-so-humble brag about how '*he knew they would hit it off from the get-go, so he might as well get the credit.*'

Pancake manages to wriggle herself out of Gabe's arms not even ten minutes in and she winds herself around their legs, purring happily before settling down on Billy's foot. Gabe tries to coax her back but it's no use.

When they finally get to their vows, Adeline has no idea how she's still holding it together. One glance at Billy tells her he's doing just as well as she is. His eyes are glistening, *so* blue and full of love; a silent promise with every glance her way.

"Adeline and William have prepared their own vows," Tobias says, the pause that follows snapping Adeline's attention back to him. "If you guys are ready?"

"Yeah, Addie's gonna go first," Billy replies. "If that's cool?"

"It's your wedding," Tobias shrugs and Adeline nods, clearing her throat. She wrote her vows down on a piece of card and tucked it into Norah's flowers in case she needed it, but the words are so deeply ingrained in her now, she could recite her promises to Billy in her sleep. So she shakes her head when she feels the gentle tap from Norah on her shoulder.

"Okay, William– wait, no. That sounds weird," Adeline giggles. A quiet echo of laughter fills the room and she exhales deeply as she starts again. "Billy. Gorgeous, charming, sweet Billy. My stardust lover, you brought magic and light into my life and with it, you gave me the courage to face the shadows. You've given me so many moments of joy and laughter and you are my one constant in the chaos. If I can only promise you one thing, it is that I will do the same for you. I will love you, encourage you and protect you with everything I have. I am yours for as long as you'll have me."

She takes a breath and Billy squeezes her hand three times. *I love you.*

"Billy, you're up," Tobias says and Adeline beams at him, her nose and eyes scrunching up with pure joy as Billy wets his lips in preparation.

"Adeline. My sweet girl, you are a force. A gorgeous whirlwind of a human who took my world and turned it on its head in the best way. I can't imagine my life without you in it, can't imagine a future without you by my side. We're made of the same stuff, you and me, we have stardust in our souls." Billy grins, his eyes brimming with tears and he sniffles as the first drop cascades down his cheek. Adeline reaches out and catches it with the pad of her thumb, encouraging him to continue. "You have a heart of gold and a smile to fuckin' match and I swear, baby, I'm gonna put that smile on your face every day. I promise to always be in your corner, to love you and protect you no matter what. I am stronger because of you, wiser because of you and my heart is full because of you. I am yours, Adeline Gold, for as long as you'll have me."

"Can I kiss him yet?" Adeline asks through her own tears. She's itching to take Billy's face in her hands, kiss him like her life depends on it.

"Almost," Tobias laughs. "Reynolds, do you have the rings?" Stan fumbles in his pocket for the velvet covered box that houses their wedding bands. He holds it out once it's open and Adeline takes Billy's, the simple gold band reflecting the soft lights above them. "Okay, Adeline. If you could place the ring on Billy's finger and repeat after me." Adeline slides the ring on, grinning up at Billy when it meets his knuckle in a perfect fit. "William," Tobias starts, "as a sign of my love."

"William, as a sign of my love."

"I have chosen you above all else."

"I have chosen you above all else."

"With this ring, I thee wed."

"With this ring, I thee wed," Adeline breathes, dropping Billy's hand briefly to swipe carefully at the tears under her eyes.

"Okay, Billy. Now you." Tobias nods to the rings and Billy takes the remaining one from the box, a more delicate band with a group of stones that match Adeline's engagement ring. He slides it on slowly and huffs out an adorable little laugh when Adeline wiggles her fingers. Repeating the same lines after Tobias, his voice is only a little shaky as he races through. As soon as the last word leaves his lips, they burst into watery giggles, giddy and incredulous as they realise this is it, they've done it. Tobias claps his hands, grabbing their attention. "And now, by the power invested in me by the state of California, it is my honour and delight to declare you married. Go on, kids. I know you want to."

"Oh my God, finally!" Adeline dives for Billy, her teary laughs swallowed as he pulls her flush against him and captures her lips in a searing kiss. She's vaguely aware of Pancake leaping away, of people clapping and the music starting up again.

Right now, though, the only thing that matters is Billy.

ADELINE

He carries Adeline through the lobby of the hotel, earning a questioning glance from the concierge and bored-looking late night receptionist when he almost stumbles and Adeline bursts into a loud laugh that echoes through the vast space.

"Hi!" Billy says, with his brightest, most charming grin, as he stops in front of the desk and drops Adeline unceremoniously to her feet. She notices the girl perk up at Billy's infectious happiness. "We have a room, uh... the honeymoon suite."

"Sure! Can I take a name and some ID please, sir?"

"Brooks," Billy replies, and reaches into the pocket of his coat for his wallet. He hands over his driver's licence and the receptionist, Kelly, according to her name badge, spends a second flicking through the large book in front of her before tapping the page with a manicured nail.

"Gotcha." She turns around to the wall of keys and plucks the largest from the bunch. She holds it out for Adeline to take while Billy tucks his wallet away. "You have extended checkout and our special newlyweds package is outlined in the brochure in your room. Congratulations and enjoy your stay."

"Thanks, enjoy the rest of your night."

"Yeah, you too," Kelly smirks as Billy hauls Adeline into his arms again. She feels herself turn pink from the tips of her ears down to her neck as Billy throws Kelly a wink and turns to head towards the bank of elevators on the opposite side of the lobby.

They wait, impatiently, for the next one to arrive and then Billy has Adeline pushed against the mirrored wall as soon as the doors close behind them. He mouths at the soft curve of her shoulder, warm and wet and as sure as hell marking her up as he sucks and kisses each little patch of skin afterwards.

"Been wanting to get my hands on you like this all night," he admits and the gruff quality of his voice rumbles against her neck as his lips and hands roam. He clutches at her waist and explores every soft dip and sharp line of her body with lust-filled enthusiasm. Pushing in closer, Billy hitches her up off the floor with new strength and a secure grasp on her hips. The chiffon and silk of Adeline's dress bunches up as Billy shoves apart her thighs with one of his own and presses the thick muscle against the heat between them. The needy whine it elicits is quickly swallowed with a burning kiss and a throaty groan as Adeline drags her fingernails over the wrinkles of his shirt, digging them into his shoulder blades.

The elevator jolts and dings, the doors sliding open onto an empty single-roomed floor, and Billy tears his mouth away from Adeline's with a gasp. With his hands spread across the curves of her ass and carries her out into the small entryway. Adeline takes a moment to regulate her breathing as she falls slack against Billy's chest. With her face buried in the juncture of his shoulder, she breathes in, delighting in the fading scent of the cologne he picked out especially for today and the natural salt of his skin.

"You wanna unlock the door, sweet girl?" Billy asks, twisting so Adeline can reach to slot the key into the lock, turning it until it clunks. The room is huge and the first thing she notices as Billy carries her over the threshold is that it's a lot classier than she imagined. She was picturing *a lot* of pink and red, too much velvet and heart-shaped everything. Instead, the space is decorated like a palace

– cream and gold and warm shades of brown that blend in beautifully with the intricately carved canopy bed in the centre of the room. There are also rose petals on the silk sheets and towels folded to look like swans, so not *all* the stereotypes of a honeymoon suite are lost.

Billy drops Adeline to the floor, keeping her back flush to his warm body with an arm around her waist as her feet hit the plush carpet. It's so soft, the pile so thick that she sinks into it as she takes her own weight again.

"This is *so* gorgeous!" She beams as she glances up at Billy.

"Tobias really splashed out on his gift, huh?" Billy replies. His arms fall from Adeline's body and he presses a soft kiss to her shoulder before she decides to venture into the bathroom. There's a jacuzzi tub in the corner, already filled with steaming water. More rose petals float within the bubbles and lit candles like the wall. The whole room smells incredible, like an expensive spa, all soft floral oils and minerals. Beside the tub, a gold stand holds a bucket filled with ice and a bottle of champagne and two glasses sit ready on a small table.

"Did you do this?" She asks.

Billy stands in the doorway watching her, looking a little more ruffled than he did when they said their vows earlier. His hair is fluffy, the styling wax probably long gone thanks to all the dancing, and with his tie hanging loosely around his neck and top three shirt buttons open to reveal the toned expanse of his chest, he looks delectable. A small whine slips out of Adeline's mouth as she takes him in. Billy looks at her with dark eyes and a smile that can only be described as starving, his tongue playing its part a little too well as he flicks it into the corner of his lips.

"I called ahead before we left the party. Thought it would be a nice way to end the day, y'know?" Billy replies with a wolfish little glint in his eye. "What better than champagne in the tub with my wife?"

"Your wife is a lucky lady."

Billy shrugs, "I'm a lucky man."

The heat of his stare is blistering and the predatory way he eyes her up makes her feel exposed; naked already. She's sharply aware of the way her dress is clinging to her skin with the humidity of the room, and with the absolute want thrumming through her body, Adeline's senses are in overdrive before Billy's even made a move. She catches a glimpse of herself in the steamed up mirror, the wild frizz of her hair obvious even without a clear view, but Billy is looking at her like he can't wait to devour her bit... by...bit.

He grins, soft lines around his eyes and a dimple in his cheek as he moves to tug his tie from his neck. The butterflies in Adeline's belly double, hundreds of thousands of fluttering wings that send her heart skipping a beat. Letting the tie drop to the floor, Billy begins unfastening the remaining buttons of his shirt. He's painstakingly slow with it, and with a sheer determination to not look anywhere but at Adeline with his burning gaze.

"You're taking too long," Adeline whines when Billy slowly shucks the shirt off his shoulders. It slips down over his triceps, past his elbows and falls from his hands as he takes a step forward, joining his tie on the floor.

"So impatient, Mrs Brooks," he teases. Adeline pouts but she can't help the smile that breaks it as Billy stops in front of her. She reaches out, her fingertips dancing over his firm chest. He's been working out, sticking to the personalised plan Wren set up for him so he doesn't do any further damage to his arm, and it's working *wonders*. "Turn around, Tinkerbell."

Adeline obeys and Billy pushes her hair to the side. His dexterous fingers work quickly to undo the buttons of her dress, impressive considering how fiddly they were for Norah to fasten earlier in the day. The moment the material loosens and falls from Adeline's shoulders, Billy presses his lips, hot and eager on her skin. He skims over the marks he made in the elevator with determined, hurried hands and pushes her dress down her body until it pools at her feet.

"Look at you," he sighs as if he can't believe the sight of her.

Adeline feels hot all over as he helps her shimmy out of her underwear, taking his sweet time dragging it over her ass and thighs. His hands wander, groping and caressing every soft and sensitive part of her and she revels in the way he enjoys her body. She never feels more beautiful than when Billy is like this.

Once she's bare, she helps Billy out of his dress pants and boxer shorts, just as slowly and tenderly as he had undressed her, and then she takes his hand and leads him to the bathtub. Adeline sinks beneath the bubbles, the water lapping against the porcelain and Adeline groans softly as the hot water envelops her. It sloshes heavily when Billy climbs in, settling in behind her, all thick thighs and broad chest caging her in. He fusses for a moment, pouring them each a glass of champagne and hands one over to Adeline with a tender kiss and a small tug on her bottom lip.

"To us, sweet girl," he murmurs.

"To us." Clinking their glasses together, Adeline takes a sip and hums in delight as the bubbles fizz on her tongue. She twists in place between Billy's legs, wanting to see him better without craning her neck, and winds up resting against the side of the tub and curled into his body. As she makes her way through her drink, she studies his face, taking in every line – the happy ones and the faint, fading scars – and counting every freckle. She comes to the conclusion that he really is the most gorgeous man she's ever seen. Adeline sighs, stroking the pad of her thumb over the little divot in his chin.

"You know, I kinda miss the beard."

Billy chuckles, wrapping his fingers around her wrist until they settle over her pulse. "Well, that's an easy fix," he replies. "You gotta close your eyes though, baby. Otherwise the magic won't work."

"You're ridiculous," Adeline snorts and Billy drops his head to her shoulder. He grazes his teeth over the soft skin before biting lightly, teasingly. When he looks up, he narrows his gaze.

"Close... your... eyes." With a playful huff, Adeline lets her eyelids flutter closed. Every sound is amplified now she can't see; the small clink of Billy's glass being put down, the quiet fizz of the bath bubbles that grows louder then settles again. Billy hums, sounding appeased and then taps Adeline on the nose with a wet finger. "Okay, open."

Billy's sunshine grin fills her vision as she opens her eyes. His sunshine grin and a beard of white, foamy bubbles, dripping and glooping from his chin and cheeks.

"Oh, yes. That's much better," Adeline giggles, "so handsome."

Billy laughs and then it turns into a grimace as some of the bubbles catch on his lips and are subsequently licked up by his tongue. Adeline swipes her hand over his cheek, collecting bubbles in her palm and blowing gently. She tilts her head, watching as they go floating into the air and when her eyes focus again, Billy's expression is nothing but adoration.

"I love you," he whispers, "and *this* definitely doesn't feel real yet." He holds up his left hand, his wedding band gleaming in the soft candlelight. Adeline rests her glass on the edge of the bathtub and holds up her own hand, linking their fingers together so their rings meet.

"Stuck with me now, hot stuff."

"That was kinda the plan, sweetheart," Billy says, his tone hushed and gentle. He tugs her towards him and his mouth hovers over hers, barely touching as their breaths grow heavy, warm puffs against their lips. It's Adeline who breaks first, closing the gap and slotting her mouth over his with quickly burgeoning enthusiasm. Tendrils of steam wisp around their damp bodies as Billy kisses her back with long, languorous strokes of his tongue. He tugs on her bottom lip and Adeline moans as he lets go with a pop before kissing her again, quick and wet, to soothe the bite. There's a flood of desire in her belly, like a bubbling hot spring, and it spurs Adeline to clamber into Billy's lap. Water splashes as she settles across his thighs and takes his face in her hands, joining their mouths again. She's in Billy's orbit completely, so caught up in his gravity that anything outside of him is forgotten, unimportant, as he clutches the nape of her neck and his fingers tangle in her hair. The dry taste of champagne lingers on his tongue with remnants of their wedding cake. Chocolate fudge so saccharine sweet it's addicting as Adeline licks into his mouth, searching out more of it.

Billy lets out a sharp groan as Adeline threads her fingers into his hair and pulls, wanting him closer, surrounding her as much as he can. He deepens the kiss, heavy and hot before his mouth diverts, trailing across her jaw and down the column of her neck. Adeline's whole body leans with his touch, giving into him as he sucks burning bruises on her clavicle and soothes the marks with slow, deliberate swirls of his tongue.

"I can't get enough of you, sweet girl," he croons, low and rumbly, as he raises his head just enough to flick her earlobe and take it between his teeth. "Every single part of you is fuckin' exquisite."

Billy's cock gets with the program, curving up between them under the water, thick and begging to be touched. Adeline takes it in her hand and wraps her fingers around him, stretched but not quite meeting. Her hand glides over his length with ease, thumb brushing over the tip and making Billy moan. Adeline tugs him forward, kissing him quiet until he's whining against her lips. He ruts up into her hand, the bathwater almost spilling over the edge with his thrusts. Slowing down, Adeline twists her fingers and squeezes gently around the head of his cock on each stroke, the way she knows Billy likes, and he almost chokes.

"Christ, Addie."

"You need me to stop?"

"Mm–*fuck*. No, no. Keep goin'."

Watching Billy fall apart might be one of Adeline's favourite things. The way his mouth goes slack, half-lidded eyes dark and trying so hard to focus on what she's doing. He's beautiful, glistening with it. His hair, damp from the humidity and Adeline's wet hands, sticks to his forehead in curls and his cheeks are rosy, flushed with the intensity of it all. Billy's cock pulses against Adeline's palm, slick with pre-cum and oil-infused water and his breathing becomes ragged, his chest heaving as he holds back.

"Need t'fuck you, baby. Need– fuck, please let me. Gotta be

inside you," he babbles, head falling to her shoulder. He has one hand on her breast, absentmindedly rolling and flicking his thumb over her nipple as he mouths lazily at her collar bone. His other hand is curled around the edge of the bath, white-knuckling the porcelain. Adeline lets go of his cock and Billy groans at the loss.

"You wanna fuck here?" Adeline asks with a cheeky smile. "Or the bed?"

"Bed," Billy replied, surging forward to kiss her and then mumbling against her lips, "up and at 'em, Tinkerbell."

They clamber out of the tub, dripping through the hotel room as they forgo towels. Slick hands against wet skin, they stumble, giggling and kissing on their way to the bed. They don't even make it halfway before Billy's hands slide across Adeline's belly, hugging her waist as he hauls her off the floor and against the nearest wall.

"Billy!"

"Couldn't wait," he gasps breathlessly, kissing Adeline hungrily as she anchors her legs around him. Billy's mouth is eager in its exploration of her body, spending extra time ensuring every inch of her he can reach has been covered by his lips, dewy and soft and warm on her skin. He hitches her up the wall a little more, slipping his hand down between them. "Oh, *sweetheart*," he purrs as two long fingers stretch her out, sliding in nice and easy with how slick she is. Adeline whines, squirming as Billy curls his fingers steadily with each drag along her walls. "So worked up, baby."

"Billy, Billy–" she chants, a hitch in her breath between each moan of his name. "*Oh my God.*"

"Fuckin' love it when you say my name like that," Billy says as he grins, cocky and bright. "Say it again, sweet girl. Scream it for me when you come. I know you're close already, can feel it."

"Uhhh, *fuuuck*," Adeline breathes. "Mouth. Want– *shit*– want your mouth, *please*."

"You'll get it," Billy says. He laughs, rich and gorgeous, as he slips his fingers out of her cunt. Adeline whimpers at the loss until they're replaced with the firm head of his cock, pushing into her slick and hot.

That, she was not expecting.

"*Oh!*"

"Want your first one to be on my cock. Think you can do that, sweet girl?"

Adeline nods, hazy as her head rolls back against the wall and Billy ruts up into her with quick, deliberate rolls of his hips. She can feel his thighs trembling beneath her, telling of how restrained he's being. The first knot in the rope keeping her tethered pulls tight and then snaps as her orgasm rocks through her and Billy swallows her moans. He pulls out as she pulses around him, leaving her empty again in a reprieve of shallow breaths and soft murmurs.

He holds her against the wall for a few moments longer before her clammy skin meets the cool air of the hotel room as he carries her over to the bed. Adeline lands in the rose petals as Billy drops her gently to the sheets and she shuffles back until her head hits the feather-soft pillow.

"Now, since you asked so nicely," Billy chuckles as he lowers himself between her legs. Adeline instantly misses his beard as his cheek rests against her thigh; the way it would scratch up her skin and tickle with each subtle movement his head makes when he's eating her out. Not that she's complaining.

His whole mouth latches onto her as he eases his tongue through her folds, lapping her up. Adeline's body is on fire, damp and prickly heat coating her skin and burning through her veins. Lips parted, she moans, loud and high pitched as Billy hums against her clit before sucking it between her lips. The low vibrations are her undoing, the second knot unravels; a slow, smooth wave of pleasure this time.

"M'gonna come again, Billy... oh my– yes. *Yes! Billy!*" Adeline babbles, words tumbling from her lips before her brain has a chance to catch up. Billy keeps going as Adeline's toes curl and she grinds her pussy against his mouth, riding out her orgasm.

"Attagirl," he whispers. As he looks up at her, he's wearing a dimpled, boyish grin.

"Get up here," Adeline says, reaching for him with wiggling

fingers. Billy's lips meander over the soft terrain of her belly and up the valley of her breasts. She kisses him, open-mouthed and fervent, the moment his face appears in front of her; hard not to when his lips are so gorgeously kiss-bitten and glistening with her arousal.

Billy shifts, rocking against her and sucking in a sharp breath when the head of his cock nudges against her heat as they move. He reaches between them, slicking himself up with slow drags of his length over her wet folds. Every nerve in Adeline's body tingles, every sound and colour heightened as she grows impatient – but what's new?

"*Billy*," Adeline whines, "fuck me again, I wanna feel you. Want you to fill me up." Her hands weave into his hair, pulling his head back so she can work her mouth along his jaw and relishing the stuttered breaths she gets in return.

Billy holds himself up with his right arm and Adeline wraps her legs around him, heels pressed into his perfect, peachy ass. Lining himself up, he sinks into her with one torturously slow tilt of his hips and a deep, rough groan.

"Jesus *Christ*. Every goddamn time, sweetheart–" Billy grits out, "feels like the first. So fuckin' perfect, Addie."

Adeline blushes at the praise and her already clammy skin burns even more. Billy glances down at her, looking pleased with himself as he fills her to the hilt and stops.

"Baby. Move. Please."

Billy wets his bottom lip, cheeky smile blurring, and he dips his head to kiss her softly. The kiss distracts her as he pulls out almost all the way and begins driving into her, the muscles at the small of his back rippling under her heels as he thrust hard and deep. Adeline buries her face in his shoulder, mouthing at the skin to stop herself from screaming.

"Don't hide, sweet girl," Billy grunts. "I wanna hear you, Addie. Let me hear you."

Kissing his collarbone, Adeline's mouth wanders to his and they share stilted breaths between messy kisses as Billy rolls his hip. The room fills with the sound of slapping skin and Adeline chanting his name, incoherent moans and gasps getting louder and louder as he fucks her into the mattress. Billy straightens up and leans back, one hand flat to the bed behind him. Adeline's legs fall to the sheets, wide either side of him. He splays his fingers out over her belly, the pad of his thumb working in circles over her clit as he watches his cock disappear into her with his bottom lip between his teeth a deep furrow in his brow.

Adeline is a whining, writhing mess. It's dizzying, when he fucks her like this, pulling her apart like he lives to coax sweet sounds from her lips and paint a rosy flush over her skin. With a soft grunt on each long, deliberate thrust, Billy curses and pushes deeper, the hard drag of his cock forcing Adeline closer and closer to tumbling over the edge.

"Come on, sweetheart. Be a good girl and come for me again. I'm so close– oh *fuck* – need you to come." Billy crowds into her space again. He kisses her hard, all teeth and tongue, and Adeline clutches his arms, desperate for an anchor as the low rumble of her third orgasm simmers low in her belly.

"*Ugh*– fuck, Billy!" Adeline keens. Her back arches off the bed, body tense and trembling against him. "Love you, love you. Oh, *GOD.*"

Her vision whites out as her climax rushes through her, the third and final knot in her belly snapping as she cries out, cut loose and drifting with never ending pleasure. Billy fucks her through it. His hips snap with intent, shifting Adeline further up the bed into the messy sheets and rose petals as he seeks out his own release.

His thrusts falter and he moans as he comes. His cock flexes and it's the last thing Adeline feels before the warm rush that spills into her. Billy falls forward, mumbling something about needing a minute as he kisses her lazily and Adeline cards her fingers through his hair, pushing back salty, damp strands from his forehead.

"I'm never gonna get tired of that, holy fuck," Billy whispers, his voice thick and rough. "Fuck me, Tinkerbell. I am *so* in love with you."

Adeline giggles and presses a kiss to his temple as he noses at the crook of her neck with a tired groan. They're both hot and sticky with sweat, a mess of limbs and bedsheets and crumpled rose petals. Billy pulls out of her with a quiet hiss and rolls off the bed, leaving Adeline with a lingering kiss before he pads off to the bathroom. He returns a couple of minutes later with a damp cloth and two robes thrown over his arm. Adeline sits up as he approaches the bed with that lazy smile of his and in all his naked glory.

Tender hands wipe her down, cool cloth followed by soft kisses and whispered conversation as they preserve the little pocket of intimacy they've created. When they're finally somewhat clean and snuggled up in the soft white robes embroidered with *Mr* and *Mrs*, Billy hands Adeline the room service menu right as her stomach rumbles. Unsurprising considering the work out they just had. They order burgers and fries, another bottle of champagne and one of each dessert to share, and Adeline couldn't think of a better way to end their wedding night.

The bed is ridiculous. It's like sleeping on a marshmallow with its soft satin pillow and silk sheets that feel cool against Adeline's skin. She already knows she won't be able to leave it tomorrow.

She's been asleep not even two hours when the light across the street begins to flicker, somehow managing to rouse her from the deepest of slumbers at 5am. She turns to face Billy, the orange glow illuminating his features as he exhales soft even breaths in his sleep. His lips are pouted adorably, cheek squished into the pillow. Adeline counts the freckles across his nose, faint but withstanding after he spent so much time outside on the ranch, his skin still holding the last of his golden tan. She presses her nose against his, feels him wiggle it at the tender pressure, and kisses his plump lips. Billy sighs, his warm hold on her tightening as his eyelashes flutter and his mouth parts.

"I was wrong," he murmurs sleepily with his eyes still closed, "on Thanksgiving."

Adeline peers at him from where she's tucked into his side and he squints down at her. His lips curl into a smile, lazy and like it's too much effort this early in the morning.

"Yeah, what about?"

"*This* might just be the best fuckin' day of my life."

Adeline grins and presses a soft kiss to the underside of Billy's jaw, inhaling the lingering scent of the oils and bubbles from their bath earlier and snuggling closer to settle back into sleep.

"It's been pretty great, hasn't it?"

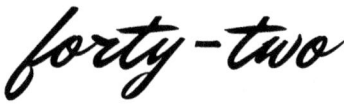

ADELINE
February 23rd, 1976
Gold Brooks Family Ranch, Georgia

DECEMBER ROLLS INTO JANUARY AFTER A QUIET CHRISTMAS
at the ranch and a not-so-quiet New Year celebration in Malibu. By
the time February arrives, Adeline feels like she and Billy have
settled into married life like they've never known any different. The
ranch house is slowly transforming into theirs with fresh paint and
thrifted furniture. All the rugs from the wedding now occupy
various rooms and the place has taken on a hybrid aesthetic of the
beach house and Billy's Brooklyn apartment. There's just one room
left to fix up, but it needs a little more thought than a lick of leftover
paint and a vintage rug.

All that is on the back burner right now though, with the way
Billy is back in full driver mode. He's spending long days out on the
track trying to get his muscle memory back. Wren is monitoring him
more regularly, changing up his fitness regime and daily exercises as
he progresses. Adeline had almost forgotten what it's like to date a
NASCAR driver after so long away from the routine of it all; she'd
gotten too cosy with the idea of Billy being around all the time that

now she misses him even when he's ten minutes down the dirt path that leads to the ranch's track and garage. So, with Norah and Gabe stopping by for a visit between races – the 1976 season well underway – Adeline hasn't seen him for most of the morning, spending it catching up with her best friend and discussing plans for Billy's 31st birthday while Gabe was all out to look at the car.

He's been driving it *a lot*, keeping it in good shape with the little he knows of mechanics, tyre changes with the help of Myles and the odd look at the engine when it happens to overheat. He called Adeline in for a second opinion on a quick rattle that started up a few days ago, hence the desperate need for Gabe to take a look.

Adeline hovers in the doorway of the garage for a while, having left Norah to use the house phone to call her parents. She watches the pair of them work in tandem, bickering playfully, before she makes herself known.

"Hey, hot stuff. Have you decided how you want to celebrate your birthday yet?"

Billy glances up from the hood of his car, where he's been tinkering while Gabe is sprawled underneath it on the creeper. The movement is so sharp with surprise, he knocks the top of his head on the propped up bonnet. Adeline whispers a soft apology when Billy rubs over his hair with a grimace and hops over Gabe's legs to saunter over to her.

"I told you, sweet girl. We're gonna be in New York so a quiet dinner with my folks is fine. You threw me a whole party last year, I'm happy just to spend it with you guys this time around." He has black oil smeared over his cheek, his fingertips grimy with the stuff, and the devil-may-care grin on his face has Adeline taking a step back as he nears.

"Billy," she says with a warning tone, "this is a new dress, don't you dare."

"It's a lovely dress," he agrees slyly. It is. Square-necked with a floaty skirt and bell sleeves, the fabric a soft velvety floral print of forget-me-nots and blue daisies that remind Adeline of Billy's eyes. She threw a loose-knit brown cardigan over the top to keep the February chill off as she walked down to the garage but she *loves* this dress which is why she shoots her husband a scolding look as he edges even closer.

"Exactly. So you can keep your dirty hands off it, Brooks."

"But, *baby*," Billy whines, and that goddamn bottom lip juts out as he takes another step, dropping his gaze so he's staring at her thorough half-lidded eyes. "You usually love my hands on you."

"You know, I may be under a car but I can still hear you!" Gabe's muffled voice interrupts. "No funny business in the garage."

"Hate to break it to ya–" Billy starts and Gabe groans in disgust.

"Oh, like you and Norah haven't done it in worse places," Adeline scoffs. "I've heard stories, Gabriel." That just causes Gabe to groan again and wheel himself out from under the car. He gives them side-eye on par with Norah's and Adeline smiles sweetly at the mechanic as he stumbles to his feet, wipes his hands on the rag tucked into the pocket of his overalls and stalks from the garage, muttering something about needing to piss.

With him gone, Billy is quick to sway forward and kiss Adeline. Warm and slow, his tongue teases though the seam of her lips, feeling her out. Adeline melts into him, kisses him back with an equally languid and deliberate glide of her mouth over his. A low, almost growl of a whine forms in Billy's throat as he backs her up against the garage wall and he cages her in with his hands to the brick either side of her. His body heat radiates from him, fingers twitching as he tries so hard not to touch her.

Instead, Billy settles for a brush of his cheek against hers and Adeline sighs at the delicious roughness of his stubble over her jaw as their mouths slide from one another. Billy makes his way south with a deep hum against her skin and Adeline's hands in his already wild hair. Kissing Billy like this feels like home; when he tastes like his morning coffee and his skin holds the faint smell of motor oil mixed with the warm, woodsy fragrance of his cologne.

The clearing of Gabe's throat pulls them away from each other, breathing heavily with parted, dewy lips and flushed cheeks. Billy rolls his eyes and huffs out a disgruntled chuckle.

"Hi, Gabe. Back so soon?" he says through gritted teeth.

Gabe ignores his tone for the most part and jabs a thumb in the direction of the car.

"I'm nearly done with this if you wanna gear up?"

Billy nods in thanks and starts getting himself ready. Adeline watches him, admiring the regained muscle tone in his arms as he swaps out his mucky overalls – dug out from the rusting metal cabinet in the corner of the garage – for a driving suit and gloves. He still gets aches, days where his muscles seize and Adeline has to work the knots out, massaging his shoulder for hours or soaking in the tub with him until they're both sleepy and prune-like. It beats the alternative they could have been dealt with – a lost limb or worse; a lost son, brother and partner.

"I'm gonna try to match my last official race lap time today," Billy tells her with a lopsided grin, his eyes lit up like a kid at Christmas, and it shakes her out of her reverie. "Gabe's just makin' sure the car's good for it."

"Are *you* good for it?" Adeline blurts without thinking and she winces when Billy's grin turns into a frown, his brows pinched with hurt.

"Addie, if I wanna make it to next year's series..."

"I know, I know. I just worry, and I know you're more mentally prepared now it's just– that's *fast,* Billy, and so soon."

"I can't expect to qualify after a setback like this with just a few months of quality driving under my belt. I gotta get back to where I used to be, get racing on the smaller circuits again first. If I don't do this now..."

Adeline nods. He's right, of course he's right, but it doesn't do much to offset the unease she feels. Nor does the notion that it's not just herself she's thinking about anymore when it comes to her fear of losing him. She's not about to stop him from living out his dream, though, not when it was almost ripped away from him. Billy wipes his hands on the discarded overalls and steps closer.

"I wish I could go out there with you," Adeline mumbles softly as

Billy cradles her jaw in his hands, thumbs delicate in the way he brushes over the apples of her cheeks.

"Not a chance in hell, sweetheart."

"I know, just– be careful, okay?"

"Hey, I'm always careful!" Billy laughs, surging forward to slant his mouth over hers. This time the kiss is tender, *I love you* and a promise in every soft, measured peck of his lips.

"Stardust, Billy," Adeline whispers.

"Stardust, sweet girl."

Adeline follows as he heads to the car, the engine already rolling as Gabe polishes off the hood and gives the roof a gentle tap.

"She's all set, B. The track surface looks good too so you should be in for a nice lap."

"Thanks, Gabe. Hey, you wanna time this one? Addie's a little shaky."

Adeline dares a glance at her hands, betraying her with a subtle tremor that *of course* Billy would pick up on. Norah enters the garage at that moment, nodding at Billy in a subtle exchange of good luck as he pulls on his helmet and drops the visor over his eyes.

"He knows what he's doing, Addie," Norah says softly as her arm settles around Adeline's shoulders and she gives a gentle squeeze of reassurance. Billy climbs in through the open window of the car and straps himself in, adjusting the net over the gap once he's settled. She can do nothing but watch as he drives to the start line, the undeniable hammer of her heart against her ribcage setting a steady rhythm to the rumble of the engine echoing across the ranch.

They all follow, standing back from the track as Gabe holds up a hand and signals a countdown. The car revs and Adeline subconsciously grazes the pads of her fingers over her belly. She's watched Billy drive this track countless times, but never this fast, never with the intent of driving like he would in a race. That said, when she catches sight of him through the windshield, he looks as in control as ever. Hands poised on the steering wheel, fingers wiggling in anticipation and suddenly Adeline gets it. It's what they both know after all; they're both drawn to the rush, the thrill and adrenaline despite the probability of the crash.

She doesn't have time to ponder over it longer as Gabe's hand flies down, his thumb hitting the stopwatch as Billy is off, burning rubber. Adeline can't tear her eyes away as he heads down the first stretch of the oval track with a consistent build in speed before he executes the first bend neatly. Despite her heart still being in her throat, her pulse softens a little then and the corners of her lips curl into a proud smile. There's only one, minuscule moment when his tyres skid on the next bend but Billy saves it with the kind of ease that shows just how good he is. Then he glides along the black stretch in what feels like the blink of an eye. Somehow, in that time, Adeline can picture it all; the crowds, the noise, Billy back where he belongs. It's only a few seconds later that he speeds past the finish line and Gabe stops the watch with a beautiful, toothy grin blooming across his lips.

"He's one of a kind, I swear," he says as he holds the stopwatch out to show them.

43.2 seconds.

Billy drives once around the track again, cooling down until the car slows to a stop beside them.

"You fuckin'-- what magic juice are you drinkin', man?!" Gabe shouts as Billy clambers out, a little unsteady on his feet. He hastily pulls his helmet from his head and jogs over.

"That felt good. Was it good?" He asks, breathless and jittery.

"Was it fuckin' good? You just beat your time by a whole second and a half, B. First lap at full speed and– *Jesus Christ.*"

Billy catches Adeline's eye as Gabe continues to rant and she realises she's been gawking at him this whole time, eyes wide and lips parted in awe.

"Tinkerbell?" He reaches out and suddenly Adeline is falling into his arms, fingers weaving through his hair as she crashes her mouth to his. Fervent and hungry, she nips at his bottom lip and Billy groans. It's low, in the base of his throat, and Adeline grips onto him tighter in response. The rough palms of Billy's racing gloves skim over her skin, cupping her cheeks as he softens the kiss.

Breathless, and with the brightest, most sunshine smile she's ever seen, Billy pulls away from her mouth with a content sigh. He noses along her cheek and Adeline giggles, delirious laughter bursting from her lips. She knew he would do it, but seeing him come back after everything and be just as good, better even, has knocked her for six completely and she clings to him, peppering soft, sweet kisses over his cheeks and up to his ear.

"You're something else, Billy Brooks," she whispers as she falls in love with him for the thousandth time over.

BILLY
March 8th, 1976
New York City

"ARE YOU ALMOST READY?" ADELINE ASKS, HER FINGERS busy hooking in her earring. Her expectant gaze slides to Billy's reflection in the mirror and he almost feels bad for being caught staring at his own wife.

Adeline turns around on the small stool she's positioned in front of Billy's mirror and lifts an incredulous eyebrow at him across the room. In fairness, Billy has been standing in his underwear with his shirt undone and socks pulled up to his calves for the better part of five minutes and they do have somewhere to be. His hair is still damp from his shower, curling at the nape and around his ears, and he's nowhere near ready to leave the apartment. In his defence, he got a little caught up in watching Adeline fix her hair and applying lipstick that he's sure he's just going to kiss off her plump, pretty lips by the end of the night.

"Have I ever told you how gorgeous you are?"

"Nice try, hot stuff. But I promised my dad and Tobias we'd get there early and at this rate, we'll be lucky to make it before the entrees come out."

Billy sighs. He should be excited about tonight really, it's his first NASCAR event in nearly a year and it's an important one; a chance to network with the execs and meet brand reps from the Shaw & Gold partners. It's time to show the world that Billy Brooks is back and preparing to race again.

"I'll hurry, promise," he says as Adeline stands, smoothing out her dress, and Billy's gaze tracks her hands over the gold fabric.

"Is it okay?" She asks, turning to the side.

"It's perfect, sweet girl. You look like a goddamn dream."

Adeline beams and Billy abandons the pressed slacks he was about to pull on, instead grabbing his Super 8 from its current home in his small suitcase. He's been using the camera a lot lately, getting Adeline to film his driving progress and capturing their newlywed life. He loads a new reel of film and points it at his beautiful wife. Adeline is halfway to berating him already.

"Baby, we don't have time–"

"Give me a twirl, sweetheart."

"*Billy.*"

"Just one spin, you look too good not to document it."

Adeline concedes, spinning so the skirt of her dress flares out. The glimmering gold catches the soft light of the bedroom in a blur of ethereal shine and suddenly she lives up to her pixie nickname. Billy keeps the camera trained on her as she turns and twirls, youthful and happy. It's moments like these that remind Billy why he's so in love with her and the little life they're building together. Giggling, Adeline comes to a stop with a cute little curtsy and Billy clicks the camera off, dropping it to the bed.

"Are you sure we have to go to this thing?" He whines as he struts towards her, flashing her the smile he knows makes her crumble every time.

Or so he thought.

"Yes. We've declined every event so far this year."

"For good reason," Billy counters.

"You need to show your face and shake some hands," Adeline says in a tone that brooks no argument. "Just a few hours. A few hours and we'll come home."

"Okay. Yeah, okay," Billy agrees, his hands landing on her hips as he tugs her forward and dips his head to kiss her softly. Adeline's lips are like silk with her creamy lipstick, no doubt now tinting his own mouth red, and she tastes of those godawful dill pickle flavoured chips that she's currently in the habit of keeping a handy stash of by the bed. As Billy breaks the kiss, she pats him gently on the pec and steps out of his hold.

"Get dressed, Billy."

"Clean your teeth, Adeline," he shoots back and she pokes her tongue out in defiance on her way to the bathroom, lingering long enough to blow him a kiss as she disappears behind the closing door.

Once they're both finally ready to leave, they make their way across the river and into Manhattan. Billy peers out the window as they drive past his old haunts and familiar tourist traps. He *has* missed New York. Coming back to the city feels like a tiny missing piece of him clicks back into place, the piece that lives for the noise and the rush of the city that never sleeps. One look at Adeline though, smiling softly across the back seat of the town car Tobias sent and wearing Billy's large leather jacket over her golden dress, and the feeling fades. He can miss places where he once belonged but as long as he's with her, he feels grounded, loved, and lucky as hell to call her home.

The NASCAR event they're about to walk into – a three-course meal and mixer – is being held at the Palm Court at the Plaza Hotel. Billy remembers the last time he attended an event there, just one of the many Delilah refused to accompany him to. He remembers seeing Adeline flit around the room, cosying up to drivers and dancing with Norah and Gabe. If he was a braver man, he would have introduced himself to her back then. But she was gorgeous in an otherworldly sense and a little intimidating to a younger Billy Brooks.

This time, he's walking in with her on his arm, matching rings and a secret.

"There's my favourite couple!" Tobias all but bellows across the space. He has two martinis in his hands and an exasperated-looking Norah following after him.

"Hey, sorry we're late," Adeline apologises with a brief kiss on Tobias' cheek.

"You're good. They're only just bringing out the appetisers," Norah informs them as Tobias palms off one of his drinks to shake Billy's hand, abruptly pulling him in for a hug.

"It's good to see you back at one of these, Brooks," he says and Billy might even detect a little emotion in Tobias' voice before he checks himself. "Follow me to the bar, I wanna talk comeback."

Billy glances at Adeline, bewildered and silently hoping she'll get him out of it. To his chagrin, she shoos him away and signals for him to get her a drink while he's there. He pouts and manages to steal a kiss before Norah is pulling Adeline away to their table in the opposite direction.

"So, '77." Tobias gets straight to it as Billy leans across the bar, gaze drifting to the other man once he's got the attention of a free bartender.

"Yep."

"It's gonna be your year, Billy. I can feel it," Tobias grins.

"I thought the same about '75," Billy replies, his tone light despite the implication. "I'm learning to just take things as they come, Toby. I don't even know if I'll be racing next year yet." He turns away from Tobias and the noise beside them to relay his drinks order clearly. Tobias is still talking, obviously.

"No reason why you won't be, Addie told me your lap times– well, Addie told Michael your lap times and he relayed them to me but you get it. Get reacquainted with the adrenaline of competition, a few amateur races under your belt and you'll be qualifying with flying colours. There are companies chomping at the bit to sponsor the team, but *you're* the kicker. It's you they want to sponsor. Pepsi, Billy. *Pepsi!*" He's practically jumping up and down and even Billy can admit that's kind of a big deal, but he hums noncommittally and thanks the girl behind the bar as she hands over his drinks.

"Takin' things as they come," Billy repeats with a raise of his eyebrows and tight-lipped smile. "My lap times are good, I know that, but I'm not in the right mindset to compete *just* yet."

"Well, you know where to find us when you wanna talk. At least mingle a little tonight, make a connection or two but the ball's in your court, Brooks."

"Got it, Toby. Thanks. I wanna race again, just don't wanna push it, y'know?"

"Yeah, I understand," Tobias says, his eyes softening a little as he glances around the room. "You better get that drink to your lady."

Billy follows his line of sight to meet Adeline's gaze, her red lips upturned into a tender smile as she watches them. She knocks him off his feet with just a look and if his hands weren't full, he'd pinch himself.

"Yeah," Billy says, slightly breathlessly, "yeah, I better."

Tobias claps him on the back and Billy makes his way over to their table for the evening.

"You okay?" Adeline asks as he sits down beside her and hands her drink over. He inches a little closer and throws his right arm over the back of Adeline's seat, his fingers brushing softly over the nape of her neck. The fingers of his left thread with hers under the lace trim of the tablecloth, hidden enough that he can keep his hand on her protectively without it being obvious.

"Yeah, sweet girl. Just Tobias being Tobias, you know how it is."

"Sorry," Adeline murmurs, "I thought it'd be better to get his spiel out the way."

"Trust me, it was–" Billy pauses as Adeline inspects her drink and he leans in to whisper, "it's just orange juice and Sprite, Tinker-bell. I got the girl to add a cherry and orange slice so it looks like a Harvey Wallbanger."

"Look at you; not just a pretty face, Brooks."

Billy chuckles softly and presses a kiss into Adeline's hair just as Stan and Gabe rejoin the table looking sheepish. Stan slides into the chair beside Wren, kissing her hello and murmuring something in her ear that causes her to giggle, her pale skin flushing a rosy pink up to her ears.

"Where've you been hiding?" Adeline questions, her head tilted in that interrogative way she's so good at. It's usually directed at him so when Stan catches his eye, Billy just shrugs and takes a sip of his whiskey, much to his friend's annoyance. Adeline's gaze is unwavering until Stan cracks.

"There's a poker game out back. Christ, Goldilocks, you could squeeze a confession out of a serial killer with that stare."

"Thank you, it's taken years of practice."

"I take it you lost," Billy comments and Stan's shoulders sag as he holds up his wrist. The Rolex he wore so proudly is now missing – the watch Stan blew a good chunk of his championship winnings on – and Billy quirks an amused eyebrow.

"Don't tell Norah," Stan begs, "she'll make fun."

"Don't tell Norah what?"

"Hi, Nor," Billy grins as Norah reappears at the table with a cigarette between her lips and a full glass of wine in her hand, and he can see Adeline's mouth twitching before she looks up at her best friend.

"Gabe and Stan lost in a poker game."

"Addie!"

"What? That was payback for telling everyone I was upstairs when I asked you not to the day Billy got signed."

"That was over a year ago, oh my God!"

"You didn't wanna meet me, sweetheart?" Billy asks, teasing her just a little and relishing the way Adeline cringes in response. Her cheeks are flushed and when she opens her mouth, words tumble out of it with a squeak of embarrassment.

"I had a big, fat crush on you, okay? I needed time to prepare before I met you properly so I was happy hiding at the top of the stairs until *Stan* opened his big mouth."

Billy hooks a finger under her chin, guiding her to look at him.

"I'm glad he did," he says, tender and sweet as he kisses the corner of her mouth.

"Yeah, me too." Adeline squeezes his hand, her thumb rubbing over the gold of his wedding band as she plants a soft reciprocating kiss on his cheek.

The rest of their evening is enjoyable, and if anyone notices Adeline isn't as rambunctious as usual, they don't say anything. Still, Billy takes her for a gentle spin around the dance floor and he schmoozes and shakes hands as promised. When the empty dessert plates are cleared away, Billy sneakily drains Adeline's glass of sweet wine that accompanied her tiramisu, and his own dregs of whiskey, before announcing their departure.

"Can we get hotdogs?" Adeline asks as they leave the hotel. She bats her eyelids and pouts adorably as she hangs off Billy's arm. Tobias offered his car to take them home again but as they skipped out early and the evening is mild enough, a pleasant walk through Manhattan seemed like a good idea.

"Hotdogs? After a three-course meal?"

"Um, yes. I'm *hungry*, Billy."

"Well, we can't have that," Billy laughs, "c'mon, Tinkerbell. I think there's a cart on the next street."

Adeline hums in satisfaction, pressing up onto the balls of her feet to kiss him gently. Her thumb is quick to follow her mouth as she swipes fading lipstick from his stubble, not for the first time tonight.

With their food secured – extra mustard, ketchup and all the toppings for Adeline and crispy onions for Billy – they wander further along 5th Avenue, along the outskirts of Central Park and the upscale buildings that line it.

"My dad's thinking of retiring," Adeline says around a bite of hotdog, ketchup oozing from the bun and onto her bottom lip. She sweeps it up with her tongue and Billy swallows his own mouthful down thickly, suddenly wishing they'd bought sodas too.

"Yeah?"

"Mhmm. In a few years, he said. He's nearly fifty-five, and has been in the game a long time. I think he wants to get out before he's sixty. He, uh, he asked me earlier if I wanna take over. He was all like," she lowers her voice, hand on her hip as she mimics her father, "*'it's not Shaw & Gold without a Gold, sunshine'.*"

Billy laughs at her impression, one of those quiet laughs where his face scrunches and his eyes squeeze shut. When he opens them again, Adeline is looking at him and waiting for his response.

"And do you? Wanna take over?" He asks, because it's her decision. He learnt a long time ago that he's just in it for the ride when it comes to Adeline. Where she goes, and what she does, Billy will gladly follow. All whilst shouting from the rooftops about how incredible she is.

"I mean, I did approach him about it years ago. I think he always knew his half of the team would be mine one day. But then I met you and well now..." she trails off as she lowers her gaze, "I don't know if I should."

"Women can be more than wives and mothers, Addie. If you wanna run the race team, you run the fuckin' race team." Adeline huffs out a quiet chuckle and shakes her head. Billy's pretty sure he knows what's going through her mind, finding the whole thing unbelievable no doubt and trying to picture herself working alongside Tobias in that capacity. "Your dad did it, didn't he? With a kid too. And I know you've said he didn't have much of a life outside of NASCAR and you when you were growing up but we could make it work, Tinkerbell,"

"I'll think about it," Adeline says, as they circle back to 59th Street and she follows Billy down into the subway station. "See where we're at when he actually decides to retire."

"Okay," Billy replies, an arm around her waist as he holds her close to his side and they step onto the 4 train towards Brooklyn Heights. "Marriage is about compromise though, baby. If you decide you wanna do this and we have to make some changes, that's okay."

Adeline's reply comes as a soft kiss and murmured sweet nothings into the curve of his shoulder as she huddles closer and Billy finds his hand slinking protectively beneath her – *his* – jacket for the remainder of the ride home.

When they get back, Billy helps Adeline out of her dress. He takes a second to admire her like this, all soft curves and glowing skin. Her panties sit high on her stomach, her cotton bra just on the right side of too small now. Billy likes it, Billy likes it a lot, the subtle evidence of how her body is changing.

He stands behind Adeline, chest flush to her back and his chin resting on her shoulder as he sways slowly, manoeuvring them both so they're in front of the mirror. Their reflections smile back at them as he wraps his arms around his wife's middle, his hands settling flat over her barely-there baby bump. The gold dress she wore did a good job of disguising the neat little curve of her belly. Humming quietly, Billy places a warm, open-mouthed kiss just below Adeline's ear and watches as her chest expands and falls with a sigh, her head falling back to his shoulder as she closes her eyes.

"When are we gonna tell 'em?" Billy asks, lips trailing along the line of her jaw.

"Soon," Adeline whispers, "I like that it's just for us right now."

"My mom's gonna know, y'know," Billy chuckles. "She'll take one look at you and be able to tell by the tiniest thing."

"Then we'll tell her before your birthday dinner."

"Yeah?

"Yeah."

"Don't move," Billy whispers, removing himself from her warmth to get his camera from where he left it on the bed. He resumes his place behind her once it's rolling, only a few frames left of this reel to capture this week's bump progress.

Adeline blushes, her hands covering her eyes when he zooms in on their reflection in the mirror, dragging the focus down to her belly and back up to her flushed face.

"*Billy.*"

"Look how beautiful you are, my sweet girl," he croons as Adeline peeks out from behind her fingers, tilting her head as she rubs a hand over her stomach.

"I'm only gonna get bigger."

"And you'll be beautiful then, too."

"You have to say that," Adeline scoffs, "we make out and stuff."

Billy laughs, "we do a little more than that now, Tinkerbell." Adeline raises an eyebrow as if to say *'no shit, look where it got us'*, and then her expression changes as she gasps softly.

"They're moving," she breathes, "oh my God, it's like really intense butterflies."

Billy discards the camera on the dresser next to them. He wraps both hands back around Adeline and she moves them to her belly, giggling every time she feels a flutter. He knows he won't feel it this early on but it sets his heart pounding all the same. They stay like that for a while, whispers and soft conversation between them and their unborn child.

"Y'know," Billy hums thoughtfully after a while, "I think racing can wait."

Adeline meets his gaze in the mirror with a hard frown, "What?"

"I'm gonna wait, maybe a year or two. I wanna be around for this."

"What? But you've been itching to go back, you belong on the race track, Billy. It's what you've been working towards and you've been away for so long already," Adeline says and Billy shakes his head, breathing out a soft chuckle.

"Nah, sweet girl. Right now, I belong right here. With you and our kid– shit, Addie, *our kid!*" He's still so giddy over it, two months after finding out and sixteen weeks in. He'd be stupid to put racing before this, and in truth, Billy's been thinking about holding off on it a lot recently. It's not a new revelation to him.

Finally saying it out loud though, and to Adeline, makes the decision feel terrifyingly real. He's a little worried about her reaction but he needn't be, not when she spins in his arms, her lips meeting his in a gloriously slow, all consuming kiss. She gets out mumbles of *'only if you're sure'* and *'are you serious?'* between kisses and Billy just nods as draws back and meets Adeline's glistening hazel eyes. He sinks to his knees, cradling her bump and pressing his lips to her tummy, humming softly as the love of his life cards her fingers through his hair.

He'll race again, one day, but all the dreams he's had – to race, to win, to be the best at what he does – they all mean nothing without this one. The one coming true right beneath his palms. He can win or lose on the track, but Billy knows one thing for certain.

He struck gold the moment Adeline came into his life.

ADELINE

January 15th, 1979

Malibu, California

Eyelids flutter open to the early morning darkness of the bedroom, the curtains drawn but doing little to block out the shine of the moon, still hanging high and bright in the sky. That's not what stirs Adeline from her sleep though. It's the soft, warm mouth trailing across her shoulder blades, the fingertips taking a leisurely meander up her thigh under the sheets.

She shuffles onto her back, blinking blearily at Billy. Billy whose hair is flopping across his eyes, and whose lips are curled into the lazy smile Adeline is greeted with most mornings.

"Mornin', baby," he breathes, low and husky and thick with sleep.

"What time is it?"

"Five-thirty," Billy replies, pulling Adeline up and on top of him. She buries her face in his shoulder, groaning as his arms circle her waist and he begins running his hands up and down the expanse of her bare back. She would be mad that he's woken her so early but without this little window of reprieve before Frankie inevitably requests their attention, Adeline knows they won't get any proper alone time before the race later. So she lets herself relax into her husband and savours the gentle pressure of his large, warm hands roaming over her.

Pressing a kiss to the divot of his shoulder, Adeline mouths at Billy's bed-warm, freckled skin; a lingering tan from last summer and their two weeks in Mexico just before Christmas – a belated honeymoon-cum-family vacation. They documented the whole thing with grainy, over exposed photos and video footage. The reels of home movies sit neatly in a cabinet at the ranch, stacked along-side others labelled with *Frankie's First Steps* and *Baby Brooks Turns 1!* in Billy's messy scrawl.

"Are you nervous?" Adeline whispers into the quiet, turning her head so she can kiss softly at the smattering of stubble on Billy's jaw. She lifts a hand from where it's tucked under the covers and strokes her thumb gently over his chin where a small collection of greying hair sits amongst the dark – the beard of a man parenting a trouble-some two-year-old.

"No," Billy answers, "and before you say it, I know I'm allowed to be."

Adeline hums, accepting his response.

"How long do you think we have?"

"Thirty minutes maybe. Why? What're you thinkin', Tinkerbell?"

Adeline glances up to see Billy wiggling his eyebrows; a playful, lopsided grin illuminating the small space between them. He dips his head, nose brushing against Adeline's cheek before he glides his mouth over hers. The kiss starts off sweet, a tentative *Good Morning Kiss* as Adeline's come to call them – slow and lazy, just feeling each other out as they wake up.

Billy hums, his tongue sliding over Adeline's bottom lip before he makes his play, waiting for the inevitable gasp as the muscle tickles the sensitive skin just at the seam and Adeline parts her lips, right on cue. From then on it's a desperate, toe-curling kiss. All soft breaths and whimpers between nips and sucks. Adeline moans as

Billy's hands move to cup her ass, and he nudges her legs open above him so she can feel his cock, heavy and hot, against her cunt.

"Gonna wish me good luck, sweet girl?" Billy purrs, "like old times?"

Adeline's skin prickles with heat and she drags her bottom lip between her teeth as she nods. With one last kiss to the corner of Billy's mouth, she ducks beneath the sheets with a giggle. Needy hands and lips travel the length of Billy's torso, tongue exploring the dips and hard lines of his stomach as she works her way south. Billy tenses beneath her as she peppers his hips with tiny kisses, and his fingers weave into her hair – the blonde tresses already wild from sleep – as he bucks his hips up eagerly.

With a teasing kiss to the base of his cock, Adeline's thumb catches a bead of pre-cum from the tip and she drags her fist to meet her lips. She gets a low moan from Billy in return, a licks a long, slow stripe following the thick vein that runs along the underside of his shaft. Billy is practically vibrating with anticipation as she prepares to take him in her mouth and then–

"Mamaaaa!"

"*Fuck*," Billy sighs. His body falls slack on the bed and Adeline works her way back up to his lips, collapsing against him.

"Tonight," she whispers, "whatever you want."

"Mmm, lucky future Billy."

Adeline chuckles, just as another shout from Frankie echoes across the hall.

"I'll go," Adeline says, even though they both know a call for mama right now doesn't necessarily mean it's *her* he wants. "You... sort that out." She gives Billy's cock one last stroke and he groans, chasing Adeline's grinning lips as she climbs out of bed and collects her robe from the seat in the bay window.

The beach house is quiet when she pads across to Frankie's room. Of course, it is still early and only Stan and Wren decided to stay whilst everyone else opted for a hotel closer to the raceway. They're in the guest bedroom down the far end of the hall.

"Hey, trouble. You're up early today," Adeline says, and Frankie –

with his wide, hazel eyes and head of soft, chestnut curls – grins at her from where he's standing on his chubby toddler legs, clinging to the top bar of his crib. He's almost outgrown it, they'll be shopping for little beds soon.

"Mama, mornin'," he mumbles sleepily and continues chattering away as Adeline hauls him into her arms. He's so big now, and holding him like this only ever makes Adeline miss when he was small. They would swaddle him to her chest, sometimes Billy's, and take him on evening walks around the ranch to get him to settle. Now he needs tiring out with big boy games before he even begins to yawn. What she'd give to have a tiny baby again, but she and Billy have decided to wait until Frankie is out of his terrible twos before giving him a sibling.

"Mornin', sweet boy," she echoes, nuzzling her nose into his hair to get those good baby pheromones before planting a tender kiss on his temple. "Did you have a good sleep?"

"Mhmm... sleep good. 'Nana and podge?"

"Yeah, Franks. You can have banana and porridge. Let's get your diaper changed first, huh?" They're in the process of potty training but right now, night times are easier with a terry cloth diaper and a quick change in the morning. Especially on a day like today.

"No, no. Want 'nana and podge," Frankie grumbles, his little hand balled into a fist as he grips her robe. Adeline tenses. She's not as patient as she would like to be with him but he's been like this lately, defiant in what he wants and when he wants it. Not that he doesn't have his sweet moments. In fact, there are more of them than anything else, but she and Billy discovered quickly that two is definitely a difficult age.

"In a minute, Frankie."

"No. Want 'nana."

With a sigh, Adeline moves to the changing table by the window, clinging on tight to a wriggling Frankie. She can tell he's just on the verge of a full-on, wobbly lip meltdown when Billy pokes his head around the door. It's obvious he heard the start of a tantrum; the man has a sixth sense when it comes to their son. He ambles in, his handsome face bright and cheery as he runs a hand through Frankie's hair and dips his head to blow a raspberry on his cheek.

"Dada, mornin'" Frankie says through a giggling squeal.

"Mornin', bud. You want me to make your 'nana and podge just how you like it while mama gets you cleaned up?"

"Yeah, 'nana like a face?" Frankie checks, waiting with a curious tilt of his head for Billy's confirmation.

"You got it, Franks. A big smile for our big, good boy, right?"

"*Me* big, good boy."

"Sure are, buddy," Billy smiles, "so let Mama change you and your breakfast will be ready when you come downstairs."

"O-day, Dada." Frankie beams, suddenly calm and agreeable, and Adeline whispers a quiet '*thank you*' as she kisses Billy softly before he turns to leave the room.

One clean two-year-old later and Adeline makes it to the kitchen just as Billy finishes up Frankie's breakfast. Creamy fine-rolled oatmeal sprinkled with a little brown sugar and topped with banana rounds in the shape of a smiley face stares back at her as she deposits Frankie in his chair and pushes him close to the table. Frankie wiggles happily in his seat, picking up his little plastic spaceman spoon and digging in.

"You spoil him," she says quietly as she joins Billy on the other side of the kitchen. "It's why you're his favourite."

"Smiley face banana is hardly spoiling him, sweet girl," Billy replies, palming off a cup of coffee to Adeline as she scrunches her nose up at him. "And he loves you, you're Mama."

He presses a kiss into her hair and they lean against the counter and each other, all fond eyes and soft smiles as they watch their son absolutely devour his breakfast. You'd think they'd be used to it by now but Adeline still has pinch me moments, usually when she walks in to Billy snoring on the couch with Frankie atop his chest and almost cherub-like as he sleeps.

"Is that yummy, Franks?"

Frankie nods, flashing them the sweetest smile. It's filled with smushed banana and oatmeal but he's happy so Adeline will take it.

Stan and Wren emerge a few moments later, early risers on race days. Stan pads into the kitchen bleary-eyed and yawning while his fiancée grins, bright and awake for six-thirty in the morning. She makes a beeline for the coffee pot and Stan slides up to Frankie, holding his hand out. Adeline rolls her eyes.

Here we go, she thinks.

"Good morning, young Franklin," Stan says and Frankie shoves his podgy, oatmeal covered hand into his. They shake twice before Stan gives him a soft fist bump and they both wiggle their fingers.

"Stanley, mornin'!" Frankie shouts, "cool dude shake!"

Stan wipes his grubby fingers on his pyjama pants, shrugging when Adeline grimaces, and ruffles Frankie's hair with his clean hand.

"We'll whip up breakfast if you guys wanna go get ready?" Wren offers as Adeline whisks Frankie's empty bowl from the table before he topples it to the floor and remnants of oatmeal get stuck between the tiles.

"Are you sure?"

"You go get dressed, Tinkerbell. I'll watch the troublemaker," Billy says as he appears beside her, his warm palm rubbing slowly down to the small of her back. "We'll swap when you're done." He swoops in with a cloth to Frankie's mucky cheeks and fingers before chucking the gleeful two-year-old over his shoulder.

"Billy, he's gonna be sick if you do that!" Adeline calls after him, shaking her head, but Billy's already bouncing Frankie into the living room, the sounds of their matching giggles floating back to the kitchen. Stan chuckles as Adeline rolls her eyes fondly.

"Y'know, he's exactly the kind of dad I thought he would be," he says and Adeline grins, nodding in agreement.

"He's a natural, that's for sure."

"It's been good for him," Stan says softly, "after everything I think he needed a little perspective and having you beside him, then Frankie coming along… it kinda feels like he's in the best place he can be for his comeback."

"Big day," Adeline breathes, and before she can get too emotional about it, she leaves Stan and Wren to make breakfast, sneaking through to the stairs while Billy has Frankie occupied with his toy cars.

She makes it halfway up before she stops and turns around, selfishly stealing a secret moment to watch her boys together. Billy is lying on his front, helping Frankie lineup all the cars in colour order, getting the little boy to name each colour as they go. Frankie picks up his favourite, a tiny model of his dad's old Dodge Charger, and pretends to rev the engine before he makes it zoom along the floor. Billy glances up then, catches Adeline's eye and flashes her a lopsided grin.

Big day.

BILLY
Riverside International Raceway, California

Four years.

Four years and yet nothing has changed. Gabe is still calling across the garage for last-minute engine checks, Stan is on the receiving end of a pep talk from Tobias, and Norah is walking in circles around her car. The chaos is the same, the hum of the building adrenaline that shakes the garage is there and filtering its way through Billy's bones. But he ignores the noise, ignores the flurry of people who all seem to slow down as he hones in on the only constant he's actually searching for.

Her back is to him as she lowers down to talk to Frankie. The two-year-old is laughing, his face lit up as he scrunches his cute button nose. He's the perfect combination of them both when he does that and Billy can't get enough of it.

The Brooks Scrunch, he calls it.

He watches them for a little longer while he still goes unnoticed in the doorway. His adoring gaze lingers as Adeline tucks a curl behind Frankie's and thumbs at his little rosy cheek, peppering kisses to his other one until he squirms. Billy's whole world is crouched low amongst the madness, as if there aren't thirty people trying to prepare for the first race of the season around them.

He doesn't manage to hide for much longer, Frankie's wide eyes clock him over Adeline's shoulder and before either of them knows it, a blur of brown hair and red and yellow stripes is heading straight for him.

"DADDY!"

Billy scoops him up, throwing him over his shoulder as the garage is filled with Frankie's delighted squeals.

"Where have you been hiding?" Adeline asks as she joins them, pressing up onto her tiptoes to kiss Billy softly.

"Oh, uh–"

"Billy, we told you to wait for us, you absolute knuckle– oh, hey Addie! And my *favourite* Brooks! Come 'ere, trouble." Frankie wiggles in his arms, reaching excitedly for Rosie, and Billy has no choice but to drop his son or hand him over.

With Frankie happily chatting away to his aunt, Billy watches on amused as Adeline gawks at his sister. He can practically see the cogs turning behind her eyes before she shakes herself out of it.

"Wait, are you all here?! I thought your flight was cancelled?"

"I begged Tobias to send a charter plane," Billy says sheepishly. "It didn't feel right not having them here."

Right on cue, his parents enter the garage and Billy stands back as Adeline engulfs them in bone-crushing hugs. He's already had his moment with them; a quiet pep talk from his dad, a prayer from his mom, and a ribbing (that comes from the heart) from Rosie.

"Oh, look at my little squish!" Eleanor coos as she plants a smacker of a kiss to Frankie's cheek. "William, he's gotten so big!"

"He is *three* this year, Ma," Billy chuckles, "and kids tend to grow." He's about to say something else when Stan suddenly appears beside them, suited up and ready to go as he flashes everyone a smile.

"B, it's almost time."

"I guess that's my cue," Billy breathes. The nerves he denied this morning are seeping in slowly now, trickling down his spine like liquid gold in the cracks of a broken pot. He's sure once he's out there, back in familiar territory, he'll be fine. He's just gotta *get* out there first.

"Well, we better go find our seats," Eleanor says, "Roseanne, give your nephew back to your brother." Billy laughs when Rosie grimaces at the use of her full name and accepts Frankie with open arms.

"I'm really glad you guys are here," he smiles as he brushes his hand through the soft waves of Frankie's hair. He still smells of baby some days and Billy inhales as he kisses his son tenderly; a comforting gesture for himself more than anything.

"Give 'em hell, my sweet boy," Eleanor murmurs, cradling Billy's cheek.

"Always do, Ma."

After another round of bone-crushing hugs, his family disappears off to the stands and it's just him and his little family, huddled together.

"You got his ear defenders?"

"They're in my bag," Adeline replies, gesturing for him to hand over Frankie. Billy does so reluctant, squeezing him just a little bit tighter and pressing a collection of sweet kisses to his son's face as he's passed between them. The whole day has felt normal until now, until he has to part with them, even if only for a few hours. "You're more than ready for this, Billy. It's okay to be nervous, use it."

"Yeah...yeah. I will. I just– it's hard, leaving you guys."

"We'll come with you to the car," Adeline says as she hitches Frankie up on her hip. "You wanna go see Daddy's fast car, Franks?"

"Uh, yeah!" Frankie grins, all that's missing is the implied '*duh*'.

"He got that from you," Billy says, cocking his head accusingly.

"I will kiss you quiet," Adeline threatens and Billy laughs because he would like that a lot, actually; especially right now as they near his car and the pre-race jitters have well and truly set in. He makes sure his suit is secure, his gloves comfortable on his hands as he stops beside his new Dodge, decked out in Pepsi branding. Without a word, he takes Adeline's jaw in his hands and his mouth slants over hers as he kisses her, slow and soft and deliberate with every swipe of his tongue and brush of his lips. A thousand ways to say *I love you* are present in the way he strokes her face and runs his thumbs over the apples of her cheeks. When he breaks away, it's with heavy breaths and a full heart.

"I love you, sweet girl."

"I love you," Adeline sighs, swaying forward for another kiss, cut short but a tap to their faces by a little hand.

"Fwankie kiss now, Daddy!"

"Oh, of course! How silly of me to forget!" Billy smothers Frankie with more kisses, tickling him and revelling in the gorgeous sound of his laugh. He commits it to memory, stores it away to replay it if things get tough out there.

"You better head to the grid," Adeline says, her soft palm cupping Billy's smooth cheek as she brushes a thumb over his bottom lip. "Be careful."

"Always," Billy murmurs as he pulls his helmet on. "Hey, Frankie, what are we made of, buddy?" Frankie scrunches his nose, his little gappy smile lighting up his whole face as he looks up at Billy like he's the best thing since sliced bread.

"We made of stardust," he says proudly.

Billy grins.

Yeah, he's gonna be alright.

THE SOUTHERN
SPORTS DAILY

January 16th, 1979　　　　　　　　　　　　　　　Tuesday

BILLY BROOKS: THE COMEBACK KID

By Grant Buchanan
MOTORSPORTS WRITER

RIVERSIDE, CALIFORNIA – NASCAR golden boy, William 'Billy' Brooks drove his first professional race in almost four years this past weekend, competing in the Winston Weston 500.

The crowds at Riverside International Raceway were lucky enough to see the long-awaited comeback of the Shaw & Gold driver after the crash that brought his career to a grinding halt back in 1975.

Brooks, 33, was seen pre-race in the team's garage, mingling with fellow drivers and getting in some last minute family time with wife, Adeline, who he married in a private ceremony at their Georgia ranch three years ago, and their young son.

With young blood like Patrick Peters taking up pole position after his record-breaking qualifying lap last week, and fellow Shaw & Gold driver Stan Reynolds and Apex Motorsport's Rick Matthews keeping Brooks on his toes, it was a tight race. The pair of veteran drivers each have a championship win under their belt to live up to, after all.

It doesn't look like Brooks has anything to worry about though. With a well-earned place on the podium just one race in, 1979 could well be his year.

> **RELATED**: ADELINE BROOKS SET TO SUCCEED FATHER, MICHAEL GOLD, AS THE SHAW & GOLD RACING FOUNDER RETIRES.

acknowledgments

Becs, the Steve to my Bucky. Thank you for graciously and patiently listening to me whine and complain and whine some more. You always know exactly what I need to hear and I will be forever grateful to have had you a text and a meme away throughout this whole process. Lub u.

My mum, who has always let me do my own thing and encouraged it. Look, I wrote a book! Thank you for always believing I can do stuff like this, even when I struggle to believe it myself.

My beta readers; Shic, Ale, Chrissie & Jess. Thank you for taking the time to read this and giving me honest, wonderful, hilarious feedback. It meant more than you know.

The Sugar Club; you wonderful, brilliant humans. I feel very lucky to be a part of something so special. It's you guys who showed me this was possible so thank you. I can't wait to see what else we all accomplish.

about the author

Rebekah Buckley is a British romance author based on the south coast with a penchant for gentle fictional men and iced coffee.

She's had a passion for history and creative writing from an early age and as an adult has been relearning her love of telling stories in her spare time. When she isn't writing, you'll find her singing badly to Taylor Swift and daydreaming about living in New York.

Gold Rush is her first novel.

Printed in Great Britain
by Amazon